ADVANCE PRAISE FOR *The Butterfly and the Violin*

"Cambron's debut novel is rife with history, faith, and hope. It will entrance readers with its poignant characters, intriguing plot, and unpredictable love story."

—SUZANNE WOODS FISHER, AWARD-WINNING, BEST-SELLING AUTHOR OF THE LANCASTER COUNTY SECRETS SERIES

"Fresh. Fascinating. Unforgettable. *The Butterfly and the Violin* is a masterpiece of a debut. From stunning cover to satisfying conclusion, this poignant novel marks Kristy Cambron as an author to watch."

—LAURA FRANTZ, CHRISTY AWARD FINALIST AND AUTHOR OF *LOVE'S RECKONING*

"*The Butterfly and the Violin* held me captive from first note to final moment. Just like the beautiful violin Adele plays, Cambron lyrically weaves words and emotions, carries you through a simultaneously heartbreaking and uplifting story, and leaves you yearning for more. Absolutely spellbinding!"

—KATHERINE REAY, AUTHOR OF *DEAR MR. KNIGHTLEY*

"*The Butterfly and the Violin* is a powerful debut novel that weaves together a touching contemporary story with dramatic events in World War II. A compelling plot and an intriguing cast of characters illustrate that even in the darkest times, when evil seems impossible to overcome, hope can be found through trusting God and using our gifts as an act of worship. Readers of historical fiction will be captivated by this inspiring novel!"

—CARRIE TURANSKY, AWARD-WINNING AUTHOR OF *THE GOVERNESS OF HIGHLAND HALL* AND *THE DAUGHTER OF HIGHLAND HALL*

D0951587

CALGARY PUBLIC LIBRARY

SEP   2014

"Cambron's debut, *The Butterfly and the Violin*, is a wonderful read! I loved deciphering the mystery of what really happened, and the novel revealed a piece of World War II history I'd never heard before. Original and enthralling."

—COLLEEN COBLE, *USA TODAY* BEST-SELLING AUTHOR OF
THE HOPE BEACH SERIES AND *BUTTERFLY PALACE*

"In *The Butterfly and the Violin* author Kristy Cambron weaves together two intriguing stories: one set during World War II in Auschwitz, and the other set in present day. The past and the present intersect, revealing profound truths of how there is beauty to be found in the darkest moments of our lives—and reasons to trust God even when it seems wiser to abandon hope. Cambron's novel touched my heart and challenged me to think more about the meaning—and the cost—of love and courage."

—BETH K. VOGT, AUTHOR OF *SOMEBODY LIKE YOU*

"*The Butterfly and the Violin*, with its skillfully woven modern-day and World War II storylines, instantly put Kristy Cambron on my 'favorite authors' list. Her characters captured my heart right from the start, and her wonderfully paced plot fed my love for both historical and contemporary fiction. Cambron's portrayal of Auschwitz, especially, stunned and impacted me. Truly, one of the most moving novels I've read."

—MELISSA TAGG, AUTHOR OF *MADE TO LAST* AND *HERE TO STAY*

The BUTTERFLY and the VIOLIN

A HIDDEN MASTERPIECE NOVEL

KRISTY CAMBRON

THOMAS NELSON
Since 1798

NASHVILLE   MEXICO CITY   RIO DE JANEIRO

© 2014 by Kristy Cambron

All rights reserved. No portion of this book may be reproduced, stored in a retrieval system, or transmitted in any form or by any means—electronic, mechanical, photocopy, recording, scanning, or other—except for brief quotations in critical reviews or articles, without the prior written permission of the publisher.

Published in Nashville, Tennessee, by Thomas Nelson. Thomas Nelson is a trademark of HarperCollins Christian Publishing, Inc.

Published in association with Hartline Literary Agency, Pittsburgh, PA 15235.

Thomas Nelson, Inc., titles may be purchased in bulk for educational, business, fundraising, or sales promotional use. For information, please e-mail SpecialMarkets@ThomasNelson.com.

Scripture quotations are taken from the Holy Bible, *New International Version®, NIV®.* Copyright © 1973, 1978, 1984, 2011 by Biblica, Inc.™ Used by permission of Zondervan. All rights reserved worldwide. www.zondervan.com

Publisher's Note: This novel is a work of fiction. Names, characters, places, and incidents are either products of the author's imagination or used fictitiously. All characters are fictional, and any similarity to people living or dead is purely coincidental.

Library of Congress Cataloging-in-Publication Data

Cambron, Kristy.
 The butterfly and the violin : a hidden masterpiece novel / Kristy Cambron.
   pages cm
 ISBN 978-1-4016-9059-5 (trade paper)
 I. Title.
 PS3603.A4468B88 2014
 813'.6—dc23   2014002836

Printed in the United States of America

14 15 16 17 18 19 RRD 6 5 4 3 2 1

For my dad.
And for Jeremy, whom Yahweh has uplifted.

Whether you turn to the right or to the left,
your ears will hear a voice behind you, saying,
"This is the way; walk in it."

ISAIAH 30:21

CHAPTER ONE

⁓

Present day, New York City

"Is this it?"

Sera James bounded through the front doors of the Manhattan gallery, so excited that she nearly slipped for running across the hardwood floor in her heels. She came to a flustered stop in front of the large canvas hanging on the back wall. Breathless, she asked, "You've confirmed—this is her?"

"Did you run all the way here, Sera?"

"Yes. Wouldn't you?" She wasn't ashamed to admit it. From the second she'd received the phone call, Sera had pushed and shoved her way off the subway in a frenzy and had run the eight blocks back to the gallery, dodging taxis and cracks in the sidewalks all the way.

Penny nodded. "The guys in the back just opened the crate. Can you believe it's been there for a week and we didn't even know it?"

She shook her head in disbelief. "Unfathomable."

Sera unwound the chiffon scarf from her neck and shrugged off her trench coat as she stepped away for a moment, draping them both over the antique wooden counter stretching across the back of the room. She twisted her long ebony hair and tucked it into a loose bun, then secured it atop her head with a pencil she found nearby. It wasn't until she turned back to her assistant that she noticed the girl hadn't moved an inch. Penny stood like a statue, her only movement an index finger that twirled a lock of strawberry blond hair at her nape.

Sera laughed. When her assistant took to whirling a strand of hair around her finger, something had to have completely captured her attention.

"You're doing it again, Penny."

The action was telltale. But Sera didn't blame Penny in the least. This moment was special. If the painting was what they both thought it was, standing in awe was warranted. The rest of the city could have flown by outside the front windows and neither one of them would have noticed. Or cared.

"I'm just sorry it's not the original." Penny offered Sera an envelope without looking away from the canvas. "But it is another step closer and that's what matters."

"You've inspected the borders?"

"My hands were shaking like crazy the whole time," Penny admitted, tilting her head to one side. "But yeah. Even though I knew this was paint on canvas, I still checked to be sure. The negatives are inside."

Sera opened the envelope and held the negatives up to the light. Penny was right—the painting before them was eerily similar to the one they sought. Checking the borders was the only way to distinguish the original from a copy. And if the borders didn't match, then this couldn't be the one they'd been searching for. Her heart almost sank a little before she realized that while it may not have been *the* portrait, it was still a portrait of *her*. The borders didn't matter much when those piercing eyes continued to stare out, haunting the viewer.

Sera swallowed hard, thinking how long they'd waited for the moment to arrive. She replaced the negatives in the envelope. "It may be a copy, but I still have to know. How did you find it?"

"An estate sale," Penny answered, her voice sounding almost dreamy. "Just north of San Francisco."

"And do we know for whom?"

Penny nodded again, and this time cocked an eyebrow in a curious fashion. "That's the mystery—it's some businessman. A financier in real estate. William Hanover is his name. I called his office with a basic inquiry and he contacted us back immediately. Said he was liquidating his late grandfather's estate. The name doesn't ring a bell for me at all and I've been chasing this painting for more than two years, same as you. Nobody in the art world has ever heard of him."

The name was foreign to her too. Who was this William Hanover, and how did he manage to get his hands on a painting that was a virtual copy of the one she was looking for?

"And did we make an offer?"

"Mmm-hmm. I figured you'd want to, so I made a generous one."

Penny's answer didn't inspire a lot of confidence. Sera shook her head. "Then why do you sound as if you've got some bad news for me?"

"Because he said he's not going to sell. Money isn't enough, apparently."

"But you just said it was an estate sale."

"Right," Penny cut in. "But it was a chance encounter that I found the painting on an Internet auction site. It was the image and not a bill of sale that caught my attention. I was sifting through old photographs of estate sales from last fall, jewelry and such. You know, the usual. I'd been through an exhausting file of artwork when I came across a photo of this—faded and barely noticeable in the background, behind a vase that had been high-lighted for sale. But there's no doubt—it's her."

Her assistant stood back and eyed the painting, then pulled a clipboard up to her chin as if entranced by the vision of the ethe-real beauty.

"It was her eyes, Sera. They pierced right through the computer screen and pulled me in, if that's possible."

"It's possible." The same thing had happened to her the first time she'd seen the painting. Only hers was a patchy memory, of an image she'd once seen as a young girl. Thinking back on it now made the moment all the more surreal.

"I spilled a whole mug of coffee down my front when I saw it on the computer screen." Penny smiled, one of those youthful, dimple-cheeked grins so characteristic of the young art student. "Remember that ivory sweater I borrowed? Hope you didn't want it back anytime soon."

"No," Sera answered honestly and, lost in thought, took a step closer to the canvas. "Forget about it. This is better."

"It is, isn't it?" They stood for a moment, speechless, transfixed by the beauty of the portrait. Penny shook her head and on a hushed breath whispered, "After all this time. She's finally here."

It had been far too long, that was for sure.

From the moment Sera had laid eyes on the work of art when she was eight years old, she'd been haunted by the otherworldly beauty. A simple three-quarter silhouette of a young woman of perhaps twenty years of age, with flawless, iridescent skin and those ever-piercing, almost animalistic blue eyes. The softness in the mouth, the sadness in the features . . . the stark coldness of the shaved head, showing a young beauty who had been shorn of her crown and glory . . . the tattooed numbers, shouting out from the left forearm that cradled a violin.

"So, let me get this straight." Sera stood tall in her pencil skirt and classic white oxford, with arms folded and foot tapping while she tried to work things out in her mind. "We found a painting by chance, but it's not the original. And though it happens to be an image of our long-lost girl, it's not for sale. The owner won't take money for it."

"That sums it up. I wish I could say it didn't."

Sera stood back for a moment, puzzled as to how the painting could be in her gallery under the circumstances. "So . . . how did it end up here again?"

"It's been sent here on loan."

"Why on loan?" Sera leaned in, nodding at the exquisite brushstrokes.

"That's just it." Penny paused with a hitch in her voice.

With her attention piqued, Sera half turned to find Penny chewing the edge of her thumbnail. Penny furrowed her brow as if she were staring into the bright summer sunshine. Sera stood up straight then, as her hands found their way to her hips. She almost smiled at her friend's behavior.

"Penn—what on earth is the matter with you? Is there something you're not telling me?"

"He wants to talk in person." Penny looked close to cringing. "About his terms."

Sera did smile then. The man had terms? "His terms for what?"

"For hiring you," Penny admitted with an almost too reluctant smile herself. "Or us, rather. He's willing to pay close to an obscene amount of money for the services of the gallery that's looking for the very same thing he is—the original painting of our girl."

"Did you explain why we're looking for the painting?"

"Yes, of course I did. I told him we had interest in acquiring Holocaust era art for the gallery, but I had to soften it a little. After all, something to the tune of 'She's been dreaming of finding this painting since she was a girl' didn't seem appropriate to confess to a complete stranger we might have to negotiate with. I mean, if he has a copy of the painting, then he may be our ticket to finding the original. I told him the truth." Penny pulled a paper free from the clipboard and handed it to her. "Enough of it, anyway, to get you an invitation and a plane ticket to the West Coast. Your flight leaves tomorrow—on his dime."

Hesitating, Sera toyed with the idea that the man could have his own agenda.

"Okay. We both know why I'm looking for the painting. But why does this William Hanover want it? Did he say?"

Penny shook her head. "I guess that's what this ticket will help us find out."

Sera reached for the ticket with trembling fingertips.

Two years.

It'd been two years since her world had fallen apart, since she'd thrown herself into work and once again found herself consumed by the intrigue of the painting's mystery. She may have first learned of the painting as a girl, but her real dedication to unraveling its mystery hadn't come until she had nothing left. If finding the last piece of the puzzle meant that Sera had to work with this William Hanover, then she was game.

Thank You, Lord. The unspoken prayer somehow made her heart feel light. *We're this close to finding her.*

"Penny." Sera smiled. "We're finally bringing her home."

CHAPTER TWO

—

December 3, 1942
Vienna, Austria

"She is in shock."

The doctor had poked his head out into the cold, looked up and down the deserted city street, then tugged her into the house. Adele heard the sound of bolts locking as he secured the door behind them. He led her into the front parlor where a faded brocade sofa sat against the back wall across from two plum-colored armchairs with sagging cushions, polished wood arms, and clawed feet. A fire crackled on the hearth.

"Here, bring her over to the fire."

He spoke to someone—she didn't know who. All she knew was that she was safe for the time being. No one had followed her. She'd looked behind her every few steps and, as a precaution, had doubled back in the shadows of several snow-covered streets before she came to the doctor's front stoop.

"What is wrong with her?" A woman's voice cracked. Adele couldn't blame her for the fear. She was scared too. Everyone in Vienna was scared. "Look at how she's shaking."

Adele's hands indeed shook.

The trembling ran from her fingertips to the crook of her elbows like she was being jolted with shots of electricity. Whether it was from the cold or astonishment at the events just witnessed, she couldn't know. Adele had never been in shock before. She'd never seen anyone killed. Not until tonight.

"It hurts," she managed to whisper, for she felt pain. It had been numbed, but now that she was safe, her senses had returned. An almost unbearable stinging now burned like fireplace embers had been laced beneath her skin.

"Yes, I know."

"I'm sorry, Doctor. I had nowhere else to go." He had to know something terrible had happened or she wouldn't have been pounding her bloody fist upon his door in the dead of night. Doctors were awakened at all hours, she knew. But it wasn't likely he'd been awakened like this before.

"Hush. Sit here, child," he said, and pulled a chair nearer to the fire. "You'll be warmed by the hearth."

The doctor settled her into the chair and went about issuing orders to two women who moved to stand behind him, flanking his shoulders. Adele could just make them out in the dim light of the front room; a young woman of maybe fifteen and an older woman with a severe scowl and layers of wrinkles marking her brow.

"Pull the drapes closed tight. And get her a glass of wine, please," he continued, his deep voice floating out from beneath a weighted gray mustache. "Then bring a basin of hot water, bandages, and some blankets. We must warm her up."

"But the wine is nearly gone," the young woman whispered.

"Then we should have enough for one lady who has need of it."

Adele listened to them whispering back and forth. Wine was hard to come by. They'd have been cautioned to use it most sparingly. Who knew if the war would ever end and supplies would be available again?

"I can think of no greater reason to use it up. It is for Miss Adele," he offered. "Please, Daughter, do go and get it."

The man patted her cheek and turned his attention back to the older woman who had taken to pacing about the room. She wrung her hands as she marched back and forth. She glanced over at Adele from time to time, shaking her head and muttering under her breath. She finally stopped to peek out the heavy woolen drapes, examining the darkness of the street.

"Dieter, what has happened to her?" The older woman approached and whispered low, her thick Austrian accent pronounced even though the words were hushed.

"I do not know. You heard the knock upon the door same as I did. When I opened it, I found Miss Adele shivering on our front stoop."

"Was she alone?"

He didn't answer. Instead, he gave Adele a respectful smile before turning back to the fidgeting woman. He whispered several indiscriminate words while the woman continued eyeing her.

Adele had met her before. She was the doctor's wife. Ava was her name, and though it had been several years since they'd crossed paths, her expression had not changed. The circles painted beneath her eyes matched the graying color of the hair tucked up in her faded paisley kerchief. She looked unkempt and severe, like everyone in Vienna, for years of war had taken their toll on those left in the city. But it was her haughty disapproval that Adele remembered most. Those pinched lips and that cemented scowl were as uninviting back then as they were now.

"You know who she is." She spat out the words like an accusation. "All of Vienna knows the orchestra's sweetheart. How can you think to hide her here? She will be spotted on sight. They will question why a woman such as she would be taken into our home in the state that she is."

He shook his head.

"Dieter—"

He cut into his wife's pleas with a hushed but firm reprimand.

"I cannot turn her out! This is Miss Adele. I would not send a stranger from this house, let alone the daughter of Fredrich Von Bron himself. I owe my life to the man. Have you forgotten that? He saved me in the Great War. This is his daughter and that makes her as good as family. If she needs our help, then she shall receive it without question."

"But they will come and take us away too. Your own daughter could face deportation! Do you not understand what this could mean?" The woman twisted her hands in knots as her gaze darted from her husband's face over to Adele. "She must go. Give her wine and bread and then send her away."

"No one will be deported. Go now. Please do as I've said." Dieter returned his attention to Adele's hands. The woman's heavy steps pounded the hardwood floor as she walked away.

"Adele. You are hurt." He swept a wooden stool up under him and began picking at her wool coat and woven scarf as both garments dripped stray drops of blood upon the floor. "Let us get this coat off so that I may have a look, hmm?"

Ava came back and laid a stack of bandages nearby. She didn't leave—the woman lurked back in the shadows, staying put like a ghost haunting the doorway.

"Good," he said, smiling and nodding when the coat was discarded. "Your sweater—arms and torso—there is no blood." His hands squeezed up and down her arms. "No broken bones. You're not injured anywhere else. This is good."

"My hands." Adele could say nothing else. She held out her hands to show him the cuts that continued bleeding red droplets over the light camel dress she wore.

"Yes, yes. I can see that must hurt a great deal," Dieter replied, and cradled her hands in his to dab at the wounds. "Let's see to that right now."

"The wine, Father." His daughter tapped his shoulder, then

handed over a chipped tumbler that was not quite half full. She set a black medical bag at his feet.

"Here, drink." Dieter brought the glass up to Adele's lips, but she couldn't force herself to drink. It was the last thing she wanted to do. Anything she swallowed would come right back up again.

"I cannot." Adele pushed the glass away. "Please."

Dieter glanced over his shoulder as his daughter retreated to the doorway with her mother. The two looked on like nervous vultures.

"The basin? I need water," Dieter remarked, his words sounding tinged with frustration. "I cannot clean her wounds without it. Then blankets and a charger of bread, Astrid. She needs nourishment and warmth. We cannot let this chill go unchecked or she'll catch her death by morning."

Again Ava looked as though she wanted to argue, but he cut her off before a word could be uttered.

"And blow out the candles in the entry before you wash the blood from the door." He pulled a small table up closer to his side and set the tumbler of wine upon it. "Go, please. Both of you."

The older woman sighed and tugged her daughter back through the archway from the parlor, the sounds of her huffing echoing down the hall.

Adele watched the women go, then turned back to the doctor. "Have I caused you difficulty by coming here?"

"No, child. No," he answered, and shook his head. "Now, let me see to your hands, Adele. What has happened to you?" He once again went about gently wiping the blood from her hands.

After all that had happened, she needed someone to confide in. Her life now depended on it.

"They . . . shot . . . them," Adele said with a pause after each word, struggling against the bottom lip that quivered with her admission.

"Shot? Who's been shot?"

Adele shook her head. It all seemed so different now. She'd been innocent. A fool. What did she think, that men with guns wouldn't use them?

"The Haurbech family." Adele mumbled the words. Shuddering, she added, "Elsa, my friend. Her husband used to play with the orchestra sometimes, that is, until . . . they shot them! Even little Eitan . . ."

He tilted his chin down and peered back at her over the top rim of his bifocals. "Who are the Haurbechs? And how did you come by them out on a night like this?"

Adele squeezed her eyes shut on the questions and shook her head. Visions of the night's horror flashed through her mind—the running, dark alleys all around, the violent odor of fish down by the docks, icy wind burning the insides of her nostrils. And silence. There was an eerie silence that had been undisturbed around them, except for her ragged breathing and shoes pounding the wet pavement. Then suddenly, noise. Ripping through the night. And falling bodies . . . shock. Her heart stopping and then, all at once, thumping again until she thought it would burst out of her chest. The anguished screams and pops of gunfire piercing her ears . . . young Sophie's hand being torn away from hers . . . glass shattering . . . her feet, slipping on blood that had pooled on the ground as she tried to run away . . .

A tremor predicated her next words.

"They were being loaded into a bread truck."

"Where?" If he was stunned by her short admission, he didn't show it. He held her hands, still dabbed at them with the strips of cloth, and waited for her to respond.

Adele dropped her tone to a whisper. "Not far from here, down by the fish market. They'd waited so long to come out of hiding." Her voice hitched on a muffled sob. "And I promised them that everything would be okay if we tried it tonight."

"Adele? What on earth are you saying?" Dieter looked her straight in the eyes, the shock she'd expected now evident as he searched her face.

She knew what she was admitting to.

It was a death sentence if the Germans found out. No, her fate would be sealed if *anyone* learned the truth. Austrian Adele Von Bron, the daughter of a high-ranking member of the Third Reich, society's darling and the gifted violinist with such a bright future ahead of her, was involved in the secret transport of Jews out of the city? It was a shocking revelation that was unbelievable even to her. If they knew . . . if anyone knew . . . she was as good as dead.

"I have been working with Vladimir. You know of him?"

He nodded. "Yes. Vladimir Nicolai. And he plays in the orchestra as well?"

"He's a cellist in the Philharmonic," she admitted, though Dieter couldn't know how much more he was to her. "He has contacts in the south that were prepared to accept the family, to smuggle them to Switzerland."

"And how long has this been going on, young Adele?"

"For nearly two years," she breathed out. "I learned of Vladimir's activities by accident, though he tried to shield me from them."

"And he convinced you to go along with this scheme?" Dieter sounded not only shocked but somewhat defensive on her behalf, as if he was angered that the rebellious young cellist had lured her into the activities by deception—or force.

"No. I chose it." Adele felt renewed strength as she shook her head. "And I know what you must be thinking. By God as my witness I was not coerced. Vladimir did not seek me out. I knew of the Haurbech family's whereabouts and I wanted to help them escape."

"How did you learn of them?"

"That doesn't matter now." And it didn't. What good would it do to endanger more lives when the family they'd hoped to save was now dead? "We were helping them for many months."

Dieter looked back over his shoulder before whispering a reply.

"But I thought there were no Jews left in the city. I'd have thought they'd all fled or been taken away long before now. Most all that I knew left Vienna more than three years ago. The ones that didn't leave, well... How could any still be in Vienna? Is it possible?"

"Yes. There are some left." Adele looked up at him, hoping her eyes would entreat him to help in some way, maybe even to tell her that she was living out a dream instead of being in the world's broken reality. "Vladimir was there with me. He told me to run when the Gestapo arrived. They came out of nowhere. I had been under the cover of the buildings by the fish market, leading the children from the alley to load them on the truck, but then—it all happened so fast."

"And what did happen tonight?" he asked, and pressed her hand to her lap in order to begin stitching one of the cuts. She winced against the pain.

"It was the older child, Sophie. She screamed when they shot her parents, and though I tried, I couldn't cover her mouth in time. They—" Adele choked on the words and shook her head.

"You got away." Dieter took his hand and tilted her chin up to look at him. "How did you escape without them seeing you?"

"Vladimir pulled us down the alley and he went the opposite direction with Sophie. He picked her up and told me to run. To run and not look back. He'd instructed me beforehand that if anything went wrong, to go to a place that I knew would be safe. So I came here."

Dieter nodded.

"Vladimir is a good man. He will look after little Sophie," Dieter assured her.

"But I don't even know if he got away. They ran the other direction. And when the bullets started to fly around us, I heard him scream." Adele reached up with her bloodied hand and touched fingertips to her trembling lips. *Heavenly Father, is he even alive? Or is my Vladimir shot dead in an alley somewhere?* The fear was too real. "He yelled for me to keep running, so I did. I ran all the way here through the snow."

"Did he say your name?"

Adele hadn't even thought of that. Had Vladimir screamed it out when he'd ordered her to run away? She couldn't think straight to know whether he had or not.

"I don't . . ." Adele closed her eyes. Somehow it helped to remember. "I don't think so."

"You are certain?"

Was she?

With eyes closed and mind reeling, Adele relived the shuddering few moments over and over again, listening for her name to be called out in her memory. The screams were real, as were the gunshots, but she didn't hear him call for her.

"No. He didn't say my name."

"Good." He patted her wrist. "And your hands?"

That's right. She still hadn't managed to tell him what had caused the cuts that now covered her palms.

"I looked back. He told me to run and I did, but I turned around when I heard gunshots." Adele allowed Dieter to pull her hand back to him. He inspected it, then bent to retrieve something from a medical bag on the floor at his feet. "I tripped over a crate and fell. There had been glass from a broken window on the street and my hands caught my fall. I felt the glass cutting into them but I got up and kept running."

"There now." Dieter turned back, shushing her as tears began to roll down her cheeks. "We'll see to this. I know you are worried, but you must have trust in him. Hmm? Vladimir Nicolai sounds as if he is a capable man. As for the hands of a concert violinist—they will be good as new, I promise."

"But until then . . . how can a violinist play with hands she cannot use? They'll know something happened and they'll question me. The guards saw that someone was there helping them escape. And they chased after us. It won't take long for them to figure it out. They could be searching for us even now." Adele entreated him, the tears now having been replaced by a breathless plea. "What do I do?"

"You're quite sure no one saw you?"

She nodded.

"Adele, you are known in this country. I can appreciate your heart for wishing to help those poor people, but how could you take such a risk with your own life? You know who your father is as well as I do. It would only take one person to recognize you and report it."

He was right.

Adele's musical talent was just one of the reasons she was well known in Austria. As the granddaughter of a renowned violinist and daughter to a famous concert pianist and a high-ranking Austrian general, it was assured that she was known. It was also her wheat blond hair and the family's trademark blue eyes that had made her known beyond the stage. Had a streetlight cast a glow upon her features, there was a great possibility she'd been recognized.

"My father knows nothing of my actions," Adele admitted. "If he did, I suspect he'd turn me in himself."

"I expected your father would have been ignorant of these activities."

"But will anyone believe I have been home all night? My mother and father are likely to learn of this from the staff. What excuse can I give if they enter my room and find the bed empty?"

"How did you take leave of your house, then?"

"I feigned a headache and retired to my room after the evening meal. I asked not to be disturbed."

"Good. That may buy us some time." He seemed satisfied with her excuse and continued. "You will stay here until we've figured out what to do. We have a woodstove and a nice cot in the kitchen that will be yours," Dieter directed, his attention focused on the strips of gauze he was winding around her hands. "Don't worry. You are safe here. We'll determine what's to be done by morning."

She couldn't think of anything to say but "Thank you."

Adele said it, as softly as she could, but he didn't acknowledge her words. When he continued dressing the wounds, she whispered it again, this time with all of the raw emotion pent up inside her.

"Thank you."

He looked up. Adele met his gaze and was shocked to see that gentle tears had glossed his eyes. The passion grew more alive as he spoke. "This is not Austria, you know. What we've become? This is not God's path."

Searching the face of the sweet gentleman doctor she'd known all her life, she leaned forward and gave him a grateful kiss on the cheek. How could such a humble man exist, one with great honor and compassion for the injustices of the world, when her father lived as such an antithesis to those same virtues?

"If this is not God's path, then we must find it again."

He smiled and patted her cheek just as he had done to his own daughter's only moments before. "Be heartened that you are alive. That is God looking out for you, I think."

Adele would have smiled had she not remembered something. She tried to submit to the man's attempts at calming her frayed nerves, but all at once, the fear came flooding back. He didn't understand, did he?

She had a concert for the Third Reich the next day.

CHAPTER THREE

———

December 4, 1942

*S*leep became a welcome escape.

The doctor had convinced her to swallow some of the wine, and as soon as Adele had lain down and closed her eyes, it had taken effect. She'd been lulled into the deep blackness of sleep, to a place where she was forced to remember nothing. There were no gunshots or fallen bodies, no fear of faceless officers who chased her down dark alleys with guns drawn. It wasn't until she cracked her eyelids open that she could recall anything of the night before and where she lay now, which was on a cot hidden in the back of the doctor's kitchen.

She blinked, remembering where she was, and glanced through the opening in the brocade curtains that shielded the small alcove in which she'd slept.

As dawn broke through the kitchen window, she could see a black-and-white checked flooring ran the length of the large but sparsely decorated room. White farmhouse cabinets, a butcher's block, and a small shelf with canning items were the only things she could see lining the walls. An extended oak dining table was positioned in the center of the room, curiously sporting only three chairs. She wondered if at some point the others had been used to feed the oversized woodstove in the corner. A large pot boiled upon it, with liquid that splashed over the sides and sizzled when the drops reached its hot surface.

Her stomach growled in response to seeing and smelling something cooking on the stovetop. When was the last time she'd eaten?

A light rap at the door suddenly drew Adele's attention. Forgetting her bandaged palms, she grabbed onto the sides of the cot and struggled to pull herself upright.

Dieter approached, his face grim. He appeared weary around the eyes.

"Miss Adele," he said, and motioned to someone in the shadow of the hall. "You have a visitor."

Her heart began pounding in her chest.

Was it her father? Surely not. The German authorities who had come to question her? No, they'd push their way in if that's what they wanted. Perhaps it was another member of the orchestra. But who else knew she was there?

When the tall form stepped into the dim morning light, her questions faded and a wave of relief washed over her.

She finally exhaled. "Vladimir!"

In her joy at seeing him, Adele tried to stand but fell back on the cot. Her hands gave out in their support of the rest of her body. Yet he stood there, tall and handsome, staring back at her. Thankfully, he wasn't as grim-faced as the doctor. His smile was faint but still welcoming, so much so that she could almost feel the warmth in it. It was akin to the usual smiles she lived to receive from him.

Dieter stood by quietly, a look on his face that she couldn't read. He seemed distant somehow, and much more solemn than he'd been the night before. He looked from Vladimir to her and exhaled low.

"I'm sorry, Mr. Nicolai," he said. "I can give you no more than five minutes. Then we've got to get her out."

With steps that creaked upon the floor, he left them alone in the room.

Vladimir rushed forward and pulled her into a hug, burying his face in her hair. "Thank God you're safe."

She squeezed her eyes shut, loving the feel of his arms around her.

Thank God you're safe too.

"I couldn't come to this part of the city before now," he whispered against her ear. "I had to find a place to keep Sophie. And I came back for you as soon as I could."

"What time is it?"

"It's early still. Just after seven o'clock."

"You're alive." She whispered the words aloud, finally able to let her heart believe he was really there with her. Adele pulled back from his hug and brushed a bandaged palm over his cheek, rejoicing over the fact that they'd both run for their lives the night before and, by the hand of God, had survived.

He seemed to understand that she needed to look him over as she began checking his arms and hands and face while he knelt before her. She noticed a cut under one eye, but other than that she found no indication of injury. Truly, he appeared to be no worse for wear.

"What happened here?" She ran a fingertip along the skin beneath his cut, the feather-light touch upon his skin medicating to her frayed nerves.

"It's from the glass of the shop windows."

Adele felt breathless, affected by how close they'd come to death.

"How?"

"The shots." She dropped her hand, having only just remembered her palm was covered in gauze that she didn't want him to see. And he must have seen it, because his countenance changed.

"And that's all?"

"Yes." He offered a slight nod. "Just the one cut. I am well."

"But what if they ask—"

He cut into her worries. "They won't. Who would ask after a paltry cut on the face of a merchant's son?"

She nodded, then immediately contradicted the action. "But if they do?"

"I'll make an excuse."

Was it that easy to erase such things?

The stove top sizzled and popped again, the liquid from the pot hissing behind them. It brought an uncomfortable silence to the conversation. She felt she had to say something, anything to keep her throat from closing up.

"Did you sleep?" Why was she asking trivial things?

"No."

"And what about—"

"Adele, stop this idle conversation." He cut off her question with the soft reprimand. Still kneeling beside the cot, he took her bandaged hands in his. "The doctor's already told me."

She attempted to pull her hands back but he held on, giving them a gentle squeeze. "I'm fine."

"No," he said, staring back with eyes that spoke only of concern. "You are not. How in heaven's name will you play tonight?"

"I don't know." Adele shook her head at him, her thick blond waves falling soft about her shoulders. In her sleepy haze, she'd forgotten about the concert. Now she was faced with the fear of uncertainty again. What would she do?

"I've been speaking with Dieter. He thinks you shouldn't play with your injuries. You risk infection or even permanent damage if the stitches come loose."

Vladimir's hazel eyes almost stared through her. He looked tired. For how upbeat he was attempting to appear, she could see now that he was exhausted. And worried. Though they'd been through a close call the night before, he looked like he was concerned about the cuts on her palms more than anything else.

"I must play," Adele admitted, forcing a smile and shrugging her shoulders a bit. "I have no choice. My father expects me—no, he demands that I play. 'It's for Austria!' he says. He'd never allow me to miss a performance, especially not one as important as this."

"Adele, you don't seem to understand the gravity of the situation." A lock of dark hair fell across one of his eyes as he leaned in toward her.

She wished their world were different, wished she could brush the lock away from his face whenever she pleased. But in what world could someone of her family's position offer their daughter's hand to a merchant's son, no matter how gifted he was musically? No matter how much she cared? Their relationship would have to stay secret.

"I understand. I saw the same things you did last night. I know what is happening, Vladimir." She choked on the emotion of the night before. "I know what the risks are."

"No, you don't, Adele. You couldn't possibly."

Adele was confident she wasn't misreading the compassion in his eyes as he looked over her bandaged palms. He still thought her innocent, didn't he? And shielded. And unaware of what occurred outside of the perfectly arranged life her parents had created for her.

But all of that was gone now. In the blink of an eye, everything had changed.

"I put you at risk by coming here, but I didn't have a choice. I had to know if you were all right . . ." Vladimir's voice trailed off, as if the truth was too difficult to admit. "The Gestapo has questioned my father. I believe we're all being followed."

"No." Adele whispered the single word, shaking her head, knowing full well what it meant. They'd landed their sights on him as a possible traitor to the Reich.

"And the doctor? What about his family?"

He shook his head. "They have not come to question him, thank God. They have no reason to tie him to me." He glanced over his shoulder and lowered his voice. "But his wife pressures him."

She almost couldn't breathe. "To turn us in?"

"She's scared," he answered, looking a bit scared now himself.

"She wants us to leave, then?"

He nodded and began gathering the things that had been set upon a nearby chair. He shoved bandage rolls in his coat pockets. "We can only stay a few moments. We have to get you home and somehow sneak you in before breakfast. If you call for the staff to bring a tray to your room, you'll be able to hide your bandages. You couldn't do that at a dining table."

"I feigned a headache as an excuse from dinner last night. I can carry that over to this morning."

"Good." He lifted her coat from the back of the chair and stopped when the bloodstains were washed in the soft morning light.

"You can't wear this home. We'll have to get you another." Vladimir turned his attention to the hall before he whispered, "I wonder if his daughter has an extra one."

"And are you going to play tonight?"

He turned back, giving her a forced smile. "I think playing the cello for Austria is the least of my worries right now."

"If you're there, then I think I could play." Adele held up her hands. "Despite this, I think I could do it if I knew you were across the stage from me."

Thoughts of the upcoming victory ball were about as far away as one could get from the bloodshed she'd witnessed. Adele had no idea how they could go back to ball gowns and flutes of bubbly champagne. The luxury of the night ahead made her feel sick to her stomach. Even now, she could look back at Vladimir's eyes and see that he was struggling with the same reality. They had to go. They had to perform. They had to sit and play and then mingle amongst some of the same men who may have pulled the trigger on her innocent friends the night before.

"I'll go." Vladimir brushed a hand across her cheek. "I will go if only to keep a watchful eye over you. Because all of this is my fault, you know."

"How could what happened last night be your fault?"

"Not last night, Adele. I should never have allowed your stubbornness to overtake my better judgment. You never should have been involved from the beginning. And if I can help it, you never will be again."

She chose to ignore the fact that he'd called her stubborn.

"Who is going to help you, then?" Adele challenged him, wishing her hands didn't hurt so—they'd have fit nicely on her hips at the moment. "Someone has to help you get Sophie out."

"You cannot. I won't let you."

"You can't stop me," Adele countered. "I was responsible for Sophie last night. Her mother—my friend Elsa—she trusted us. I can't forget that trust just because she's gone. How can you think I could go on without seeing her daughter out of this godforsaken place? Sophie is the last survivor of her family. We must help her."

"I didn't say I refused to help her."

"She's only a child."

"And she is also a Jew." Vladimir's face revealed nothing but a stony resolve in response to her pushing. "For that, they'd kill you for even knowing she is alive, even with your family's connections. They wouldn't think twice about sending you to one of the camps or, God help us, doing something worse to you. I can't let you go any further with me in this."

"Where is she?"

Vladimir sighed and shook his head. "I can't tell you."

"So you expect me to go to that ball tonight, to wear some

pretty dress and a smile and act like last night didn't happen? Whether I play or not, you know me well enough to know I cannot stand by and do nothing."

Adele could not believe he would try to shut her out now.

"Look at your hands, Adele. This was bad enough." Vladimir kissed one of the bandages and braced an arm under her elbow as if to help her stand. "We had a close call last night and I won't let that happen again."

"You can't protect me from everything," she insisted, swinging her legs over the side of the cot so she could stand up to him on her own. "This is my life. I can do with it what I choose."

"You're correct. I can't protect you from everything, but I can protect you from this. *This* is within my control." Vladimir turned toward the doorway of the kitchen, their voices having alerted the doctor's wife to come and check on them. He addressed her with a weary sigh. "My apologies, ma'am. We were just leaving."

"That's it? We're supposed to go back to our old life like nothing's happened?"

Adele had wanted to hug the life out of him when he'd walked through the door. Now she wanted to wring his neck. How dare he presume to shut her out! Didn't he understand that she had more than a passing attachment to him? Didn't he know that she wanted to do something meaningful with her life, and with him?

"You said you would play tonight, Adele, and I believe you will. You're far too stubborn to let them ever get the best of you." Vladimir tilted his head down in a formal nod to her. "But as for the rest of it? That was the first and last time I allow you to be put in harm's way."

She folded her arms around her middle, feeling a void that had opened up between them.

"You need a coat," he said before stepping from the kitchen.

He returned but a few seconds later with a long wool coat in a deep claret. "Here," he whispered, and slipped it over her shoulders.

Adele looked at the pearl buttons that lined the front of the coat. She ran her wrist over the softness of the ivory satin lining. "It's beautiful."

"It's his wife's."

She nodded. "She's taken great care with it. It's probably from before the war, isn't it? It looks like an opera coat."

"It's all they had." His voice was quiet and unusually rough. It sounded laden with emotion.

"Vladimir." Adele's heart felt heavy. "I've taken her best coat, haven't I?"

Vladimir didn't acknowledge the truth. He looked back at her with an all-too-evident softness in his features and whispered, "Come on. I've got to get you home."

CHAPTER FOUR

———

$\mathcal{M}$arina Von Bron declared her daughter to be nothing less than a perfect vision in her ball gown.

The specially purchased champagne satin had been flown in for the occasion all the way from Berlin, and tailors had labored throughout the week to ensure the shoulder-grazing design had been perfectly stitched down to the very last shimmery detail. Now Adele stood in front of her boudoir mirror, feeling like a statue as her mother flitted about, dousing her with flowery perfume and touching up the last of her makeup for the concert.

"Here, my darling daughter." She plucked a tube of lipstick from the vanity and motioned for her to push out her chin. "Pucker."

Adele did as she was told and received a thick layer of cherry red to stain the natural pout on her lips. She rubbed them together and made a soft *pop* when she parted them.

"Lovely," Marina declared, and turned to raid the jewelry box on the bureau. "You're wearing cocktail gloves tonight?"

Her mother tossed the lighthearted question over her shoulder, her French accent bubbly. Adele couldn't help but feel startled at the mention of the gloves and tried to cover quickly.

"Just until we go onstage."

"Oh yes, they're quite nice. Can you imagine appearing at a Vienna Philharmonic concert without gloves? I know you cannot play in them, of course, but they are proper to wear the rest of the time." She made a *tsk tsk* noise under her tongue as she continued searching through the jewelry box and mumbled, "Ah . . . *Cherie!* Where are those pearl earrings?"

After a few seconds, she turned with a victorious smile, holding up pearl studs.

"Your grandmama's earrings," Marina chirped happily, and began tugging at Adele's earlobes. "She wore them on a night like this—the very night she met your grandfather. I hope you should have as much luck as she did." Her mother's voice trailed off as the earrings were slipped into her lobes and attention was given to the last details of her hair. "There will be hearts breaking for you all over Austria tonight."

Surely her mother could hear the audible beat of her heart. The woman was making idle conversation; how could she know that the words were cutting into Adele's chest, frightening her all the more?

Marina leaned to the side, meeting her gaze in the reflection of the glass. "Adele? Have you a young man, then?"

Yes. His name is Vladimir.

His name is Vladimir and I'm dying inside because I don't know if he'll show up tonight . . . if he'll stay in Vienna . . . if he'll even be alive tomorrow.

When Adele shook her head, her mother turned to busy herself with brushing the back of her skirt, fearful as always that she should appear the least bit wrinkled in public.

"Ah well, do not worry. You shall have one after tonight. A young Austrian from the city. Or perhaps a German officer? I know that one or two have asked your father if they could come calling. Wouldn't that be nice?"

Adele looked back at their reflection in the mirror, shocked at her mother's nonchalance. There her mother was, preening as if their greatest worry in the world was planning a future wedding party. How delusional was she? Did she not know what was happening outside their window? Did she not hear the rapid cadence of gunfire tearing through the streets at night?

The horror Adele had witnessed the night before was just a taste, she was sure. If what Vladimir had told her was correct, then the Germans were not experiencing as much victory as they'd have the world believe, despite the lavish victory concerts they always hosted. Each public event added to the deception that they were not being increasingly routed by the Allies. Why, the Germans were feverishly building fortified watchtowers all over the city and had been since September. Why would they take such measures if they weren't fearful that a wave of the Red Army was about to wash over them?

"There. *Magnifique!*" Marina clapped her hands together. "My beautiful, perfect girl. They shall be stunned by you tonight— every officer in the audience—first with their eyes and then their ears." Her mother tapped a finger on the tip of her nose. "Mark my words, Adele."

"Thank you, Mama."

Adele looked at her reflection in the mirror, feeling dead inside. How could she be dressed in such finery yet know that there was so much suffering all around? The contradiction took her breath away.

"Why so quiet, pretty girl?" Adele's mother always meant well, though her affections were usually placed in extolling the virtues of a polished and graceful persona. "Are you nervous about tonight?"

"No. I'm not nervous." Adele admitted the truth. She'd played onstage a hundred times before. Her mother wasn't likely to believe that nerves had overtaken her anyway.

"Your headache has not returned?"

Adele shook her head against the lie she'd told to sneak out of the house the night before.

"Then what is wrong?" Marina turned her daughter to face her and tilted her chin up with her hand. "Tell your mother."

Adele knew she could never tell her mother the truth. Marina Von Bron was too taken in by the glitz and glamour of their place in the Third Reich to care for any of the Jews in the city. Adele had heard her going on about Vienna's "Jewish problem" at cocktail parties. She thought them wretched, soulless creatures and the sooner Austria had sent them all away to useful employment at the work camps, the better.

Preoccupied, her mother stepped away and then returned and, with a marvelous white mink shawl outstretched in her arms, prepared to grace Adele's shoulders with it.

"Do you not wonder, Mama, what is happening out there?"

Marina seemed confused and looked to the closed bedroom door, even as her hands smoothed the fur around Adele's neck. "Downstairs? Well, your father has guests to accompany us to the concert hall. If you'd rather we go on our own, we certainly may. I can have a car brought around."

"No—I meant out there." Adele tilted her head toward the windows that overlooked the charming Viennese street below. The streetlamps cast a soft glow outside. "Beyond our home, beyond the borders of our city. Where our boys are fighting and dying and coming home in caskets. Out there where our world is falling to pieces. Beyond parties and victory concerts . . . far beyond playing the violin on a stage. What does it look like out there? Do we even know?"

Marina looked disturbed by Adele's words. The talk of death and war was too weighted a subject for her view of the light evening ahead.

She came round to stare her point-blank in the face. She grabbed onto Adele's upper arms and squeezed hard, as if to shake her from her momentary stupor. "What in heaven's name is the matter with you?"

"Nothing, I—"

Another squeeze and a shake. "Tell me this instant. Does this have to do with your departure from a room full of dinner guests last night?"

"I just . . ." She paused, fearful of the wild look that had taken over her mother's usually lovely eyes. "I don't know if I can play, that's all."

"Hush your mouth this instant!"

The sudden outburst caught Adele by surprise, so much so that she couldn't even manage to utter a response.

"What an insult to your father and the rest of the men downstairs, and to the Führer!" Her mother's face contorted as if the very thought pained her. "What happens beyond our walls is no concern of yours, do you understand me? Your job is to play. That is what you will do for Austria. Play. You will honor the Führer and your family. You will not make fools of us tonight."

"I hadn't thought to make a fool of anyone."

Her mother eyed her, the intensity of the glare working to shred her resolve.

"Where is this coming from, Adele?"

"Nowhere, I—"

Her mother cut in with force masked as elegance in her tone. "You have been gifted a rare talent, and I'll not have you waste it because you've decided to become interested in philosophy all of a sudden."

"But we are Christians, are we not?"

Marina huffed. "You see me pray in church every week. I light a candle for all of Austria. What else has God to do with what happens out there, except to protect the fighting sons of our country? I pray for their courage, just like everyone else."

Adele didn't understand why her mother was so upset. She'd never seen Marina Von Bron swat at a fly, let alone grab her by the arms until there were bruises pinched into her second layer of skin. And now she scoffed at her mention of God? He had everything to do with it, hadn't He? Adele felt they had every right to question what they were doing after the murderous display of evil she'd witnessed the night before.

"Mama." Adele wished she could tell her the truth, that if they followed Christ, they couldn't hope to follow the Nazis in the same breath. She knew what was happening out on the streets of Vienna, and all over Europe, for that matter. They couldn't look away any longer. "How can I play in the midst of such suffering? How can I turn a blind eye to what is happening? I didn't know what it was until now. But what we're doing to the Jewish people, it's"—she almost couldn't say the words out loud and instead whispered them—"it's *evil*, Mama."

The smack hit her across the cheek without warning. Her mother had pulled back and let her hand burn the left side of her face with as much force as she possessed.

Adele was stunned.

She brought a gloved hand up to the side of her face and held it there, unable to believe it had happened except for the painful throbbing that had already begun searing her cheek.

"Are you a coward or are you Austrian?"

With her cheek on fire and thoughts racing, she whispered, "I am Austrian."

Marina brought her face in closer until their noses were but an inch apart. "Then I suggest you *act* like it."

Adele stood with her hand on her face, watching as her mother turned to tidy the makeup that had been strewn about the bedroom vanity. She dropped tubes of lipstick and blush brushes into the top drawer, then collected hairpins and deposited them in a mother-of-pearl box on the bureau.

"I expect you to be downstairs and ready to go in five minutes."

She swiped her fur wrapper up from the vanity chair and without so much as a second glance left Adele in the coldness of her room.

CHAPTER FIVE

Sausalito, California

*S*era stepped out of her rental car and looked up—way up, at the towering Bay Area estate home before her.

She turned in a circle as she glanced around at the pristine grounds. An expanse of lavish architecture stood tall over the weaving cobblestone walkway that led to the blue coast below. Several rocking chairs along the length of the back porch had been lulled into a gentle ebb and flow by a sea breeze that perfumed the air with a fresh saltiness. It made her want to drop into one of the chairs and rock the day away.

This hideaway was like nothing she'd ever seen. She was from Manhattan, an island with some of the most impressive real estate around—but not like this. Not like the pile of California bricks in front of her. It looked exactly like one of those sprawling California wineries she'd always seen in the calendar pictures that hung above her desk at the gallery.

She looked to a grassy area overlooking the bay. There was a large white tent pitched in the center. It had a lengthy stage and an archway with an outrageous amount of flowers, elegantly draped ivory gauze curtains, and strings of Italian lights being laced up all around. A commercial van sat to the side of it, where workers were unloading silver candelabras and an endless stream of wooden crates that were being carried into the tent. What was going on? Clearly some sort of event.

She pulled off her sunglasses and took a long look at the expanse of the house, the tent, and the bay beyond, murmuring, "Just what in the world do you do, Mr. Hanover?"

"He was in real estate."

Sera thought she'd whispered the question under her breath.

She spun around at the voice and was met by a man who had walked up behind her. He stood there, a thirtysomething Mr. California Cool with a soft blue T-shirt, matching eyes, and a Red Sox cap pulled down over his forehead.

He wore gardener's gloves and had a rake in one hand, with a leaf or two still stuck to the prongs.

"Edward Hanover owned a real estate investment company," he said, leaning on the end of the rake in a casual manner. His mouth curved with the slightest hint of a smile tucked under the shadow of the hat's brim. "Heard you coming up the drive," he said, and motioned to the tree-lined gate she'd driven through.

"Oh, right." Sera nodded and looked blankly at him for a moment.

"Can we help you?"

"Uh, yes. I'm here to meet with the Hanovers. I have a gallery sheet in here somewhere." Trying to cover her embarrassment, Sera fumbled about her oversized handbag for the printout Penny had given her before she boarded the plane. The one with all of the information regarding the painting. The one that had fallen into the black hole of her purse and was presently missing in action.

She tossed her hair back over her shoulder, now wishing that the kick of coastal wind would calm down enough so she could see what she was doing. After an awkward moment of silence, she gave up the search and plucked a business card out of her purse instead.

"Yes. I am, uh—" She leaned in, squinting in the sun, and offered the card to him. "I'm Sera James."

He stared back at her as he took off the gloves and shoved them in his back pocket, a half squint evident on his face too. Her name didn't appear to ring any bells.

"Of the Sera James Gallery in Manhattan?" she said, eyebrows raised, although if this guy was part of the grounds crew, why was she bothering?

"Oh yeah. The art thing." He accepted it, then flipped the business card against his knuckles as if lost in thought. "They said someone from the gallery would be flying in soon. I didn't expect it to be today."

He motioned the end of the rake past the driveway where the tent stood, bustling with workers. Sera's gaze followed, and finally it clicked. Except for the blush pinks and muted greens of the flowers, every last detail was set in a pristine ivory. And ivory could only mean one thing.

"They're having a wedding?"

He nodded.

There was a wedding at the estate and no one had bothered to tell her. Sera gritted her teeth. She was going to kill Penny when she got home. How could her assistant fail to mention a tiny detail like a wedding, especially when the painting was at stake?

"I'm so sorry. I didn't know . . ." But before she could finish the apology, his attention was diverted.

"Hey, Manhattan—would you excuse me for a moment?"

Manhattan?

He walked toward a younger man, midtwenties maybe, with a tan and a giggling girl positioned at each elbow. If this guy was also a member of the grounds crew, he seemed to have forgotten it. Sera noticed a rake leaning up against the side of the florist's truck as he chatted with the girls.

Sera watched the group. It gave her a moment alone to stir up her confidence.

Breathe, Sera. She straightened her blazer and inhaled. *It's awkward, but not a deal breaker. If you still want to find the painting, you've got to go in there and convince this family that they want to help you.*

She watched as the man in the ball cap dispersed the group. He spoke to the younger guy and tossed a nod her way. Were they talking about her? The girls snatched up baskets overflowing with French peonies and scurried away as if their apron tails were on fire.

When he walked back up to her, she asked, "What did you say to him?"

He rubbed a hand against the back of his neck and turned toward the younger man who'd moved to the front stoop. "I suggested that he might be better served seeing our guest into the house if he couldn't keep his mind on his work."

Sera tilted her head toward the tent and frowned. "No one told me that there would be, well, this going on. I would have scheduled a better time for the Hanovers."

"What, that?" He shrugged. "Don't worry about it. There's always something going on around here."

"Yes, well," she answered, her hand going back to the bottom of her bag. He smiled as she continued digging.

"Not exactly ready for a day at the beach, are you?"

Sera looked down at her tailored black suit and then back up at him. "You mean to say I look like I'm from New York?"

"Not at all, Miss James. Just an observation. How about we show you around, since you're here on estate business."

"Um, are you the gardener?"

"Sometimes." He chuckled under his breath and tipped the brim of his ball cap as he walked away. "Go on in, Manhattan. The guy on the porch is Paul. I told him about you, and he's waiting to give you the dime tour."

〜

"Paul!" A lovely blonde sailed down the spiral staircase the moment they walked through the door. She darted into his arms and he welcomed her, hugging her tight as they turned in circles. She was a tiny flip of a thing, petite and with a youthful glow that couldn't have put her at more than twenty years.

"Macie!"

"I didn't know you were going to be here this early. We expected you tomorrow." The young woman beamed at him and pecked a kiss to his cheek. "No one told me a thing."

"Then it wouldn't have been a surprise," he teased, and flipped the sunny waves that bounced over her shoulder. "When did this happen?"

Macie grabbed the back of her hair and shrugged. "The first second Mom had her back turned, I had it all chopped off."

"And how'd our dear mother take it?"

"Like a champ." The girl winked at him. "She only cried for a half hour before she was calling the stylist with the new short-haired bridal theme. She had to reorder the flowers and change the neckline of the bridesmaids' dresses at the last minute, but it's kept her occupied at the very least."

"I'm surprised she's still talking to you after that stunt."

"Nah," she said, and waved him off. "I'm still in her good graces, don't forget, because at least I'm getting married. That means someday, Eric and I will give her grandkids and you'll still be all alone in that Boston apartment of yours."

He coughed rather uncomfortably and quickly stood aside, exposing Sera to the bride's sparkling, dimpled smile.

"Macie, this here is . . . Manhattan. She flew in from New York for the occasion. Manhattan, this is my sister—our bride."

The young bride looked shocked. Her eyes popped open a little wider and she grinned from ear to ear.

"Really." Macie turned to Sera, who'd been eyeing the front door as an escape route. That plan was dashed now that the bride was smiling and checking her out from top to bottom. "Your date, Paul?"

"Nope," he said with a slight shake of his head. "Here on estate business. I have orders to give her a tour of the house."

Macie contorted her face in an animated frown.

"Well, keep her away from William, that's all I have to say. He woke up in a rotten mood and has been in his usual take-charge mode ever since. He's even managed to issue orders to the wedding planners. If he finds out she's here in the midst of it, you might not be able to vouch for her safety."

Sera was taken aback by the comment. Wasn't William the person she was supposed to meet? He should have been expecting her.

"Look at her." Paul slugged his sister's shoulder with a mock punch. "She's turned into a deer in the headlights. Five minutes and Manhattan is already thinking about hightailing it out of here."

Had that all shown on her face? Sera had to think it was possible, because that was exactly what had been flying through her mind.

Macie leaned in to shake her hand and whispered, "Manhattan? Is that a real nickname or one that this guy gave you?"

"It's Sera," she said, offering a smile in greeting.

"The Hanover men fancy themselves clever with handing out nicknames. No one else likes it either. Paul here's called me Spacey-Macie since I was five and got lost at the grocery store. Word to the wise—they'll never let anyone forget a nickname once they're branded."

"I heard that." Paul stepped up and issued her a stern frown. "And for your information, I'm not the one who gave it to her."

Sera looked back and forth between them. "I'm here on

business, actually. Estate business. I'm supposed to meet with a Mr. William Hanover? I believe he's expecting me."

"You're here to see William?" Macie said, and exchanged glances with Paul. His face was covered with a curious grin.

It made Sera even more nervous. "Is that a problem?"

"Oh, believe me, honey, he's not expecting you," Macie answered, shaking her head rather sorrowfully.

"He's not?"

"Well, not really." Paul echoed his younger sister's statement, but with something lighter about his voice. He seemed to be close to laughing. "But I'd say he probably knows you're here."

"But my assistant said—"

"I'm sure your assistant had it right. It's about the painting?"

Sera nodded, not sure what to make of the odd reception the Hanover house presented its guests.

"When he finds out you're here, it's going to send him into hyperdrive." Macie gave her a weak smile as she reached out to pat Sera's elbow. "I'm so sorry."

"Well, he might already know she's here, Mace."

The bride shook her head. "No way. He would have said something."

"So I'm guessing, Miss James, that you had no idea my grandfather's will is being contested and that all of his holdings are tied up in the hands of the court." Paul's face dropped when she was rendered speechless. "Classic. They didn't tell you?"

"No, not a word." Sera shook her head, befuddled by the revelation that the painting might be unattainable even to the Hanovers. Getting involved with legal proceedings was messy business. "What's going on?"

"Well, I'm sorry to tell you this." Paul shook his head. "But there's only one thing standing between my family and our inheritance, and that something is the painting. William is unlikely to be happy to see you."

At his words Sera did a double take, looking from the blushing bride back to him. "Why . . . ? He doesn't even know me."

"He knows everything he needs to, Miss James. You just happen to be searching for the painting whose owner is set to inherit the entire hundred-million-dollar Hanover estate."

CHAPTER SIX

⎯⎯

his was bigger news than Sera was prepared for at the
moment. Not in the first hour of her having landed in
California. And not as she sat waiting in a chair across from the
massive desk, tapping her feet like a schoolgirl who'd been sent
to the principal's office. But here she was, suit-clad Manhattan,
waiting for the head of the Hanover clan to step into the estate's
downstairs office and turn her ordered world upside down.

As promised, Paul had given her a tour of the house before
he'd deposited her in his eldest brother's office. Nine bedrooms.
Twelve bathrooms. A pool here, a library and media room there.
The house was palatial, with a beautiful view that spanned the
California coastline, but she was used to wealthy clients and had
prepared herself for it.

Finding out the value of the family estate, though—that had
thrown her a bit.

It couldn't be true. *The painting* was the sticking point? Sera
thought she'd been searching for a lost painting that couldn't
have been worth anything to anybody. Now it was worth the
equivalent of one hundred million dollars? That was more than
the price of an original Monet. And way out of the price range
that could make it attainable to her.

Sera could hear the clock ticking on the wall. She'd come all
this way because of the mystery in a painting that had stolen

her heart years ago. Now she'd landed in an even bigger mystery and the patriarch of it all was coming in the office—to see *her*.

The door creaked and Sera turned toward the sound. What she saw was nothing short of a cruel joke. It wasn't the fire-breathing Hanover monster that Macie had warned her about. Neither was he the boorish family boss that Paul had described. Instead, in walked one of the handsomest men she'd ever seen.

Blue dress shirt, matching eyes. Dark hair. He'd discarded the Red Sox hat and had managed a quick change of clothes, but there was no denying it. Her heart sank when she realized who it was.

Are you the gardener? Sera thought back to the embarrassing question she'd asked him outside and almost melted to the hard-wood floor.

Lovely. What else could go wrong?

"Miss James, is it?" He walked in the office with a studied air and sat down behind the desk. "I'm sorry to have kept you waiting. As you know, I was busy working with the grounds crew." He tilted his head toward the windows overlooking the front lawn and flashed a brilliant smile. "So to speak."

She nodded politely and tried to return a confident smile to his teasing. "That's all right. I haven't been waiting long."

Smile. Yes, that was it. If she could smile, maybe she could convince him that she wasn't a total ditz.

"I'm sorry to be an imposition at such an important time, but as I said outside, no one informed me there would be a wedding here. I expected to meet with you in person and settle this business of the painting in one afternoon. Had I known the legal troubles surrounding the estate, I'd have opted for a more appropriate time."

"Ah," he mumbled, and leaned back in his office chair until the wood creaked. "Then Paul told you about the inheritance."

"He did."

"And you think there's a better time to tell a man you're trying to take a hundred million dollars out of his pocket?"

She squirmed uncomfortably. "I'm not sure what you're refer-ring to. I just own an art gallery. Anything decided regarding the estate is out of my hands." Those would be the hands that were twisting in her lap at the moment.

"Well, that is where you're wrong."

"I am?"

"You're in an unusual position here. I find that my grand-father, however noble his intentions may have been, has caused a rather deep rift to form between the members of our family. When he passed last November, the family—including my father and his younger sister—well, we all had an understanding about where the money was going. There was a will. It was signed and notarized in 2007 when his mind wasn't in question. But in the last couple of years, he'd changed. Enough so that we have to believe he wasn't in the full use of his mind when he made cer-tain decisions regarding the estate."

"Is that lawyer talk for 'He changed his mind and you're not happy about it'?"

He opened a desk drawer and took from it a manila folder, which he laid open-faced on the desktop. Then, without hesita-tion, he leaned in and eyed her directly.

"May I speak plainly, Miss James?"

"Is that not what you've already been doing, Mr. Hanover?"

Something tightened in his face. She noticed the almost nondescript twinge of a muscle that flexed in his jaw once she'd decided to answer him with a bit of moxie.

Score one for Miss James.

She could see by his response that there was a lot at stake. This guy was polished, comfortable in his own skin, and impos-sibly good looking. But despite his subtle efforts to see if she'd be intimidated in an office that was bigger than her entire Lower East Side apartment, she refused to fold.

Sera coughed over the nervous tickle in her throat and notched her chin a little higher in the air. She'd be confident in front of him if it killed her.

"Do you know what I have here?" he said, drumming the folder with his fingertips.

"I'm sure I don't."

"It's a copy of my grandfather's will. Signed little more than a year ago, stipulating that the entire estate should be left to someone none of us have ever heard of. Someone without a name. The owner of a certain painting. We have a painting in our possession, but it's a copy of the original. What's more, we don't know where the original is or who owns it. Now, you can imagine what kind of surprise this was to us, the unsuspecting family members who now have to keep my grandfather's business afloat with no assets to do so. Would you think that as president of my grandfather's company I might be a bit, we'll say, taken aback by this turn of events?"

"I suppose so."

"Would you say that I have the right to be concerned when some anonymous gallery owner waltzes in with a story that she's searching for a lost painting, our painting, mind you, and positions herself to clean out the estate my grandfather worked his entire life to build up?"

Sera's palm flew up on instinct, asking for a pause to the accusation. "Wait—you think I'm here for your money?"

He didn't flinch. "Aren't you?"

"Of course not!" Surely he wasn't serious. The man thought she was there on a mission to find the painting so she could cash out on the family estate? "You can't think I'm capable of doing such a thing."

His eyes sparkled a little. "I think anyone would be capable of it given the one-hundred-million-dollar paycheck involved. That's why we've sought to keep this matter quiet. No media. You understand. If it got out that the estate goes to the owner of some lost painting, we'd have every fortune hunter and news outfit in the country descending on the estate in a matter of minutes."

It was a difficult situation, no doubt. Having heard a bit of the backstory helped her make some sense of it all. But that was where Sera's compassion fizzled. This man was a stranger, yet he possessed the ability to stare straight through her.

Sera could feel her temperature starting to rise hotter than the California sun outside. "Listen. My gallery stumbled across your painting by chance. We've been searching for the original for the last two years and had hoped this was the key to finding it."

"For two years?" He cocked an eyebrow. "You've been after the same painting I'm looking for?"

"It would seem so."

William paused and, tilting his head to the side, said, "Then your explanation for wanting it is . . . ?"

She couldn't tell him the truth. Not now. Best to gloss over the fact that she'd do just about anything to find the one link she had to her father's memory. "The fact that this painting is named in your grandfather's will has nothing to do with me. I am merely doing my job as an art historian. We're acquiring Holocaust era art for the gallery. My job right now is to find the painting—end of story."

"Has someone hired you to find it?"

"No."

"Well, Miss James. It seems you and I have a common interest in this story, then."

"And that would be?"

"Whatever our motives, I want to find the rightful owner of this painting as badly as you do. And when I do find them, I'll have the pleasure of presenting him or her with a summons to appear in court. Our family has to contest the will. We have no other option."

"You'd take someone to court over this?"

He didn't answer. He didn't need to. She could see it all around them. Money. Inheritance. The lavish lifestyle that had been showered upon him. Of course the Hanover family wouldn't want to give it up. Who would? In fact, William would probably do just about anything to protect his family's fortune, and she could be instrumental in that.

"Why did you ask me to come here?"

"I told you—when I heard you were looking for the painting, I assumed you were after our estate and I figured I'd better have a chat with you."

She sat in silence for a moment. A memory flashed before her eyes. Her dad, leading her into a Paris gallery to talk to an old colleague. And there it was, hanging on a back wall. Not in a place of prominence, but tucked away in a dusty corner, as if the lovely violinist had been forgotten by time.

Sera stood and shrugged her purse up over her shoulder. "Well, if you think I'm of the fortune-hunting type, I won't stay and dampen your sister's wedding with my presence. But if you decide you want to talk business, the address of where I'll be staying is on the back of my business card."

Sera walked toward the door with as much confidence as ever. Inheritance or not, she would find the painting. With or without his help.

"Oh, and if you call the hotel, I'll be under the name Manhattan."

CHAPTER SEVEN

—

December 4, 1942

Could snow hold memories? Adele wondered. It fell down around her now just as it had on so many other nights she'd waited for him. And though it was years ago, she could still remember the first time she'd sat upon the bench, waiting in the garden hideaway as she watched the minutes tick away until it was time for her first concert. She'd been young, faith untested, so different from who she was now.

"Here you are." She could hear Vladimir trudging up behind her, his feet crunching on the ice-tinged grasses with each step. "I know—we were supposed to meet more than an hour ago."

"I was going to stay right up until performance time, hoping you'd come."

She half turned on the bench then, enough to see him walking up behind her in a pristine black tuxedo. Vladimir Nicolai was steadfast and strong, his dark hair falling over his forehead enough to tip his lashes. He wore an overcoat of black wool and an ivory tucker that danced out on a light gust of winter wind.

"Tell me you haven't been out here all this time." He rubbed his hands together and blew into his palms. "It's freezing out here."

"No. I went in for a while." She shrugged. "But I don't mind."

And she didn't, even though her legs felt like blocks of ice. Who ever thought of waiting in a snowfall while wearing paper-thin satin? But facing the painfully cold night was nothing in comparison to waiting, hoping, and praying he would arrive. In truth, she'd have stayed out there all night, concert or not.

She stood then, watching him, fearful of her own reaction whenever he was near. Adele had been in love with him from the moment they met more than three years before. She'd been young then, and had probably seemed like the kid-sister type to him. He'd been young too. And clueless as to her affection. But something had changed. And now the tall young man had grown up. He had grown up in the midst of war and was taking her breath away with each step in her direction.

He stopped in his tracks, holding back from her by several feet.

"Why are you wearing that?"

She looked down at the fur shawl that draped over her satin gown. "What, this?" she asked, holding the edge of the fur out.

"Yes. That, the dress—all of it."

"Is there something wrong with it?"

"No—" He almost smiled, but instead tilted his head to the side as if in thought about something. "Where did you find satin?"

She lifted her shoulders in a light shrug. "My mother."

After what had happened moments before she'd left for the concert, she hated to even think of her. But the rest needed no explanation, she guessed. Everyone knew Marina Von Bron and her taste for over-the-top finery. Adele had never felt so ridiculous as she did wearing satin and pearls in the midst of a war zone.

"Doesn't she have you wear black for a performance?" He took several steps forward again, but this time seemed distracted and stopped just short of the tips of his shoes touching hers.

He looked down at her.

She hadn't remembered him being that tall. Had he always looked down on her like that?

"It's a victory celebration to honor the Führer, as you know. And I have a solo," she said, nervous all of a sudden. Why was this night so different from all the others? "Is it too much?" She had to ask. Lavish satin, pearl earrings—she'd grown up around her mother's taste for them but had never found a liking of them for herself. No doubt she looked like a child playing dress-up.

"No. Not too much. Not too much at all." He looked down at her still, curiously quiet. "So, are you able to play? Your hands?"

She'd been twisting them without even noticing. The pain medicine the doctor had given her must have been doing the trick, for she scarcely felt a twinge. "Dieter gave me some pain medication to get through the performance." She held up a gloved hand, which he took and cradled in his own.

"You hide your hands in gloves because of me." He brought it to his lips and pressed a brush of a kiss against her palm. "I am so sorry. You can't know how sorry I am."

She looked away, finding that his gaze was too intense.

"Did you hear me, Butterfly?" *Butterfly*. He'd given her the nickname the first time they'd ever played onstage together. "Everything will be all right."

Vladimir always said that to her.

He was older, had played with the orchestra many times. She was barely seventeen that first night, and inexperienced, and scared out of her mind. He'd been late for the performance, but just in time to keep her from passing out before she took the stage. He'd been running in the back entrance and had bumped into her as she came outside to the very garden in which they stood now. It had been spring then, and warm, their view of the world warm and innocent with it. She couldn't help but think how everything had turned cold now.

"Do you remember how nervous you were? That first performance?"

She nodded. So they were thinking of the same memory.

"Of course I do. You told me that I would have to play like I did in rehearsals—to feel the music, to let it float from my soul in honor to God. And we saw a butterfly. It was doing the same thing, floating around, dancing from perch to perch right here in our garden. It landed on our bench." Her fingertips grazed the back of the bench as she spoke, recalling the memory like it was yesterday. "You said that I had to go in there and not be afraid to play, to share the gift that God gave me."

"I did say that." He smiled. "And what did you do?"

"I went inside and played."

"And showed all of Austria what a beautiful genius you are," he said, a laugh escaping his lips. "I was impressed by the youngest member of our troupe. She showed them that a little butterfly of a girl could upstage a group of arrogant men. And that, Adele, is when Vienna found her sweetheart."

"I don't remember it like that." She turned her eyes and, in distraction, looked down at her strappy heels, their gold color sparkling in the moonlight.

"Adele, I won't let you be put in harm's way. I meant what I said this morning."

"I know you did."

"Then why won't you look at me?"

"Because I am afraid you did mean it and I will never see you again." Her chin quivered. She felt it, was moved by her own unconscious reaction to saying the words aloud.

"Adele, look at me." He tilted her chin up until her eyes met his. "I'm leaving right after the performance tonight." He paused, perhaps knowing that he should ease into the admission, that this was a moment they wouldn't get back for some time to come. "I'll be gone until this war is over. But I will come back."

"You've been called into service, then?"

He shook his head. "You know my health makes me ineligible. That won't change, Adele."

"Then why do you have to leave?"

"Because so many young musicians were conscripted into service, they elevated a musically inclined merchant's son to play in one of the world's greatest orchestras. I'm told that I can play the cello for Austria. That is my purpose. It is for the Third Reich, they tell me. To show my allegiance. And all while I'm looked at as a coward."

"You're not a coward. You can't help a heart condition you've had since childhood."

He shook his head in defiance. "You don't understand, Adele. Whether others look at me as a coward or not, I'd not have fought for Germany. No matter how much I love my country. But I have to use my life for something. I have to fight in some way. And playing on a stage in front of Hitler's stooges isn't the way to do it. A ticker that beats out of sync can't prevent me from doing what I know to be right."

"And what is that?"

He shook his head. "I can't tell you."

She didn't ask where he would go, or what he would be doing. He wasn't likely to tell her no matter how many times she asked. Instead, she needed to know only when he would return.

"But what if this war never ends?"

"It will."

"How do you know? You don't know that."

Did she sound like she was pleading? She didn't care. Her words were frozen on air, the last bit of warmth leaving her body with them.

"You must have faith," he said, the words simply stated and giving the appearance of being deeply felt. "Have faith that God will use the evil of this war for His good. Somehow, He will."

"And how will I know you're safe?" Her voice hitched on

emotion that had long been bottled. She released it now, almost stuttering, "How will I know you are even *alive?*"

After the agony of the night before, of not knowing if he was alive or lying in an alley somewhere, she couldn't relive that fear. Not again.

"When you see me onstage"—he breathed the words and inclined his head toward the back door—"in there. That will always be our place. It's in both of us, isn't it? The music? This call to play . . . we will always have it together."

She trembled as a gust of wind wove around them with its icy dance.

Adele Von Bron in love with a merchant's son? Her parents had already tried to stop it, but they'd send her away immediately if they learned their little violinist was ready to give up everything for this man. They found him unsuitable, without even knowing the events of the night before. Had they known the truth, that she loved him even more for the bravery he possessed in attempting to save the Haurbechs, they'd have turned him in to the Germans right then and there.

"What are you thinking about?" he asked.

"Last night. And now this—an extravagant victory concert even when Vienna could fall siege to the Russians. They are building watchtowers all around the city. They are doing it for a reason, aren't they?"

He nodded. "The Germans are scared."

"We're all scared." She shook her head. "Our entire world is going to change."

He shocked her then by wrapping an arm around her waist and pulling her in close, closer than he'd ever dared before.

"I think it already has," he whispered against her mouth, and led into a kiss that could have melted the snow at her feet.

She fell against him, inviting the warmth of his strong arms to shield her from the shockingly cold night around them. She clung to him with the passion she'd felt anytime her soul connected with his. He was, after all, her closest friend, and though the future seemed uncertain, he was the man she wanted to spend it with. The blackness of Nazi Germany flooded into their dreams for a future, but still she dared hope it would someday end, that she could one day love him freely.

Adele dared to hope their first kiss wouldn't be their last.

Vladimir wound his hand through the curls at her nape, the softness falling down in a curtain around her neck. She melted further, leaning in, coveting every second of the kiss she'd always wanted from him. And suddenly, Vladimir pulled back.

The void left her speechless. Perhaps he was aware that if he did intend to leave, the kiss was only making it more difficult. Adele looked back at him, the hazel eyes she'd long ago memorized looking down on her so sweetly.

He lifted a finger and traced the outline of her chin.

"Was that a good-bye?" she asked. The only courage she had left was in those few short words. "Tell me it wasn't a good-bye."

"I'd take you with me if I could." He brushed a hand over the hair at her temple, smoothing it back from her brow. "You're safe here, with your parents."

"But even when you do come back, my parents won't let me see you."

"I know, Butterfly."

She blinked, knowing fresh tears were glazing her eyes. "Take me with you."

"I can't. Not where I'm going." He squeezed her hand. "Anything that connects us now would only implicate you, and I won't let you be hurt again. Do you understand me?" He pulled back sharply. "Never again."

He tried to turn, but she spun him around, forcing him to look at her again.

"I chose this, remember?"

He wouldn't acknowledge her words. Instead, he stood stone-faced, looking back at her.

"You didn't know what you were doing."

"Yes, I did. I was the one who brought them to you, remember? I was friends with them. I was the one who promised we would get them out—all of them. And I came to you. Why do you think I did that?"

Because I trusted you, her heart willed him to understand. *Say it. Say you know I trusted you then and I trust you now . . . Tell me I haven't imagined the love between us.*

Tell me that, and I'll live on it forever.

A clock chimed in the background, breaking the silence with its aching, lonely tone. It signaled what they both knew.

"We have to go," she whispered, the fur suddenly inadequate to prevent the cold night from producing a chill down her spine.

She turned and he caught her at the wrist. Lightly. With the softest hold on her sensibilities at the same time.

"I promise this is not the last time we'll see each other. I swear it to you." His eyes searched hers, looking over her face with a fervency she wasn't prepared for. "Do you believe me?"

She couldn't say yes. Her heart couldn't commit to it. She was too afraid this was the last time.

"Two blinks." She offered the onstage signal they'd always shared. From that first night they'd played together, he'd blinked at her to give her courage to go on and it had been their silent message ever since. "I'll give you your two blinks when I see you onstage, as usual."

He shook his head. "I don't think that's going to work for me anymore. A signal to mean 'my friend' doesn't seem appropriate," he said, and offered a sudden, heart-stopping smile. "Not after the way you just kissed me."

Adele blushed. She knew her cheeks were as red as her lips when she felt them flood with warmth.

"Now, as for our friendship—I'd like that to continue." He tapped the tip of her nose with his finger. "The rest? We'll see if we can change that to three blinks when I return."

Three blinks? I. Love. You?

Adele smiled in spite of the world that threatened to fall around them.

For the first time in months, she had something to look forward to. She could look out in their future and finally see an end to war and a start to the life they might have together. It was hope filled, the promise of those three blinks, and she had a feeling it would get her through to his return.

"I see you're considering it?"

She nodded and wiped a frozen tear from her cheek with her gloved hand. "I am."

It was all she had to say.

"Good," he said, putting an arm around her to lead her inside. A barely there whisper caressed the side of her ear: "You can do it, Butterfly."

And the snow continued to fall.

CHAPTER EIGHT

—

*A*dele walked onstage.

She could feel the eyes of everyone in the auditorium boring into her. Her mother, no doubt finding something inappropriate in her dress. Her father, puffing up like the proud peacock he was. And the rest of the affluent guests, the ladies dripping in jewels and furs, each clinging to a Nazi officer's arm.

All of it sickened her. It was the first time in her life she could remember hating her gift. She didn't want to use it like this. Surely God wouldn't want her to play for this crowd?

The click of her heels echoed off the ceiling as she walked across the stage and stood out in front of the rest of the orchestra.

Nerves set in. Her hands, shed of the protective gloves and gauze, now lay naked at her sides, their blistered and puckered appearance tucked beneath the folds in her gown on one side and cradling her violin on the other. And when she thought she could not play, when she thought of forgetting what she must do and walking offstage, she looked up. Not with her entire head, just with her eyes. She looked at the second chair in the back row.

And there he was. Vladimir. Smiling. Urging her on. Telling her it was okay to play, to love the gift of music God had crafted in her heart, and to not be ashamed to share it with the rest of the world, even if that world was filled with SS officers. He tilted his head down in a light nod and blinked three times. And as if by magic, Adele smiled in return.

She felt something come alive, and if only for that night, it was okay to play. She felt as if God was granting her permission through Vladimir's accepting gesture. She wasn't playing to honor the Führer. Instead, she was playing for the honor of another.

Adele vowed then to play for the lost. She'd play for Elsa, her friend. For Elsa's husband, Abram, and their little boy, Eitan. She'd pick up her violin and touch her bow to it, playing the haunting melody for the little Jewish girl, Sophie, hidden by Vladimir somewhere in the darkness of the city. And she'd play for the rest of them, for the world's loss of innocence and the coldness of hate that fought to overshadow the love she knew to be born of God.

She would play.

The conductor raised an arm and they were brought to attention, all of them prepared to do their job for Austria, to play as they never had for the leader of the Third Reich. And Adele joined them. She let the notes dance from her heart and out her fingertips. She allowed the pull of creation to take over every breath in her body as the notes cried from her innermost soul.

Then came the moment for her solo.

Adele played each note with precision. Brought to tears, feeling as if her soul had finally expended what God had called her to do. She knew then that an artist could feel it, could know when her craft is practiced, when it is used to its fullest potential. Adele felt it, maybe for the first time. She felt the music come alive from the inside out, pulling her away from the fear of the night before and pouring a measure of peace upon her.

It felt like hours that she stood up there, whisked away in the moment, sailing through her act of worship to her Creator. And for how fervently she gave in to the magical dance of the notes upon her soul, she felt no physical pain. Adele was astounded that her hands didn't hurt at all. No, they weren't an impediment as she thought they'd be. They moved with dexterity to every note she wished to play. They flew back and forth, with the speed of the music and the haunting notes of each melody.

It felt wonderful to conquer her fear, to play without the instability of the future hanging over them like a threatening tyrant. She felt exhilarated and alive onstage, alive like she'd never expected. Adele stopped on the last note, lowering the violin and bow. She accepted the thunderous applause with the rest of the orchestra as the blood began dripping from her hands down the sides of her gown.

CHAPTER NINE

———

The phone was ringing when Sera stepped through the door to her room at the Ivy Ridge Bed and Breakfast. She dropped her bags in a heap on the floor and sailed over the bed to answer it, slamming her hand against the bedside table in the process.

"*Ow!*" She wedged the phone against her shoulder and began rubbing the stinging pain out of her fingertips. "Hang on."

She almost lost the phone again when she tried to reposition it against her chin. "Penny, I am so glad you called," she said, assuming her assistant would be the only one calling. "I just ran into the room and I smashed my hand on the bedside table. And my meeting at the Hanover mansion was disastrous. You won't believe this—he actually thinks I'm after his money." She shook her head and let out a weary sigh.

"Who is Penny?"

She stopped, startled to hear a male voice on the other end of the line.

"She's my assistant," she backtracked, with her gut telling her to shout, *Wrong number!* and hang up quickly. Or permanently button her lip. Either way, she dreaded confirmation of who waited on the other end of the line. "I'm sorry. Who is this?"

"You'll be disappointed to hear that it's William."

She closed her eyes as her chin sank to her chest. Could

things possibly get worse? He'd never help her find the painting if he thought she'd insulted him.

She began tripping over an apology at once. "Mr. Hanover, I assure you I meant nothing by that comment—I only meant that I didn't . . . that is to say, I expected someone else to be on the line and—"

"It's okay." Was he laughing? It almost sounded like it. His voice was much lighter than it had been in the office. "Am I disturbing you?"

"No. I just got in."

"Well, I don't want to take more of your time than is necessary, so I'll state the reason for my call. I was hoping to come to an agreement with you."

She repositioned the phone in her hand, the words having caught her attention. "I'm listening."

"We both want to find the original painting."

"I agree." Yes. If she learned more about his painting, then it might lead to what her heart longed for, to see the original painting once more. Regardless of their different motives, they both wanted the same thing.

"And we both know that my grandfather is the place to start."

Sera had to concede that point as well, no matter how much she preferred not to admit it. "That is why I came all this way."

"Exactly. I have a connection to the painting and you have the means to find it. We each have something the other wants."

"So what is this agreement you're after?"

"We work together. I hire you, and you share what you already know."

"Keeping your enemies closer?"

"Not exactly." He said it so lightly that Sera caught the hint of a smile evident in his voice. "I'm calling to invite you to dinner."

"Dinner?"

"Is that a question?"

"No," she said, completely taken aback. Sera drifted down to sit on the side of the bed. "I just didn't expect—"

"That I could be civil when it comes to my family inheritance?"

"I wouldn't describe it in that way."

"I won't mention the fact that I can tell you're lying. In any case, I thought we could talk over dinner. And if you are still interested, we can be of some help to each other."

"Dinner tonight?" She had a plane to catch in the morning, so it would have to be that night, if at all.

"Yes. If you're free."

"Casual or, uh, dressy?" She couldn't believe she was agreeing to it. Dinner with the patriarch of the Hanover clan could prove intimidating. And she only had one outfit suitable for dinner—a little black sheath and strappy heels. She hoped it would do.

"It's up to you. Just so you're comfortable."

What could it hurt to have dinner with the guy? Sera shrugged her shoulders. She had to eat. But with a handsome man while the California sun set in the background? A smile covered her mouth as Penny's voice echoed in her ears. Yes, her assistant would have been gleeful over the fact that a man had asked her to dinner—even if it was platonic in nature. She'd have screamed, *"Go!"* without missing a beat.

"Miss James?"

"Yes. I'm here," she said, jarred from her thoughts.

"So, what do you say? Pick you up at seven?"

Sera smiled in spite of herself.

"Seven it is."

"Good. See you then," he said, sounding more sure of himself somehow. "And, Miss James—better go ice that hand."

⁓

William's car pulled up to the Ivy Ridge Bed and Breakfast at precisely seven o'clock.

She looked down from her second-story window in a state of instant panic when she saw him hop from his Jeep in khaki shorts and a T-shirt.

William had instructed that she dress comfortably, but Sera had taken that to mean something appropriate for a business dinner worthy of the Hanover luxury she'd witnessed earlier in the day. Where was the suit? Wasn't this a business meeting? She always dressed up to meet clients.

Sera glanced in the bureau mirror. Her reflection said office cocktail party, not California casual. There was nothing she could do about the black sheath now—the dress was the only thing she had that wouldn't have her baking in a Jeep with the top down. But as for the rest, she had to do something.

With only thirty seconds to fix her appearance, Sera pulled the pins out of the elegant chignon at her nape and flipped her head over, running her hands through her long hair. She stood up straight again and let the loose waves fall down to cascade about her shoulders.

She turned to survey her appearance in the boudoir mirror.

Hmm. Not enough.

Off came the chandelier earrings and the gold cuff at her wrist. Sera discarded them and tossed them back in her suitcase. She put simple diamond studs in her ears and traded out the heels for a pair of sleek red-patent flats. One last look in the mirror and she figured her outfit was about as casual as it was going to get.

She snatched her clutch from the bed.

"Well, Mr. Hanover," she whispered aloud, and headed for the door. "Here we go."

~

Sera wasn't prepared for where she'd be having dinner.

Not prepared at all.

William had driven his Jeep right down onto the sand and stopped not far from a group of people scattered around a huge beach bonfire. Guests were mingling over plates of food and glasses of champagne, some dining at the tables and chairs that had been set up while others lounged on blankets in the sand.

She rubbed her hands over the goose bumps that had popped out on her arms. Whether it was fear or the cool breeze kicking up off the water, it didn't matter. He'd still brought her to a beach party and she, not knowing a soul and wearing a black cocktail dress, felt like the odd woman out.

William looked over at her for a moment but didn't say anything. If she could have judged his thoughts, she'd guess he wondered how in the world anyone could be comfortable in a cocktail dress at a beach. No doubt he thought she looked ridiculous. Pity, then, that she answered her thought out loud.

"Well, in my defense, you never said we were going to a beach party to talk business."

He half smiled, a curious grin that tipped the corners of his mouth, then reached in the backseat and tossed a khaki jacket in her lap.

"It might be a little big, but at least it will keep your shoulders warm," he said, and hopped out of the Jeep. Sera looked down at her lap, sheepish, it seemed, every time she opened her mouth in his presence. She shrugged the jacket up over her arms as he came around to her side of the car.

Add gallantry to his list of unforeseen virtues, she thought, and stepped out the door he held open for her.

She stood in front of him then, noticing how he towered over her. And in her little black dress and jacket that fell down to balloon about the hem, she looked up, probably with an all-too-blushed look to her face.

"And for the record," he whispered, and leaned in to close the car door behind her with a *click*. He lingered there for a few seconds, looking at the contours of her face before he spoke again. "I would have said you looked nice, had you given me the chance."

Sera swallowed hard and tried not to get caught up in the openness of those eyes that were looking down at her. He smiled and tilted his head toward the group on the beach. They'd broken up and one faction lingered, chatting and laughing over a collection of blankets and driftwood logs, while a group of younger guys played football. The sun had bled in a cascade of blues and golds as it stretched out to the west, creating a perfect canvas backdrop.

"Come on." He motioned for her to follow him and began plodding through the sand in his flip-flops. "Macie will want to say hi."

Sera caught up to him and tugged at his sleeve to turn him around. He looked back at her, eyes wide.

"Wait a minute. You brought me to a family dinner?"

"Yeah. Is that a problem? You've already met them, so . . ." A casual shrug pinned his shoulders up with the last words. "I didn't think you'd mind."

"A dinner with family, right before a wedding." Understanding was quick to dawn. "You brought me to your sister's rehearsal dinner?" Sera stopped in her tracks, panic freezing her with her feet half buried in the sand. The man couldn't be that clueless about such things. "I can't intrude. Not like this."

He looked to the group and then quickly turned back to her. "It's okay, Sera. They know you're joining me. I thought under the circumstances it would be okay."

"Under the present circumstances, they think I'm taking their inheritance away."

"I thought you said you weren't."

"I'm not," she fired back.

"Good. There's no problem then, right?" he said, taking her

hand in his as he tried to tug her toward the group around the fire. She wiggled it free from his grasp and stood, feet planted like a statue in the sand.

"Like it or not, I'm the enemy. I'm looking for the painting that could ruin their lives."

"You're not the enemy if we hire you."

Sera shook her head. "But I thought everyone would hate me . . ."

This was worse than she'd thought. A rehearsal dinner with the people who thought she was there to empty their bank accounts? There was no way they'd accept her.

"They don't hate you."

"No?"

"No," he confirmed, shaking his head.

She stiffened her chin. "But you do."

William smiled again, but this time, the heart-stopping grin gave away the fact that he was amused by her comment rather than just trying to be polite.

"I never said that," he sighed. "Paul may have, and I will kill him later for it, but I never did." He paused and, with some discomfort, kicked the sand at his feet. "Look, I owe you an apology."

He did?

"You do?"

"Yes. I realized after you left that this isn't your fault. You may be a part of it now, but you never intended for any of this to happen. And I was . . ." He looked like he was somehow familiar with making apologies. He must have been a shoot-first-apologize-later breed of man. "I was rude, and I apologize. As your potential employer, I think I can ask you to let first impressions slide."

She eyed him with a bit of speculation. Something inside told her to stay guarded with him, although he certainly seemed genuine.

Obviously having seen the faint smile she offered in acceptance, he nodded and reached out for her to take hold of his arm, then led her over to the crowd.

Macie was the first to spot them and, with a burst of youthful energy, hopped up off her blanket and sailed in their direction.

And with that, Sera was welcomed.

Macie took her by the hand and introduced her to her fiancé, Eric, and then to the large group of groomsmen and bridesmaids gathered round the fire. Surprisingly, Sera found she wasn't quite the stranger she'd expected to be. The group smiled at her. And talked. And asked questions about her life in New York. What had brought her there? And how long did she plan to stay? And what was she doing with *this* guy? (The latter question coming from Paul, of course, as he pointed at his stiffening older brother.) Over a plate of crab cakes and fried clams, Sera found something she'd never have expected. This family, the one that was in danger of losing everything, was willing to receive her without question.

Sera wasn't sure she knew how to take this kind of acceptance; she wasn't used to it, that's for sure. After more than an hour of cheerful conversation, a toast to the bride and groom, and some live guitar music by Paul, she felt even more relaxed. Relaxed and grateful.

A fluttering memory whispered to her heart, reminding her of the God to whom she hadn't turned for so long. She'd breathed out a thank-you to Him when the painting had shown up in her gallery. But the realization now that Sera wanted that openness with God again—well, it surprised even her.

Thank You.

"Do you want more?" William walked over and took a seat next to her on the log, holding a plate of fried seafood out in offering.

Sera shook her head. "No thanks. It was wonderful, but I've eaten far too much already."

He sat quietly and set the plate down on the buffalo plaid blanket at their feet.

"I tried to tell my mother that she'd ordered too much. But, well, mother of the bride and all . . . you can't tell her anything. She insisted we'd be feeding some small West Coast army and cleaned out all the seafood from here to Seattle."

William ran his hand through his hair.

Sera picked up on the action as telltale. It was akin to vulnerability, which was surprising for the oldest, almost patriarchal Hanover. It set her to wonder why there was no father of the bride in attendance at the rehearsal dinner.

"I heard you're stepping in to give the bride away." Her voice was barely loud enough to be heard over the crashing waves. "That's rather noble if you ask me."

"Ah. That." He seemed to find embarrassment in it, for he shook his head and laughed softly. "Macie told you, huh? She shouldn't have done that."

Sera smiled in spite of herself. "I think she was trying to convince me that you're more than the figurehead of the Hanover family. And she followed up by telling me not to give in to you about the painting."

"So she thinks I'm a tyrant." He laughed and held up his glass of iced tea in a mock toast. "Nice to know someone's on my side."

"I think she was hoping I wouldn't hold this morning against you. I really didn't know about the will."

"I know you didn't," William agreed, and moved his view from a point out over the water to cast his gaze in her direction. "And despite what my siblings say, I'm not all work. Macie's a good girl. She means well. But she's young," he said, and looked over at the bride and groom sitting across from them. Sera watched them too as the firelight danced, illuminating the faces of the couple who were all smiles on the eve of their magic day. "She has no concept of the real world. For better or worse, we've shielded her from that. She's been through a lot in the past year. Eric seems to make her happy, so I'm glad someone is there for her."

"She's been through a lot?"

"Well, the last year has been trying. Thank goodness she's not alone."

"Yes," she said, watching as Macie tucked a lock of hair behind her ear and then laughed out loud at something her fiancé had said. She was young. Sweet. And endearing in a way that only a bride could be. "Thank goodness for that."

Eric draped his arm over Macie's shoulders and pressed a kiss to her temple. "And she seems to make him happy too," Sera noted, lost in the view of the happy scene.

William nodded in agreement. "She does."

Sera turned away, suddenly overcome by the memory of being a young bride herself once. It came flooding back but she didn't want to think about it. And though she'd sought God's healing for it once, she no longer had the inclination to think much past the busy life she'd made for herself at the gallery.

Staying busy hid the pain. Forgetting she'd ever been in love, that she'd ever been a would-be bride herself . . . it all had been buried deep when her fiancé called off the ceremony the day of their wedding, and she hadn't looked back since.

"My father left about a year ago."

William's words shocked Sera out of her memory. She looked up, blinking, as he stared deep into the dance of the firelight at their feet.

Had she heard him correctly? "He left?"

Something in William's face hardened as he confirmed the truth, nodding. "Right before Macie's twentieth birthday. He left our mom, the company—everything. After nearly thirty-five years of marriage. He just decided one day that he didn't want to do it anymore. He expected he'd receive a large sum of money when Grandfather passed, but that didn't happen. My grandfather was a good man, there's no doubt about that. But the relationship between him and the men of the family was often strained."

"Why is that?"

He shook his head. "A number of reasons."

He didn't seem inclined to share them.

"Where is your father now?"

William shrugged and tossed a shard of driftwood he'd found at his feet into the mouth of the fire. "Not sure. Last we heard, he moved back to London. My grandfather was from Great Britain and so my father spent time there as a kid. I guess he wanted to go back to someplace where he had fond memories."

"But he'll come home, right? Surely with the wedding—"

"He knows all about the wedding."

Sera was horrified that a husband and father could leave his family. And poor Macie. Her own father had abandoned her on what should have been the most important day of her life. And for what? Freedom from responsibility? She wasn't sure why the elder Hanover had made such a decision with his life, but it felt like a waste.

She hated to see the toll it was taking on the family.

"I'm so sorry."

"Mom tries to stay busy." William looked up at the woman with brunette hair and a welcoming smile on the other side of the fire. "The wedding has been good for her. You know. To take her mind off things. And Paul—he's his own animal, I suppose. I never worry about Paul. He could make a smile out of any situation. Laid-back is just his way."

She looked at Paul, who was entertaining guests across from them, then glanced back to the bride again and felt a wave of guilt wash over her. She understood what it meant to be discarded, to be abandoned by the man she'd expected to live the rest of her life with. Sera knew the loneliness that Macie and the rest of the family must have been going through. And somehow, seeing the

Hanovers from a new perspective gave her a clarity that changed something in her mind.

"So it's not all about the money." She whispered the statement.

"No. It's not," William answered immediately, and stood. "It's my job to keep this family together, and if we lose everything we have left, I think that would be the last straw. I can't let that happen."

He held out a hand for her, to help her up. Sera took it, gratefully accepting the tiny glimpse into his private life. It made him seem familiar somehow, and not as severe as she'd first thought.

"Want to take a walk?" He tilted his head up the beach. "Talk business?"

Sera nodded, appreciative to have something else to think about.

She walked by his side, saying nothing, feeling the salty air fill her lungs with each breath. It was a sweet, calming walk, unassuming for the moment and refreshing in a way she couldn't explain. And she didn't feel so disconnected from him anymore. William Hanover had evolved from a foe into a friend with a few careful steps through the sand.

"I'm sorry. I had no idea what your family was dealing with."

"How could you?" He tossed a rock she didn't know he held. It sailed out into the black night and dropped down into the stirring darkness of the sea.

Focus, Sera. You're leaving tomorrow. Do not allow yourself to become too personal with this man.

"So your grandfather—how long did he have the painting you sent me?"

"As long as I can remember. It's always been hanging in his office. But I never knew it was a copy of an original painting. That's new information."

"Did he tell you anything about how he acquired it?"

"He had it all these years. I just assumed he liked the painting," he said, shaking his head. "I never even thought to ask him." The last words were whispered, almost as if they were uttered in regret.

Sera watched as he stared out at the water.

"Well then. Is there anything you want to know about the painting? You brought me all this way. You might as well get some information out of the deal."

He paused, then asked, "The girl. Do you know who she is?"

Sera wrapped her arms around her middle as the sea breeze whipped in around them. She turned her face to it, allowing her hair to blow back over her shoulders. "Yes. Her name is Adele Von Bron. She was Austrian, a concert violinist prior to the war."

"Prior to the war? Then what happened after it?"

"You mean her shaved head and the tattoo?"

"No. I could guess that much," he replied, and shoved his hands in his pockets. "I wondered if you have any information about what happened to her inside the concentration camp. I may never have asked my grandfather about the painting," he said, exhaling. "But that doesn't mean I didn't really see it."

"I think that's what we're trying to find out."

He turned to look at her then with an almost boyish enthusiasm that had taken over his face. "Okay. Let's start there. Can we find her? She might still be alive, right? That's not out of the question. So we should be able to contact her, find out if she knew my grandfather somehow."

Sera shook her head. "We can't."

"Why not?"

On a sigh, she said, "Because we believe she died at Auschwitz in 1944."

CHAPTER TEN

⁓

*A*dele sat in her father's study, her hands bandaged in her lap.

The room was quiet. And eerily dark. Much darker than she'd have anticipated, even given the situation she now faced.

She glanced over at the immense marble and carved-wood fireplace on the wall. The dancing flames against the opulence of the room had once seemed so warm, so inviting when she curled up on the settee to read books as a young girl. But now? She imagined the fireplace with an intricate web of carved gargoyle-like creatures, all with menacing superiority as they mocked her, and a blazing fire that licked up to consume the entire wall. Suddenly, she felt evil all around her. It was as if the loving home she'd always known had morphed into something that threatened her with imminent danger.

The door creaked open. She heard heavy, clipped footsteps and the door slammed. She jumped at the sound.

The hard-nosed Fredrich Von Bron walked by her and slammed his uniform hat and gloves on the desk. He addressed her without looking up from the desktop.

"I am going to ask you this once, Adele, and you will answer me."

Adele sat there, terrified out of her mind.

From the moment her hands had begun to bleed down

her dress, the spotlight of guilt was cast in her direction. She hadn't known it before the concert, but the German authorities had learned that someone—whoever had been helping the Haurbechs—had fallen in their haste to run away from the docks. The blood evidence on the broken glass at the scene told them they'd be looking for someone with injuries similar to hers. But they'd been just as shocked as everyone else in the concert hall. No one would have thought to turn their attention to the general's daughter as the guilty party.

Of course, they didn't want a scene onstage, before all of Austria.

Adele had been whisked away to a dressing room where she was ordered to change into a simple navy frock that had been retrieved from the room's closet. With blood darkening her front, the lovely satin gown was no longer wearable; it was tossed in the nearest trash bin. She'd stood in the dimly lit room, hands shaking as she stripped out of the soiled gown and pulled the day dress over her head. She was surprised that the pain wasn't worse. No, her hands shook with fear now. Adele knew it, could feel it quickening her pulse and sending her fingers to fumble with the buttons that lined the front of the garment.

She recalled breathing out nervously as she affixed the last button at her collar.

Oh God . . . what have I done?

Getting dressed was all she could do other than wait.

Guards had been posted at the door, so there was no chance of fleeing that way. She checked both of the windows in the dressing room and was once again denied any chance for escape—they were tightly latched.

All she could do was sit. And pace. And wonder what would become of her. Would the Germans come and take her away? Oh heavens, would they come with guns drawn like she'd seen the night before?

Adele had paced the room, wondering what they would do with her, feeling like a trapped animal that awaited the return of the hunter.

It was a surprise then that her father came to fetch her at all, which he did more than an hour later. He'd not said a word, just walked stone-faced as he led her through the back hallways of the concert hall and tugged her into their waiting car. They drove through the snow that had once seemed so sweet in the garden with Vladimir; it had turned to a miserable ice-tinged rain that pelted the car windows on all sides. Then she arrived back to her prison of a home, was tossed into her father's study, and had seen no one but their family physician in the hours after. The doctor had attended to her wounds but said nothing. He held on to an awkward silence, no doubt because he was ordered to do so, and then left the room.

All of this she recalled as her father was now there, cold as ever, demanding she answer whatever it was he would say.

"What is the nature of your association with Vladimir Nicolai?"

Adele swallowed hard.

Her father hadn't asked about whether she was out on the streets with a Jewish family the night before. He didn't demand to know whether she'd stopped at the house of the doctor they both knew. He didn't even seem to hold any concern for what had happened to injure her hands. No—it all went back to Vladimir, and that was a dangerous thing. If she admitted having involvement that was any deeper than the platonic association with the orchestra's events, then she'd be admitting to everything. And if she admitted everything, it would implicate the man she loved.

It felt now like her own father was attempting to bait her.

Adele answered carefully, "He is an acquaintance from the orchestra."

Fredrich shook his head. "Do not lie to me."

The words were clipped, and flat, and without the least bit of warmth.

So he did know. She guessed he knew everything. What good then would it do to paint pictures of the truth? He was her father, after all. He'd not allow any harm to come to them. Perhaps she could appeal to that side of him.

"Whatever they've told you—there is an explanation."

"I come back from fighting a war only to have been told an outlandish story about my only daughter. That she sustained injuries while committing a crime that carries a harsh punishment. Knowing it cannot be true, I now seek to hear your denial of it."

"What story, Father?"

His intake of breath was sharp, his stance rigid as a fireplace poker. He stared back at her, the bushy mustache strangely unmoving when he spoke.

"Where were you last night?"

Adele's heartbeat began to thump in her chest, for she'd begun to doubt. She'd half quipped to Dieter the night before that if her father knew what she'd done, he'd have turned her in himself. Now she was fearful of that extreme becoming truth.

She opened her mouth to speak, but was silenced by guttural screams that rang out from somewhere out in the hall.

Adele turned her eyes toward the closed door, though she could see nothing through it. The high-pitched wails, however, were frightening. The sounds were coming from a woman— her mother? She was screaming uncontrollably, "This cannot be happening!" And was she hitting someone? It sounded as if someone was attempting to restrain a wild animal, not a refined concert pianist who was well respected in the social circles of Vienna's elite.

Her father did not flinch through the entire tirade. He stood quite still as fists pounded upon the door and something shattered—the porcelain vase on the table in the hall, perhaps? Before long, the animalistic wailing descended the stairs and became but a faint memory on the first floor.

God . . . , Adele's heart cried out to Him. *What is going on?*

Her father must have seen the display of emotion cross her face because he addressed it.

"Yes. That was because of you."

"But what—" Adele couldn't say it. What did this mean? What were they going to do to her?

Her father stared back at her with empty eyes. There was no depth of feeling there, nothing of the man who had tucked her into bed as a child. No, he was the general now. This was the man others had—and whom she now—feared.

Nothing but coldness predicated his next words.

"Bring him in."

Adele turned toward the door, and in a split second, her world crumbled.

She jumped to her feet as Vladimir was dragged in, barely able to stand for the beating he must have taken. His hands were shackled in front of him, his lip bleeding onto his white tuxedo collar and the bow tie dangling from his neck. One eye was swollen but still open, looking back at her with as much emotion as she'd ever seen.

They couldn't touch, didn't dare try to talk . . . There he was, her love, broken and bruised, and all she could do was accept the crushing apology displayed on his face.

"Tell me your association with this man."

"What?"

Vladimir shook his head, telling her without words that she had best keep quiet. The guards who held him stood still, like iron statues at his sides. One shoved him and barked a command when they saw him attempt to communicate with her. Vladimir quieted but kept a steely resolve on his face.

"All I need is confirmation of what I already know to be truth, Adele." Her attention was brought back to her father.

"I don't understand what you're asking."

"Answer me! Were you with this young man at the docks last night?"

Adele looked from her father to Vladimir and back again. The instinct to flee was overpowering. Couldn't they try to get to his contacts in Switzerland? Could they run and hide somehow? Perhaps Dieter could hide them. Surely this was not the end?

When she could say nothing, when the only movement that could be felt was the quivering of her chin, the quiet shattered. Without an ounce of remorse, her father issued the order: "Kill him."

"What?" she screamed, but the officers had already shoved him down to his knees, and one raised a pistol to the back of Vladimir's head.

She had the instinct to scream, "No!"

Even then, Vladimir fought to shield her from the horror of what could happen were she to say anything further. "Look away, Adele!" he screamed, head held high with the gun barrel pressing up against it. "Don't watch!"

"Shut up!" One of the guards smashed the butt of the pistol against the back of his skull. Vladimir fell to all fours, his cuffed wrists keeping his body from crumpling on the floor.

"Stop!" Tears stung her eyes. Could this be happening? *Oh God, what can I do?* "Please," she sobbed aloud. "Father?"

Adele looked to him, hoping, begging even, that she would find some glimmer of compassion yet alive in his eyes. But she found none. Her father looked through her and nodded to the guard with the gun. With a split second to make a decision, she screamed out the words she'd always wished to say and threw herself on the ground in front of Vladimir.

"I love him!"

Adele's words cut into the air, bringing a severe silence with them.

Her father looked like he had molten lava flowing under his skin, his red face giving way to a display of acute rage. His hands balled into fists at his sides as his chest rose and fell with each intense breath. The guards, equally astounded, looked back and forth between her father and her body on the floor, waiting for a sign of what to do next.

She looked to Vladimir alone and with shuddering emotion mouthed the words *"I'm sorry,"* for they both knew what she'd done.

Vladimir was attempting to be gallant. If she admitted nothing, then he could take the fall alone. He'd have kept their secret to the grave to protect her. It made her love him all the more—made the fading dream of a future together all the more gut-wrenching as they knelt on the ground, their hearts exposed as they faced each other.

Vladimir shook his head at her, ever so slightly, tears glazing his eyes.

"This is out of my hands now, Adele." Her father stepped over to the French doors of the office and flung them open. She gasped to find the second-story landing of their grand home full of armed SS guards. Vladimir hung his head in defeat when several guards came in, one yanking her up from each side while another shackled her wrists in front of her. She was hauled up to standing as her father watched, emotionless.

"You already knew?" She directed the question at her father, with nothing left to lose.

Fredrich gave her a curt nod, though she thought—hoped—she saw a glimmer of sadness in the eyes that stared back at her.

"But how?"

Not one for illusions, he replied, "Dieter's wife. The fool. She turned you both in, thinking it would remove suspicion from them. But you went to their home, put them all at risk. If they are executed, the blood is on your hands, Adele."

"But the doctor? He is your friend . . . We've known him all of my life."

"A friend who is a traitor to Austria." He paused, but only for a split second. "As are you, Adele. Austria will forget you after tonight." His voice was layered with emotion, his resolve cold as ice. "I hope you understand the fate you have chosen." And with that, he walked out of the study, leaving them behind with the terrifying group of SS officers.

And it began.

Vladimir was hauled up and they were forced out into the hall, then down the stairs. A wool coat was wrapped over her shoulders, though she wasn't even given time to force her arms into its sleeves.

"Where are they taking us?" she tried to ask Vladimir, then turned to the guards standing around. No one could or would answer. She was given no opportunity to retrieve anything from her room—not her grandmother's earrings that she'd taken off after the concert, not her Bible or the journal she'd always kept. She'd be allowed nothing and instead was ushered to the marble entry of the grand home where the etched glass front doors had been opened, the depth of the black night before her.

"Give her this." Adele turned at the sound of her mother's voice.

She could scarcely breathe for the terror building in her heart.

What would they do to her? Was this the last time she'd step through the threshold of her childhood home? Would she never hear her mother's voice again? However much she needed a glimmer of compassion from one of her parents, the violin case was all that was forthcoming. It was shoved into her hands by one of the guards as her mother turned her back, tears glistening on her cheeks, and walked away into the conservatory.

It was her practice violin and not as grand as the one owned by the orchestra, but it was a companion of sorts nonetheless. She hugged it to her chest as they were ushered out the front door, the rain unyielding as tiny ice pellets stung her cheeks.

Adele turned once more to look at Vladimir. He turned too, perhaps his soul having connected with hers, and looked across the top of the car to where she stood. She didn't know what she expected, for everything had turned out opposite of what she'd thought. Would he be angry because she didn't save herself? Would he deny her a last look as her parents had?

Vladimir looked at her with the same eyes, those lovely eyes of her friend that were now full of heart-shattering emotion, and mouthed, *I love you too*, before his head was tucked under the roof of the vehicle and he was swallowed up by the night.

And her new world began.

CHAPTER ELEVEN

*S*era was relieved when she saw William trotting up the walk to the bed-and-breakfast.

Until the Jeep pulled into the drive, she wasn't sure whether he'd show up. In fact, she wasn't even sure if she would be there. The alarm clock had sounded a good two hours before she was due to head to the airport and she'd lain awake in bed, agonizing over what to do.

The possibility that they could work together and find something that would break the mystery wide open was more than tempting. Sera had, after all, been searching for the painting, coming up with no new leads. But if she stayed now, what would the gamble be? Spending the previous evening with him had surprised even her. William Hanover wasn't a cold businessman. He'd shown a tender side, and that scared her to death.

With the wedding happening tonight, she'd doubted whether he would show. But he surprised her yet again by greeting her with two paper coffee cups and an easy smile.

"Morning," he said, coffee cup held out. "I took a shot and ordered you a mocha. I hope I was right."

It wasn't lost on her that she found it easier to smile in his presence now, for he seemed a bit more relaxed too. She guessed it was because of the peace they'd made the night before. His jeans were worn-in, as was his T-shirt, matching the casual smile he offered as he settled in the Adirondack chair next to her.

"Thanks." She took the cup from him and tipped the warm confection to her lips. "Don't think I've met a latte I didn't like. I'm from New York—we practically live on caffeine."

"I kind of wondered if you'd be here this morning or if you'd be jet-setting your way back to the East Coast."

"Why is that?"

He shrugged and took a sip of his coffee. "Last night it seemed like you may have said everything there was to say—about the painting, I mean. I thought maybe you'd be about ten thousand feet up right now."

Sera almost smiled, but bit her bottom lip to cover it. "In truth, so did I."

He nodded. "But you're still here."

"You offered to change the plane ticket, so, yes. I'm still here. But you—are you sure it's okay that you're here? With the wedding and all."

"It's hours away—I'm fine." He looked at the virtual home office scattered around her: laptop, files, cell phone, and a legal pad with notes scrawled on it. "Already deep in research, I see."

"Up to our necks in research is what we've been for more than two years," Sera said and dropped a folder down on the coffee table in front of him. "And like I said last night, we've hit a dead end."

He set his coffee cup down on the table and picked up the folder, flipping through the stack of papers inside. "What's this?"

Sera exhaled. "That is a file with the last known records of our girl. Everything we can find on her stops after October 1944. Records weren't always kept if someone was sent to the gas chambers or was one of those randomly executed by SS guards. It's horrible. And we're not sure what happened to her."

"Orchestra records . . . photographs . . ." He held up several printouts of black-and-white photos, turning the snapshots from horizontal to vertical to view each image.

"Yes. The ones on the top are from her early years. Whatever I could find. And in the back of the folder are these." Sera took another sip of her coffee. "You'll understand what we're looking at when you see them."

She sat and watched him. William's face was stoic as he sorted through the stack of photos. He looked at each for a moment, photos of a young Adele with her barrel-rolled blond hair and bright, youthful smile. There were group photos of the Vienna Philharmonic, shots of her with her violin, even shots of her while playing onstage. Sera had found one or two pictures of Adele's family, one of her with a group of schoolgirls at the university she attended in Vienna, even a candid of her as she'd been lost in the magic of playing her violin in a practice studio.

And then William froze. His hand brought a photo up closer to his eyes and Sera watched, knowing which photo he'd found.

"This isn't real . . . is it?"

The photo was of a performance of the orchestra within Auschwitz, with Adele just one of the group of those playing while a gaggle of SS officers smiled on.

"Yes." Sera nodded and pointed to a female sitting off to the side of the photo. "That's her."

"I had no idea that there was anything like this in the concentration camps."

"Most people don't. I didn't for quite a while," Sera admitted. "I heard mention of it while in an art history survey course, that there were musicians, even artists who hid the art they created. When the camps were liberated, the armies that came in found art that had been left behind. Paintings . . . sketches . . . poems even, scratched into barrack walls. And they had musicians who played in orchestras right there in the camps. I didn't know much about it until I went back to research the painting. That's when

I found all of this. And in the past two years we've learned what she must have gone through."

"How did you find out about her?"

Sera figured he'd ask. She tossed a photocopy of the painting on top of the stack of photos. "We found her by the serial number," she said, pointing to the numbers scrawled on her forearm. "The tattoo."

"And you're sure she is this Adele Von Bron."

"Quite sure."

He held another photo up to her. "When was this one taken?"

Sera took it from him and looked over the image. "Well, this image is unique. We're not sure why, but there are some photographs that were taken inside the camps. This one was actually taken by an SS officer. It's a photo of what we believe was one of her last performances, from late September 1944. She's there in the first row, first chair from the left."

William looked shocked by the explanation. "They had concerts in the camps."

He didn't make a question out of it. Rather, he made the quiet statement as his eyes moved over the span of musicians in the image, all with instruments in hand.

"I think performing the occasional concert was the least of what was forced upon them."

"What do you mean?" William leaned in, his eyes fixed on her.

Sera turned away, feeling a connection building between them again. Deflecting, she turned her laptop around so that they could both see it and typed something into her Internet search browser.

"Have you ever heard the term *selection* in reference to what happened in the camps?"

"I don't think so." He shook his head as the search results popped up on her screen. "But I think I can guess what it was."

She turned the laptop toward him once the search results

popped up. "That was it," she pointed out. "Selections for who would live and who would die."

William began clicking through a series of photographs from a Holocaust archival site. Image after image went by, of weary prisoners arriving at the camps, of mothers with little children, some in coats with the large Star of David sewn on the front, others with families huddled in groups as they unknowingly walked the dirt roads to the crematorium.

"The SS guards would have selections when new convoy trains arrived at the camp. In Auschwitz, those deemed able to work were herded to the right. Those who were doomed to the crematorium were often sent straight to the gas chambers, which were in the holding area on the left."

"Unbelievable," he said, still clicking forward through the pictures.

"Stop—right there." Sera brushed her hand over his to stop him. Surprised at her own comfort level, she pulled her hand away and dropped it back into her lap. "That's the orchestra. It's debated by some historians, but many believe they were forced to play during the selections. Adele would have been with them."

"They played, knowing people were being sent to their deaths?" Sera could hardly believe it herself. But yes, it was true.

She nodded.

"They were forced to play cheerful music—German marches or Hungarian folk music—to keep the prisoners upbeat as they marched out to work and returned to the barracks each day. Can you imagine? Day in and day out, as thousands of people walked past them. Mothers. Unsuspecting families. Children . . ." Sera's voice trailed off as she tried to envision what it must have felt like to be forced into such a horrific situation. "It was the worst in 1944 through 1945. That's when the Germans began transporting Hungarian Jews to Auschwitz. Hundreds of thousands of them went straight to the gas chambers upon arrival. And the orchestra played through it all. It's said that the musicians had some of the highest suicide rates of any prisoners in the camps. I wonder how they could even go on."

"Now I understand the depth of the sadness." William turned and looked at her. "In the painting? Adele's eyes look as though they go deeper than the back of the canvas. It's because of what she saw, because of all the people who walked by her and she was powerless to stop it."

"We can't know the full extent as to what actually happened. And she was there for almost two years before our record of her goes cold."

William shook his head. "So she was a Jew? That's why she was sent there?"

"No. That's just one layer of the mystery." Sera sailed into action, feeling the rush of energy that came with the unraveling of the story a piece of art could tell. "Look at this."

She opened another file folder and dropped it into his hands. His eyebrows arched up the instant she presented him with a picture of the uniformed man.

"Who is he?"

Sera pointed to the name at the bottom of the photo. "Fredrich Von Bron."

"Her father was a member of the Third Reich?"

"Austrian. A general," Sera confirmed, nodding. "And because of his position, we know that whatever happened must have been severe. It was kept quiet too. We haven't been able to find any news reports about it. Adele was sent away as a reeducation prisoner. That meant she would have been a labor worker as punishment for some sort of offense. She was sent to Auschwitz-Birkenau early in 1943—that was well within the time frame that prisoners were tattooed as a means of cataloging them. Those who were sent straight to the gas chambers weren't registered or tattooed, but another group that wasn't tattooed was the reeducation prisoners."

"But she was tattooed anyway."

"Exactly."

William leaned back in the chair and folded his hands behind his head. "There's a lot here that doesn't add up."

"Right," Sera agreed. "The rank of her father and her notoriety alone should have assured that someone like her would never have been sent to the camp. She was known in Vienna—all over Austria. She was a concert violinist, beautiful, talented, with her whole life ahead of her. So how in the world did she end up there?"

He looked at her curiously and dropped the photo back on the file folder.

It was his close inspection of her face that started tying her stomach into knots. Maybe he was feeling a familiarity, same as she?

"What?" She grabbed the pencil that had been tucked behind her ear to jot down a date on the back of one of the photos.

"I just realized something," he said, leaning in close to her as he dropped his voice down to a whisper. "This is about more than money for you too, isn't it?"

Sera noted how softly those blue eyes smiled at her, with enough of a hint of openness that she couldn't turn away. And she found that she didn't need to answer him; somehow he could read the words that weren't yet on her lips.

"Why?" he asked so easily, so openly this time. "Why does all of this matter so much to you? Because I can see that it does."

Sera dropped the pencil and, trying to cover the nervousness, tucked a lock of hair behind her ear.

The truth was, she'd taken the case of Adele's painting out of pure necessity. She'd been broken and needed an escape. With her heart shattered, she needed something—anything else to focus on. She'd felt the sting of hurt, and though she was a Christian, her faith had been shaken. Her fiancé was a Christian man. He'd promised to love and honor her. But instead, he walked out on their life and left her holding her broken heart in her hands.

The mystery of the painting had been the perfect diversion.

"I suppose it's the great history of it all . . . to see that a piece of human expression is still alive in something that's been left behind for us . . ." She shrugged. "Most people would think I'm crazy, that it's just paint on canvas. But . . . it speaks to me. It's a living, breathing record of the lives that have gone before us."

She ran her fingertips over the edge of a photograph, this one of Adele and several other musicians from the orchestra. "Look at this," she said, and handed the photo to him. "It was taken in the spring of 1942, for the college newspaper. Look at how happy she is here. So different from the painting."

William nodded. "So that's why you're doing this? For her?" He paused, then said, "Or is it for you?"

Funny how this man, who was still a virtual stranger, could pinpoint the one thing Sera didn't want to admit. His ability to read her thoughts was unnerving. It had her desperate to hold back. She couldn't tell him that she'd seen the painting once before. The memory was far too personal.

"Let's find out about Adele first," she said and took the photo back from him. She looked for something to do to distract her. Tidying up the stacks of photos around them seemed an appropriate task. "I'll work on myself later."

"After you've found the painting."

The statement was simply put. It was so simple, in fact, that it drew her eyes to his. He took a last drink of his coffee and then set the cup off to one of the side tables.

"Let's get started then," he said, rolling up his sleeves. "Put me to work."

"Well, I've pretty much told you what we know, and where the snags are. I was actually hoping that by coming here, we could find out what your grandfather has to do with this. Anything would help."

"Well, I confess that when I learned what the will stipulations were, I went looking for any connection to the painting. I'm embarrassed to say that I came up without much to go on." He cocked an eyebrow and continued. "That is, until I received a call from your assistant and you came into the picture."

Sera nodded. "And we'd hit a dead end ourselves. I can still share what we do have. I know it's a long shot, but maybe we should check these photos to be sure there's not a young Edward Hanover in there somewhere. You said your grandfather traveled quite a bit in his younger years."

"He did." William continued looking through the photographs without looking up. "But that's not what I'm looking for."

His words piqued her interest. "What?"

He'd begun lining up several pictures in a row. They were all photos of Adele, of course, the same ones she'd seen before. "There." He lined up the last photo and then glanced back at her. "Notice anything?"

Sera leaned in to take a closer look.

Adele was in each photo, smiling and looking happy as she always did in the photos with the other musicians from the Vienna Philharmonic. There was nothing out of the ordinary. Just a sea of smiling faces. If there was something there, she wasn't seeing it.

William took his finger and pointed at one of the young men in the first picture. Then he pointed to the same man in the next picture. And another. Another after that. On and on down the line, until he'd found the same man repeated in every one.

A shiver ran the length of her spine.

William held up the last photo in the line and pointed to the young man's face. "Who is that?"

Sera couldn't believe she hadn't noticed it before. But now that the photos were laid side by side, it was as clear as day. The young man with the cello and the dashing smile was in every picture.

"I don't know who he is." Sera finished his thought without missing a beat. "But he seems to be in almost every picture that she is."

"Right. But why?"

Sera's breath caught in her lungs when she realized exactly what they were looking at. Bravo to the real estate financier for finding it. William was busily going through another stack of photos.

"This guy—he's in all the photos, but not always right next to her. Maybe that's why I never noticed it before, because we were always looking at her."

He nodded. "So maybe we need to stop trying to uncover something in the dead end and instead try digging from a new angle."

"Track down who this man was, and see if the trail leads to Adele. Do you think he could still be alive?"

"The thought crossed my mind."

William was lost in another stack of photos and computer printouts from a nearby folder when she saw it. The evidence was tiny to be sure, and overlooked unless someone was on the hunt for it. But now that they were, what she was seeing fairly took her breath away.

Sera dove into her computer bag and tore through each pocket until she found the magnifying glass she kept there. Putting the glass to the image made her one hundred percent certain. They'd been looking in the wrong place.

With a manicured fingertip, she slid the photo across the tabletop until it was right in front of him.

"Look," she said, pointing to the miniscule evidence in the

picture. "It's small but you can still see it. Look by the folds of her skirt. She's trying to hide it but it's there, plain as day."

William looked and almost immediately took in a sharp breath.

"She's holding his hand."

CHAPTER TWELVE

———

March 12, 1943

Surely the snow held memories.

Adele didn't question it anymore. Not after she'd been loaded on the train to the work camp—she knew it to be truth now.

She stood huddled against the inside of the cattle car, the wood agonizingly rough and splintered even through the thick wool of her coat. But leaning against it was the only way she could endure standing for so long. All of the people were packed in so tight around her. One couldn't have thought to sit. Or think. Or even breathe in the stagnating stench of the car. They'd been herded in like animals with no food or water and no heat to protect them against the elements.

That was an agonizing two days ago.

Adele's old reality was gone. The scratching pain of the wood and the falling snow outside were the only remaining links to the former world she'd known. Everything else was a terrifying dream. A frightening new reality that had been whisked in around her.

The Germans had assigned her to the labor detail, though she didn't know exactly what that meant. They'd been benevolent enough to give her a trial, one not attended by her parents or anyone else she knew. She knew in her heart the conviction was certain before it had begun—a mere formality. A courtesy, perhaps, because of her family name and father's military rank. Although she'd forever shamed her family, the name still held some value. The assignment of reeducation in a work camp, however, was a foregone conclusion. Adele's offense had been serious enough to carry a death sentence and she knew it.

Her sentence had been eight weeks of labor in one of the Germans' camps. Eight weeks and she'd be released back to her parents. But it seemed odd that she'd been ushered so far from Austria to Poland for only two months of work. Why would they take the trouble to ship her so far, with the obvious cost associated with transport, when she could have been made to work not far from her home?

Around her, some people cried. Others were strangely quiet. A child would occasionally ask, "Where are we going, Papa?" or "When will we get there?" Some spoke in languages she didn't understand. She heard praying, mumbling, muffled sobbing on the long journey that the bumpy train took through Poland's bitter landscape.

Adele was close to a window, if it could even be called one, and at least she could feel the air. The iron bars marring the view did little to give comfort. They revealed nothing but an endless sea of frozen fields and the occasional tree, always looking like a predictor of death with its bony trunk, stark, leafless limbs, and backdrop of gray sky. It was as haunting outside the train as it was inside, and for that, the nearness of the window made her feel unlucky.

Adele's hands shook as she gripped the bars. For though she kept a tight hold on the window, she'd not be able to grasp the night outside. She could no longer feel freedom, and that, combined with the deathly, frozen silence, terrified her all the more.

Silence.

That was the ever-present companion for them all—a stony

silence that was pierced only by the occasional wail of someone on the other side of the car. Buried in sorrows, one couldn't have thought ill of the person for crying out, but it was too much to endure. Some of the others silenced the wailing man, whether through coaxing or threat, and the rest of the journey once again became a path void of any sound.

God?

The word left her lips on a shuddering, frozen breath. And then a muffled sob. Adele summoned courage from somewhere deep inside. Then the cycle began again. Each time she tried to pray, the same cycle of terrified breathing started, over and over again, until all she could do was say His name and nothing else. She muttered the words, whispered them . . .

"Abba . . ."

"Where is my son?" A stuttering old woman with no teeth and frightened eyes had asked her the same question over and over for the past day. She was pitiful. Terrified. Shocked and unable to cope with reality. "My son. Do you know where he is?"

Adele shook her head for what felt like the hundredth time.

"No, I'm sorry. I'm afraid I don't know your son."

She'd mumbled his name too many times for Adele to have forgotten it now. But she said it again anyway, tears rolling from her eyes as the last flicker of hope faded from them.

"Viktor. That is his name."

"I'm sorry."

The whispered response was all she could offer.

She'd tried holding the woman's hand earlier in the night and had patted it so as to offer comfort, but it only served to further the woman's regression into mania. She was soon clinging so that Adele thought she would suffocate. She'd peeled the woman's hands from her own some time ago and had shrugged her side up against the painfully rough wood of the cattle car wall instead, trying not to cry out of guilt.

Mothers. Lost sons. Violinists who had no concept of the real world before that moment. Daughters. Frightened families. So many strangers. They were all packed in together, young and old, never having met but oddly connected by their crossed paths on this terrible, frightening journey.

All starving. Craving water. Or the awakening from a dream.

"I see something," someone yelled.

The strange turning of all heads in unison precipitated the electric jolting of her heart. Adele saw smoke through the bars on the tiny window. It was off in the distance—nowhere near the tracks on which the car rode. Someone screamed when they saw it. Another wailed. Adele heard a man crying next to her, his wretched sobbing more terrifying to her than the open shrieks of women and children.

The car slowed. She gripped the iron bars for support and, with her other hand, hugged the violin case ever so tightly to her chest.

A high-pitched whistle of the brakes predicated the slowing of the train wheels upon the tracks. Dogs barking? She hadn't expected that. And the smell of sulfur on fire, cutting through the air with a sickening ferocity, filling every crack in the frozen walls of the car with a putrid stench that turned her stomach. One or two coughs. Someone was weeping again and others told them to hush. A baby cried out—from hunger? Its cries fought with the dogs' barks, both demanding nervous attention from the captives packed in all around her.

And they finally came to a stop.

The smothering existence in the cattle car was over and they'd soon find a new reality.

The doors flew open and on the gust of air that came with it, all she sensed was a maddening flurry of activity. More dogs. Yelling. Someone shoving her from behind. Guards with guns. Another wail from the person in the back of the car. Dawn having passed some time ago. The puttering woman in front of her asking the guards where her son was.

"Out!" The order was shouted. Faithless and cold were the voices that offered their greeting. *"Out! Out!"*

Adele was yanked from the car. She nearly turned her ankle as it twisted down on the cold mud by the tracks. She was shoved from behind again. She turned to find a sea of ruddy brown or gray wool coats with yellow stars and miserably pale faces looking back at her. Weak, empty faces, emotionless as fate called them to march forward, moving with an anguished ebb and flow that was faster than she'd have imagined for the swarming masses of people all around her.

Through terror, she mumbled, "Heavenly Father . . . what is happening?"

Adele's heart began reciting His name over and over again with each beat, like a mournful dance, like the haunting sound of the violin crying in her ear. It was her one comfort. The only sure thing she knew in that moment. God. Was He there? If she called out to Him, would He follow her anxious steps through the mud? Would He sustain her through what her eyes were seeing?

She turned back around, not knowing which way to walk, following the crowd of women who were being parted from the men and boys.

"Women and children—left!" It was shouted. Barked. *"Recht! Recht!* Men to the *recht!"*

She heard wretched crying, saw the anguish as mothers' hands were torn from their children's and they were pushed to the left, the tears of anguish and the cry of their souls upon each face. Everything was happening so fast, yet it seemed as if the world turned round her in painfully slow motion. It felt like she was stuck in some terrible film. Or a frightful dream.

A sea of people walked to and fro as they discarded bags and suitcases marked up with scrawled names and former street addresses, tossed in mountainous piles upon the platform. And there were men with striped uniforms, almost like pajamas, herding the crowds past long lines of barbed wire fencing. Were these men prisoners too? Why so many fences? What in the world was going on?

What she was seeing—it couldn't be happening. Would it do any good to pinch herself now?

Oh God. Do You see?

More families fractured. Sobbing. Others had agonized faces. Stunned. Painted with disbelief.

Adele shuddered and wrapped her arms tighter around the violin case in her arms. It was almost too cold to breathe, even for a spring morning in March. She could barely think. She no longer had hunger or thirst . . . all she could do was see. Her eyes still worked. They tore through the mist, looking ahead to the tall brick beast of a building that loomed up beyond the tracks. Though her other senses were numb, she could and did see what was happening, as the greeting of the camp was menacingly dark. And she had a feeling she'd remember it always, as if her soul would be burned with the memory.

"Women—this way!"

She was pulled into a line. Closer, closer they came to the beast.

A little girl walked by, head down, fighting against the cold, never looking or laughing or skipping along as all children do. She was holding her mother's hand. That darling little girl with the kerchief tucked over her hair and tied in a knot under her delicate, porcelain chin. A baby she was. Tiny. Taking two steps to her mama's one, her legs far too little to keep up with the quick pace of the barking guards' instructions.

What would happen to her?

Adele had never felt so alone in her life. Was this what her Vladimir was seeing? Was he being ushered forth too? Did lines form for him in some cold, lifeless camp?

Oh heavenly Father, is he one of the strong men who crumbled to weeping in his own cattle car?

She stepped forward, looking at the mouth of the great brick beast. The wide doors welcomed their prey as an eerie snow fell down, the memories of each flake the only witness to the scene except for her. And was it snow? Something else? Why wasn't it cold like an early March snow should have been when it drifted down and melted upon her exposed skin?

It fluttered on the breeze like paper-thin cinders from the fireplace at home.

Ash falling down?

Adele breathed out in terror. *God . . . what is this place?*

Auschwitz.

—

They allowed Adele to keep her violin.

This she hadn't expected.

The Germans had rushed her through registration—the horror of which she was still numb to. She'd been taken through a line with the other women from the car. But most of them, especially the ones with children clinging to them, had been ushered through a wall of buildings and barbed wire and she'd been left behind.

Adele wasn't sure where they were headed, but she wanted to go with them. At least she could have asked what was happening, could have felt a connection to some earthly being who had taken the long train journey with her. But it wasn't to be. They were led away and she was pushed and pulled in another direction.

The SS guards spotted her—did they recognize her as Austria's Sweetheart? Adele had always hated that name, the product of careful marketing by her parents. But it hardly mattered now. No one appeared to have been able to pick her out of the group she'd arrived with. She was just as starved and dirty,

just as despondent as all the rest. They appeared to be interested
in the violin, however. The black case she clung to had been the
subject of immediate conversation when she made it to the front
of the line. The other women and children slowly trudged away
through the early-morning mist as she looked on, wishing she
wasn't alone.

They demanded answers to question after question, all in
German, of course, and she was expected to give quick answers.
Did she speak German? Yes. Once that was surmised, they continued at a feverish pace. Was she a Jew? No. Good. And what was
her name? Nationality? Why did she have an instrument? So it
was hers? Interesting. How long had she played? Was she a professional or an amateur?

Why wouldn't her brain work?

Adele squeezed her fingernails into her palms, hoping to
wake herself from the dream. Or shock her mouth into action.

She answered that she was Adele Von Bron, she was Austrian,
and she did in fact play the violin. She'd had experience playing
with the Vienna Philharmonic. They seemed to doubt this, likely
because she was so young and because the Viennese orchestra
did not take women as members, but she persisted through their
skeptical glances. Yes. Formal training. No. Not a professional.
She played with the Vienna Philharmonic on invitation. She'd
been a student at the university in Vienna. How long? For three
years. She was in the music performance program.

The SS guards whispered something, both of them in front
of her looking back at her only once.

What was happening?

Adele was then ushered away from the group. This so terrified her that she could scarcely breathe. An SS officer ordered
her to follow him, which she did, though her feet felt like lead as
she tripped and stumbled over pebbles on the road away from the
train platform.

Short, quick breaths. Shuffled steps. No words from the young man who walked in front of her, his back stiff as a poker, the gun in his belt all too visible. They passed three-story brick buildings. Barbed wire fences hummed with the electricity that coursed through them. All the same in look and eerie feel. The buildings and fences were stark, ghostly, and somehow threatening with their lack of emotion.

She glanced around, noticing that other than the guards, there were no men or boys in the area where she'd been taken. She was inside Auschwitz-Birkenau, which she'd learned while awaiting trial was a work camp for women. But some of the women on the platform were quite old and others had several children, babies even, bundled up in their arms. How would they work? Did the Germans have child care in this camp? Perhaps the older prisoners cared for the young ones while the mothers worked.

And then Adele's thoughts were torn from looking around the camp to the sudden terror of where she was going. The path the SS guard led her upon took them past a two-story building, one that had a large brick wall that was shielded from view of the registration lines.

They walked upon a deserted, snow-powdered road.

And then suddenly—everything stopped. Breathing, thinking, even a slight halt hitched in her footfalls, which she covered for fear the guard might notice. She kept walking, but her eyes were pierced with a vision to her left.

Screaming out from the long brick wall was the unmistakable mark of death: blood spatters, head high, in clear succession as if poor souls had been lined up against the bricks but moments before. The earth was reddish-brown, the cold March ground still frozen, mud mixed with a shade of blood red in dusted piles of latent snow. She knew what it was. She'd seen it the night that the Haurbech family had been gunned down. The scars on her hands seemed to burn with the memory of it even then.

Death was here. Like the life-altering scene she'd witnessed at the docks in Vienna months before, the blood told a story other than this place being a work camp.

Oh God! Is he going to . . . kill me?

She felt her stomach lurch even as the SS guard led her past the brick wall. Whether he'd noticed the death stains, she couldn't know. He seemed unconcerned with it. He walked by at a quick pace. He didn't stop, yet he didn't pull the pistol from the holster on his belt to use it on her either. All the while it stayed there, the glint of metal flashing, punishing her with fear for each heavy step he took.

She breathed deep for a moment, willing herself to walk and not faint.

Should she try to run?

Adele doubted she could get away. They were walking through a maze of buildings and scattered electric fences. She'd not have known the first place to go if she tried to run away from him. And then just as quickly as terror had covered her, a temporary sense of relief rained down. He wasn't going to kill her, at least not now, not against the horrible death-stained wall.

The SS guard ushered her into one of the buildings. She stepped through the paint-peeled door into a shocking scene—bins of clothes, glasses, and shoes overflowed everywhere. The ground floor of the two-story building was dark, lit only by the overcast sky outside the windows, the air as chilled inside as out. It smelled damp and musty. More bins. They were everywhere. And was that . . . hair? Piles of it. All around. Suitcases were stacked up against the wall until they reached the ceiling like a sad wall of aged leather wallpaper, some well made with gold leaf initials on the top and others looking quite worn.

What was going on? Were they going to cut her hair? Give her new clothes? It was hardly possible that she could have had a more threadbare dress than the ruddy-brown one she wore. It scarcely covered her. And while in somewhat good condition, her coat did little to supply real warmth. Perhaps they would issue her a prison uniform like the men at the train platform. If she was to work here, Adele supposed that the inside of the building would be in the same condition as she'd become used to on her journey—bone-chilling cold would likely be a companion for some time.

Adele clutched her violin closer as she walked through the warehouse, remembering what was inside the velvet lining of the case. She'd hidden her treasure there long ago so her mother wouldn't find it. And now, in this place, it was the only thing in the world that brought her comfort. If she couldn't have her Bible, then the small token would serve as her only link to her old life.

She hugged the case in a death grip.

"Halt," the guard barked, and pointed to the ground in front of her feet.

Adele obeyed and froze her steps, stopping in an aisle between the bins.

Where was everyone? The room looked like an unused warehouse. There were no people. No registration lines. No other guards. Just inanimate objects made of wool and leather piled up to the ceiling, the only witnesses to what might happen to her here.

Her heart thumped wildly in her chest, almost like a bird flitting, about to be let out of a cage.

The guard opened a door at the end of the aisle and went inside. The door was cracked enough that Adele could see an older woman standing there, could hear hushed voices. He turned and gestured toward where she stood amongst the bins of discarded wares.

Adele swallowed hard.

Was this where she was to work?

None of it made sense.

But then, standing in the damp warehouse on a frigid spring morning didn't make much sense either. Seeing blood on the brick wall outside—that was sheer madness. Perhaps she'd been transported through the looking-glass to some hellish Wonderland? She'd read Carroll's classic children's novels, never imagining that one day she'd meet the same fate as Alice, tumbling down into the depths of a grotesque nightmare world where nothing made sense.

The older woman nodded to the guard, and not requiring anything further, he whisked past them both and began marching back down the aisle. Adele could hear his boots clip against the concrete floor and seconds later the outer door slammed, leaving her and the woman inside.

"Your name?"

The woman took several steps toward her, then stopped and opened the door wide. Adele could see inside what looked like a common room of sorts. There were plain plank beds lining the side walls, two barred windows high up on the walls, light emanating from two bare lightbulbs hanging on wires from the ceiling, and a tiny black stove in the center of the back wall. The room was dim and appeared to have been deserted save for the woman who stood before her now. She was middle-aged and of normal height, her brown hair tinged with gray at her temples. Her eyes possessed laugh lines that appeared unused in a place like this.

"I asked your name." The woman wasn't harsh, just matter-of-fact. "Here you must answer questions immediately. Truthfully. And do exactly as you are told or you will not survive. Do you understand?"

Her mouth finally worked, though the output was stuttering. *Not survive?*

"Adele. Adele Von Bron."

"And you play the violin?"

She nodded. "Yes."

"Good. Come in."

Adele was led into a stark room, the wooden door closed behind her. There was no one else there, just as she'd thought. And so it seemed the time to ask at least one question—anything to make sense of the lunacy that had been playing out all around her. But what should she ask first? What was the odd snow that rained down as she'd stepped from the train? Had this woman seen the bloodstains on the brick outside? Thinking of Sophie and Eitan Haurbech, she feared for the gruesomeness that the young ones would be exposed to in such a place. Where were all of the children who had been on the train platform? She'd seen none as she walked through the camp just then.

"What is happening here?" That one question seemed to cover all things and so she asked it, rather wildly, eyes searching the wrinkled face before her. The woman seemed driven by purpose only and, rather than answering, reached for a wooden chair and set it in the center of the room.

"Sit," she ordered Adele, which she did, the violin case still clutched in her arms.

The woman took a chair and positioned it across from her.

She sat and with a quiet, controlled voice said, "I need you to take your violin out and play it for me. If you've lied and cannot play, then I am to send you back outside to the guard. He'll smoke a cigarette while he waits to hear your playing, no more than five minutes. If I do not send you outside, then he will go about his business and you will stay here. Now, I need you to play."

Adele didn't know why she was being asked to play. But as the woman had said, she'd not question. She opened the case on her lap and removed her practice violin, the wood gleaming cherry in the dim light of the room. She removed her bow with it and deposited the case on the ground at her feet.

"What would you like me to play?"

The woman showed no emotion on her face when she said, "It doesn't matter."

Adele took a deep breath and pulled the instrument up against her chin. She placed the bow upon the strings and began to play.

It was odd that the last memory of her playing had been in satin and pearls, before a grand auditorium of some of the Third Reich's most distinguished guests. Now she played in squalor, the mold in the air stirred up by the movement of her arms. But she still played, as best as she could, for she had a feeling that the proficiency with which she did so would somehow be judged for something quite important.

It wasn't like it had been at the concert. That playing had been a release of something magical from her soul. That had been in service to the Lord, the use of her gift for something that brought worship to Him. But here? In this moment, it was only to survive. Adele played as a gifted prodigy should, though her heart was deadened further with the sound of each note.

The music here sang only of evil.

The woman raised her hand to halt her playing. "That is enough."

Adele stopped, and though her hands shook, she tried to rest the instrument in her lap as calmly as she could. Somehow she knew she sat across from the woman who held her fate.

"You play quite beautifully." Adele wasn't sure how the woman knew this, but she seemed to be learned in judging how a musician should play.

Adele nodded rather than answering. Compliments had no bearing in such a place, so much so that she couldn't bring herself to utter thanks.

"You may stop worrying," the woman said. "I'll not send an artist like you outside."

A breath that Adele hadn't known her lungs to possess was expelled, sagging her shoulders with it. She looked down at her lap, biting her lip over the tears that were forcing their way out of her eyes.

"And if you had sent me outside . . ."

"You no longer have to think on what might have happened."

"Oh God!" The words spilled from her mouth before she could stop them. "They were going to kill me!" Panic rose in Adele's throat, cutting off her airway. It happened faster than she could process the reality.

She'd come but a moment away from a bullet in the head.

"Try to breathe, child." The woman sounded kind somehow. Her words were blunt, but they were tinged with some form of compassion.

She rose and crossed the room. Adele listened to the woman's feet padding across the floor. She returned a few seconds later and placed a metal pail at her feet.

"Do you need to be sick?" she asked, and reached her hands out to take the violin.

Adele hadn't considered it until that moment. She let the violin go when it was swept from her lap and, feeling something of a release, retched into the bucket as the woman stood over her. But after having nothing to eat or drink for more than two days, there was not much to come of it.

"Better?"

She nodded, though she felt empty. The pit of hunger in her stomach had grown so that she felt physical pain in the act of getting sick.

The woman knelt down at her side and placed the violin back in its case with gentle and almost loving hands.

Adele found the woman to be an immediate source of peace in the darkness that surrounded her. And something in her heart wanted to cry out, to throw herself in this woman's arms and beg to be let out of the hellish nightmare that plagued them both.

"Thank you." It was all she could manage to say. But like that night so many weeks ago, when she'd gone to Dieter for help and he'd so willingly stitched up the wounds of her hands, she could think of no other words. Nothing else mattered in that moment.

The woman gave a slight nod. She stood and began moving around the room. The bucket was discarded in the far corner. She came to the row of wooden planks against the wall and began folding a sheet on one of the beds. The others had what appeared to be straw mattresses covered in dingy sheets, for the concrete floor under each was littered with the telltale straw dust that collected as if someone rolled around on top of the mattress.

"Where are the others?"

"Others?" The woman had a habit of speaking without turning around.

"There are six beds." That meant that at the very least, they could accommodate four more workers in the moderately sized room. If what she suspected was the case, they'd soon find the room filled with far more than four other women.

"These beds have just been brought in." So that was why there was straw on the floor. "And you are the first."

Adele didn't understand. "The first of what?"

The woman paused. Would that be the hallmark characteristic of this woman? Few words spoken, and those would be carefully chosen? "You know where you are, yes?"

"Auschwitz."

"You are in Birkenau. It is the second of the main Auschwitz camps."

Adele stood and moved across the room toward the woman, her hands clenched in tight fists, her soul begging for answers.

"What is happening here? I heard about these places when I was in jail, awaiting trial. And knew I was being sent to work and that these people could be ruthless, but—"

"But you never expected this."

The woman had read her thoughts. Another trait that seemed born of more than just experience in the camp.

"No. Nothing close to this." Adele didn't know what to say. And maybe nothing needed to be said. The train platform. The horrific wall of death along the path. The despondent guards and prisoners in striped uniforms. The families being ripped apart at the train platform . . . What could she speak of that this woman wouldn't have seen or heard herself?

There was one thing.

"What is your name?"

The older woman looked as though the creases in her face wanted to smile. Maybe they wished to form the lines that had once been born of joy? But not in this place. Not in Auschwitz. She'd not smile. No one would.

"My name is Omara Kraus."

"And what am I the first of, Omara? Why am I here?"

The woman looked her straight in the eye and with the most emotionless of words said, "You are to play in the Women's Orchestra of Auschwitz."

CHAPTER THIRTEEN

—

There's an orchestra?"

Omara went about tidying up the room, almost as if she hadn't heard the question.

"But why?"

To her question, Omara's answer was clipped, immediate. She didn't look up as she dropped wood chips on the fire in the tiny stove. "Because they are smart."

Cold. That could describe them. Inhuman, perhaps? Merciless. Murderous. Adele could think of an entire list of characteristics to describe them. But not smart.

"You have heard the name Maria Mandel?"

Adele shook her head. Then, realizing the woman hadn't turned to look at her, answered, "No. I have not."

"She is as devoted a Nazi as any of them. Believes in the Germans' mission. But she also understands the value of music, like any good German would have been taught to. She became the cruel caretaker of the women's camp last autumn, and though it is unfathomable to you and me, she has high regard for musical talent among the prisoner population. The other Auschwitz camp has an orchestra, so she decided that Birkenau must have one as well."

"The orchestra is her idea then?"

"It is her necessity, I believe." A muscle flexed in her jaw, as if hatred had spilled over from her insides and burst forth upon her face. "The main Auschwitz camp has a men's orchestra and she wishes to have her own project here. So in this way, they are smart. They exploit the gift of music given by God. They understand how the arts can be associated with many things—with happiness in a life once lived. Not that they care whether we remember joy or not. We are animals to them. But they do care that the prisoners be primed for manipulation. That our spirits be quelled into doing nothing but mindless work, as if we were machines. Music will be one of their tools to do this. They take away our names, our very identity," she said, and lifted the sleeve of her rust-colored dress to reveal a number harshly tattooed on her left forearm. "And replace it with a number. They take our joy and turn it into something evil."

"How do you know?"

"Because I have seen it."

Adele resisted the urge to pinch her arm and tell herself to wake up. This was real. Omara had seen the atrocities inflicted upon the Jews, much like Vladimir had once described to her. It seemed so far away then.

Now it was staring her in the face.

"What have you seen?"

Still kneeling on the ground, Omara finally turned. She looked as though she'd been doused with a bucket of ice water. Any softness in her features had become pinched and her lips terse, as if the angry memories within her mind were fighting to escape through the pores in her skin.

She crossed the room, saying, "This camp opened in 1942. I was one of the first here."

"You've been here for more than a year?"

"Nearly."

Adele was stunned to silence.

She began to consider the possibility that her reeducation

sentence of fifty-six days could be longer and much more terrify-ing than she'd thought. Omara had been in the camp a year and the notion no longer fazed her. What could that mean?

"I was a professor of humanities at the university in Berlin," Omara said, finally sitting on the edge of one of the straw mat-tresses. She did not appear weakened. Rather, the middle-aged woman gave the impression of a wise old storyteller who owned her craft and would find comfort in sitting through the tale she must repeat. She folded her hands in her lap and gazed out into the room, almost as if the brick wall had melted away and some vision of her memory had come alive behind it. "We were not free to speak out. Certainly not if the voice came from a Jew. All of the rights of the public were taken away in the early 1930s. It was the Nazis' way of gaining control over us. That was when it all started, against the Jews, I mean."

"Which you are?"

"Yes." Omara's chin rose a little higher in the air. "I am a Jew. One of the creatures of the same God. Of the same matter. Of bone and blood and the same human flesh as they. One who is alive by His hand to this very moment. And when I see a growing hatred for any race of human being, no matter the justification, I cannot stand by in silence."

"So you stood up and spoke against them? The Nazis—you condemned their practices?"

"Yes." She nodded, chin still proudly notched. "I did."

It was all that Adele required to feel the pit of regret take form in her stomach.

She remembered a night at the dance hall, almost four years ago now. She remembered when Vladimir told her that Germany had invaded Poland. "Taken charge of" Poland, her father had called it, because Germany and Austria with her would now be strong again. They could have pride once more. But Adele remem-bered what it felt like that night. Shame had crept in.

Now the shame filled her. Guilt that she'd blindly followed along, and regret that she'd not done more to help others like the Haurbechs.

"You condemned them and now you pay the penalty."

"No more than anyone else who passes through the barbed wire into the gruesome belly of this camp. And I give far less than they, the poor souls who are sent down the hill."

"Sent down the hill?"

Omara's eyes looked toward the far north corner of the building. She tilted her head in that direction.

"Never go to that end of the camp, Adele. The end that is lined with the birch trees and the small brick houses."

"Why? What's there?" Adele pictured a hundred brick walls identical to the bloodstained one she'd seen outside. Could there be anything worse than what she'd just seen?

"It is death. There, you hear it. Wailing, down the small hill that is shielded by those scraggly, lifeless trees. The condemned—they cry out. Screaming. Unaware of what is happening to them until it is too late. It is horror in smoke and ash."

"But what kind of horror—" Adele swallowed hard. "Tell me. What kind of death is there?"

"The kind your music will protect you from. You need not know more than to play. They have requested that we form an orchestra, which we will do. And we will play. To survive, we must do it. It is our only chance."

Adele stood there, staring, wondering when the shock would leave her body. It hadn't receded yet.

"Do you see, child? Your music is a ticket to life."

Adele glanced around the room as Omara continued readying the beds for their new occupants. It was stark to be sure, with the cold brick wall, the tiny barred windows, and the damp air. She coughed over the strong odor of mold and wrapped her arms around her middle.

How in the world would they stave off illness in this place? She felt its chill even then. Hoping that the room would be temporary, she asked, "Where are we?"

"Canada." Omara's one-word answer was surprising to Adele.

She looked around at the musty back room of the warehouse, having remembered the bins, full to overflowing with cast-off wares that no longer had any owners. "And what is Canada?"

"It is a land of plenty."

Omara walked to the door and opened it, exposing their view to the long rows of bins she'd seen when the guard brought her in.

"Look around you. The bins hold great stores of wealth but the prisoners cannot reach any of it. You will find that in winter, many a prisoner will die without shoes or a coat, but here in this warehouse, they could each find aids to survival. Be glad you are here, in this one-room penthouse. The other barracks are overrun with rats and lice, the bunks dirtied, the straw teeming with death and disease. The prisoners die of starvation while at least the orchestra may be given food. They have soiled uniforms they wear year-round, yet you have a dress, haven't you? And they did not make you cut your hair."

Her hand instinctively flew up to the thick blond mane at her shoulders. It may have been dirty after several torturous days on the cattle car, but at least it was still there, laying soft as it grazed her trembling shoulders. "Why would they make me cut my hair?"

"The hair of a Jew is infectious, they say. But it is not because you are a Gentile that they've left your head unshaved."

"Shaved?" Was that what all the hair was from in the warehouse? Her head turned as if pulled by a string and she glanced over at the mound of hair in the far corner.

Omara scoffed, with mock humor lacing her tone. She reached up and feathered the hair at her brow. "And you thought I wore my hair like this by choice, cut short as a man's?"

"They've all been shaved like this?"

"Yes."

Adele tried to understand but couldn't hope to. "Everyone?"

"Those in the regular population have been shaved. Numbered. Tattooed. Dehumanized. The imprisoned will work. Day in and day out, whether ill or hungry or driven mad. They line up for morning counts, sometimes for hours, in the driving rain or blasting heat of summer. I've even seen them standing in the snow. Agonizing as the ice gathered around their ankles." She coughed over what seemed to be a hitch in her throat, then continued. "And when they die, which they will, their body will still be a number as it is heaped into a mass grave."

"I . . ." The words hardly came to her trembling lips. It was so . . . cold. Unreal. And the word she'd once spoken to her mother came alive on her lips. She breathed it out—*evil*.

Adele shook her head. "I can't believe you. Men could not be so cruel. This isn't real."

Omara placed gentle hands on Adele's shoulders and squeezed until she was forced to look up. "It's not important that you believe me. What is important is that you work and that you play when you're told. That is the only way you will survive in this place. Do you understand?"

Survive?

"But I was sent here to work." Adele bit her lip, stopping it from voicing childish ideas. Naïveté was a luxury she could no longer afford. "I thought it was just to be a punishment. They'd assign the formality of a work detail to humiliate me, then send me back to the care of my parents."

"They don't waste their time with humiliation. You'll work in Canada," Omara instructed, tilting her head out toward the stocked warehouse. "And in the orchestra, when the time comes."

She glanced over at the bins, feeling haunted by the abundance before her. "But if the Germans have all of this, why not give it to the prisoners? Surely they have no use for old cast-off suits and worn shoes. Wouldn't it make the prisoners better workers if they were kept from illness? A jacket and shoes would aid in that."

Omara walked up to Adele and laid a hand on her elbow. "My dear, you will learn quickly that they have no use for us. Any of us. Even if we can play, we are not worth being alive to them." She closed the door, a look of disgust on her face. "They'd sooner burn the warehouse to the ground than give a coat to a Jew."

CHAPTER FOURTEEN

*S*era, what in the world is going on?" Penny sounded worried through the phone line. "I haven't heard you like this in a while. You're a nervous wreck."

"I'm at his little sister's wedding! He invited me—what was I supposed to say?"

"I would have said yes too." Sera heard a chuckle through the phone.

"Penn, you're laughing at me."

"You bet I am. And enjoying it, I might add."

The irony wasn't lost on her.

Penny was the one who made impulsive, flighty decisions when it came to men. Why, the girl had had more boyfriends than they had paintings in the gallery. But when it came to having any kind of love life, Sera was the complete opposite. She was guarded and—yes—all work and no play. So the fact that she was shut into one of the Hanovers' massive estate bathrooms, nervously scrutinizing her appearance and pacing, wasn't a good sign.

"Penny, this guy hired me—that sort of makes him my boss." Sera's strappy black stilettos clicked as she marched back and forth across the marble floor. She stopped when she heard Penny laugh on the other end of the call. "Thanks for taking this seriously."

"You have to admit, it has a funny ring to it. Sera, you're huddled in the bathroom of your new employer's California mansion, calling your assistant—"

"Friend."

"Okay, friend. The point is, you're chatting on your cell phone when you should be out there enjoying yourself. Eat cake. Sip champagne. Dance. Laugh and let yourself have a good time for a change! You deserve it."

"Seriously?" Sera almost shouted, then lowered her voice to a rough whisper when she heard guests moving about in the hall beyond the closed bathroom door. "You know I can't do that!"

"You can't enjoy yourself, just for fun's sake? Do I ever know that."

"You know what I mean, Penn. I don't know if this is a date—or what. I'm desperate for some advice here."

"You'd have to be close to desperation to call me. I had three dates with three different guys last week," she countered. "I haven't figured it out either."

"Then tell me I've lost my mind. Tell me I can't start to like this man. This is business—it's crazy, right?" When Penny offered no reply, she stopped and lightly stomped her foot. "I am not moving a muscle until you answer me. As your friend I am ordering you to give me one good reason why I should stay. Go ahead. Give me just one."

There was silence on the other end.

Then Penny said the exact thing Sera would have expected from her younger, much more freethinking assistant: "What's he look like?"

"Penny!"

"Oh, come on. You can tell me. Is he a looker?" Sera could hear her mad typing in the background. "Forget it. I'm Googling him. It's faster than trying to get answers out of you."

"Stop Googling him this instant!"

Penny was about as subtle as a red costume at Christmas. The girl honestly couldn't restrain herself from saying and doing whatever was flitting around in the recesses of her boy-crazy mind.

"Penn, looking for a picture of this guy isn't going to help."

"Oh yeah? I need to know what kind of situation we're dealing with here. I mean, if he's gorgeous, then you might never come home and then I'm out of a job. If the guy's got ears that stick out or a huge nose, then I can at least read a fashion magazine at lunch instead of poring over the classifieds. Besides, I'd like to see the face of the man who's managed to crack the brick wall around Sera James's iron-clad heart. This is unprecedented. I am therefore forced to conclude that this guy is tasty enough to be on the cover of *GQ*."

"No one's cracked anything," Sera whisper-shouted, still hearing the clicking of the laptop keyboard in the background. "And he's not tasty!"

No, he hadn't managed to break down a single wall. Not at all. Considering she'd run out this afternoon and bought a designer outfit for the occasion and she now stood, smoothing wrinkles out of the tea-length pink dress while she tried to convince herself that she wasn't a basket case.

After a pause, and the continued staring in the mirror, she caved in to the tug of honesty. "Penn, I bought a dress."

"You bought a dress for this guy? This is more serious than I thought."

"Not for the guy—for the wedding!"

The line was silent then, so much that she wondered if the call had been dropped. She then heard a clicking noise in the phone, almost as if Penny was absentmindedly tapping a pen against her teeth.

"You there, Penn?"

"Are you going to tell him about Michael?"

"Michael? Why on earth would I tell him about Michael?"

Penny paused for a moment, then continued, "Oh, I don't know . . . A new guy might find it interesting that you were hours from walking down the aisle when your fiancé called off the wedding and you've sworn off dating since. Like, for more than two years?"

"I haven't sworn off dating!"

"Could have fooled me," Penny huffed lightly. "Listen, Sera, you may not realize it, but you've shut practically everyone out of your life. You never go out of your apartment except to work. You haven't gone home to visit your mom in almost a year. And I distinctly remember the last time I set you up on a double date, you called it quits and left the pub by seven thirty, even though I dug up a marginally cute guy who was willing to pay for dinner and a movie. You could have at least stayed through the spinach dip."

"When was that?" Sera was trying to remember three boyfriends ago. "Was that the date with Brent's cousin?"

"Yeah. And it wasn't Brent. It was Brad," Penny chided. "Beside the point."

"Then what is the point? I think a line is forming on the other side of the door." Sera could hear guests clamoring even louder outside in the hall.

"You're hiding out," Penny declared.

Was she? The dress was stunning, she hoped. It had taken her more than an hour to find one that she thought would do.

"You're right, Penn." She was hiding out from William. Hiding out from having a life. All because she was terrified of getting hurt again.

Had she been hiding out from God too?

"So what are you going to do?"

"The only thing I can do—flee the confines of this bathroom and join the reception." Sera grabbed up her black alligator clutch from the marble counter. "Off I go."

"Okay. Call me later if you need to."

"I will."

Sera almost hung up, but Penny's voice chimed through the phone again.

"Oh, and, Sera?"

"Yeah?"

She could hear Penny's snicker through the phone. "Stay away from staring into those baby blues of his."

—

"Is everything okay?"

William held the chair out for her and pushed it up behind her when she sat down.

"Yes. I just had to take a quick phone call."

He sat down next to her. Close. A little too close. She could smell the coolness of his aftershave.

In the midst of twinkling lights and the sound of laughter and joy all around, it was funny to feel like they had a moment to themselves; it was a hopelessly crowded wedding, after all. As they sat there, he quiet and she wondering what in the world he must be thinking, it almost seemed like they were alone.

"May I ask you something?"

"Of course."

"Why did you say yes? When I asked you to the wedding, I mean. What made you agree to come tonight? Because I almost had the feeling that you'd have rather avoided it."

Sera thought about it for a second, then shrugged. "Free dinner. A beautiful view. And cake? A lady never turns down cake."

"Is that right?"

"Famous words of my assistant." She tilted her chin a bit, offering a light smile, hoping she appeared more in control than she felt. "Or I could always be buttering you up. You know, so you'll give me the painting when this thing is all over."

"Buttering me up, huh?"

"That's right, Mr. Hanover."

"And tell me, Manhattan." He turned and looked her dead in the eyes. "Just where did you get that dress?"

Her hands flew up to rest on the collar of the exquisite pink sheath. "My dress?"

Sera swallowed hard.

"It wasn't lying around in your suitcase, was it?"

She tried to wave him off with as much nonchalance as she could fake.

"Well, a Manhattan suit wouldn't do for a wedding. It would be a dead giveaway to all of your guests. But lucky for me, California has stores like New York does, and I could quickly walk out with this."

"Who knew?" He smiled, the sarcasm tinged with her same brand of light humor.

"Right. Who knew? I bought the first dress I saw in the window." *After I tried on twenty in between.*

He sat back, looking at her with an open stare. And though he looked handsome in his tux and smelled even better, she again reminded herself to shut off any feelings before they started.

A faint ocean breeze blew in. Some of the strands of roped twinkle lights stirred in the vault of the tent above them. The candles on the table flickered. And it rustled her hair, sending a few long waves to dance about her shoulder. She calmed them with one hand, fighting the inclination to let them go in the event he might be bold enough to smooth them himself.

"Do you enjoy being so formal?"

"Formal? I don't think so." Her Friday nights were spent eating Chinese takeout while cuddled on the couch in front of an old black-and-white movie. Sera couldn't help but laugh a bit, thinking of her favorite pair of navy sweats with the small hole in the seam.

"Then we agree you can stop calling me Mr. Hanover? I only hear that at the office and I don't like it even then. It's William. Or Will to my family and friends."

"Ah, are we to be friends now? I hadn't thought of that." She tried to sound light and teasing. The serious look on his face didn't match that one iota.

"I'd like to believe so, Sera. We've spent roughly the last forty-eight hours together, haven't we? Maybe we could be friends in this? I can see this is important to you."

The breeze danced again, rustling his hair this time. It didn't break the connection between them. She took a deep breath as the blue eyes searched her face.

Okay, God. Whatever You're trying to tell me, You've got my attention.

When she didn't answer, William's face changed. "But there's more to it, isn't there?"

"Yes."

"Sera," he whispered, tilting his head to one side. "What is it you're not telling me?"

She turned her eyes from him, changing her view to the expanse of the starry sky and the illuminated tent overhead. It was a beautiful scene. Too beautiful to darken with a memory she'd kept buried for so long.

The band cued up, breaking the silence she'd put between them.

He must have felt the change, because instead of saying anything further, William stood and removed his tuxedo jacket. He tossed it on the back of his chair, then looked down at her. And with possibly the most tender voice she'd ever heard, he whispered into the space between them, "Dance with me."

He stretched out his hand.

"What?"

"Come on. You agreed we'd be friends. Friends can dance."

He kept his hand out to her, though she hadn't made a move to accept it.

"I haven't danced in quite a while," she whispered so no one else would hear, but still couldn't seem to stop her head from shaking under the embarrassment. Hopefully he couldn't see that the hands she'd buried in her lap were quivering so badly they were nearly convulsing.

"Good. Neither have I." When she made no move to accept, he continued with a boyish smile. "I'll lead with the wrong hand and you can even step on my toes if you want. Come on. We'll fumble through it together."

The music began to play, a vintage melody that most guests seemed to know well. He turned his head toward the direction of the stage. A singer began belting out the jazzy tune of "The Very Thought of You" with her silky voice, and they both instinctively smiled.

"Sounds like they're playing our song," he said, still waiting, his palm open. "Are you going to tell me no? When I'm standing up and everything?"

Sera stopped thinking. She stopped running and analyzing for once, and did what her heart told her to do. Two years or a hundred—it didn't matter how long she'd been closed off, hiding her heart away. Maybe she could think about trusting someone again.

Maybe she could trust him.

Sera laid her clutch on the tablecloth and placed her hand in his, walking alongside him as he led her out to the dance floor.

With the slight graze of his fingertips on the small of her back and the other hand cradling her palm, she suddenly felt right. They danced. Swayed with a deliberate softness. Moving without words, melting together, absorbed in the magic of the vintage 1940s song as if they'd danced together for years. And somehow, as he held her, Sera forgot that they weren't the only two people dancing beneath the blanket of the starry sky. The dance floor was full, but neither noticed.

Somehow her eyes drifted closed as they danced. As he held her. As she was wrapped in the stirring potential of what love *could* be. She worried that her heart would forget it was treading on dangerous ground while waltzing in William Hanover's arms.

"Do you think they danced to this?" He whispered the question against the hair at her temple. Her eyes popped open.

"Adele and the young musician?" she asked, on a whisper.

"Yes. The song would have been popular during their time, wouldn't it?"

Sera felt the warmth of his breath burn her forehead and shivered. He must have thought her chilled because he gently pulled her closer, until she was cradled up against the heat of his chest, her head nudging his chin with each melodic sway.

"I believe so. Probably sung by Billie Holiday or another popular singer of the era. But I always think of this song as sung by Nat King Cole."

"In the fifties?"

"Mmm-hmm."

He nodded, his chin bobbing against her forehead.

They danced silently, swaying to the chorus with its enchanting words.

"And do you believe in second chances?" William's words were faintly whispered.

What was he thinking? She wished she knew.

"Second chances?"

"If they were a couple as we suspect, wouldn't they have given anything for one more chance to do what we're doing right now, especially given what might have happened to them?"

She shook her head. She'd been searching for a painting of Adele—not looking to uncover a decades-old romance. Love had been taken off the table long ago when her heart was shattered. So was she supposed to care about fresh chances now? What did they hold but broken promises?

He seemed to notice her pause, but chose to ignore it and whispered closer to her ear, "What should we do with this stolen moment?"

Sera felt a pit forming in her stomach. She was leaving in twelve hours. That was it. She'd be on a plane flying thousands of miles away from California and those blue eyes of his.

"William, I'm leaving tomorrow and—"

He tightened his grip at her back and laughed softly. "See? You didn't call me Mr. Hanover. I knew you could do it if you set your mind to it."

"It doesn't matter what we call each other," she admitted, trying to find the right words to soften the truth. "I'm just . . . not sure I'm ready for this."

"Is it because I've hired you? Or is it something else?" William leaned back, enough so that their eyes met. Their dance became slower, each step more intentional. More connected, even. "Something more than the painting?"

She tilted her chin in a soft, singular nod. "It always has been."

As if waiting for something, he whispered, "Who hurt you, Sera?"

She stared back, feeling the weight of his eyes as they searched her face. So she wasn't able to hide everything.

"Someone who was supposed to honor a promise until death do we part." She sighed. "But he couldn't honor it even to walk down the aisle."

His voice was heavy, laden with tenderness. "I'm so sorry."

Sera took a deep breath against the emotion that threatened to pinch her eyes to tears.

"I've thought about this. A lot. And—"

William's mouth flipped into a sudden grin. "You thought about me?"

"No." She shook her head, embarrassed that she couldn't think straight around him.

"No, you didn't think about me?"

She fumbled her steps and nearly took off the tip of his oxford with the heel of her shoe. "I'm sorry," she apologized, and halted their swaying. "We've both got baggage, William. Just different kinds. We're both searching for something outside of what happened to Adele—your search happened to cross with mine. And given the fact that there's the painting between us, and your family's future at stake, it's not a reality that we can be friends."

"Good."

He surprised her with the one word.

Really? He thought it was good?

Sera popped her head up and looked him dead in the eyes. "Good?"

"I thought that might get your attention." The words were whispered a scant second before his lips brushed hers. It was soft, sweet, and a blink of a kiss that she hadn't expected. "I don't think I want to be friends with you either."

CHAPTER FIFTEEN

———

September 1, 1939

$\mathcal{S}$ee? He's looking at you again."

Margie kept tugging at the sleeve of Adele's blue-and-white flowered dress as she whispered about the tall, dreamy-eyed gentleman who'd walked into the dance hall a few moments before. He stood across the room, casually leaning against the wall and looking every now and then in their direction. The band played, couples danced, and the overhead lights dimmed over the dance floor in between them, but he appeared not to notice.

Margie and the rest of the girls thought it was a chance sighting, didn't they?

Her heart quickened as he stood there, leaning to one side with his long legs crossed, looking toward where she sat with her gaggle of red-lipped friends.

"Did you hear me?" Margie poked her in the shoulder. "That hotsy-totsy over there keeps giving you the eye. I'm sure of it. He turns this way every few seconds. See?" The bright-eyed brunette raised her brows and smirked. "He did it again! He's looking at our sweet little violinist, I do believe."

Adele stirred the straw in her cola bottle, trying to appear as nonchalant as possible. "Really? I hadn't noticed."

Margie could see through her. Always did. She was the first

friend Adele had made when she'd started college that autumn, and boy-crazy though Margie was, Adele enjoyed her caring nature. The other girls, Faye and Greta, were both studious musicians in the music program. They were lovely and proper, and far more reserved than their unofficial brunette-haired leader.

"I think he's going to ask you to dance, Adele." Greta winked, her long lashes upturned on a smile that softened all the contours of her face. "And on your birthday, no less."

Adele felt her cheeks tinge with a blush.

Of course she hoped he'd ask her to dance on her birthday. What else could she want?

"He'd better ask, after all the staring he's doing. You haven't noticed?" Margie rolled her eyes, causing a chorus of giggled sighs from the other two friends at the table. "You'd better start noticing, Adele. Look at him—he's perfect. Austria's Sweetheart may have been gifted with more than a seat onstage for her special day."

"Leave her alone, Marg. She's trying to forget who she is for one night. Can't she just be Adele? Why does the orchestra have to be brought into it?"

"He plays for the Philharmonic, doesn't he?"

Adele nodded and tried to steel herself from looking over at him in return. Instead, she looked down at the cola bottle she'd been turning in her hands. "Yes. He's a new cellist."

"See, Faye? She's playing coy with us. Our Adele is officially falling for mystery man number one over there and . . ." Margie exhaled noisily and sagged into a playful sigh against Adele's shoulder. "Let's face it. I can't blame her. I'd be smitten with that one too. I've been trying to get the dirt on him for weeks, and curiously, she never has any details to share. Don't you think that's a bit odd? I think they're secret friends and she refuses to tell us."

Adele had to smile.

Her eyes had clamped on Vladimir's tall form the second he'd strolled in through the front doors. As a matter of fact, Adele had been waiting for him all night, though she'd never have admitted it to her group of friends. They sat around like lovesick kittens, purring over every dark-haired man who gave a half smile in the direction of their table. But when Vladimir had strolled through the doors, a collective sigh rose up from the group.

For some reason, Adele was reluctant to share much.

Maybe it was because she feared her parents would find out about their friendship. Or maybe she didn't want to admit to the mad crush that was building on her part? Surely the older Vladimir wouldn't notice her as anything more than the orchestra's young guest violinist.

Adele wore a pearl comb in her hair that night. She'd rolled her hair high on her head and let the back trail down her neck in a riot of curls about her shoulders, like many other girls there. But the comb? That was for him and him alone. She hoped he noticed it, hoped he didn't see her as the little college girl who played with him onstage. Could he see something of the woman in her?

"The odds are that he'll be walking over here within the next five minutes." Margie, always romantic with the swoony daydreams about happily ever after, smiled at her knowingly. "And you, miss, will find yourself swept away."

"But one of us might not be here to see it," Faye whispered, shoving her with an elbow. "Look."

A handsome officer was walking in their direction. He stopped before the table, inclined his head to the group, and then turned . . . to her.

"Excuse me, miss. Might I have the honor of a dance?"

Margie kicked her leg under the table, the heel of her shoe knocking her shin. Adele glanced across the table to see her brunette friend smiling wildly and bobbing her head in a hopeful nod. *"Are you crazy? Say yes,"* she mouthed. Faye and Greta stared back at her too, their eyes wide while the officer waited for his answer.

On instinct, she moved her eyes to glance at Vladimir, hoping he'd see the exchange and swoop in to ask her to dance instead.

The wall was empty.

Her eyes scanned that side of the room but found no evidence of him. When had he moved?

The sound of someone clearing their throat brought her back to the table. She turned her attention back to the officer who was waiting patiently and the friends who seemed breathless while the agonizing seconds passed for her to render a response.

There was nothing else to be done. Vladimir hadn't asked her to dance. Surely he didn't want to or he'd have intervened.

Adele nodded slightly and rose up out of the chair. The officer beamed a smile back and offered a gloved hand, which she took, and they moved to the dance floor.

Though seeming a bit nervous, the young man was an expert dancer, likely as schooled as she'd been in her youth. Her mother had always planned that she'd have a moment like this, a chance encounter on a dance floor with a young man as privileged as she, and they'd drive off into the sunset together in a Rolls Royce with Nazi red flags flying. But though her mother's wishes for grandeur would no doubt have been found in the polite and handsome young man, he'd never hold the slightest candle to the penniless cellist Adele wished had asked her to dance instead.

She nodded politely to the officer's conversation, listening as intently as she could. She danced almost robotically, feeling not the slightest spark as he continued talking. And while she hoped to feel something, it was no use. Her eyes wandered the room every second while the young man held her so stiffly in his arms.

Adele could scarcely wait for the song to be over so she could escape. But each time she tried to excuse herself, another eager young man would fill the place of the one before. It was three more dances before she had a moment to catch her breath. And still, with each twirl around the floor, Vladimir had never come back into view.

She needed some air.

The moment the notes of the present song stopped and the applause began, she gave the last young man a polite thank-you and turned on her heels toward the door.

Thank goodness it wasn't too cold out. She didn't have the will to go back to the table for her coat. Her friends would have noticed the tears building in her eyes and questioned her.

Adele burst through the front doors without a look back.

She nearly bumped into a couple of young officers standing near the entrance, smoking and laughing about something. One of them whistled when she walked by, causing her to quicken her pace.

Maybe she'd just walk all the way home.

It wasn't that far. And it would give her time to compose herself before she had to walk through the door. No doubt her mother would be up, waiting to hear every detail of the night out. Who did she dance with? Had there been any eligible young men there that night? It always occurred in the same manner.

There was no way she could hide tear-streaked cheeks.

"Adele?"

She heard footsteps clamoring behind her. She stopped, her heart quickening to the sound of Vladimir's voice. After hastily wiping at her eyes, she turned to face him.

"Where are you going?" Panting, he came to a stop in front of her.

"I'm going home." She gave him a forced smile. "I'm tired."

"But you left your things," he said, holding her peacock blue coat and leather purse out to her. Confused, she took them from him and mumbled, "Thank you," as she shrugged the coat up over her shoulders.

She didn't understand him at all.

He stood in the dance hall, looking at her for the longest time, yet never asked her to dance. One after another, other young men had asked her. She'd been good enough for them to waltz around the floor.

Vladimir was older. And probably more experienced with matters of the heart. Adele knew she must be a child to him. Having realized it, she now wanted nothing more than to tear the pearl comb from her hair and march off into the night away from him.

Hers was a schoolgirl crush, plain and simple.

"I was looking for you." He pulled a handkerchief from his pocket and offered it to her. "Are you upset?"

"No," she lied, but accepted the handkerchief and used it to dab at the corners of her eyes.

"It's okay. Everyone else was. I saw several of the other girls crying too."

What was he talking about? They'd stopped in the middle of the street without even realizing it.

He must have read her thoughts, because he looked around and then tugged her over to the sidewalk next to a park. They stood under a lamppost, the light illuminating his face. And suddenly, she wasn't mad anymore. Vladimir had a look of genuine concern on his face. She could see it now.

"Vladimir, what's wrong?"

"Didn't you just hear?"

She shook her head. "Hear what?"

He tilted his head and stood back a step with his arms folded across his chest. "You mean you don't know what's happened?"

"No—" she said, but stopped short.

She looked around then and felt an eerie pit begin to form in her stomach. After a glance down the street, she could see a crowd pouring out of the front doors of the dance hall. Some people were cheering and skipping about the sidewalks as they tugged on coats and hats. Others were comforting young ladies with an arm around their shoulders. And for it being late evening, it seemed that an inordinate amount of traffic was now passing them by on the street.

"Vladimir," she said, looking around at all of the activity. "What in the world is going on?"

He didn't seem inclined to answer her question. He seemed fixed on her instead. "If you didn't hear what was going on, then why did you run out of there?"

"You saw me run out?"

He shook his head. "No. I stepped away from the dance floor for a few moments and when I returned, you'd gone. Your friends saw you go outside."

"Were you watching me?"

He ignored her question to ask one of his own. "Why are you crying?"

She sighed. "I'm not."

"Did that last creep in there try something with you, because if he did, I'm going to—"

"No. He didn't try anything with me," she said, tugging at the sleeve of his trench coat even as his hands formed into tight fists. He looked like he was ready to turn around and end the young man's life if she didn't stop him. "I'm just tired."

He looked like he didn't believe her, but he did relax considerably.

"You cry when you're tired?"

Adele knew she looked embarrassed. She could feel the heat rise in her cheeks until she had a telltale blush. It was something she hated about herself—her emotions were always so easily splayed across her face.

He raised his eyebrows as he looked down at her, waiting for an answer that made sense.

"Unless you want me to go back there and deck that jerk on principle, I suggest you tell me what made you cry."

She could have laughed in that moment. The jerk was standing right in front of her.

The only thing left to do was attempt to change the subject. People were moving so fast around them, shouting from car windows and running down the sidewalks with excitement clicking at their heels.

"Vladimir, tell me what's happened." People continued bustling by them. A uniformed man bumped her as a couple rushed past, and apologized in his haste to comfort a weeping woman in his arms.

Vladimir pulled her farther away from the busy sidewalk and turned to face her.

"It all happened so fast. One second the dance hall was alive, then the band stopped playing in the middle of a song," he said on a sigh, and ran his fingers through his hair. "I'd heard about it only moments before. A friend had his car radio on and he'd come in to tell me the news."

"What news?"

"Hitler has invaded Poland."

Adele's hand flew up to her mouth on a gasp.

Then that's what all of the people were so stirred up about. But it didn't make sense. If the German army had invaded Poland . . . why in heaven's name would anyone be happy?

"Invaded Poland . . . That's terrible! Why do they celebrate?"

"Because it's war. That's inevitable now. It's only a matter of time before France and Britain declare it."

She shook her head in disbelief. "We're at war? Or you mean to say that we've started a war?"

He too must have noticed the irony of the youths from the dance hall showing such jubilance around them, for he glanced back over his shoulder and shook his head.

"It looks that way."

"But why are they happy?"

"I don't think they're happy." He turned back to her, concern heavy in his eyes. "They're young and brash. And stupid. They don't know what it means."

"It means a lot of these boys will be going off to fight, doesn't it?"

"Yes. I'd say so."

"And you?" She was breathless with the prospect. "You'll go with them?"

Vladimir paused a moment before he responded. "If they call the boys into service, I'm sure I'll be called too. But I don't think I can go and fight, not for this Austria at least."

"What do you mean? You won't desert, will you? They'll throw you in prison!" She shook her head, trying to understand what he was telling her.

"I'll do what I have to do. Adele, you don't have any idea what's going on here."

"Then tell me so I can understand."

He shook his head. "You've been sheltered. I'll not ruin that."

"Ruin what? Don't presume to treat me like a child."

She wanted to stomp her foot at him but that would seem childish. Instead, she folded her hands in front of her waist and waited, chin up.

"I never said you were a child. You're just . . . innocent."

Innocent. That was as bad as saying she belonged in pigtails on a hopscotch square chalked out on the playground. She stood with as determined a constitution as ever, staring up into his eyes without the slightest flinch. She had to show him she wasn't as young as she seemed.

"I'm not leaving until you tell me."

He hesitated only a moment.

"Remember the Anschluss last year? When Hitler marched into Vienna and took control?" He shook his head, seemingly in disgust. "I saw what happened to the Jews after that spring. Good people. Shopkeeper friends of my father. Boys I'd grown up with, their families expelled from this city and their businesses burned or confiscated. After the *Kristallnacht* programs, they had nothing left. The lucky ones got out then. I worry for any who remain. It might be too late for them to escape now."

Kristallnacht.

It meant "night of broken glass."

She'd heard of it in the newspapers, only not explained the way Vladimir had. It amounted to dirty accusations made by those who refused to support Austria—at least that was what her mother had said. The degenerates and criminals of Vienna. They supported the Jews and propagated this *Kristallnacht* idea as an excuse to wreak havoc on the city. The lawless Jewish communities claimed it explained the broken glass from Jewish shop windows that had been shattered across Germany and Austria the previous November. But those shops had been harboring criminals. Criminals who didn't support the government during the Great War and who didn't support it now.

But as for men being killed just for being Jews?

Adele had never heard of such a thing.

"But Hitler's government has helped the people. He's built up our nations again. Made them great after the depression of our childhood. My father told me stories about the Great War. How terrible it all was. We've been saved from that."

"Not really, Adele. Not when people are being killed for being Jewish."

"You're sure of this? There is proof?"

He shook his head. "I don't need proof beyond what I've seen with my own eyes."

Adele wasn't sure what to believe.

Surely the Jews couldn't have been so ill-treated as that? Their entire livelihood taken away? Senseless acts of violence that led to their being killed without just cause? She couldn't believe her father would have been so blindly supportive of such a government. Why, she and her mother had accompanied her father to the very parade Vladimir spoke of now.

She even remembered seeing the Führer. He looked quite severe, that was true, but she thought him only a misjudged military strategist. He was a powerful speaker, she remembered. And masses of people had come out of their homes for it. They'd lined the streets to celebrate with flags flying. They loved him. The sea of red had actually pulsed with excitement that day in March, the crowds alive with the energy and prosperity of a once-more prosperous empire.

Germany had the right to be a world power once more, didn't they? Why shouldn't Austria go along with them?

Adele remembered playing at a party that night in March 1938. It wasn't anything like playing for the Führer, of course, but her mother and father had both been proud that their sixteen-year-old daughter was such a symbol of patriotism and triumph—she wore the German swastika band proudly on her arm. The Führer the symbol represented couldn't have been so evil as to have supported the killing of innocent people.

"You've seen Jews killed?" She couldn't believe Vladimir had harbored such a horrible secret. He'd never spoken of it before.

He nodded. Slowly. Just once.

"I can't believe God means *this* path for Austria—or for us." Adele mumbled the words, somehow knowing that it was okay to be herself around him. "I suppose I have to question the things I've been told. It's a new life that's dawning for us. War is going to change things, isn't it?"

"Yes. It will," he agreed quietly.

Adele didn't even wait a breath before she added, "Then I hope it changes me."

And in that moment, Vladimir surprised her.

He smiled.

It wasn't one of those heart-stopping grins of his. But this time he actually looked . . . proud? Was that it? Did that easy smile and those inviting eyes mean that he was somehow proud of her?

He took a finger and tapped the pearl comb in her hair.

"When did you get this?"

She shrugged. New combs. Birthdays. How could such things matter now that they faced war? "Last week. My mother took me shopping again."

Vladimir shoved his hands in his pockets in an almost boyish fashion.

"It looks nice."

So he had noticed her, but simply chose not to act? What a miserable prospect.

"But then if you wear it, what will I do with this one?" When her eyes shot up to meet his, he shocked her by pulling a small box from his pocket. "Happy birthday," he said, presenting her with a little silver trinket box wrapped in a lovely, cherry red satin bow. "Butterfly."

She took it from him with genuine surprise in her heart. "I thought you . . ."

"I know. You thought I forgot." He shrugged, almost sheepishly. "Someday we're going to have to change your assumptions about me. I can remember the important things."

Though her hands shook as she took the delicate box, Adele tugged the ribbon loose and opened the hinged lid to find a soft white satin lining with a tiny golden clip resting inside. He took it out and with careful fingers exchanged the pearl comb for the small golden wings of the butterfly in her hair.

"There. Now you look like the woman I've come to know."

After all of the rehearsals they'd played together, and all of the nights meeting in the garden to talk about the weather or other little things that probably seemed unimportant to him, she knew her heart was gone. It wouldn't matter how many officers asked her to dance; she'd only ever be able to think of him.

"Come on, Butterfly," he said, and slid his arm around her shoulders. "I'll walk you home."

How easy it was for him to offer to walk her home.

Despite how Vladimir tried to keep the conversation light, a darkness had crept in around them. It was time to grow up, not just with a birthday. War was coming. It was coming quickly, and she felt something tug at the innermost recesses of her heart.

They'd never even danced.

CHAPTER SIXTEEN

April 2, 1943

The golden butterfly clip and the small picture of Vladimir had been hidden in the crushed velvet lining of her violin case for the last couple of years. Her mother had never thought to pull back the plush red fabric of the case, just like the Germans hadn't when she'd been registered in the camp. And now, after almost a month in Birkenau, the small photo and clip were her prized possessions. In fact, they were her only possessions to speak of, except for the brown dress she wore and the shoes on her feet that were two sizes too big, since she'd lost her own shoes on the first night.

No one had told her to sleep with them under her or they would be stolen right off her feet. Lucky for her, she'd slept with the violin case tight in her arms or it might have gone missing too. Adele remembered waking that first morning, her body aching from sleeping on a hard wooden plank bed, her back raw from the repeated poking of dried stalks of straw, feet bare and cold as ice.

Even in the room of women who had joined them, no one would own up to the theft in the morning. Omara was the one to tell her she should have slept on her shoes. It sure didn't help much after the fact. And though they'd been laboring in a warehouse full of shoes in all shapes and sizes, stealing a pair of replacements could mean death for any of them. They couldn't risk it. The replacement shoes she'd been given would have to do until Omara could procure something better.

Each night she took the photo out and tucked it up in the cracked brick next to her bunk so Vladimir's smiling face could look down on her. She'd hold the clip in her hands, running her fingertips over the smooth wings as she prayed. She only hoped her prayers floated up to reach him, wherever he was, and that he was safe somewhere far away from the horrors she'd been forced to endure.

Oh God. Is he alive? Is he in a place like this?

Adele lay in her bunk on her side, her face pressed toward the wall, her back tight up against Omara's. With only the barest sliver of moonlight shining through the tiny window to illuminate the photo, she mostly imagined the tall man with the dashing smile and the tender eyes she knew so well.

"We never danced. Do you know that?" She whispered the thought aloud, to no one in particular, just so she could hear it and remember that night at the dance hall nearly four years before.

Omara stirred beside her but said nothing.

"After everything that has changed, I never imagined that dancing would be the one thing I'd long for." Adele breathed out the words like a heartbeat, as her mind had them dancing circles round a grand dance floor far away from the stark reality of a concentration camp.

"She's talking nonsense." Marta was a tough-as-nails violinist from northern Poland. When it came to anything Adele said, she seemed to find a complaint easily.

As Omara had predicted, their little orchestra had grown. They now had twelve women packed in the room rather than the six they'd expected. They were doubled up in their bunks, irritable for sleep after a long week of work and late-night rehearsals. And though she hadn't repeated the thought very loud, Adele didn't expect the reception she received floating up from the bunks.

"It's not nonsense, is it? To think of a happy memory?" She whispered the words, almost willing them to form an image of a dancing couple whirling around on the fog of a dream in the darkened room.

But just as before, Marta's irritation was evident and shattered the memory in an instant. "Someone tell the Golden Girl to shut up and go to sleep."

Adele hated Marta's nickname even more than the one her parents had given her. In Vienna, being dubbed Austria's Sweetheart had been an embarrassment to her. But once the rumor circulated among the other orchestra girls that she'd had a privileged life in the Third Reich before Auschwitz, they made no attempt to hide the fact that they loathed her for it.

The obviousness of the cutting nickname referenced more than just her hair.

Adele expected the rest of the girls to follow Marta's gibe as they usually did, so she thought to cry herself to sleep. But Omara surprised her by not advising against the conversation. Instead, she turned onto her back and whispered into the night.

"I danced once."

Adele moved her cramped body so that she faced Omara. She saw the moonlight casting a soft blue glow on her features. "Tell me?"

"It was long ago . . . too long for remembering tonight." Omara's attempt at finding a pleasantry was noticeably weak, her voice sounding tired. "But I applaud you for thinking on it. You will need such memories to get you through what is ahead, when you will long for many things."

"She has been here four weeks. Wait until she's been here for months. She'll pray for moldy bread before she ever does for dancing shoes. They'll make sure of it. Killer of souls, they are."

One of the other girls spat the words at her from somewhere in the black of the room. Several new faces had come from one of the ghettos in Poland and they were quite versed in starvation. And the actions of soulless SS guards.

"Go get the guards. Tell them she disturbs sleep for the rest of us," Marta said, the words cutting.

Fränze, their little flute player from Warsaw, added a cautious *Sshhhhh!* to the bickering.

"Leave her be," Omara issued sternly, quieting the room. She then spoke more softly. "Don't listen to them, Adele. They'll only scare you. And don't think harshly against the hardened ones. We can't know what they've been through—Marta especially. She was in a ghetto before this and she's lost her entire family."

Adele was chastened. "No."

"Yes. It is so, I'm afraid," Omara said, sighing. "They had no food or water when things got bad in the ghettos. Some people tried to escape through the sewers. They tried to get her to go with them, but she couldn't leave her ailing mother. Her mother was all she had left."

"And what happened?"

Omara sighed. "She lost her at the train platform." Which meant she'd been deemed unfit for work. And deemed unfit always meant the same. She'd gone to the chambers.

The heart in Adele's chest contracted with the thought of what Marta had gone through. Adele's parents may not have forgiven her for betraying Austria, but at least she'd not been forced to stand by and watch them die before her eyes.

"Thank you." The gratitude was whispered, mainly so Marta wouldn't hear and think she was trying to win Omara's favor.

"Go to sleep now, Adele. Three thirty in the morning will come too quickly for us all."

Adele couldn't stand the thought of the morning counts being mere hours away. But soon they'd all be lined up and playing, ushering the laborers to march forth to their long workday. And though she was exhausted, she couldn't find sleep. The exhaustion bled down to her soul like water seeking a drain. It made her as tired as the others who had to endure the exhausting fear of death, day in and day out.

She lay there, photo now clasped between her fingers, staring up at the aged wood ceiling. "What do you do when you're too tired to sleep?"

Omara seemed to understand the meaning of the question and paused before her answer. When they barely ate and struggled to practice the eleven hours that were sometimes required of them, they couldn't possibly wish for anything but to close their eyes in sleep. It seemed wrong somehow, didn't it, not to be able to find it now?

"Sleep for him."

The suggestion so surprised Adele that she felt emotion rise up in her throat.

"What did you say?"

"You heard me, child. Do you love the man in your photo?"

She nodded once, her eyes wishing they could produce tears.

"Then close your eyes in sleep for him. Stay strong. Fight to survive."

Adele ran her finger over the edge of the photo, pretending it was the side of his face. "I remember the first night he walked me home. He asked if he could court me. Can you believe that? He was such a gentleman that I almost laughed. He didn't even try to kiss me that first night, though in truth, I would have let him. He gave me a gift—a butterfly clip," she remembered, smiling through the darkness. The memory of his face warmed her. "He stood under a streetlight and told me he intended to ask my father's permission. He wanted to do things right. He said I deserved it."

When she paused, Omara exhaled, "Yes? And what did your father say?"

Adele pressed the photo in her palms, as if to hide the secret of her love for him. "He said what any well-bred father would say. Vladimir Nicolai was a gifted musician. But as a suitor for Adele Von Bron, he was nothing better than a common laborer with dirty hands."

"He put a stop to your relationship then?"

"Only the relationship he knew about," Adele whispered, remembering the harshness in her father's voice when he advised that she not see the merchant again. "We met in secret after that, in our garden whenever we could. And by then, I already loved him."

"If you want to dance with him in the future, then live today. Pray for God to give you the strength to endure each day, for it will be called upon in this place. It will be called upon for all of us," she said louder, her voice obviously carrying to the ears of all the girls in the room. "Strength? That begins with sleep."

Adele hadn't thought past the momentary for weeks.

In the camp, you never dared to think about tomorrow. You lived in the here and now. It had all become clear. She'd expected to find an end to her reeducation in the hellish place. Yet something told her that reeducation was not as simple a thing as walking out the front gate when one's calendar said it should be over. Had Adele owned one, the date would have been boldly circled in red.

What did it matter now where, or even how long, she slept? She'd never see the world from outside the barbed wire walls of Auschwitz.

"I'm never going home, am I?"

"Why would you say such a thing?" Omara's words registered surprise.

"I was nearly killed upon arrival. Do you not remember that?"

"We're all nearly killed on arrival."

There was no veil of innocence anymore. Adele asked and

Omara could always be counted upon to give her a truthful answer, even when the truth stung.

"How did you get in such a position of power?"

"I have no power, Adele. Not here. I do what they tell me. I keep their musical pets in line."

"And if I'd not known how to play, if I'd been a frightened young girl who had walked in here and begged for mercy because of a lie, they'd not have given it. So what if I had walked in here and couldn't play?"

Omara looked at her with a stony constitution and admitted, "Then I would have taught you quickly."

Adele couldn't believe her ears. Did this woman actually mean that she would have lied? To the German SS? If anyone would have found out, it likely would have meant instant death. Would she have risked that for a violinist from Vienna? Her own parents would not have risked so much.

"Why?"

"Why what, Adele?"

She needed to know the truth. No matter how gruesome the details might have been, Adele needed to know why she'd been saved. "Why would you have not sent me back outside to the officer that day?"

She answered on a breath laced with feeling. "Because I believe that this too shall be used by God. Somehow, this story He is writing will live on."

"How does He tell the story?"

Water dripped in the background, punctuating the question. And though no one stirred around them, Adele knew the other girls were also waiting for Omara to offer some shred of hope in her answer.

"He tells it through the art of creation. *His creation.* He tells it through each one of us who survives."

CHAPTER SEVENTEEN

$\mathcal{N}$ ice tan." Penny tossed the comment out the minute Sera walked through the office door on Monday morning.

"Thanks."

"Where were you yesterday?"

Sera dropped her handbag on the desk. "Flying home."

"Uh-huh. So . . ." The girl twirled her swivel chair around to face Sera's desk and allowed it to roll partway across their shared office. She leaned forward, elbow on her armrest, and dropped her chin into her hand in the fashion of a bubbly middle school cheerleader. "How was California?"

Sera was not about to get into any of that, not first thing in the morning.

"It was sunny," she said, and took a sip from the salted caramel mocha in her to-go cup. She set it on the desk and went about her normal routine—turning on her monitor, hooking up her laptop before switching on her desk lamp. She did anything to act as busy as possible.

"Sunny." Penny didn't appear to be accepting the brush-off.

Sera shrugged off her jacket and hung it on the antique iron hook behind the office door.

"Yeah. California is sunny in April. A little cold along the coast, though. I had to borrow his jacket."

Penny hopped up from her chair and nearly tackled her when

she turned around, playfully grabbing her by the shoulders. "You can't leave me in suspense like this! What happened?"

"Nothing."

"Nothing?" Penny shot her a disbelieving look. "I don't buy it."

"I sent you an e-mail with details of everything."

"Oh, I got that. I'm used to receiving work e-mails from you on a Sunday. And I read it. I admit I almost fell over when I did. It said you were coming back a day later than expected, with a hundred-million-dollar problem, I might add."

Sera felt a surge of nervousness blast her veins. She wasn't quite ready to talk about what had occurred between William and her. Talking about it might make it seem more real.

She glanced around the empty gallery. "Isn't there something that needs to be done around here?"

"Nope." Penny shook her head and dropped her hands down to her hips in a domineering fashion. "Not until you spill, Sera."

Sera sighed and wiggled out from under her friend's intense glare. "There's nothing to spill," she said.

"Oh yes, there is—you called me from the guy's bathroom. His mansion bathroom, I might add. And you just happen to leave out the part where we're hired to find a painting that's wrapped up in his family fortune. That phone call was telling. You've never cracked like that, and I've known you for, what, three years?"

"Four." Sera settled into her wooden swivel chair and dove into a rather listless tapping on the keyboard. She could feel Penny staring a hole through her and finally looked up. "Four years."

"Fine. Four." Penny sat on the edge of the desk and looked down at her with expressive eyes. "And in those four years, I've only known you to act this way about one other guy."

"Michael."

Penny seemed to realize she'd brought up a painful memory. "Look, I didn't mean to bring it up. But I haven't seen you like this in so long. I almost dared to be happy—"

Penny broke off as the office phone rang.

They both glanced over at the phone in unison. It was barely nine o'clock on a Monday morning. Who could be calling that early?

Who else?

Penny picked up the handset. "Sera James Gallery, Penny speaking."

Sera had hoped, at the very least, for a few days to prepare herself for the next time she'd hear his voice on the other end of the line. It was strange to think the same lips that would speak from miles away had brushed a butterfly's kiss on hers just a day ago.

She touched her fingertips to the pout of her bottom lip, lost in the memory.

"Yes, just a moment, please." Penny pressed a button on the phone, then held it out to Sera. "It's him."

"It is?" The *him* part required no explanation.

Penny gave a long, exaggerated nod and pulled a chair up closer to the phone. She plopped down in it, fully intending to stay through the conversation.

"So?" She nudged the phone closer to Sera, giving her a gleeful smile. "Do you have any idea what time it is in California?"

"Don't you, uh, have some work to do?"

Penny shook her head. "Not a thing. This gallery practically runs itself."

Luckily for her, the brass bell above the front door chimed and an elderly couple walked in off the street. Sera's heart leapt. *Customers!* She could have kissed them. Given them a free painting. Anything to show gratitude for their absolutely perfect timing.

She tilted her head toward the door, raising her eyebrows at Penny.

Realizing her plans at listening in had been conveniently thwarted, Penny rose and playfully mumbled, "By all means, Madame James. Allow me." Her heels clicked against the floor as she walked away. Her hand rested on the antique knob of the glass-paned office door.

"Open or closed?"

Sera almost rolled her eyes. Did she really have to ask? "Closed, thanks."

"Six o'clock in the morning. That's what time it is in California." She winked and closed the door behind her, almost trotting away on a cloud. Sera knew why. Penny was practically gleeful to think that a man had any kind of effect on her love-starved boss.

Penny disappeared around the corner and Sera stared at the phone, the continually blinking red light toying with her already frayed sensibilities. She tapped a pencil on the tabletop while she debated answering.

The prospect of speaking to William was nearly as bad as the prospect of him not having called at all. But she had no clue how to formulate words on her lips.

She picked up the handset and pushed the button to answer the call. "This is Sera."

"Good morning."

A softness was evident in his voice and that, along with the easy way he greeted her, brought an instant familiarity that warmed her cheeks with a blush. The fact that William hadn't felt the need to state who he was said more than she'd expected.

In hearing his murmur in the phone, she could tell he was smiling. It was one of those things a woman knew—a smile could never be hidden in a voice.

"You must be busy there in your Manhattan office. I've been waiting for a while."

"Have you?"

"Yeah," he said on a pause. "Almost two minutes."

She heard the teasing in his voice and played along. "Well, I'm sorry about that, *Mister* Hanover. I'm sure you're not accustomed to such outrageous waiting." She fumbled through the file folders at her desk, sticking a pencil in the chignon at her nape, and fluttered around for Adele's case file. "But I've got my file right here. I was reading on the plane and found something that might help. I know it's around here somewhere."

"Would that something you found be his name?"

Her hands froze. The young musician in the photographs? "You know his name?"

"Mmm-hmm."

"How? I mean, I just left California and—"

"And you think the only thing this businessman can do is sit behind a desk and issue orders all day. Or rake leaves in the yard."

Sera leaned back in her chair, the antique wood creaking with the action. "And?"

"Uh-uh. Not until you acknowledge the fact that you didn't think I'd call with anything more than questions."

"Okay. I didn't," she admitted, almost laughing. "That's fair enough, isn't it?"

"Good." He seemed satisfied with her answer, because she could hear that he began typing on a computer keyboard while he talked. "I'm e-mailing you right"—he paused and she heard a click—"now. Check your inbox."

Sera sailed into action and pulled up her e-mail program.

The urge to stop breathing toyed with her, the excitement was so great. After months of dead ends, after the hours Penny had spent poring over art auction sites and the many late-night hours they'd both spent at the gallery elbows-deep in research, they were finally on a hot trail again, one that might lead her to the real painting of Adele.

She entered her password, fingers trembling slightly.

And suddenly there it was. His name. Staring back at her from the computer screen.

"Vladimir Nicolai."

"Yes." She could almost hear William smile again through the phone.

"And you know this is him because . . . ?"

William's voice turned all business. "I contacted the Austrian national archives in Vienna and spoke with the curator of the museum. She put me in contact with a colleague at the Vienna Philharmonic, and after a couple of conversations, we were able to do a little cross-research over e-mail. I sent pictures and he sent the name."

"You make it sound so easy," she mumbled, still scanning the paragraph of information that accompanied the name in the e-mail. "Penny and I have been looking for a link like this for a while."

"But you didn't know the connection between Adele and Vladimir. Now we do."

"You're right. Now we do."

William cleared his throat. "Maybe we can talk about it in person," he said, pausing slightly. "I'll be in New York next week."

"Really?" She kept reading, hardly noticing what he'd said.

"Yes. A week from Friday," he said.

"William, it says here that there is no record of Vladimir after January 1945. That's when the Soviet army liberated Auschwitz, isn't it? So if he was a concert cellist before the war, I wonder why he didn't go back to it after? It says here that there was no record of any performance with his name in the program after the war ended. Dear God." She stopped, wondering if the same fate that had taken Adele had snuffed out Vladimir's life as well. "Maybe he didn't survive Auschwitz either."

She began scrolling down through the rest of the information in the e-mail, looking for something, anything that stuck out.

"I thought maybe we could have dinner."

Sera supposed that William's asking shouldn't have surprised her, given that he'd held her so close on the dance floor.

The wedding had made its own magic around them . . . Despite their differences, he'd kissed her and, heaven help her, she hadn't been able to think of much since.

"Dinner?" She swallowed hard. "You mean to talk about the painting?"

Was he wondering the same thing she was—whether what they'd felt on that dance floor was something real? A picture of Michael flashed before her eyes. The memory of a discarded wedding gown and returned gifts . . .

"It's just dinner."

"No, I know. It's . . ." How could she tell him what really bothered her? "I didn't expect you'd be in New York quite this soon."

She dropped her free arm down on the desktop and rested her forehead against it.

"Sera." He said her name so softly, without the reproach she'd expected. "Do you think you'll ever be able to trust again?"

No, no, no, her heart rebelled. *I can't trust anyone. Please don't ask me to.*

She bit her bottom lip so she wouldn't say the thoughts aloud.

He didn't wait for an answer, just said, "Keep digging. I'll call next week for an update."

CHAPTER EIGHTEEN

June 30, 1943

Adele and the rest of the members of the fledgling orchestra had been moved from their one-room barracks to block twelve—which they called the music block—in the general camp population.

When she'd first arrived, the quick decisions of the Nazis might have surprised her. But now? Adele had seen the truth of what was happening in this place. And she didn't question. To stay alive, they went where they were told, stood at attention or knelt for hours, lined up in the sweltering heat, or played their instruments at the SS guards' whims. The prisoners in the orchestra, whether Jew or not, had a distinction amongst the general population. It became clear that the orchestra was her means of survival.

The ragtag group of musicians had grown almost organically. Adele couldn't remember how exactly they'd formed, but when they'd come together as the camp orchestra, she was surprised at the instruments that ended up in the block. Violins. A cello or two, one of which Omara could play. Even a mandolin and an accordion had been brought in from the train platform and now rested with the pile of instruments they looked after.

Though they'd been relocated to live and rehearse in the

music block, Adele had spent the last few months working in Canada during the day and playing at the whim of the SS. Their group expected that the rehearsal schedule would increase, but whether that meant the work in the warehouses would decrease with it, none of them could know.

None of them questioned. They just did. They worked. Walked where they were told. Never stepped out of line or had an original thought—especially not with the daily roll calls in the yard. The orchestra was a part of it, but they were sheltered from some of the horrors that other prisoners were subjected to . . . standing for hours in the rain. Kneeling, unclothed and without dignity, as the camp doctors walked through the lines of souls and determined who would be pulled out and sent to the gas chambers.

Adele tried not to think how naive she'd been when she'd first come to the camp. She knew nothing of the truth. She'd thought the brick wall was the worst of it.

It was painful that Adele and the rest of the girls in the orchestra were forced to catalog the useful items in the block, teeming with provisions while thousands of prisoners wore scraps and walked barefoot, then ship them back to Germany.

It was where she stood now, thinking on the naïveté of her first months in Auschwitz, wondering how she'd become so hardened in so little time. Her feet registered sharp pains up the length of her shins after weeks of standing on the concrete floors. She picked up an old woolen suit coat with cracked leather elbow pads and a small hole in the lapel where a hungry moth had left a telltale mark and ran her hand along the seams. Despite the rather sad condition of the suit, it was known that the Jews hid money, family jewels, heirlooms, and modest pieces that would bring even a small sum of much-needed money in the hems of clothing to keep them from the Germans.

Adele ran her fingers over every seam, paying special attention to the bottom of the coat and inside the pocket holes. The wool was scratchy, but smooth underneath the surface. Finding no evidence of hidden items, she tossed the coat onto a nearby pile so it could be cataloged. Those wares deemed unfit for shipping back to Germany would be destroyed.

Always cataloging. And filing. And re-cataloging.

The Germans certainly liked to use up paper. Adele doubted there would be many trees left in Europe based on the way they recorded such trivial matters. It seemed important to them, to a dizzying degree. Adele could not figure out why keeping track of every last item that had come into the camps was of such importance—yet the people, the living and breathing souls who worked their fingers to the bone, were treated with such wretched abhorrence.

"Have you finished with this bin?"

Omara approached her, clipboard in hand.

Adele nodded.

"Good. You may go," she said, and scribbled something on the clipboard paper. "We have an early morning ahead of us. Go get rest, Adele."

"I will."

"And, Adele," Omara added, giving one of her strictest mothering glances. "Be sure you wash. I can't have you falling ill. Understand?"

With another nod, she was dismissed.

Adele trudged back to the musicians' block with a few of the others and entered the bunk room. They must have been as tired as she was, for no one much favored talking. They shared a wash bucket, each cleaning up in silence as they prepared for bed. No one quipped about her hair now. Some of the others had been shaved, the Jews of course, but others had not. And they had a small collection of wares, dresses and such that had been pooled between them.

For whatever hatred had emanated from the girls in her first weeks, there was none of it now. They may have resented her still, but none of it was spoken aloud. Barring illness or selections, the musicians had no choice but to stick together for their survival. If one played, they all did.

She'd barely closed her eyes in sleep when she heard Omara's voice, the urgent words pulling her awake. "You must wake, Adele. *Wake up.*"

Her lids blinked until Omara's face came into focus, and on instinct she shot up from the straw mattress with the cloud of sleep still lingering upon her.

"What is it?"

"Get up," Omara ordered, tugging at the sheet to uncover her legs. "Put these on."

In the dim light of the barrack, Adele could see that Omara was clad in a fine dress of dark velvet with a white lace collar, and her short hair had been combed.

Before Adele could comment on it, Omara dropped a pair of heels and a pile of cloth on the bed. The fabric glimmered in the moonlight. She ran her hand over it to find the softness unmistakable.

Chiffon? Where on earth had she found chiffon?

Adele picked up the garment and the length of it fell out to reveal a long dress of a pale color. "What's this?"

"Hush," Omara scolded lightly. "Don't wake the other girls."

"Why not?"

"Because no one is to know about this."

Adele had no idea what was happening. Omara had done everything she could to ensure the safety of all the girls in the fledgling orchestra, and though it was quite strange to be awakened in the middle of the night with a party dress tossed in her lap, she had no choice but to trust the woman.

Adele leaned in and lowered her voice to a whisper. "What's going on?"

"They've asked for us to play."

She looked up at the window and saw that the moon was high outside. "But it's the middle of the night."

"We don't ask questions, Adele. Remember?" Omara began laying items out on the bed: a comb, what looked to be a handful of hairpins, and a tube of lipstick. "Here," she said, and tugged her elbow to get her to stand. "Take off your dress and put that on." Omara's eyes then rounded in her face, and she noted, "We must do something with your hair."

"My hair?"

Omara nudged her on, tugging Adele's hands up to the top buttons on her dress. "Hurry." She then moved over to a box they kept in the corner with the paltry hygiene items shared by the girls. Adele could hear her rummaging through it as she shrugged out of the ruddy-brown dress. It reeked of sweat and mold. She crinkled her nose at the smell when the garment fell to her ankles, leaving her dingy slip underneath. Washing up with water had done little to help with it the night before.

"I have soap." Omara wasn't one for mincing words. But who would hold pretenses in their circumstances? They all smelled like they lived in a musty warehouse.

Adele hadn't seen actual soap in nearly five months. "Soap? But where on earth—"

"No questions. Just wash." Omara approached and dropped the small lump in her palm, then continued puttering about with the wares she'd placed on the plank bed.

"Thank you." Adele took the soap and washed, feeling, for the first time in months, like a woman. The faint scent of roses perfumed the air around her.

Omara tried fussing with her hair while Adele dried and pulled the dress over her slip. It zipped up the side, which she noticed as she inspected the fit of the garment.

"How does it fit?" the older woman asked, still tugging the

comb through her hair. She stuck a few pins in the back of Adele's waves.

Adele ran her hands down the length of the gown to shake out the wrinkles.

"It's a little big." She ran her hand over the liquid softness of the fabric, trying to ignore the feel of airy chiffon against her bony hips. "But it's . . . beautiful."

So many weeks ago, she stood in a gown as elegant as the one she wore now. It had hugged her curves, dancing at the hem with each graceful movement and accentuating an hourglass figure. It was difficult to fathom that before Auschwitz, her life had been full of parties, concerts, scores of elegant gowns, and red lipstick. There had been food and drink in spades.

She tried not to think about the ever-present ache in her belly.

Oh God, please don't let me have to see them eat . . .

"It fits? Good," Omara said, and turned her around to face her. She unstoppered the tube of lipstick and twisted it to reveal a bright poppy red. "Here, put this on."

Adele was handed the lipstick so quickly that she hadn't time to process her own reaction. The last time someone had helped her dress for a concert had been the night the Germans took her into custody, the very night her mother had presented her with a specially tailored satin gown from Berlin.

The open tube from Omara hadn't been in her possession more than a second before her trembling hands fumbled, and it clanged down to the floor and rolled under Marta's bed.

"Adele!" Omara whispered, but it still held the severity of a reproach. "What is the matter with you, child? They are waiting for us!" She knelt down on the ground and ever so quietly reached her arm out under the sleeping girl's mattress. Adele knelt too, hoping to help retrieve the lipstick.

"I'm sorry . . . I think I'm nervous."

Omara waved her back. "The shoes," she whispered. "Put the shoes on. I'll find the lipstick."

Adele gave an embattled nod, which her friend wouldn't see with her back turned, and carefully lowered herself down on her cot. She sat on the side of the bed, her heart beating and tears painfully stinging at her eyes. She should have felt lovely in a gown such as the one she wore, with glittering gold heels to put on and lips that would soon be rouge red. But it was the stark contrast of the moment that made her soul burn from inside her chest. It cried out, manifested in tears, finding that she'd been barely coping for months only for her defenses to be broken down by something as simple as a tube of lipstick.

Her heart was breaking, hinged on the memory of that last night of the concert. It had been the last night she'd seen her parents. It had also been the last night she'd seen Vladimir, and her heart felt the weight of it at that moment.

She'd come to Auschwitz alone. She'd been ripped from her family, from her former life, as everyone else had.

Omara returned to her side with the lipstick in hand.

"Here, child," she said, holding the lipstick to Adele's pout. "Pucker."

Adele swallowed the growing lump in her throat.

Through the silver-lined moonlight, she wrapped her hand around Omara's and together, with her hand shaking and Omara's working to steady it, they brushed the waxy color over her lips. She pressed them together, softly blending the color without making a sound.

Omara knelt before her, and with a depth of feeling Adele hadn't expected in this hell on earth, she brushed a hand over Adele's cheek.

"You can do this, Adele."

She nodded. Then sniffled as quietly as she could. "Can I?"

"You must."

Omara handed her a swatch of fabric and motioned for her to dab at her nose with it. She did as she was told, noticing the softness as the handkerchief brushed her skin. Everything about the moment—the dress, the softness of the fabric at her face, even the scent of roses hanging on the air . . . she couldn't comprehend that lovely things, or even a tiny glimpse of kindness, could still exist.

"I know you don't wish to hear this, but you look beautiful."

Adele couldn't say thank you. Not when she was terrified to have to play—for *them*. She closed her eyes, fear threatening to take over and shatter the softness of the moment. The hands in her lap clenched into tight fists.

God? Abba . . . go with me. I am so scared . . .

She fought the instinct to burst into tears, willing her emotions to retreat back into the deadened state in which they'd been for so long. If she couldn't feel anything, then she thought she was safe. She could make it. She could focus on survival and nothing else. But the fear was so great now, the memories once again alive.

The warmth of Omara's hand shielding her own knotted fists caused her to open her eyes. Her friend nodded, eyes warm through the moonlight, and nudged the violin case up against her side. Adele hadn't even known it was there.

"Here." Omara lifted Adele's hand and placed it on the top of the case. "Take him with you."

Vladimir's picture.

Like a heartbeat, she breathed in unison with the intensity of the moment. All the time she'd been holding on, talking to his picture, willing him to stay alive . . . and never had she understood that the memory of their last night onstage might be all that she had left of him. The one stolen kiss in the garden, that one flash of their future, might be all they'd ever have together.

Adele curled her fingertips against the top of the case until her nails were digging into the leather.

"Then you understand," Omara whispered, "that they take everything from us. But what they can't take, it is alive in here." She pointed a gentle finger to Adele's heart and began shaking her head. "*He* is here. Whatever you do, don't let them get at him."

Adele nodded.

She couldn't, didn't want to cry anymore. She didn't want to feel anything. It was too risky to her survival. She rose to her feet and, with a numbed resolve to stay alive, straightened the lovely gown on her hips. She took a long, deep breath and declared, "I'm ready."

⸺

Chocolate.

It was the first thing Adele noticed when she was led into the party room—chocolates stacked in elegant mini towers that dotted the length of the grand banquet table.

There were baskets of crusty breads and honeyed pastries. And fruit! She counted several bowls of fresh blueberries and great stacks of apples and pears. Adele couldn't remember the last time she'd seen such delicacies, or had tasted anything but tepid soup made from turnips and horribly bitter grass. And the intoxicating scent of oranges—it filled her nostrils as if it were the finest incense, the sweet smell of citrus nectar torturing her aching stomach with each intake of breath.

What did oranges taste like now?

Both she and Omara had been ushered by automobile to Solahütte, the SS recreation center mere miles away from Auschwitz. It was nestled in a grove of trees along the river, with air fresh and decidedly unpolluted by the stench of filth and vermin they'd become used to. Adele had asked Omara where they were going. It was less from fear and more from sincere curiosity, as she knew they'd not have taken the time to dress her up for a date with death. Omara had answered that they were being

taken to a retreat of sorts, the place SS guards who had exhib-
ited meritorious service were gifted with earned days of rest and
relaxation. There the men and women would lounge along the
river, as evidenced by the rows of deck chairs she saw overlooking
the tranquil scene. And they attended jovial parties apparently,
as she saw when they were ushered into a large banquet room
with abundant trays of food overflowing on nearly every surface.

Omara had cautioned her that this excursion was not a privilege. It was an order, another performance and nothing more.
She'd been noticed by several of the SS guards, and when one
recognized the young musical prize of Austria, he'd told his supe-
riors that their next party should be graced with her presence.
All of this Omara had whispered to her on the drive to the resort.
She was not to speak to the guests. She was to play, proficiently,
of course, and that would be it. They would play and then return
to the camp.

There would be no discussion, no diversion from this. No
food or offer of luxuries extended from the SS. And the guards
who drove the car made it quite clear that any attempt at escape
by either of them would result in both being shot. This Adele
didn't question or take lightly. If they took the time to caution of
it, death was not a threat but a certainty.

Adele sat in the crowded hall, staring at the hordes of food.

Her hands clutched the violin as they awaited the order to
begin playing. Omara had been given the chair beside her and
she too appeared to be waiting for the instruction to begin. But
while Adele was awed by the opulence of the party scene, Omara's
constitution was quite different. She appeared to be seething.
Her usually soft features were pinched into bitter lines that made
her look a decade older than she was. Her eyes were squeezed
until they were almost closed, the acrimony all too evident as she
looked around at the smiling young guards mingling with the
female members of the SS.

She couldn't believe that the usually controlled Omara could be so obvious with her display of hatred toward them. "Are you all right?" she whispered.

"Yes." Omara looked away from the partygoers in seeming disgust. She adjusted the cello in her arms.

"They said we were waiting for two more musicians from the other camp," Adele said, looking around at the bustling scene. "But should we not begin? And perhaps play a duet until the other members arrive?"

When the older woman didn't answer, Adele prompted again. It was strange. Omara was showing some genuine depth of emotion she'd not given a hint of in the months that Adele had known her.

"Omara?" She leaned in to her friend, urging her to do something other than glare at the scene with abhorrence. "Shall we play? Bach, perhaps? Beethoven's Fifth?"

Omara shook her head.

"Or one of the German marches? They favor them when they are played at the gates each day. A march is fitting for a party," she whispered.

It was true. Though Adele couldn't say she recognized any of the guards at this particular party, she did know that the guards at Birkenau seemed to enjoy the jovial marches.

"Omara?" She still hadn't answered. "The *Arbeitslager marsch* perhaps? It is one of their favorites and seems more upbeat."

"No."

The word held such ferocity that Adele was taken aback.

What was wrong with Omara? Could she play? Oh, heaven help them if she couldn't. Adele's fear had abated when Omara was so steady, so strong in helping her prepare for the party. But now? The uncharacteristic behavior the woman displayed made her fear return in haste.

"I think we should play something." Adele whispered the

words through somewhat pursed lips. She looked around, noticing that some of the uniformed partygoers had now turned their
attention toward them.

Some whispered.

One or two shouted, "Play!" with hands cupped around their
mouths. All seemed irritated that their musical talent was pretending to be statues rather than doing what they'd been brought
in to do. She pictured guns being drawn from belts and felt goose
bumps cover the length of her arms in response.

"Omara, they are staring at us. Shall we not pick something?"

"Do you know the *Handel-Halvorsen Passacaglia*?"

Adele's head snapped back to look at her friend. "Yes," she
said, surprise fluttering at her heart. "But it's an incredibly ambi-
tious piece of music for a duet, especially for a violin and cello."
In truth, she doubted her dulled mind and woefully tired arms
could keep pace with such an involved piece.

What was Omara thinking?

"Is there nothing else?" she urged. "Something less involved,
perhaps? A march or a popular ballad?"

Omara ignored Adele's obvious attempt at placation.

"Do you know your part well enough to play it without sheet
music?"

She could have lied and said she didn't know it. It was a chal-
lenging piece, to be sure. But something told her to take direction
and go along with it.

Nodding, she said, "Yes. I do."

"Good," Omara said, and raised her bow. "On the four count."

With both of them at attention, Omara counted them off.

On her cue, their instruments cried out the first notes
in unison. The music began with a rush of energy, with their
bows soaring over the strings as if they'd light the roof on fire.
And soon, heads began to turn. Adele could gather that much.
Though she focused on the music and only had a sense that eyes

were perhaps turning in their direction, the bustle of the room had died down considerably and all that she heard was the sweet sound of resin and string dancing out on the air.

They played the entire piece of music, alive and triumphant as it was, until nearly every guest was sneering at the unbelievable sight of two worthless prisoners playing such angelic music.

Adele saw them out of the corner of her eye, for she didn't play as she usually would. She wasn't lost in the magic of the moment, refused to allow the music to carry her away. No, this was playing of a much emptier, more formulaic kind. She played only at the bare minimum of her abilities, with eyes open, sure that God would curse the use of her gift for such an audience. What's more, Omara's strange behavior had caused her to take much more of the stand-up role in their present circumstances. She felt that under some sort of weight, Omara's usually solid resolve to survive was cracking.

Perhaps being forced to play for such a group had been the last straw.

The last note carried off the end of her bow and she stopped, almost breathless, and looked around at the scores of eyes staring solidly at her. What was surprising was the look on each face. None carried the slightest hint of derision. Instead, the faces of the uniformed men and women around her seemed . . . impressed?

The silence broke into riotous cheering then, with shouts of exclamation coming from their audience. Adele refused to be caught up in the moment. She didn't care what any of these people thought of her playing. She was almost void of any emotion. But Omara? Adele looked at her friend to find that she still seethed. She seemed sickened by the show of approval from the Germans, repulsed that they could find anything of beauty in the same people who had been treated like dogs during the camp's daytime hours.

"Shall we play another?" Adele whispered, now looking around for the two other members of the Auschwitz orchestra who were supposed to join and make them a quartet.

They never arrived.

Adele and Omara played several more selections, all upbeat, patriotic tunes for the half-drunk revelers. It was deep into the night, and the first light of a new day would soon be upon them. As the party was thinning out, they were given the orders to pack their instruments and leave.

Omara went to talk to their accompanying guards and driver, to arrange for the ride back to the camp, leaving her quite alone in the banquet room. She felt relieved that there were few party-goers left. But the fact that she was the only prisoner there, one who had been plucked and primped to look like a normal musician, made her feel exposed.

She turned her back to the rest of the room and began a methodical gathering up of their instruments so that she could appear occupied and they could depart the instant Omara returned. She moved with great care, hoping it would take every second until her friend was back at her side.

"I remember you." She heard a young man's voice from behind.

Adele turned, heart thumping. She kept her eyes down, as was expected, but she had no wish to speak to him. She inclined her head, hoping that would placate him.

It did not.

"You are Adele Von Bron, are you not? The famous violinist from Vienna?"

It had been ages since she'd heard her entire name, since she'd been more than a number on a page . . . How would she answer? Again, she nodded, not wishing to carry on a conversation with anyone.

Omara had warned her long ago, "Become invisible if you wish to survive. Make them forget that you've ever existed."

That advice was a far cry from a young German SS officer saying her name aloud.

"Is that your name?"

She gave an automatic nod and out of fear mumbled, "Yes."

"I knew it. I heard you play in Berlin more than two years ago. You were with a traveling troupe, were you not? You were fantastic! I still remember how the crowd called you back for an encore."

Adele thought back to the memory of two years ago.

She'd traveled through Germany on a goodwill tour, some months after the war had begun. It seemed like forever ago now, and that young girl traveling with her mother was someone else entirely.

"Yes. I played in Berlin."

He shook his head, his eyes perhaps clouded with drink, and gave her a dopey smile. "I knew they'd call you here. When I said that the famous Viennese violinist was here at Auschwitz, they fairly lost their lunch. And I knew you'd turn up at one of the parties." He laughed. Actually laughed as he was talking to her!

Something about his manner of speaking seemed light, as if they were both guests at a party and he was planning his best pickup line. Was it even possible? She had a hard time not allowing the disgust to show on her face, like Omara had for the majority of the evening.

Thinking to get as far away from any familiarity as possible, she tried to turn around. He caught her at the elbow and on instinct she jerked back, almost like a fawn being chased by a hunter. She'd pulled her violin case up between them as a sort of sad leather shield.

"I'm not . . . ," he said, seeming taken aback by the swiftness of her reaction. "I'm not going to hurt you."

"I'm sorry, sir."

Had she just apologized to a Nazi?

Adele's tongue felt like it was swelling in her mouth. God help her, she hated that the manners of her mother had been so ingrained on her sense of propriety that she'd actually apologize to the next person who might end her life. Or Omara's. Or any of the girls in the orchestra.

"No, I'm sorry. I'm sorry you're in this mess," he said, looking around. "You're a Christian, aren't you? It's obvious you're not one of them. You don't deserve this. Don't belong here with the rest of them."

The words cut through her ears like a hot knife through butter.

Because she was Austrian, and a Christian, she had some value in their eyes. Little, perhaps, because she was a prisoner. But there was no doubt that he thought the Jews far beneath everyone else.

He turned and glanced at the picked-over buffet. "I was going to offer you something to eat."

The chocolate towers had been toppled, the fruit scattered, and the pastries consumed, but nevertheless, it was a feast of kings that lay spread before her eyes. He took a porcelain plate from the stack by the buffet and held it out to her.

"Please. Take some. It'll just get tossed in the waste bin if you don't."

Adele had no idea what to do. Her hand would not move. She stood, still as a statue, staring at the plate in his hands.

"We must go now." Omara sailed in and took her by the hand, tugging her along.

Adele tucked the violin case under her arm, and with Omara taking the lead, they were quickly ushered toward the door. She hadn't a moment to attempt to say good-bye to the officer, much to her relief. The last thing she wanted was familiarity with any of them, especially if they were guards she'd have to see issue a beating to a prisoner the very next day.

Omara was practically dragging her along. Adele followed, half frightened but half relieved to be going back to the music block. She'd not have any sleep before work commenced the next day, but no matter. It was better than being forced to hobnob with the SS. To smell their oranges and be forced to look at their towering stacks of chocolate . . .

"Wait!"

Adele heard the young man's voice behind them and all at once felt terrified again. Would he force her to come back and play for them again? Would he see that she thought him a monster? Was the revulsion showing all over her face? All of these things sailed through her mind before she realized that he'd not said another word. Instead, something was slipped in her hand. She turned and saw that his face held a look of interest.

Adele peeled back the napkin in her hand to reveal a generous handful of blueberries he'd gathered up.

"For you. To say thank you for playing for us," he said, and stood in the doorway, watching as Omara tugged her toward the waiting car.

She was shoved in the backseat alongside Omara and their instruments were loaded in with them, tossed in on top of them without care.

"What was that?" Omara asked, eyeing the young SS officer still lingering in the glow of light from the retreat center doorway.

"Nothing," she said, hiding the napkin full of blueberries down at her side. "He was just telling me where I belonged."

"Which was?"

Adele looked her friend straight in the eyes. "Not here, that's for sure."

The duet she and Omara played had felt like an anthem for life. They hadn't perished. The music had sustained the gift of breath in their lungs for another day. And whether Jew or Christian, Adele was one of them, the prisoners, a part of the orchestra that had become her family. That was something the young SS officer could never understand.

"They'll try to make you their pet, now that they know the famous violinist is here."

"I don't want any part of it," Adele whispered, feeling weighed down by the burden of the barbed wire fences they'd soon enter again. She hated the glimpse of freedom they'd had at the party and now, with the world falling down around them, they were forced back into captivity.

As for the other gift she held in her hand, Adele felt it was an anthem for life in another form. Before the guards joined them in the car, she cracked the window and tossed the napkin out into the darkness.

Whether the blueberries landed in the ditch or not, she didn't care. She didn't think of the fruit again once the car was speeding down the road to deliver them back to their barbed wire cage.

—

"Where have you been?" Marta's voice was shaky and she nearly tackled them when they returned to the block with the dawn spilling over the horizon. "We thought . . . when we didn't know where you were . . ."

She hugged Omara round the neck. Fränze trailed behind Marta and hugged Adele.

"Girls. We are well."

Adele heard Omara's words, but her behavior didn't speak of anything close to being well. She doubted the woman who stood before them, though she was once again composed.

"Go now. Hurry to play," Omara said, releasing Marta with a soft pat to the cheek. "Adele and I will join you shortly. We must change."

The girls had noticed the wispy chiffon dress she wore, and now Fränze, the youngest and sweetest of the group, looked puzzled. Marta too seemed confused, but her means of coping was always to bristle first, apologize later.

"Did you have a date with the Führer, Adele?"

Before she could respond, Omara stepped in between Adele and the other girls. She eyed them with a stern glare, the intensity ushering them outside without the necessity of words. When they were alone, Adele finally exhaled. The words had been cutting, especially after the night she'd been through. But to lash out at Marta in return—what good would it do?

She turned from the door and began focusing on the task at hand—once again, to play.

Though she'd had no sleep, was aching in her limbs and exhausted in spirit, she had to mentally prepare herself to be strong through another day of playing. She said a quick prayer as she began stripping out of the party dress.

"What happened back there?" Adele persisted, though Omara did not appear the least bit inclined to explain her odd behavior at the party. She pulled the chiffon dress over her head and, still whispering, carefully laid it on the side of the plank bed. "You seemed so much more than angry."

"I suppose I did," she said quietly, her hands busied in removing the pins from Adele's hair. "It was too much to have to entertain them."

"But we entertain them every day."

"Yes. At the gates when they march out to work each day and when fewer march back in. Perhaps that is entertaining to them."

Adele shrugged her soiled dress up over her shoulders, instantly feeling the difference between the buttery soft chiffon and the dirtied fabric. It layered a film of dust over her skin.

"Was it because the other musicians didn't show? You were worried about them."

"Of course. Who wouldn't be?"

"Is that it?"

Omara gathered up the things from the bed as she answered, "Adele, I have come to respect you more than you know. You have been born to privilege, yet you carry yourself as anyone here. You have a most compassionate heart. But what I caution you is to mind yourself with them."

"You mean the SS guard?"

"Yes. What did you say to him?" Omara stared back, her eyes wide and searching.

"Nothing. He was talking to me."

Omara paused. It was cold that morning, strangely cold for dawn in summer, and her breath almost froze out on a fog. "They will make you their pawn if you're not careful. That you don't want to be."

Adele had endured enough scrutiny at the hands of Marta. It didn't seem warranted to receive it now from their trusted den mother too.

"What must I do to prove my loyalty to this group? To you, even?"

Omara stopped. Her eyes drifted up to meet Adele's. She had no family. She barely had air in her lungs. If Adele had no trust from those closest to her, then what was left?

Omara spoke gently. "The building right outside—it has no back door."

The crematorium.

Adele knew it well. They could see Crematorium IV from their block, passed it daily as they marched out to play, kept their heads down as they passed the scores of unsuspecting Jews lined up to feed the fires that coughed black smoke from the smokestacks.

Omara was right. The crematorium had no back door. It was the beast of death in the midst of this hellish place and she knew that only God saved them from it.

"You understand my meaning?"

Adele nodded. "Yes."

"And that is all I need to say. I care for you to live. That's all."

"But how could I be a pawn to them?"

"Pawn. Pet. Ornament paraded before the international arts community—they care not. You have talent and a name. They are masters of exploitation. And in here? They are the gatekeepers of death. In this place, you have no power over either of those truths and they will use you if they can, to your last breath."

Thinking of the blueberries and the SS guard and the oddly tranquil resort that was but miles from the throngs of death all around them, Adele could make no sense of it. But it stood to reason that if there was a prisoner of notoriety, they would attempt to use that.

To use *her*.

"I understand." She turned her attention back to dressing quickly, her fingertips tired and cracked to near bleeding after having played through the night. But the paltry pain and exhaustion that she felt was nothing compared to the fate of those lined up right outside the block. She knew they would be there and she would be forced to walk by them with the knowledge of their fate.

It was almost too much to endure.

"How can we walk by them? Play at the selections? All the while, knowing that the elderly, the mothers and their sweet babies are all being sent straight to the gas chambers? And the ones who do live will slowly starve. They're crying for food. Parched with thirst. Changing from people to skeletons before our eyes while we play melodies for them to march to. I can't bear it."

Omara took her hand, and with the characteristic strength that had helped them all endure for so long, she squeezed Adele's palm. "God is here. He sees. He knows what is happening in this place."

"But how? I've prayed every day, poured my heart out to Him each night while we shiver, packed like animals in the block. Yet we receive no answers!" Adele fought tears, felt them burning her cheeks like acid, knowing that weeping had no home in a place like this. "I always thought I championed God in my heart, yet

I'm ashamed that I question Him now. Where is He? Why does He not answer the prayers of the many here?"

"He answers," Omara assured her. "He has heard your every cry, witnessed your every tear. He is a God of vengeance and they will learn this soon."

She found the last thought a curious thing to say aloud. "But how do you know He will enact vengeance upon them?"

Omara nodded slightly, as if she knew, but was reluctant to share. "Because if need be, we will do it for Him."

CHAPTER NINETEEN

I can see that she's being taken care of."

William had slipped into Sera's gallery when she'd been tackling her always monstrous e-mail inbox and caught her notice only when he commented on their painting of Adele. Sera had been watching the door all day, waiting for him to walk through it, and somehow he'd managed to sneak in.

He stood there, handsome and relaxed in jeans and a worn-in tee, smiling at her from the center of the deserted gallery. He gave a halfhearted glance at his wristwatch and shrugged.

"I know. I didn't exactly give you a time."

"Hi." Oh-so-unimpressive for a greeting, but there was nothing else she could manage. It was all her jittery heart would allow her to say.

"Hi yourself." He said it back, and there was nothing contrived in it. He buried his hands in his pockets and gave her a congenial grin.

Sera's lips parted on their own, and she felt the warmth of a blush as she broke into a smile. Yes, she was glad he was there.

"Nice weather you're having," he said, and took several steps toward her desk, looking around as if the building's old ceiling were instead the backdrop of a beautiful starry sky. "Fancy a walk through Manhattan on this spring night?"

She nodded and sucked in a breath as he walked closer.

"Sure. Just let me close down in here," she said, fumbling around as she quickly closed up shop for the night.

"It suits you."

"What?" She turned off her laptop and dimmed the table lamp.

He'd taken several more steps until he was just inside her office and casually leaned against the doorjamb. "The gallery. All the art and the wide-open space. Something about it really suits you."

She grabbed her purse from her bottom desk drawer. "Oh. Thanks."

"And the painting." He kept talking as he followed her from the office. "It looks like it belongs here somehow."

Sera stopped and looked at Adele, the intensity of her eyes staring out into the open room as if she knew someone was watching her.

"I'd be lying if I didn't admit that Penny and I have grown rather attached to her. We may have even plotted an idea or two to convince you that you want to sell. But then, professionally speaking, that's not meant to sway you. After all, we're looking for the same thing, aren't we?"

He walked up beside her and, staring back at the painting before them, said, "The original."

Sera nodded. It started with finding the original painting for her, but that was by no means where it ended for them both. It also included learning the identity of the painting's owner and the true heir to the Hanover estate. And the full story of what happened to Adele and Vladimir all those years before . . . Sera had a feeling she wouldn't have peace until she found out the fate of the young musicians.

Did they ever feel nervous and unsure as the prospect of love bloomed?

William broke into her thoughts. "This is a business expense, by the way, and I'm paying. So where am I taking you?"

The question was simple enough. But the answer? Not simple at all.

It depended on whether this was a date. If it was to be purely business, they could go to one of the posh bistros that usually impressed clients. But a date—that was something else entirely. She couldn't see spending the evening with him in the midst of a hundred business suits and noisy cell phones. But how did she know what it was?

He'd said it was a business expense, so it couldn't be a date.

"I thought maybe we could go to one of my favorite restaurants," she said, and clicked off the lights at the nearby wall switch. She stepped by him and walked out into the open gallery, flipping off the rest of the lights as she went. "It's a few blocks away, but if you like authentic Italian, I'd say the walk to Little Italy is worth it."

They stopped at the front doors. He did the gentlemanly thing, of course, and opened the door to the street.

"After you," he said, holding it wide.

She locked the door, trying not to notice that he stood so close to her as she turned the key in the lock.

"Which way?"

Sera felt her face warm with another telltale blush. Would she ever not do that with him?

"It's down here." She motioned to the glow of city lights a few blocks down on her right and took a step in that direction. He joined her, walking along as the warmth of the spring evening welcomed them to explore the blocks between the gallery and the restaurant.

Sera let her hand hang down at her side, wondering if he'd think to hold it in his own. They lingered through their walk, noticing the sky overhead, becoming lost in their own world. Chatting, laughing every now and then, passersby going unnoticed as they talked. They came to a charming old three-story brick building with outdoor tables, ropes of lights hanging as a makeshift awning against the sky, and the wonderful smell of roasted tomatoes and garlic wafting out from inside.

A neon sign overhead blinked in red with the green map image of Italy's boot behind the word "Mickey's." It was Sera's favorite place, a lazy little eatery she'd drop by once a week because of the amazing eggplant Parmesan and quiet tables tucked back in little nooks of the vintage-inspired dining rooms.

"This is it."

They both stopped at the glass front door.

"In or out?" Sera asked, and tilted her head to the options.

"Outside, I think," he said, reading her mind. He reached for the door handle. "I'll go in and tell the hostess we're out here."

"It's Gino, actually. The owner. He prefers to seat everyone himself." She smiled, letting him go through the door if he chose. "He'll be the only man in there wearing a tuxedo. You can't miss him."

"Been here on dates before, huh?"

He winked and cruised through the door, not giving her a chance to respond.

Sera turned and sailed her eyes heavenward the instant he was gone.

Oh Lord—this is a date. He thinks this is a date.

Even Sera had to admit that the potential of dating again held a certain amount of promise. But she was terrified. Despite how much of a gentleman he could be, she wasn't sure she could give in to trusting anyone again.

Lord . . . calm me down.

Sera exhaled just in time for him to return.

He stepped through the door and pointed her over to a table tucked in the back of the patio area next to an old stone fountain with green moss peeking out from cracks in the bricks. The sound of water dancing down the building's outer wall welcomed them to their little table.

"Are you sure you're not his long-lost relative? He said to take the special table by the garden," William said, his hand grazing the small of her back as he guided her forward. "And he's bringing out two chef's specials—whatever that means."

"That's Gino." Sera grinned, a light laugh escaping her lips. "And it'll be two eggplant Parmesans and a Caesar salad. I hope that's okay."

"I think it will have to be. I only had to mention that I was here with Sera James—he went into a frenzy and disappeared into the kitchen."

"Well, I've been coming here for years," she said, leaving out the fact that Mickey's had once been a date spot that she and Michael had shared. "He was friends with my father. Kind of took me under his wing for a time."

William pulled the iron patio chair out for her and she sat, a cascade of flowering trees at her back. He took the chair next to her, the light of the restaurant windows dimly illuminating his face. Music of old Italy was piped outside, just loud enough to be heard against the backdrop of the trickling fountain. There were other guests dining outside on the warm evening, but they seemed miles away from their tiny corner of the world.

It was a quiet, lovely spot.

He must have noticed the tranquility of the surroundings, because he too glanced around and smiled. "It's nice. Not exactly what I'm used to in Manhattan," he admitted, the smile turning into a welcoming grin.

"Good or bad?"

"No, good. Definitely good."

She unfolded her napkin, then dropped it into her lap. "Been to New York much?"

"Yeah, a few times. But I rarely left the hotel except for meetings in stuffy offices." He shrugged. "All business. No gallery stops or Little Italy with art dealers."

"So what kind of business brought you here?" she asked, then immediately thought to backtrack. Not good to corner him into answering the question, though she was dying for an answer. "I don't really know what it is that you do. For work, I mean."

"I manage the family business in my father's absence—I think that's enough for right now. It's all purchases and restructuring of companies. We buy real estate to invest, then sell off to make a profit. Let's say it puts Paul in his leather jackets and keeps my mother as the top banana at her country club," he said, then leaned back to allow the waitress to place water glasses in front of them. She set two small plates and a bread basket on the table with a quick smile, then left them alone again.

"You don't sound enthused."

He surprised her by nodding. "Maybe that's because I'm not."

"But I thought . . ." Sera couldn't get that first picture of him out of her mind—the man who had entered the office in his California estate had been all bristle and brash. If he wasn't happy with his place as head of the family business, he wore the mask well enough to hide it from her. She wondered if anyone else in the family knew.

"You thought I was a suit, and that's it."

"I didn't say that."

William shook his head. "No. It's okay. Most people do. I know I come off as hard-nosed," he said, making her knees shake when his blue eyes stared back at her. "But I don't have a choice. I have to keep this business going mostly on my own, so that doesn't leave me time for much else. Except for gardening, that is."

Sera laughed, remembering how they first met. "All right," she conceded, laughing in between bites of bread from the basket in front of her. "I admit it. It was an original way to meet a new client. But why the façade? Even with the painting. You were pretty guarded when you walked in the office that first day, but it doesn't seem to be who you really are. Is it deliberate, to appear more rigid than you really are?"

"No. I think I may have some . . . trust issues." He grinned.

"Sounds familiar." Sera smiled. "In business or in your personal life?"

William paused and tilted his chin to one side as if he'd figured something out. "Which William do you really want to know, Sera? The one who wants to get to know you, or the one you're sure is only here for the painting?"

Though she'd averted her eyes from his, she knew he was watching her, waiting for a response. But how could she say it? How could she explain that she did want to know more about him, but that her heart was locked tighter than the front door of the gallery they'd left behind? And then, in a moment of sheer horror, she found herself blurting out the truth before she could stop it.

"I was engaged," she spat out, the words feeling like fire in their effort to fly off her tongue. "Two years ago. He left me at the altar."

And that should do it. He knows the whole story and that I'm still not over it. He'll see I'm damaged goods. That I'm not ready for this . . . He'll catch the next flight back to California where he belongs.

Sera picked up her handbag, even pushed back on her chair ever so slightly, fully expecting to flee when he ended the date right then and there. But if he was shocked, it didn't show.

Instead, William reached across the table and, as gently as one might approach a skittish horse, took the purse from her hand. He placed it on the other side of the table and, with a loud scrape of his chair against the concrete, nudged his up closer to her.

Sera's gaze was redirected to her lap. The humiliation was too great to look him in the eye. Here he was, a gorgeous man with everything going for him, and he was playing nursemaid to an emotionally frazzled art historian who hadn't anything but a small apartment and a broken heart as her list of notable possessions. She was sure he could have any woman who caught his eye. So why was he being so nice to her?

"William, I like you but—" She couldn't continue, afraid that the emotion welling up would humiliate her further by generating waterworks from her eyes. But she felt the surprising warmth of his hand even before she could get her next words out. His thumb brushed the inside of her palm, then his fingers wrapped around the side of the hand she'd dropped in her lap.

"What a relief." His voice was soft, whispered even, and almost carried out on the breeze around them. He leaned in closer as the trees rustled overhead. "I had the most terrible feeling that this whole thing might have been one-sided."

"But after what I've just said, how can you be sure you even want to—"

"I'm a businessman, Sera. I'm used to contracts and paperwork. But I assure you that no one is asking you to sign anything here. We're just two people getting to know each other." He took his thumb and nudged her chin up, until they were once again staring eye to eye. "Talk to me."

Sera had tripped over her words enough in front of him. She'd meant that there was already a combustible situation to contend with. Who knew what would happen with the painting and the inheritance?

Was it smart to get involved?

"Sera, we're both looking for the owner of this painting. And since you showed up on my doorstep, we're joined by this mystery of Adele and Vladimir. I understand that there's a lot riding on this. You don't need to tell me that my family has skin in the game here to the tune of everything we own." His hand reached up to calm a long lock of her hair that had danced out on a soft breeze. He tucked it back against the side of her face. Her cheekbone tingled with the touch. "What I'm trying to say is, I want to talk—to *you*."

"And why is that?"

"Because I flew here all the way from California to do so."

Sera nodded softly.

So she'd guessed right. Work was work, but he was in New York to see her. "But what if it doesn't work out? I can't lead you to the painting only to find that you're serving its owner with a court summons at the end of it all. I can't bring myself to do it, no matter how much I want that painting."

"You can't trust me?"

There was no point in beating around the bush. She'd already laid her cards out on the table when she'd mentioned Michael. "I'm not sure I can."

He seemed to be considering what she'd said, for he brought his hands behind his head and stretched out in his chair in a casual manner.

"So, what you're saying is that I can ask you out again for roughly the price tag of a hundred million dollars?"

Sera closed her eyes on instinct, her heart sinking. That was how she'd said it, wasn't it?

"I didn't mean it like that."

"I accept." His interruption was easy. "Or I should say—I'm asking. If you agree to dinner with me tomorrow night, I won't pursue legal action until I've spoken with you about it. We'll find the painting together, and I promise to consult with you before any further steps are taken. Agreed?"

She looked up at him, eyes searching every corner of his face for any indication of manipulation. "So you'll make me a full partner in this."

"Yes. I'll up your fee."

"I don't care about my fee," she admitted, waving him off. "I probably shouldn't mention it to a client, but for this painting, I'd pay you."

"Can't argue with that."

"So we decide what the next steps are, together." She paused, then said, "And I have your word on that?"

William smiled, easily it seemed, and nodded. "You have my word, Sera."

Sera smiled and for the first time in a long while felt a genuine release of a fear that had been walled up in her heart. A fragrance-laden breeze sailed in then, rustling the hair on his forehead. He leaned in and opened his hand palm up on the table, offering it to her.

She accepted it, lacing her fingers with the warmth of his.

"How long are you planning to stay in New York?"

"I don't know, Sera. You tell me."

CHAPTER TWENTY

————

June 22, 1940

Adele had traveled to Germany with her parents on multiple occasions. They'd gone on holiday several summers ago. She'd even played in Berlin a time or two. But this trip with the troupe of musicians from her college made her feel far more grown up. It was the first time she'd left her home behind and had toured without her parents' watchful eyes glued to her.

She adored the new traveling suit her mother had bought for her. It was one of the only outfits that actually fit both of their tastes. Wearing the black-and-white hat with the bright red poppy and the tailored pin-striping down the length of the fabric, she felt fashionable and older than her eighteen years. Margie must have felt the same, for she'd also donned her best dress in a deep jade and a new black-feathered hat for their dinner in the city.

"Isn't it exciting, Adele?" Margie's usual bubbly enthusiasm couldn't be contained. She glanced around like a child on Christmas morning, her eyes popping at the bustle and color of the city outside the car windows. "Look at him," she whispered, playfully nudging Adele in the side when a rather dashing suited officer walked past their car. He tipped his hat to them in respectful greeting. "Wouldn't your mother be happy if you met someone like him?"

Adele forced a smile at the sight of the German officer, likely on furlough for the weekend. He was handsome, to be sure, and tall and catching every woman's eye as he crossed the street—except hers.

Margie sighed next to her. "In dreams, right, Adele?"

"No. My dreams are different."

It was true.

She wanted nothing more than to walk across the street on Vladimir's arm, but that dream had been snuffed out. The night he'd walked her home from the dance hall the previous September had been the last time she'd entertained the thought of actually having a future with him.

She recalled the horrified look on her mother's face when she waltzed through the front door, feeling like she was dancing on air, though the world was in chaos around them. Vladimir Nicolai had been every bit the gentleman on their walk home, of course, but something stirred in her heart that his affections had indeed been turned toward her on that night.

Adele had twirled around the dark entryway, unaware that her mother watched from the second-story landing, ready to pounce on her hope of seeing more of the dashing cellist.

But it wasn't to be.

Both her father and mother had taken it upon themselves to smother her from that moment on. She was escorted nearly everywhere. As her father was in active duty for the empire, her mother had taken the primary role in her surveillance. She'd been escorted by her mother or a carefully selected driver assigned to report everything back to the Von Brons personally. There was no way she could meet Vladimir at college, a dance hall, or anywhere in between without them hearing about it.

So they'd taken to meeting in secret, in their garden before performances, up until that summer at least. For some reason, he'd been avoiding her. He hadn't shown up in their garden for weeks, though she waited for him before each performance. The only time she'd seen him had been onstage, and even then he'd avoided making any eye contact with her.

She felt the sting of tears weighting her eyelashes and turned away, gazing out the window as the flash of city lights passed by.

"You're thinking of him again." Margie broke into her thoughts with the knowing comment. "Aren't you?"

Startled from the memory, Adele raised a gloved hand and smoothed the curls beneath her hat. "Who?"

"Vladimir. You're here in beautiful Munich, surrounded by nearly every handsome man in Germany, and all you can think about is that merchant's son."

Defensive at once, she scolded, "Don't call him the merchant's son!"

"I meant no offense, Adele. I merely thought to bring up the fact that you're blind to anything or anyone outside of him, though I can't think why."

The merchant's son? Adele hated that nearly everyone had taken to referring to him in such a manner, as if he couldn't have any worth because of it. Her mother had labeled him so with a revolted sigh and an upturned lip, as if the very manner of his existence disgusted her. Her father, always distant and authoritarian, had forbade the mention of his name in their home, expecting that his every order was to be explicitly followed. And after Vladimir had severed association with her weeks before, Adele's friends had jumped on the defense and no longer thought him to be quite as dashing as he'd once seemed. To them, he amounted to the number of coins in his pocket and nothing more.

"There is more to him than his station, or his father's pile of money."

Margie scoffed in a silly, flippant manner. "Or lack thereof?"

"How can you be so unfeeling, Margie?" Adele's voice rose

enough that the uniformed driver took notice. He cleared his throat loudly.

"Hush, Adele." Margie issued the light reprimand and tilted her head to the front seat. "Your mother may not be here," she said, leaning in closer to Adele's side, "but he is. You don't want him carrying tales back to your parents, do you?"

Adele noticed the driver's quick glance in the rearview mirror and once again turned her eyes out the window. "No. I suppose you're right."

"Look, I know you liked him. We all did," Margie said, patting a gray gloved hand to her elbow, almost as one would do to comfort a grieving widow at a funeral. Perhaps she thought the action was being supportive. "He's got a dashing smile—I'll give him that. But it's just not to be. He's not good enough for you."

"Not good enough?" Adele rolled her eyes. She might as well have been traveling with her mother, because Margie sounded like her carbon copy. If anything, Adele felt she was the one chasing a prize. A diamond in the rough maybe, but something special nonetheless.

"Come on, Adele. Look around you! We're in the city," she noted happily, then lowered her tone to a barely there but excited schoolgirl whisper. "It may not be Berlin, but Munich is just as exciting, I'm told. And we're alone . . . It must be fate that your mother had a concert in Berlin this weekend. She's playing her piano half a country away! Can you believe it? Let's meet some cute officers." Her whisper pitched an octave higher as she continued. "And after we ditch the driver up there, let's go have the night of our lives, huh?"

Adele didn't want to have the night of her life, that was for sure.

They'd finished playing a performance for the college. That had been magical—she always felt alive when she was playing, like she'd been transported to heaven somehow, and was lost in the beauty of the music until she had to come back to earth at the end of the piece. But to try to go out on the town now in her painted smile and dolled-up clothes felt empty. Especially since she'd left her butterfly clip at home—this time, on purpose.

Margie flitted her lashes and unfurled her rouged bottom lip in a girlish pout.

"Please?"

Adele laughed, unable to fight off her friend's amiable charms. She caved as she always did when her friend broke out the sulk.

"Fine. We'll have dinner and I promise to smile the entire time." She beamed at her friend with an exaggerated wide-toothed smile. "There. Happy?"

"And dancing?"

Adele shook her head. "Don't press your luck."

Margie shook her head and giggled as she looked around the busy streets. "We don't need luck tonight, Adele. We're on a single girl's holiday if there ever was one."

Whether fortuned with luck or not, Munich's nightlife was certainly eye-opening. They had the driver drop them off at a respectable dining room that had what Margie described as "the stale look of a family restaurant." No doubt the oblivious driver still sat reading the newspaper out front while they'd managed to sneak out the back of the establishment and scurry over to one of the bustling clubs a few streets over.

Sneaking into the *Blaue Kaskade* club hadn't been Adele's idea, nor did it sit well with her to risk getting caught and sent home on the next train just for a night of glitz and glamour. But her apprehension was short-lived. Always the master of persuasion, Margie used her wiles to convince the young man standing guard at the entrance to allow them to pass, but only after she'd promised him a dance once his shift was over.

"Are you really going to dance with him later?" She had to shout over the band's riotous music. She grabbed onto Margie's arm and was tugged along, fearful that the swarm of people would envelop and separate them if she didn't hold on for dear life.

Margie's eyes danced around the room, her eyes sparkling with the lights and glamorous entertainers on the club's small stage. "Are you kidding? I plan to be in a quiet corner with an officer long before then."

Adele's heart thumped in her chest. If it was staying away from the wrong kind of men they wanted, her parents had made a gross miscalculation in allowing their only daughter to parade around a strange city with the man-attracting Margie.

"Blue cascade indeed," Margie said, noting the establishment's name. "I see an ocean of dark uniforms all around us, moving like a sea of eligible men. Take your pick, honey." She tugged on Adele's sleeve to pull her closer. "Come on. Let's go get a drink."

Adele exhaled and followed, though she couldn't say she really wanted to. She had a feeling she was going to be a young musician-turned-den-mother in short order. Margie had a bit of a wild streak that being apart from her own parents for a few days had evidently loosed with striking speed.

"Are you sure you want a drink?" Adele looked around, noticing the eyes of several groups of anxious young men washing over every inch of their forms. She reached up to close the top button of her jacket in response. "Can't we just have a quiet dinner together?"

"What?" Margie half shouted over the band.

"Dinner," Adele repeated, wishing the trombone players would take a rest so she could think for more than five seconds. "Can't we have a quiet dinner?"

Margie scoffed. "A quiet dinner? In an exciting city far from home? You're crazy, little Miss Sweetheart. I want to dance."

It turned out Margie was more correct than she knew.

Adele was paraded in front of scads of young men as Margie carried her along, introducing them as musicians from Vienna.

Adele politely declined the drinks that were placed in front of them and ordered a soda water, but she watched as her friend downed tumblers of gin and hopped out to the dance floor like a desperate bird freed from a cage. She flitted around the oversized main hall of the club, moving from officer to officer, having the time of her life while Adele sat at their table and watched. After the fourth officer approached and asked her to dance, only to have to be politely rejected, Adele felt that she needed some air.

Pretending to have fun wasn't working.

She made sure to check on Margie, who saw when she tilted her head toward the back door. Margie winked from the dance floor, giving a signal that she'd be fine until Adele returned. And with that, she made her way around the side of the room to the door in the back.

It wasn't until she'd stepped through it that she could finally exhale. She rejoiced to have found peace outside.

There was no cloud of thick cigarette smoke to wave through, no screaming instruments or booming laughter echoing from the dance floor. The glittery flash of sequined dresses had been replaced by the dark stillness of the club's back entrance. It was a common enough alleyway, with brick buildings on both sides and a thin strip of sky that offered a peek at the stars overhead. Water dripped from somewhere behind her, making the only sound near her.

What am I doing, Lord? I don't even want to be here.

She took off her hat and turned it over in her hands, waving some fresh air in her face. The club had been so stuffy. She was glad to be free from it, if only for a moment.

As she turned around, a faded sign caught her notice.

Dachgarten.

A rooftop garden in the heart of the city? There was a metal staircase, sturdy it seemed, and an arrow that pointed up to the top of the building. Adele gladly left the club behind and without a second thought began a slow climb up the stairs.

The sign was inadequate to describe the beauty she found on the club's roof. There was a virtual paradise, blanketed by the night sky overhead, with bloom after cascading bloom growing in abundance. Roses. Peonies. Even summer sunflowers that looked ready to explode with their own definition of yellow sunshine. She walked around the silent garden, moving between the rows of carefully tended blooms, drinking in their sweet fragrance and offer of unexpected solace. She noticed a leaded glass greenhouse at the far end, it too looking enchanted and twinkling in the streaming moonlight.

She breathed out a prayer of thanks. Though she was trespassing on a private sanctuary, it was still a tranquil moment. If she'd been gifted with any measure of peace in the midst of her uncertain life, she'd accept it, gratefully. Between her parents' fervent wish that she marry well, the space that had been growing between her and Vladimir, and the overwhelming nightmare of war . . . she just wasn't sure which way was up anymore.

"Adele."

She whirled around at the whisper of her name, sure she'd find that some eager young officer had followed her up the stairs. Her fists were instinctively balled up in front of her, ready for a fight. But before she had time to feel threatened by the presence of a stranger in the quiet garden, the voice connected with the image of a man standing before her.

She squinted in the moonlight, shocked when she recognized his face.

"Vladimir?"

He approached with quiet steps and picked up the hat she'd dropped.

"What in heaven's name are you doing here?" It was all she could manage to say.

He offered the hat to her.

"It's not safe to walk about a strange city on your own."

It wasn't until he'd taken the several steps forward that she was close enough to read the expression illuminated by the moonlight on his face. Was he . . . *angry*? Forget the fact that she'd have been delighted to see no one else in the rooftop garden, the look on his face was rather murderous.

"But what are you doing in Germany?" She asked the obvious question a scant second before the next accusatory words tumbled out her lips. "How did you find me?"

"You don't have any idea what could have happened up here? You're alone, Adele. Alone and stupid, I might add. You've got to be smarter than this." He issued the reproach easily and reached out with a hand that clamped like a vise around her elbow.

"I asked you a question."

"You're traveling on behalf of the orchestra. It wasn't that difficult to find out where the group was going after your performance."

"You followed me."

"Adele, your parents may not want their daughter to be seen with a merchant's son, but I'm sure that doesn't mean they'd rather see her traipsing around Munich with that trollop friend of yours in there."

She yanked her elbow out of his grip.

"I don't know what you're doing here, but I'm not going anywhere with you."

So he thought to usher her back across the roof like a disobedient schoolgirl? If that was his intention, Vladimir Nicolai's arrogance had grown in spades since the last time they'd seen each other. She had no intention of going quietly.

"You're going back to your hotel."

"Oh, am I? And how do you propose to make me go?" Adele stood against him, toe-to-toe, though he was quite a bit taller and more intimidating when he wanted to be. Surprise, surprise. But he'd never met the real Adele Von Bron. She wasn't easily frightened, especially when she was upset.

He shrugged and reached for her. "I'll carry you if I have to."

She slapped his hands back.

"What is the matter with you? You haven't spoken to me in weeks." She chucked the hat back at him, uncaring that the lovely white felt would be soiled when it rebounded and fell to the ground. "And now you show up here in Munich, shocking me out of my shoes and then issuing orders that I am supposed to follow? How dare you!"

He raised his voice too, frustration mounting. "Adele, have you forgotten? I'm not allowed to talk to you. The nice visit I received from your father after I walked you home from the dance hall assured that well enough. I'm only staying away on the general's orders. You can't fault me for honoring his wishes."

"But you met me in the garden before each performance after that night," she said, crossing her arms over her chest. "Except for recently. Tell me why I waited for more than an hour before each performance this month and you never showed." She looked down at the ground, vulnerability suddenly washing over her as she stared at a pile of potting soil at their feet. "You left me there alone, Vladimir. I think I deserve to know why."

She chanced a look up at him then, meeting the stony resolve of his eyes.

He shook his head. "I can't tell you. I know you don't understand—" When his hand reached out to touch her arm, she recoiled sharply.

In the car ride around the city, she'd imagined every officer Margie pointed out to have Vladimir's face. At the time she'd felt only wonder and sadness that he'd not reached out to see her in weeks. But now? That emotion turned to anger.

How dare he drop out of her life with such indifference!

"Adele, I'm sorry. You don't know how sorry I am, but I just can't see you right now."

"You still haven't explained what you're doing here." She tapped her spectator heel on the paved rooftop floor, waiting for an answer. "Checking up on me, hmm? You don't want to see me but you don't want me to be in the company of anyone else either, is that it? Well, you needn't bother with the protective act. There are plenty of young men down there who asked me to dance."

"I know," he whispered then, the words hinged on a half-hidden smile. "I saw them."

Adele didn't understand a single thing he was saying. So he'd been there the whole time, watching her?

Vladimir bent down to pick up her hat a second time. This time he brushed it off with his sleeve and, taking a few precautionary steps up to her, gently angled the hat on her head. He tipped the brim of the fedora just down to her right brow before taking a step back again.

"You saw me in the club?"

"Yes. And I saw the officers. I wanted to punch every single one of them, just like that night at the dance hall."

She felt the anger ease from her shoulders and melt down her arms.

"Vladimir." She shook her head and continued looking back in his eyes. "I don't understand. I know my parents won't allow us to see each other, but I would have waited." She stopped, afraid she'd get weepy before him. "I waited before each performance and you never came. You can't have it both ways."

"I know."

"Then why?" She chanced keeping her eyes connected with his. It didn't matter now. They glossed over anyway. "I thought we were friends. Maybe I was wrong."

"I was trying to keep distance between us." He sighed and

raked his fingers through his hair. "Adele, more is going on here than you realize."

"Fine. Then help me understand what it is."

Vladimir shook his head. "I can't tell you. Not now."

"That's not an answer. Especially not when you show up, unannounced, while I just happen to be on a trip to Munich. That's a bit odd. I think you owe me an explanation."

She notched her chin a bit higher in the air, and though she knew her voice had quivered ever so slightly, she waited for an answer. Instead, he turned his gaze to a point out over the skyline beyond her. She wondered what could have lost him in thought at such a moment but kept silent.

"Do you remember that night at the dance hall, Adele?"

How could she possibly forget her birthday? She still had the gift of the butterfly clip tucked away. He may not have asked her to dance, but for the walk home, it was worth it.

"Of course. It changed everything for Austria, didn't it?" And for her. She'd hoped that maybe it had changed things for him too.

He shook his head. "No. Not the start of the war. I'm referring to when I held you in confidence that night. Do you remember what I told you about my friends? The shopkeepers' sons I'd grown up with and what was happening to Jews in the city?"

She nodded.

"Well, that's why I'm here."

"Vladimir, you're not making any sense."

He breathed in deep. "Can I trust you, Adele? My friend. Can I really trust you?"

Her heart wanted to scream *Yes!* Of course he could trust her. But with what?

"Your father can never hear about this. If he did—"

"You can trust me," she whispered and gave what she hoped would be a confident nod. "With anything. I won't judge you."

"There are Jews left in the city and"—he looked shrouded in vulnerability as he shoved his hands in his pants pockets and gave her a wary look—"I'm helping them to get out."

Adele's heart skipped a beat.

No matter how badly she wanted to, she couldn't find words. Never in a million years had she suspected that Vladimir would be involved in something so dangerous.

When she didn't break the silence between them, he continued. "I kept away so you wouldn't be implicated. I was protecting you." Vladimir kicked at a pebble on the ground. "Please. Say something."

"I . . . I suppose I understand what you're telling me." Adele shook her head. Every other man she knew would have been proud about such an admission. It held the note of courage, to say the least. But Vladimir? He was humble about it. Always quiet and unpretentious and able to get straight into her protected heart. "But you do realize what the penalty is if you're caught?"

"Yes." He nodded.

Rumors were flying all over the city. If anyone was to hide or help a Jew, the penalty was severe, up to and including death.

"I know what's happening," Adele assured him, "what the world is saying about Germany and Austria. Winston Churchill gave a speech this week. He asked the people of Britain to stay strong. To have courage in the face of the Nazi regime. He said it would be their finest hour. Do you think that's true?"

"How do you know what Churchill said?"

"My friends at the university," she said, feeling sorrow weighing down her shoulders. "Everyone was talking about it. I think I was the only one who didn't favor bombs falling on London. I don't think war is the answer for anything."

"Maybe not, but we have to respond when something is unjust, Adele. We can't be content to watch at the same time we condemn. To condemn is to stand up in the face of a wrong and fight it. We must pick a side."

"I want to pick a side. More than anything. And my parents don't know it, but I'm questioning things myself." She reached down in her handbag and pulled out a swatch of red fabric. "I refuse to wear it."

She tossed the armband without care and watched as it floated down to the dirt at their feet. It landed with the Nazi symbol staring back up at them.

She lifted her chin up in the air. "I'm not as weak as you might think."

"Ah, Butterfly." He moved forward, one heartbeat at a time, and stood with the tips of his shoes touching hers. He brushed a lock of hair over her shoulder. "That's the last thing you could be in my eyes."

Even in the summer heat, she shivered.

"So, why are you in Munich then?"

"We're helping a family escape. They emigrated from Vienna to hide in Germany some time ago, hoping they could make it through to Switzerland."

"So you mean . . . there are others doing this with you?"

"Yes."

He'd just confessed an act of treason that was punishable by death if the Germans found out. It was shocking, but somehow it made her love him all the more.

They'd talked of God. They'd talked of faith and the Christian life they both wanted to lead. But this? Vladimir's actions spoke of someone who actually lived it rather than talked of a life's journey dedicated to Christ.

She paused, now wondering if she could trust him with her life too.

"And the only reason you're here is to see them out of the city?"

"Not the only reason." He shook his head, his eyes probing hers, sending chills down her spine. He pulled her into an embrace and she allowed her cheek to feel the warmth of his heartbeat.

He pulled back and whispered, his mouth warming her forehead with a kiss. "I can't see you anywhere but onstage anymore." He brushed curled fingertips across the apple of her cheek. "I came to hear my Butterfly play her sweet violin."

She swallowed hard, hoping beyond hope that he meant it and had traveled to Germany to keep a distant eye on her as well. To sit in the audience of the concert hall and want only to be near to her. The sentiment was staggering.

"If that's true, then I have something to confess to you too."

He seemed taken aback but stood before her, waiting for her to spill whatever it was she felt compelled to say. "Okay."

"I know of some Jews left in Vienna, and I want to help them."

CHAPTER TWENTY-ONE

———

August 14, 1943

𝒜dele remembered how it had all started that night in Munich, how she'd given up everything to follow her heart. And now, as she trudged back along the dusty road to the music block, she could think of nothing else but how her world had changed.

By autumn, the musical troupe in Auschwitz-Birkenau had become a full-fledged orchestra. It was a world away from her youthful playing with the college troupe in Munich. Here the rehearsal schedule was much more stringent, the absolutism and demand for perfection the only line drawn against death. The one solace was that the orchestra was no longer required to work in Canada during the day. Instead, they were afforded the practice time whenever they were not playing for the laborers marching out in the morning and those returning at night—or for the arrival of trains.

The Nazis had begun to transport a steady influx of Hungarian Jews in late spring. Whether or not taxed resources had anything to do with it, it was known that by summer the overwhelming majority of these people were sent straight to the gas chambers. Adele watched this with a numbing horror—the systematic parting of people to the right or left, those deemed able to work versus those deemed unable. Her soul hurt, being forced to watch families ripped apart, to see the trudging steps the doomed took toward their fate and only be able to let her violin weep with them through it all.

She'd cried during every selection. She'd prayed too, pouring out to God in words not spoken but rather sent up from her wailing violin. But for reasons she couldn't comprehend, the deaths continued day after agonizing day. This warm August morning was no exception. She had but moments to fix her violin and run back to the platform to play for another transport.

"Omara, I snapped a string." Adele burst into the block, expecting to find her friend ready to step out and join them at the gate. What she didn't anticipate was to find someone else in the block with her. Omara stood huddled at a plank bed with another woman, their heads bent over the straw mattress together.

They both stirred uncomfortably when she entered.

"I'm sorry but I snapped a string and—" Adele noticed that the women made an effort to quickly tuck something out of sight.

"You won't have time to change a string now. You know where the replacement instruments are, Adele. Go and fetch what you need." Omara stood with her back to the bed, blocking the view of whatever they'd been doing.

Adele felt uncomfortable about what looked like secrecy, but turned toward their cache of instruments as instructed without questioning.

"Then I'll just leave my violin and take the extra." She placed her violin in its box and tucked it under her bed.

Omara nodded. "Good. We can re-string yours when we return for midday rehearsals."

"We're playing at the platform again this morning . . . ," Adele said, the finality of the task hanging on the end of the trailed-off sentence. She grabbed the case and, knowing that her feet should be swift, hurried toward the door. The guards had been irritated that she had to return anyway. It certainly wouldn't do to dawdle in her return.

"Does Alma know where you are?"

Adele nodded. Their new conductor, Alma Rosé, was the one who had sent her back. "Yes. She expects me to return with you."

She looked at the other woman there in the block with Omara, her eyes appearing purposeful in diverting Adele's glance in her direction. She looked the same as any prisoner, with head shaved and a uniform splashed with an unforgiving layer of dirt. But if Adele had to guess, she thought she recognized Helene, one of the women who worked at Crematorium IV. What she was doing in the music block on this particular day was anybody's guess.

"I will be along shortly, Adele."

She paused, unsure if she should return alone. Was it safe? Would the guards think Omara was sick and quarantine them all, or worse?

"But what do I tell Alma? If I don't return with you, the guards could take out the punishment on us both."

"I will be right behind you."

Omara seemed to grow impatient with the questioning. "Hurry now, Adele. I won't be responsible for the beating they'll issue if you're late. It's risky enough to come back because of a snapped string."

Adele did as she was told and tucked the violin under her arm. With a swift glance back, she met the eyes of her friend for a split second before the door closed between them.

Marta was the first to notice that she'd returned alone. Adele shot her a look as she slid into her seat and began readying her violin for the next song.

Always the consummate professional, Alma was strict about starting on time. In spite of an uncontrollable circumstance like a snapped string, she required that every musician be on time.

Knowing this, Adele looked around, watching for Omara's form to appear over the hill and hurry to the train platform.

"Psst! Adele!" Marta was trying to get her attention from a row away. Adele turned to see her mouth the words *"Where's Omara?"*

Adele shook her head. Marta shifted in her chair and looked over at Fränze, who was clutching her flute a few seats away. Several of the other girls noticed too but said nothing. One of the other bass players picked up the cello and sat in the chair in the back, preparing to take Omara's usual notes as her own. And so it seemed nothing else remained to be said.

The conductor raised her hand, calling them to attention.

As always, Adele's eyes sailed over to the back row. With a habitual glance to the seat Vladimir would have occupied had they been playing a concert in Vienna, she set about her duty. She played as an automaton would, with no depth of feeling, no love for the music. There were only fingers that pressed strings, a bow that soared over the instrument.

God. She breathed the prayers out as she always did, through gritted teeth. *God? How can I be forced to play like this? Please don't hate me for doing it.*

Adele swallowed hard, relief covering her when she saw Omara's form appear over the hill and hurry in their direction.

Please forgive us, Lord . . . for playing for them.

CHAPTER TWENTY-TWO

*W*ell, I've got to hand it to you New Yorkers," William said on a contented sigh, and tossed a piece of pizza crust back in the cardboard box on the worktable. "You make a mean pizza."

Sera cocked an eyebrow as she brushed the crumbs from her hands. "Oh yeah? So I've finally convinced you that New York–style crust is better."

"Miss James." He leaned in and placed his hand over hers casually, as if he'd had the liberty to do so for years. "I may never find the owner of the painting, but at least I can say I've been well fed for one of the best weeks out of my life."

She smiled at the warmth of his hand and welcomed it, but felt nerves kicking in. William had cleared his calendar and after their dinner the first night had become something of a fixture in her gallery. They'd talked. Researched the painting. Laughed plenty. And had walked through the spring evenings along the sidewalks of Manhattan, hand in hand, not looking or thinking past tomorrow.

But now, tomorrow was before them. Saturday night had rolled around. It stared them in the face—he was leaving the next day. Sera felt his eyes on her and popped up from her chair. She'd welcome anything other than talking about what they were both trying so hard to ignore.

The workroom had canvases scattered around. Some were

painted. Others had been started and left with large spots of unpainted canvas. There was the occasional sculpture on the back bookshelves, positioned as a bookend between enormous stacks of art history books. Tall windows nearly two stories in height gave a backdrop of city lights and the deep recesses of the spring sky outside, the one they'd walked under for hours that week.

Sera began busying her hands with cleaning up pizza plates and soda cans instead of thinking about what could be on his mind. She moved around the room, picking up their trash and organizing folders—anything to stop her heart from beating wildly at the thought that her affection for him had grown by leaps and bounds.

"So what's that over there? Medusa?"

She blinked and turned to him after tossing their plates in the trash.

"What?"

William pointed to a tall sculpture with long, snakelike appendages that reached out in a screaming shade of garish purple. "That thing that looks like an alien coatrack."

Sera laughed. The sculpture still managed to demand attention even from a hidden corner of the back room. "Not quite," she said, remembering the day Penny had wheeled it into the gallery on a dolly. She too had likened it to a work of mythic proportion, though the young assistant's comparison had spoken more of her fascination with the young man who created it than admiration for the sculpture itself. "It was one of Penny's finds. A piece by a brilliant new sculptor she met in one of her art circles a few years back."

"And you kept it . . ." He cocked an eyebrow with the playful words.

"Not by choice, I assure you," she admitted, reaching her hands out in mock surrender. "Translation? Penny was dating a new guy and brought in that horrible thing to convince me to give him his own one-man show."

"And did you?"

Her head began shaking along with her hearty laugh. "Not on your life."

William whistled under his breath. "The professional hazards of being the owner of an art gallery. I never would have guessed."

"It all worked out. Penny broke up with him a month later. We keep the purple alien around for laughs." She took a stool across the table from him. "It holds our coats in the winter and we get a smile when we need one. It's served its grand purpose, I suppose."

William seemed to notice her choice of a seat that was no longer at his side but said nothing. Instead, he tilted his head to one side, as if looking quite hard to find something she was trying to hide from him.

He pointed to the painting of Adele through the French doors. It was hanging in the shadows of the gallery with only a soft stream of light from the workroom to illuminate her face. "That kind of art I like. The other"—he again looked over at Medusa and clicked his tongue—"I'm not sure I get it. I'm afraid I'd have to get a new hobby if the modern stuff were the only kind of art out there for sale."

"Ah—art as a hobby. It started out like that for me, but one day . . ." She shrugged. "I don't know. It just changed. Somehow this gallery and the things in it became the center of my world."

"Why is that?"

"I guess it was because . . . well, it was after I had to cancel my trip to Paris. Going was the only thing I'd ever really wanted."

His eyebrows arched and his features started a bit. "You've never been to Paris?"

"I've been there once, as a kid. I didn't get to see much. I was there with my dad, on a layover back from a speech in Germany. He was an art historian and we stopped by a gallery to see one of his colleagues. Didn't have time for anything else before our flight."

"I can see why you'd want to go back."

Leaving out mention of the painting she'd seen there, Sera continued.

"Yes. Dad and I were close. I traveled with him sometimes. My mom didn't like it much because I missed school," she remembered, smiling, lost in thought as she stared at a spot of ink that had been absorbed into the top of the ancient worktable. "But he always made me write a research report out of it, so Mom was happy." She looked up at him then and found he'd been watching her all the time. "I was happy too. Even if I never saw Paris again."

"I wouldn't have guessed it about you."

She shook her head. "Surprising, I know. An art gallery owner who's only peeked at one of the hubs of the entire art world. It's . . ." She could have laughed over her embarrassment, knowing that he was watching as every inch of her face tinged in a warm blush. Her hand went up to partially shield it from him, resting on the side of her cheek. She looked up warily. "It's not pathetic, is it?"

"No." He did laugh then, in a casual expression of amusement that was fast becoming familiar to her. "Not pathetic at all. You've got a lot going on here, right? Manhattan is booming. And what better place to find your beloved art than New York? It's not like this city is lacking in the culture department. And you've still got time to go back there—to Paris."

"Most people would think a gallery owner had spent summers there in an exchange program or something, you know? Paris for a semester, at the very least. Especially if you want to really know what you're talking about. But it's more than that."

She paused, biting her bottom lip before she could find the courage to say the words out loud. "We were supposed to go there on our honeymoon. Michael and I."

William inhaled long and low, then nodded to her, urging her on without words. She understood. Even with a table between them, he wasn't so far away that he couldn't read her like a book.

"I'd always dreamed about it. What art historian doesn't, right? Getting lost in the Louvre and finally seeing my favorite work of art, the *Winged Nike of Samothrace*, so beautifully guarding its portico. Traveling out to the Palace of Versailles. Spending time looking up at every corner of Notre Dame's magnificent vaults. All of it came together in this one dream Michael and I shared. I'd always thought it would be the two of us experiencing it together. We'd talked about it. Planned everything out down to the last detail. But after the wedding was called off, I just couldn't bring myself to go there alone."

"Why didn't you go back with your dad?"

Sera wiped a tear that escaped to her cheek, crushing it with the back of her palm. "My dad died shortly after our trip."

William inclined his head toward her and with feeling said, "Sera, I'm so sorry."

He sounded genuine. It was enough to keep her talking through the tears.

"I was eight years old. At that age, a girl's hero is her dad. I have the memories to prove it's true. And that life can change in the blink of an eye . . ." Her voice trailed off for a moment. The memories were flooding back. "And so, the tickets Michael and I bought meant more to me than just a plane ride overseas; they connected me to the girl I used to be once upon a time. I'd hoped to share those memories with my husband. But the tickets and the memories ended up going to waste. It felt like living half a dream somehow if I'd gone on my own."

"And you wanted the whole dream."

She felt the awkward fluttering in her heart, almost like she was in junior high again. Although she didn't remember the boys in eighth grade having eyes like his.

"I guess I did. But then after everything that happened with Michael . . ." She paused. Their conversations over dinner hadn't made it to the subject of her ex-fiancé since that first night. "The gallery . . . it sort of became my savior. It was wrong, but I threw myself into work here so I wouldn't have to feel anything. It was much safer to avoid all risk."

Sera felt the tingles of nervousness turning her hands cold in her lap. She twisted them under the table where he couldn't see.

"Safer to avoid risk. I know what you mean."

"You do?"

He nodded. "Who else would understand but someone who's buried himself in work at the expense of any kind of life? I wasn't close to my grandfather. That's something I sincerely wish I could change, but now that he's gone . . . I'm not sure how to dig out of this career pit I've found myself at the bottom of."

"As of late, I've taken up scripture reading again. It's helped me." She wondered how he'd receive such a remark. She'd been wanting to share that part of her life with him for a while, but . . . well, she'd been scared. So it hadn't come up.

He looked startled.

"Really?" he asked with no emotion on his face except for the tinge of warmth that remained in his features. He looked back at her with eyes widened and lips pursed.

"Well, yes. It was an important part of my life—the central part of it really, until Michael and I broke up. I can't say I've been as close in my relationship with God, but I feel I need to be again. I wasn't mad at God. But I was mad at my fiancé. He was a Christian, and I guess I thought that meant he wouldn't hurt me."

"But we do hurt each other sometimes, don't we?"

She nodded. "Yes. I think what happened to Adele is proof of that."

William didn't say a word.

Instead, he hopped off his stool and, with a sideways glance that connected his eyes with hers, walked over to the chair that held his jacket and laptop bag. He unzipped the top of the bag and retrieved a small, leather-bound book. He came back to the worktable and sat on the stool next to her.

He set a worn Bible down in front of her.

She couldn't help but be shocked. She'd never have guessed this wealthy businessman had another side that followed Christ with a worn Bible in his hand.

"You're a Christian?"

He gave her a half smile to accentuate a slight nod. "Guilty. Since I was sixteen."

Sera exhaled as she ran her hand over the cover of the Bible. "And you've had this since then?"

He nodded. "Yeah. A gift from my grandfather when I was baptized."

Sera sat and listened to William as he took her back to his teenage years. He told her how he'd been a troubled kid early on. Because of too much money and too little responsibility, he got caught in the wrong crowd and found himself headed down a troubled road. But Christ turned his life around and he never intended to look back.

"So they actually called you Preacher?"

"Yeah. My friends were creative with the nicknames, huh? Must be where Paul and I got the notion to try nicknaming people ourselves. But it fit. I'd always thought that was my calling, even back in school. I wanted to preach in some fashion."

"And why didn't you?"

"Are you kidding? A Hanover in the pulpit?" He shrugged his shoulders. "My family had other needs. Expectations. They needed a leader. I was groomed to take over for the elder Hanover men, when the time was right, of course. And when my father left the business, it was sink or swim. Paul had no interest and Macie was obviously too young, so . . ." William sat tall on the stool, his baby blues staring through her.

"So you did what they wanted."

"I did what I had to do to keep my family together. They saw it as putting aside Sunday school and having a real career."

She laid her hand on the top of the Bible. "And now you carry this around with you to all of your board meetings."

"A Bible in hand doesn't fit the picture of the company president intimidating unsuspecting gallery owners in his office, does it?" William laughed aloud, so much so that his smile revealed the laugh lines only occasionally visible around his eyes. She noticed. Warmed to his openness. And on instinct, leaned in a bit closer to his side.

"It doesn't," she said. "And you weren't that intimidating."

He'd continued smiling at her but suddenly stopped short, his face falling to seriousness like a stone through water. "You know, I don't think I've ever told anybody that. No one really knew what I felt like I was giving up."

"No?"

"No, Sera." His voice dropped to a soft and sweet, barely there whisper. "I think that was my Paris. God was always calling me back, but I never would go."

William was so different from Michael. So open. So unashamed of his interest in the pursuit that spelled something other than power and success. This man had them both in spades, but he didn't seem affected by either. He looked like he could have given up everything without a parting glance.

He had a heart that she'd never imagined when they'd first met.

"And so after all of this"—he placed his hand atop the stack of files they'd been keeping on Adele—"we're in a different place now than when this whole thing began, aren't we?"

"I think so." With her heart thundering in her chest, Sera turned back to their research. "We don't have anything new on Adele or Vladimir. Both of their trails go cold around October 1944. The only link I can think of is your grandfather."

"And we don't know what that is."

No. She didn't have a clue.

They'd talked about Edward Hanover all week. William told her what he knew, that his grandfather was a student at Oxford when the war broke out. He'd been taking photographs all his life and had been called into service as a photojournalist for the British army.

"William, we've been through these folders a hundred times. There are no photos that we can tie back to your grandfather."

"But what about when Auschwitz was liberated? Maybe he was there. Maybe he could have learned what happened to Adele, or Vladimir, for that matter."

She shook her head. "I wish it was that easy. But Auschwitz was liberated by the Red Army. A British photojournalist wouldn't have been traveling with the Russians, even though they were allies in the war. It's just not probable that he was there."

"Then what about someone else?"

"You mean another person in Auschwitz?"

"Why not? If my grandfather wasn't in Auschwitz to see Adele, then maybe someone else was. Maybe they told him what happened to the orchestra. It's a possibility, isn't it? The orchestra was so visible to the prisoners of the camp. Someone would have seen what happened to them."

The thought struck Sera then—what if there was a photograph of Adele in the camp when it was liberated? Someone painted the image of Adele, and if it wasn't from memory, maybe it was from a photograph.

"Where was your grandfather in the spring of 1945? Do you know?"

"I'm not sure."

"It's a possibility that someone saw what happened to Adele. How she died or what happened to the members of the orchestra. What if that someone told your grandfather about her? If we can find out who your grandfather knew in the war, we might be able to find a link back to her." When he didn't say anything, she continued. "So, what do you think? It's worth a try, isn't it?"

"Your face just lit up, Sera."

She raised her hands to her cheeks, hoping to cover the blush she felt burning there. "Did it?"

He nodded. "It was like you just stepped off the plane in your city of lights. You're taken with this mystery."

"Aren't you?"

"Of course I am."

"Then you'll look into it?" Sera asked, hoping they'd landed on something that could jump-start the trails that had fizzled out. It wasn't a concrete lead, but it was better than nothing. "Could you ask your father about it?"

He paused for a moment, then looked away from her and began stacking some of the files that littered the tabletop. She wasn't sure what to make of the shift in his mood. He was still standing next to her, but now she felt distance invading the space between them.

"Will?"

"I haven't spoken to my father in months," he admitted, his tone distant.

"I'm not asking you to go to your father except to see if we can learn something new. Would you do it for the sake of your family?"

"I'll think about it, Sera."

She nodded, but wasn't sure whether he saw her. She started

stacking files along with him just so her hands had a momentary occupation.

"Okay . . ."

"I appreciate your enthusiasm about my grandfather's connection to all of this, but you're asking me to do something I'm not sure I can do." He swept up the folders in his arms and walked over to the chair with his coat. The files were stowed away and in an instant he swung the messenger bag across his body.

"You want some company to the airport tomorrow?"

He shook his head. Hands buried in his pockets, standing stone still with a soft look on his face, he said, "I'll take a taxi on my own. It'll be early."

"Early?"

He nodded.

It was clear what he was doing with the quiet demeanor. William wanted her to come to him of her own accord. He stood waiting. Whether he wanted to know if it was just the painting, she couldn't be sure. But the message was clear enough that Sera slid from her stool and walked up to stand but a breath in front of him.

"You'll need this," she whispered, and tucked the Bible away under the flap of his bag.

"I will, won't I?" His face broke into a soft smile, his voice quiet but rough with feeling. "If I ever want to see Paris again." He leaned in and placed the softest kiss on her lips. She closed her eyes to the warmth in it.

Pulling back slightly, she looked in his eyes. "Will you think about it? Calling your father?"

He brushed a hand over her cheek. "Yeah. I'll think about it. We said we were partners, right?"

"That's right."

"Then I guess I've got to hold up my end of the bargain."

~

Sera stood there at the stoop, lost in the memory that lingered even as she turned the key in the lock of the gallery's front door. She felt the familiar tingle on her lips although he'd left a half hour ago. William's kiss was all she could think about.

He was flying cross-country the next morning. And she didn't want to let him go, did she? She'd finally crossed the room to him and, heaven help her, she felt like a schoolgirl all over again with each step. Even now, she could sense the unconscious smile on her lips and feel her heart flutter with the possibility of love awakening.

She hadn't felt it in a long, long time.

"Sera?"

She whirled around, turning so quickly that the tip of her sleek ponytail almost smacked her in the face. The voice was too familiar to ignore.

Now she blinked. Several times.

He had a different cut to his sandy hair and looked like he'd caught a little more sun to the face, but otherwise, he was the same man she remembered. It was Michael Turner who stood before her, sleek Wall Street suit and all.

"Michael?"

He nodded, the glow of the streetlamp illuminating his features. "Hi, Sera."

"What are you doing here?"

He walked up to the stoop and offered a faint smile.

"Can I come in?" he breathed out. "I need to talk to you."

CHAPTER TWENTY-THREE

February 8, 1941

"What are you looking for, Adele?"

Vladimir checked over his shoulder again, looking down into the long alleyway to the deserted street. The noise at the docks wasn't too far off, reminding Adele that people were never too far away to happen by and see them, even in the dark of night. "Are you sure you know what you're doing?"

She moved a crate out of the way to reveal a weathered panel of wood at the bottom of the bricks. "The entryway to the building has a false back," she whispered, then knelt down on her knees. "See? Abram told me how to get in. We crawl through here and it takes you into the butler's pantry off a back kitchen. It's been sealed off from the outside. Bricks. No one would even know it's there."

She picked up the basket she'd hidden under her coat and started to crawl in, but was stopped by a hand on her shoulder.

Vladimir shook his head. "Uh-uh. No way you're going in there first. If anything's going to happen, it's not going to be to you."

"You're being ridiculous, Vladimir. The sardine factory has been boarded up for nearly two years. There's no one inside."

"Except for the Jewish family hiding in the basement," he huffed, and leaned back on his heels. He took a lighter from his coat pocket and offered it to her. She took it with a twinkle in her eye, glad to have won at least one battle with him.

"Don't light it until I have the panel closed." He checked up the alley again, then, seeing that the coast was clear, motioned for her to go first. "Go ahead."

Adele felt her heart warm as she took the food basket from him. He was being rather noble, wanting nothing to happen to her. "Remember what we said? We're in this together."

"Nope. That's what you said. I only agreed to this long enough for you to show me how to get in so I can take over this operation. Then you're going home."

She wanted to roll her eyes at him but thought better of it. He was being protective, and she couldn't fault him for that.

Adele knelt down and ducked her head under the top of the wood panel, inching through the dusty crawl space with the basket in front of her. It was dark and full of spiderwebs, but she could see the light of the butler's pantry enclosure up ahead. The moonlight shone through in a silver haze.

She heard Vladimir close the panel behind her.

"It's just up ahead," she whispered. "This way."

"What's the light? I thought you said the pantry was bricked off."

"It's a small ventilation window on the second level." Adele shook her head and flicked on the lighter. "Don't worry. I've done this a dozen times before. It's safe."

Vladimir groaned from somewhere behind her, showing his displeasure that she'd managed to sneak in to see the Haurbechs on so many occasions.

Probably should have kept that to myself.

"Right there," Adele said, and leaned to one side so he could see a small opening up ahead. "That's where we go in. There's a stairway down to the basement behind one of the cupboards against the back wall."

Adele crawled through the mouth of the opening that was hidden under a section of worktables affixed to the wall.

She looked around.

Spiderwebs and dust. The cupboards had been raided some time ago, but the sardine cans and rat traps on the floor hadn't moved since the last time she'd come. She looked up. The window was still barred. All was as it should be.

She dusted off her navy coat and plucked the basket up off the floor just as Vladimir crawled out from under the table. She didn't even have time to finish flouncing the dust out of her hair before he darted up to her side.

He grasped her elbow in an iron grip.

"Let go of me—"

"This is too dangerous," he said, shaking his head at her. "You've showed me where they are. Now let me take over."

"I can't do that, Vladimir!" Her voice rang out in a biting whisper. "They won't be expecting you. They'll be terrified, thinking they've been caught. Remember the children? We can't scare them like that."

"Adele, the Gestapo doesn't shimmy through crawl spaces to find hiding Jews. They knock down brick walls and open fire with machine guns. If the Haurbechs had been caught, believe me, they'd know it."

"Then let me go so I can give them this food and we can leave," she said, feeling his fingertips lighten with the last words. "I have to give them something, even if it's only hope."

He nodded toward one of the wooden cupboards against the back wall.

She tilted her head on instinct. "How did you know it was that one? There's a wall of them."

"Dust on the floor." He nodded to the trail leading to the back wall. "Footprints, Adele. You never covered them up."

She looked down at the floor to find the evidence of her

former visits plain as day in front of them. The footprints led from the crawl space at the opening over to the back cupboard.

"There's no way in and no way out of this room, Adele, except for the spaces your prints lead to. Anyone looking for hiding places would have caught you and them because of it. You didn't cover your tracks very well."

She felt the weight of foolishness wash over her and closed her eyes in shame. All this time she'd been visiting the Haurbechs, bringing them food . . . she'd thought she was doing something good. But it was luck. Pure luck that they hadn't been caught with her petite footprints littering the pantry floor.

"See why I worry about you?" Vladimir leaned in and wiped a fingertip along the bridge of her nose. "Dust."

Adele brushed off her nose on principle.

He was acting like she didn't know how serious it was, sneaking in to help her friends. But she'd been the one to help them for months without anyone else knowing. He could give her a little credit.

"The stairs are here," she said, leaning in to pull the cupboard back from the wall. "Behind this."

Vladimir edged in around her, using his strength to pull the cupboard back in her stead. It didn't appear to be needed. The wood separated from the wall on a hinge that pulled away rather easily. The void behind the wall was also brick, with stairs that led down into the basement.

"After you." He didn't appear to want to scold her any longer. Instead, he tilted his chin toward the brick opening.

Adele flicked the lighter again, giving them enough light so that Vladimir could pull the cupboard closed behind them before they descended the stairs.

"There's a door at the bottom," she whispered, and pointed to the faint lines of the portal up ahead. "See?"

She took the stairs one at a time, trying to make the least

amount of noise with her feet against the creaking boards. He took the basket and followed her with cautious steps.

"Are they expecting us?"

"Yes. Elsa will be," Adele whispered, and nudged her feet down the stairs in the dark. "It's been more than two months since my last visit. I'm overdue."

They came to the door at the bottom of the stairs and were met with a cold silence. Water dripped from somewhere in the recesses of the dark basement. Adele noticed that Vladimir kept checking over his shoulder to make sure they weren't followed. How he could see anything in the dark, she wasn't sure.

She tapped on the door, six times in succession with a break in the middle, the code they'd decided some time ago would only be for her.

There was a slight rustle on the other side of the door and it slowly cracked open.

A tall man with kind eyes and thinning hair poked his head into the stairway. The flicker of the lighter illuminated his face. He looked to Adele and inclined his head to her, greeting without words.

"Abram," she whispered. "I've brought a friend. This is Vladimir. He's here to help."

Vladimir stood at Adele's back but didn't speak. He didn't make a move to step forward or offer the basket.

"I have spoken with Elsa. We do not think it safe to open the door any longer," Abram whispered, his voice gravelly, as though he needed to cough but wouldn't. "There is too much risk."

"But we've brought food," she offered, holding out the basket with bread and fish. "For you and the children. Are they well?"

He shook his head.

"We've heard the Gestapo at night." He looked to the ceiling with tired eyes. "They've been patrolling. They've not found the pantry, but they've been in the warehouse. Searching. Tearing down walls."

"But how could they know?"

Abram shook his head and lowered his voice to a cryptic whisper. "There were rumors that there were Jews hiding in this part of the city before we went into hiding. The brave ones left more than a year ago."

Adele shook her head. "I think it's the brave ones who stayed," she said, taking the basket from Vladimir to offer to the family. "May we come in?"

He looked to the ceiling again, then nodded. "For a moment only."

Adele walked into the room, finding Elsa standing in the corner. When they connected eyes, her shoulders relaxed and she stepped forward to embrace her in a hug.

"Adele." She offered an embattled smile, welcoming her. "I'm so glad you've come."

Vladimir walked in behind her and, after bolting the door closed, began looking over the room from floor to ceiling. He must have been as concerned as she was, for the living conditions were deplorable.

Their living quarters were lit only by moonlight from a shut-up ventilation window high up on the wall and a small fire lit in the woodstove in the corner. There was a brick wall along the length of the room, with large pipes and ducts that gathered dust along the ceiling. Water leaked somewhere in the corner of the room, and the air in the room hung thick with the smell of mold. There were threadbare linens hanging from a rope fastened to a pipe from one end to the other. There was a single rocking chair and a small table, with dishes and a tub for washing, pushed up against the far wall. Stacks of books created tiny mountains on top of a small bookshelf in the far corner of the room.

Adele could see the heads of the children, the older Sophie

and her little brother, Eitan, bundled up in their blankets in a bed that was squeezed up in the corner closest to the stove. The gentle cadence of their undisturbed breathing told her they were asleep.

Vladimir stepped up to address Abram, concern evident on his face.

"It's not safe to be burning wood," he whispered, and walked over to kneel in front of the stove. He pointed up to the window set high on the wall. "The smoke. Someone will see it."

Abram shook his head and pointed to where the pipe exited through the ceiling. "The flue system is adjoined with the apartment building behind the warehouse. This used to be the foreman's private quarters when the warehouse was in operation."

"Is that building in use?"

"Yes. It is," Abram confirmed, nodding.

"And the window? Won't someone see the light?"

"I only burn it on the very cold days. The children—they've not been well. Eitan has a cough," Elsa answered, stepping up to her husband's side. She swallowed hard over the emotion that had caused her voice to crack. "This room goes up more than two stories. The window is frosted glass. And the back of the warehouse has long since been gated. No one can see it from the outside."

"How do you know?"

"One of our friends used to own this factory." Elsa looked down at the ground for a moment. "He's gone now. But he suggested the back of the factory as a hiding place once, because of the extra boiler room. Said he was going to bring his family here if things got bad in the city. We remembered."

Vladimir looked from the distraught woman back to Adele, who felt tears burning her eyes. She shrugged. What could they do?

"Abram. Elsa. We can get you out," Vladimir began, his voice laced with empathy. Adele bit her bottom lip over the emotion that was building, threatening to boil over as tears. "Maybe not right away, but I'm willing to try. I have contacts in Switzerland who would be willing to receive you."

"No." Abram brought his hand up in the air, as if cutting off all talk on the matter.

Adele stepped up to Vladimir's side then, hoping to offer some reassurance that Vladimir could be trusted. "Please listen to him. Vladimir has done this before. He's been able to get others to safety."

"We thank you, but no." Abram shook his head.

"But he can help you. He'll guarantee your safety," Adele said, and looked up at Vladimir. "Won't you?"

Vladimir said nothing. Instead, he exhaled a soft breath of air that she saw leave his shoulders.

"Mr. Nicolai." Elsa addressed him with a soft, almost melodic voice. "Can you guarantee safe passage if we try to leave Vienna now?"

All eyes went to Vladimir, who stood with solidarity. He surprised Adele by reaching out for her hand and held it almost hidden at his side. "No," he admitted, and gave her fingers a gentle squeeze. "I cannot guarantee anything at this point."

The Haurbechs nodded, looking one to the other. Elsa broke into silent tears and leaned in to rest her head on Abram's shoulder.

"We can plan, though. We can get you out of here as soon as possible, before the Gestapo comes back. We can bring you forged documents, traveling papers for you and the children."

"We'll be staying," Abram said. "We can't take the risk. Not with the children."

Vladimir sighed. "You won't change your mind?"

Adele looked up at his profile again, noticing a stony resolve she'd not seen in him before. The Vladimir she knew wasn't this quiet. But then, she'd never seen him in authority over such a

situation before. She'd brought him to be the Haurbechs' savior that night. In truth, he looked quite up to the task, had they
needed one.

After one more squeeze, Vladimir let go of her hand.

He walked over to the small table and began emptying his
pockets. He set several tins on the table. "Sardines, though I know
they're about the last thing you'd want to see," he offered, then
followed with a handful of small potatoes, three small casings
of salted meat, a bar of soap, and several small paper packets.
"Aspirin and an antibiotic. Please don't ask me where I got it."

Elsa ran over to the table, grateful to have the wares he'd
brought.

"And this," he said, placing a pocketknife in her outstretched
hands. "It was all I could find. There's no metal left in the city, I
think."

In the next instant, he had shed his coat and tossed it on the
rocking chair. "Take it. It should fit one of you." He then shrugged
off his sweater, a thick weave of dark navy, and held it out to Elsa.
"At least hang this up over the window at night. Even the tiniest
light from the stove could draw attention."

Adele could have cried when she saw Elsa's arms as she
accepted the sweater. They were so tiny, with bones protrud-
ing from her wrists like a ghost. Her skin was pale and pinched,
her once rosy cheeks a shadowy gray color. Even her chocolaty
hair now seemed dull, pulled back in a stringy knot that looked
streaked with gray.

She looked over at Abram, the wonderfully gifted musician
who'd played viola in the orchestra years ago. Adele had met
them through the university, where he'd been a professor. He was
handsome, with a congenial smile and a booming laugh that the
students enjoyed. But no one had seen him in more than a year,
not since it was rumored that the Haurbechs had left Vienna for
a relative's home in the countryside. And the laugh that had been

missed in the university halls was now replaced by a hollow voice and hands that wrung until his knuckles turned white.

They looked weary. And so unlike the couple she'd once known.

Adele felt her heart breaking for what used to be.

Vladimir turned to Abram. "You have water?"

"Yes. There is an old well at the back of the property. We've been able to draw water."

"Adele? Is that you?" A little brunette head popped up from the sea of blankets on the bed, a girl with a sweet smile and lopsided braids.

"Sophie," she whispered, hoping her voice sounded a little cheery. She pulled a box from the basket Elsa held and walked over to the bed. "I have a surprise for you, my dear friend."

The little girl smiled softly, showing off a missing tooth. She too seemed tired, weary from the fear and the lack of nutrition. Adele hated to see it.

"I've brought you a box of your favorite."

Sophie's eyes lit up when she saw the box. "Shortbread!" she whispered, holding it up so Elsa could see. "Look what Adele's brought me."

Adele reached inside her coat and retrieved a small book from the inside pocket. "And a new book, as promised. *Alice's Adventures in Wonderland.*"

Sophie delighted in the gift and swung tiny arms around her neck. "Thank you," the little girl said, forcing tears to escape from the corners of Adele's eyes.

"Read it with me?"

Adele looked to Vladimir, who shook his head.

"I'm sorry, Sophie. Not today. I've brought a friend with me and we're unable to stay. Perhaps another time, yes?"

Sophie nodded, though her eyes registered immediate sadness. Adele gave a light tap to the end of her pert nose. "Good girl."

She ran a hand over the hair on Eitan's brow, careful not to wake the sleeping boy, then turned to say good-bye to Elsa. She embraced her friend in a hug.

"I'm sorry, but you cannot come back." Abram's words were firm, but he extended a hand to Vladimir. "We do thank you for your help. May God bless you in the blackness of this war."

Vladimir took the man's hand in both of his own and gave a nod that was fraught with emotion. He released Abram's hand, then looked from him over to Elsa.

"Please hear me. I know you're both afraid, but there is greater risk if I don't come back. You're dangerously low on supplies. And if the children are sick, you'll need medicine for them. I've brought you what I could find for now, but it's not going to be enough to sustain you much longer. Surely you must see that?"

"Should we leave?" Elsa's voice was a tragic whisper. She turned to look at her husband, still with Adele's arm around her waist for support. "Is it time?"

Abram shook his head. "No, my dear. It's not safe."

Vladimir's words were determined and hopeful as he continued. "There are no guarantees in war. We know this. Safety is a luxury no matter where we tread. But if you do change your mind about getting out, my contacts can help. I have a friend down at the docks. Julian. He loads the trucks for the dockside markets. When the time is right, he can help us arrange for your transport out of the city. Don't answer now. Think it over. We can discuss it the next time I return."

Elsa perked up, her eyes freezing on Adele's face. "You'll come back with him, Adele?"

"Of course."

Vladimir cut in with a stern, "No," at the same time. "Adele will not. But I assure you that I'll look in on you." When Abram looked ready to protest he added, "Only when necessary to see how you're getting on."

Abram gave a reluctant nod. "Thank you, for all you've done."

Vladimir pulled Adele away from Elsa, who latched onto her hand and kissed her palm. She finally let go as Vladimir pulled her into the stairwell.

"We won't open the door to you unless it's safe," Abram said, closing the door with Elsa standing tearfully in the background. "Please seal the cupboard on your way out."

He nodded. "I will."

"But what about the children? You won't even try to escape?" Adele threw herself against the door, even as it was bolted from the inside. "Abram, please! We can help you!"

Vladimir took her by the hand and dragged her up the stairs, her feet fumbling to find their footing on each uneven step.

"Let them go, Adele."

She shook her head and turned to go back down the stairs.

"Did you hear me?" He grabbed onto her shoulders and shook her, trying to get her attention. "Let them be! God will watch over them until I can visit again."

"Can't you convince them to get out? Look at them. Look at how they're living. Barely surviving? With no food? The children could be sick." She shook her head, fighting against the tears that were streaming down her face.

"Adele, I won't let you do this. You're in way over your head. It's far too dangerous for you to ever come back," he said, and began pulling the cupboard back against the wall.

Adele tugged at his elbows, anything to get him to listen to her. She struggled against the strength of his arms, trying in a feeble attempt to bypass him back down the stairs. But when the cupboard met up against the wall with a gentle *thud*, she stopped and stared at him.

"Adele, I care about you too much to let you put yourself at risk."

The finality of his words set in as the dust floated through the air.

"I must come back," she said, unable to stop the quiver she

felt overtaking her chin. "I have to do this. Don't you understand? My life has to matter for something bigger than myself."

Adele collapsed in his arms then. For the lost who were buried throughout the city, who had to scrape for food and hide like hunted animals, she sobbed against Vladimir's shoulder. And he seemed to understand. With the cupboard closed behind them in the dark butler's pantry, he held her. Without the necessity of words, Vladimir wrapped his strong arms around her and let her cry.

The world had gone dark.

CHAPTER TWENTY-FOUR

April 5, 1944

Spring came in on a cloud of bitter morning fog.

The sky had cried snow through February, then stayed frigid and unforgiving well into March. Adele wasn't surprised. Between the monotonous cadence of death and the playing of requiems day in and day out, she couldn't picture something as commonplace as the warmth of the sun ever making an appearance again. A cold April was the only fitting harbinger of another spring in Auschwitz.

Adele stood with the rest of the orchestra, lined up in the biting cold during morning counts, and stared back at a gaggle of squawking birds in the yard. They would fly overhead, gangly black things with horribly beady eyes and great wings that took them wherever they pleased. Adele hated them and everything they stood for; the freedom she couldn't taste, the absence of anything normal, the void of basic human decency.

She thought of visiting the Haurbechs in their dank basement. She remembered how caged they looked. How they eventually traded everything for a chance at freedom. And lost.

She thought of the things she had once considered normal. Her parents' Viennese castle of a house. Food. Water. A warm bed.

Distant memories. Adele no longer hoped to find normalcy in the world again. Even the flock of birds seemed to flit about, boastful of their freedom.

No one needed to tell her what she already knew. Their hope was shattered the moment Omara relayed the news that Alma Rosé had died the day before.

"What does this mean for the orchestra?" Marta whispered when the guards looked away down the length of the row. "Now that our conductor is gone?"

A shiver ran down Adele's spine at how normal it now seemed to talk of death. "How did she die?" Her breath froze on a fog.

"No one knows for sure," Marta whispered. "She was taken to the hospital wing after being stricken with a fever and terrible pains to the stomach. She died not two days later." Marta looked at the guards' backs before continuing. "Some say it was an infection. Others claim she was poisoned."

"Why would the SS kill a prisoner with poison?" Fränze's tone was soft with a noticeable quiver, as if she'd just realized the SS had found a terrible new way to dispose of the lot of them. "Was it because she used to stop our playing if the SS guards didn't listen? Maybe they found that action to be an impertinence." Her vulnerability was heartbreaking.

"Not the SS!" Marta raised her voice, drawing wary glances from several prisoners. She lowered it after hearing a *Shh!* echo behind them. "They wouldn't have cared enough to poison her for that. Anyone jealous of her position could have arranged to do it. But me? I don't think it was another prisoner." She shook her head. "I believe she drank that poison on her own."

"Suicide?" Adele stared straight ahead, numb.

"She's not the first one to do it in this godforsaken place, is she?"

"Poor Alma," Fränze whispered. "God grant her peace."

"*Hush.*" Omara gave the order a scant second before a piercing wind blew in over them. "Please, girls. They are pulling people out of line today."

Adele straightened her spine.

Pulling people out of line. The female guards were at work, barking at the shivering women standing before them, sending the sick to the chambers. And the orchestra was lined up among them. Adele knew what it meant; with their conductor now gone, they no longer had a distinction that might keep them alive.

The birds squawked again, drawing her eyes to their feathered turmoil in the yard.

"Adele!" Omara's voice snapped her back to attention. From her left side the older woman whispered. "Face front and pinch your cheeks," she said, her voice tinged with caution. "You need color."

Adele pinched both sides of her cheeks so that her knuckles turned white with the action. She prayed that at the very least, it would give some life back to what she knew to be a pair of woefully sunken-in cheeks and a severely ashy complexion stretched out where soft porcelain skin had once glowed.

The guards came closer.

They saw something they didn't like in a woman with pitiful coughs. She was wavering on her feet so that she could barely stand.

Adele turned away from the sight of the beating.

No more. I can't stand to see any more.

Adele saw Omara's shoulders stiffen as uniformed guards passed their row and looked at little Fränze first, then stopped to glare at the now slightly trembling Marta. None of them seemed to breathe for a moment. But the guards moved on and their fear could be abated for another morning.

"Back to the block, girls. Prepare to rehearse." Omara's voice sent Adele toward the path.

Adele began holding back coughs upon turning to the path

that led back to the music block. She received sidelong glances from one or two of the other women walking near her and turned her head down to expel a cough in the sleeve of her coat. She felt a hand fasten to her elbow as she walked.

"Are you sick?" Omara's voice was strong and steady next to her ear, yet hushed as she steered them with hurried steps down the path.

"No," she replied, gritting her teeth at the burning cold and the pain in her achy legs caused by trying to keep pace with Omara's swift footfalls. "I'm fine."

"Do not lie to me, Adele," she said, tossing glances around, tuned in to the carefully watching SS guards lining the barbed wire fenced path.

What good would it do to lie?

Adele's chest had been tight with congestion for a few days, though she'd managed to keep it hidden. Her sickly complexion could be explained; everyone else had the same gauntness where rosy cheeks had once been. But the coughing? It was a dead give-away. She was sickened with something. And whatever it was refused to yield.

"Why did you not tell me about this?" Omara asked, even as she whisked Adele into the block. The rest of the girls filtered in behind them. Omara pulled Adele to the back corner beyond the bunks and lowered her voice. "You're shaking. Even I can see it."

Adele ran her hands up and down her arms, trying to warm them.

The forced playing with the orchestra through the winter had taken its toll on Adele. Deterioration had been swift. She felt the immense sorrow when they were called to play each morning as the laborers left the camp. And when they returned in the evening, some with the body of a friend who was a victim of exhaustion or a gunshot to the head when they couldn't work fast enough, Adele could scarcely keep her eyes open to the death marching. Often she'd play with her eyes closed, refusing to give the SS the satisfaction of searing any more gruesome memories upon her heart. But though she could keep her eyes closed through the body of a song, she always had to reopen them at the end.

The fear she'd experienced in the roll call that morning was too much. "I don't think I can play today," was all she could manage to say before collapsing down on the cot, her forehead pressed up against the coolness of the wooden bunk. A couple of the girls gave her sideways glances.

Omara stood over her, her stare darting about her face. "You are sick."

Adele felt the emotion welling up in her throat. She gave a reluctant nod.

"Yes."

They both knew that typhus was running rampant through the adjacent blocks. It had been all winter, along with dysentery, tuberculosis, and cholera. And now, Adele's feverish nights and cough-filled days were becoming too pronounced to be hidden any longer. Regardless of the label put to the illness, it was a death sentence.

Omara should have stood miles away from her; it was the sensible thing to do. Instead, she took a seat next to her on the cot. Her hand came up to rest on Adele's forehead, the knotted joints surprisingly gentle and warm to the touch. "You're burning up, child."

Adele shivered and pulled the thin coat up tighter round her collar. "I know."

"Adele, I know you may not feel like it, but you must play. You know what they could do to you if you don't. They'll know you're sick."

They may as well call it what it was. "They'll send me to the gas chamber, you mean."

"Of course that's what I mean." Omara whispered as if it were some great secret, as if no one knew what was happening yards away from them. The notion made Adele want to laugh. Everyone knew, so what good was it to hide the truth on a whisper? If a prisoner was ill and couldn't work, then they were dealt with in swift fashion. But if it was typhus, the entire block could be exterminated, either by firing squad against the brick wall outside or the death chambers that were pumped full of toxic gas.

Whispering changed nothing.

"Adele, you would risk us all by hiding this from me?"

Adele sat on the edge of her cot, her legs dangling over the side, swinging with as little energy as she'd ever had. "I'm sorry. I didn't know—" Adele stopped, closing her eyes against the fear, and squeezed her hands around the bunk's wooden rail. "I didn't know whether you'd turn me in. I wasn't prepared to face it, didn't know if I could—"

"Look at me."

Omara's order was stern, but Adele still resisted. When she didn't look up, a tender caress tilted the underside of her chin. Adele's eyes popped open and she found her friend, with as much compassion as she'd ever seen, offering a gentle hint of a smile to soothe every sliver of fear that had been plaguing her.

"Adele, you are our family. Do you understand me? This family is more than the music we play for the SS. Our bond is stronger than the sharing of wooden bunks and a wash bucket in the same block. This, child, is our worship. To live and survive and play to God from the depths of our souls. This is the call that binds us. When we worship in the good times, it brings God joy. But worship in the midst of agony?" Her tongue clicked against the roof of her mouth and she shook her head. It was an action befitting the wisdom of the words she'd chosen. "That is authentic adoration of our Creator. An orchestra will worship together, as one body. As one song. A family must do no less."

"But I'm putting all of you at risk by being here." Adele stopped to cough, then returned her glance to Omara. "You said it yourself. I could cause everyone's deaths. If you don't turn me in, one of the others will."

"They will do no such thing or answer to me."

Omara stood then. She marched to the center of the block and began arranging chairs for their morning practice. Adele watched her, shocked that there could be such compassion when so much was at risk.

"But why?"

"If you have to ask, then you've learned nothing in this place."

She thought about it, hearing the scrape of the chairs against the ground and the indiscriminate drip of water from the corner of the leaky ceiling. "Tell me. Is that what I'm here for? To learn something about life? To dissect the most gruesome parts of humanity and find some philosophical meaning out of it all?"

Omara stopped short, her arms freezing with a chair still fused to her grip. "Have you not learned anything?"

Adele swallowed hard. "Tell me," she asked, burying a cough in her sleeve once more. "What were you doing that day I came back to the barracks with the snapped violin string?"

Omara's eyes shot up to meet hers. The room fell silent, as if nature too halted for an answer. The wind calmed outside. Voices along the path were lost. Even the dripping in the corner halted, giving an eerie silence to the shadows that collected around them.

"We all have our secrets, Adele."

"And I have shared mine with you," she replied softly, but with deliberate intention. "If we are to survive, mustn't we be able to trust one another?"

The elder woman said nothing for a moment. Instead, she weaved in between the other girls over to the stacks of instrument cases and retrieved Adele's violin case from the mix. She opened it and, with gentle hands that would have held a newborn with no less care, cradled the instrument in her arms. She walked back to Adele's side.

"Do you remember what I told you when you first arrived? If you want to live, then disappear," Omara cautioned her. "Do not give them a reason to notice you. If you are a member of the orchestra, then you play. Play at the selections. Play for executions. Play down to your soul at the SS concerts and then forget every single note in them thereafter. That is how you survive. Painters. Poets. Musicians . . . like every other artist in this place, you make yourself invisible to their memory but you continue to create because you *must*." She lifted an aged finger and pointed it to the center of her chest. "In here."

Invisible to a memory; how Adele wished that were the case for her now. But that would only make her think on childhood dreams, and such things did not exist. Not anymore. Her memories were real, alive and breathing, and seared onto her heart like nothing else could be. It began with that first night down by the docks and had continued in every moment since.

Adele had shut her eyes to many things since her arrival; they burned with memories now.

"Did you hear me?"

Adele stifled a cough. "Invisible. Yes."

"Your heart is still beautiful, child," Omara declared, and lovingly placed the instrument in her hands. "We will play indoors today, to stay in out of the rain. And you must rest as much as possible. Understand?"

She nodded.

Adele's hand circled around the neck of the violin and she felt the smoothness of the polished wood against her skin. It was such a contrast to the rough wood of her plank bed, its abrasive look and musty, diseased smell putrid to her senses. Her violin was so fine in contrast, so reminiscent of life before Auschwitz . . .

"I cannot do this," Adele whispered, shuddering as she cradled the violin to her chest and lowered her face to hide a flow of uncontrolled tears. "It's agonizing!"

"You must." Omara grabbed her by the wrist, not painfully so, but enough that it caught Adele's full attention. She pulled her arm down so that it was hidden between them.

"No! If death is going to take me, then I pray God allows it. After all of this—*I welcome it.*" Tears cut a path across the dirt on her face, and Adele imagined the tiny trails of water leaving her cheekbones looking striped. "It is of my choosing this way. I still have control over one thing at least."

"Adele." Omara's shoulders straightened, looking as though a rod had been placed against her back, giving her added strength. "When one enters the camp, there is a gate with a message across the road. What does it say?"

Adele closed her eyes, unable to answer.

"Answer me," Omara insisted, shaking the hand that encased her wrist.

"*Arbeit Macht Frei.*" Adele repeated the cruel message, her heart wishing to expel the words on a sob but her body not even able to produce enough strength to move beyond shedding silent tears.

"And you know what it means?"

"Yes." She could have spat at the ground each time she was forced to look at the cruel words affixed to the iron gate. "Work will set you free."

"And so it shall."

Adele shook her head, knowing that Omara was right, but praying to God that she'd not hate her gift because of it. "I'll not think of playing in that way."

"You must. Because one day we will be free. And we become free by living despite what they do to us. We live by working, and we work for God."

"But the children! Those poor souls stepping from the train ... they're innocent! Why should I live, just because I can play? Can we not exchange our lives for theirs, Omara?"

"You know it doesn't work that way, Adele," she said, her hand releasing the hold on Adele's wrist. She dropped her voice to a much softer whisper. "They'd only kill us both."

CHAPTER TWENTY-FIVE

---

*S*era spent most of her Monday morning pacing in the back office.

Michael Turner was the last person she'd ever expected to see on the front step of her gallery that night. Yet there he'd appeared, once again popping up in her life with a request to talk. After more than a year of no contact at all. And after a promising week she'd spent with a completely different man, who had stepped onto a plane for California without any idea her former fiancé had stepped back into her life but moments after he'd wrapped her in a good-bye kiss.

She looked at the antique clock on the gallery's back wall.

Noon.

How long had she been pacing? She looked over at the stool William had so casually sat on when they'd talked about Paris. She remembered his smile, tender and open. His hand, reaching out to connect with hers. She could almost picture the Bible on the worktable, with its worn and cracking binding making her heart melt for the time he'd spent studying the words within it.

Was she crazy to have pause about giving her heart to someone new?

"What am I doing?" she said aloud, stopping in her pacing to stare out the rain-speckled back windows, as if the overcast spring sky and the brick buildings in the alley would offer any kind of answer.

"You're driving yourself crazy, that's what." Sera didn't have to turn around to know that Penny was walking in her direction. She could hear the click of her assistant's heels as she moved from the doorway to the center of the room.

"You're a mess in a business suit," Penny noted, her voice softening as she approached. She placed a mug down on the desk at her side. "Brought you some coffee."

"How long have you been standing there?" she asked, unwilling to turn around and show her assistant that a few stray tears had escaped and gathered around her lower lids. She wiped at her eyes with the back of her hand.

"Long enough." Sera felt the warmth of Penny's hand as it lifted her own, leaving a scrap of paper in her palm. "Here."

She looked up, surprised that the pink notepaper had nothing but a telephone number scrawled in black ink. "What is it?"

"It's the number for Stahlworth and Martin."

"Stahlworth and Martin. Who are they?"

"His lawyers. They called this morning. Something about the painting."

"Did they say what they want?"

"No. I assumed it was something to do with payment for the gallery's involvement in the search. I saw you pacing a hole in the floor back here, so I said you'd call them back." Penny sighed. "You can't keep ignoring it, Sera."

"What are you talking about?"

"The fact that he hasn't called in two weeks." Penny plopped down in one of the chairs opposite the desk and sighed. "Because believe me, I know what it feels like to be jilted by a guy. It hurts when they don't call."

Sera doubted that seriously. "Penn, you have more dates than anyone I know. How could you understand?"

Penny folded her arms across her chest and sank back a little deeper into the chair. "That's why I understand, Sera."

Sera took a step closer and looked down at her always bubbly friend, whose eyes were brimming with tears. "Penn?"

She shook her head. "It's nothing."

"This is something," Sera said, and swiped a tissue from the box on the desk. She knelt down by her assistant's side and dabbed at a tear that had slid down her dimpled cheek. "What's the matter? Tell me."

Her assistant's voice almost squeaked out, "I don't want you to be hurt like I've been. You can still be lonely even when your social calendar is full."

"Penn—"

When Sera tried to cut in, she shook her head. "No—hear me out. Someone needs to tell you to pick up that phone. If he hasn't called you, then find out why. Something's changed in you these last weeks and I think it's because of him. You're not the same since you got off that plane from California."

Sera tried to lighten the moment by laughing it off. "Oh, I don't know. I'm still as neurotic about the painting as I ever was."

"That's not what I mean. This isn't about losing your dad, or a painting. I think you care about this guy."

"And what if I did?" She blinked. "You think I could have a future with William Hanover?"

"Don't you? Because I've seen the way he looked at you. And it's something I've never received from any man, not in all the dates I've had." Penny raised an eyebrow. "Are you willing to let your chance at happiness go without a fight? Or are you still hooked on the reemerged Michael Turner?"

Sera tugged at a stray lock of hair that had fallen across her forehead and tucked it behind her ear. "You don't know what you're talking about, Penn. I shouldn't have told you that Michael stopped by the gallery. You can't possibly understand how confusing this all is."

"I think I can, Sera. And believe me, I've looked all over Manhattan for anything that comes close to fitting William's mold. Integrity. Hardworking. A Christian man with a fierce love for his family and a smile I've only seen him offer when you walk in a room." Penny reached across the desk and retrieved Sera's cell phone, then dropped it in her palm. "So he's got some flaws. That makes him human. But regardless, guys of his pedigree just don't exist. You can't keep ignoring the truth because you're afraid of what might happen when you surrender your control. If you do that, you'll end up like your weepy assistant here." She tossed her tissue in the wastebasket and gave a hint of a smile. "And she has sworn off men. Except William Hanover. She's a fan of him for her friend Sera."

"You really think I should call?"

Penny tilted her head to one side. "You're asking me? I would have called the guy two weeks ago, for better or for worse."

"I'm going to have to tell William about the painting—that I've seen it. It wasn't a lie, but it feels like that now. I should have told him everything from the beginning."

"And if you do now, you'll be forced to trust him." Penny finished the thought with her take on the obvious. "I told you— you've been different these last few weeks. You've opened your heart to the possibility of love again. You've opened your heart back to God. I've noticed it in you. And it's beautiful, Sera. It makes me want to hope there's someone out there who might offer me more than Chinese takeout and a drink at the local bar."

Sera patted the strawberry blond waves that tipped Penny's shoulders. "You're worth it, Penn. I hope you know that."

She smiled, a soft curve of the lips that twinkled of hope and hurts that were hidden behind a usually sunny disposition. "Let's take care of your life first, huh? Then we can work on mine."

"Sweet friend," Sera said, wrapping her in a hug. "There's nothing to work on in you. God made you perfect."

Penny hugged her back, whispering close to her ear, "How can we know what might happen, Sera, unless we give God a chance to work? You could miss out on love in your life because you're playing it safe. Do you think that's what Adele did? Play it safe?"

"I don't know."

"There's only one way to find out. Tap into that strength you have. It's already there." Penny pulled back, then rose and began walking toward the office door. "You just haven't summoned it in a while."

Strength. Sera took a deep breath. *I thought I had it once, in droves. Do I have any left?*

"I'll leave you alone."

"Penn?" Sera caught her assistant just as she was about to close the glass door.

"Yeah?" she said, leaning back with her hand on the antique brass knob.

"Thanks."

"Don't mention it," she noted softly, her bobbed curls bouncing off her shoulders as she walked through the door. "At least not now. Just remember me at Christmas-bonus time."

The door closed with a soft *click*, and Sera was left alone. With her phone in one hand and the piece of paper burning a hole in the other, she exhaled long and low.

Well, Lord. This is it—time to trust.

—

"Stahlworth and Martin. How may I direct your call?"

"Yes. This is Sera James," she answered, refusing to fumble over the syllables even though she felt the annoyance of butterflies wreaking havoc on her insides. "From the Sera James Gallery in New York. I'm returning a call from this morning."

"I'll connect you with Mr. Stahlworth. One moment, please."

Sera bit the corner of her thumbnail while she waited for the secretary to connect her to the law partner's phone line. She inhaled deep, then exhaled as her feet began their usual pacing across the back of the office. It wasn't a moment before a gravelly voice came on the line.

"Miss James. Thank you for returning my call."

"Yes, Mr. Stahlworth. I'm not sure what this is about. I'd have expected Mr. Hanover to call me directly. He usually does."

"Well, he asked that we handle the formalities from this point on."

"Formalities?" Sera paused. It wasn't a word she'd hoped to hear.

"Well, to arrange for payment, of course. Even though you weren't the one to locate the painting, Mr. Hanover has instructed us to pay you a base fee of ten thousand dollars, for your trouble. And then we'll make arrangements for the wire transfer when the inheritance is settled with the courts. I understand that your rate is one percent of the estimated value of the find."

"Mr. Stahlworth." Sera sat on the nearest stool. Nothing was making sense. "I'm not sure I understand what you're referring to. We haven't found the painting yet."

The man cleared his throat but said nothing.

Sera waited breathlessly, unsure whether her heart was actually thumping right out of her chest. But to ask at all and have what appeared to be consideration on the lawyer's part was mind-numbingly suspenseful in the moment. How could she expect to breathe?

"Sir?"

"Miss James, you are perhaps used to clients who have no aversion to the public eye. The art world can be fickle, I know.

And very public. But in the interest of Mr. Hanover's privacy, we are only able to give you certain information to ensure that the media is not brought into this. I was asked to get involved to tie up loose ends on the matter."

"Loose ends?" Is that what she was? "I don't understand. My assistant and I have been doing everything we can to find the painting. If there's a problem with the fact that we haven't delivered on it yet, I can assure you that we're on the right track."

"Miss James, William Hanover filed suit against the owner of the painting this morning."

Sera's heart did somersaults in her chest. She dug her nails into the wood of the worktable just to stay upright. "What did you just say?"

"William Hanover has filed formal papers to have the owner of the painting appear in court over the matter of his late grandfather's estate. He's contesting the will that has left the Hanover estate to her."

"That can't be true." Sera's heart wouldn't believe it. Not now. Not after the time they spent together and the promise he'd offered. Not now that she'd risked everything to place her trust in him.

"I'm sorry to be the one to tell you, Miss James, but you led him right to her."

"But I had no idea . . ." She heard papers rustling in the background. The man sounded quite preoccupied.

"Yes, well. Mr. Hanover was quite sorry for the inconvenience and wished me to convey that to you." More rustling papers mixed with the sound of fingers tapping a keyboard. "Can you be kind enough to send my secretary your banking information? I've left our e-mail address with your assistant."

"I don't believe this . . ." She shook her head, tears threatening to gather in her eyes. She clenched her fist, wishing to pound it on the table. "This can't be happening," she mumbled, forgetting that the man was still on the other end of the line.

He lied to me. Lied . . . and after everything I shared with him?

Sera's hand flew up to cover a bottom lip that had begun quivering on its own.

"Will there be anything else, Miss James?"

"Yes," she answered, and moved her fingertips away from her mouth just far enough to speak. "The painting? Does he have it?"

"No. But we're sure the woman does. We've given her a set amount of time for her attorneys to respond. If she does, and we expect she will, then we go to court and the state of California will rule on the matter. And when they rule in favor of my client, Mr. Hanover has instructed that we wire you your finder's fee."

"I don't want any money." Sera coughed over the emotion she knew was in her voice. She cleared her throat. "But I would like her name, please."

Calm down, Sera. It's going to be okay.

The words flooded over her heart.

But was it really going to be okay? Could her heart take another blow?

She brushed the moisture away from her cheek, and with a straightened spine and strengthening resolve, she grabbed the pencil from the loosely piled bun at the back of her head and readied it against the notepaper Penny had given her.

"I'm not entitled to give out that information."

"I think you are. My job is to find the painting, right?"

"We're relieving you of your services and paying out a hefty bonus to soothe your injured pride, Miss James. There's nothing about the painting's owner in that deal."

Sera pinched the bridge of her nose in frustration. "Mr. Stahlworth, you're not hearing me. I don't care about the money. I just want the painting. I've been searching for it since I was eight years old. I don't want to get involved in the court proceedings and I don't want to make any trouble for the Hanovers. I assure you of that. But if this woman you speak of has the original, I have to see it. That's all I want. To see it one more time."

The man was quiet for a moment, as if thinking it over. "He mentioned that you had an investment in finding the painting. I wasn't aware that you'd already seen it once before."

"Neither was he." Sera paused. Hoping. Praying that something good would come of the hurt she'd experienced all over again.

He cleared his throat again, then began, "I want you to know that there's nothing illegal in giving you information that is now part of the public record. Let's just state that first. And Mr. Hanover gave no instruction against it, so I feel that I can share the name of the defendant."

"I'll take any information you can share. Gratefully."

"The woman is quite old. She lives in Paris, and to our understanding, her health does not permit travel. Under the circumstances, you'd likely have to go to her."

Without a second thought as to the barrier of traveling to Paris on her own, Sera laid the rest of her broken heart out on the table. What good was it now?

"Fine," she said, pencil at the ready. "Just tell me how to find her and I'll be on the next plane."

CHAPTER TWENTY-SIX

⁓

September 1, 1944

Jt had been five years since Adele had walked home with Vladimir from the dance hall. Five years since their journey apart had begun. She thought back on it now, seeing Vladimir and the old Adele she used to be, alive now only in her memories. She turned the golden butterfly clip over in her fingers as she lay on her cot and noticed how tarnished and dirty the gold was in comparison to the gleaming gift she remembered receiving so long ago.

Except for when she was required to be somewhere, Adele had spent the better part of the last week isolated on her cot. Had stopped saying much of anything to the group. In fact, if she were honest with herself, she'd quit living. She'd not ventured outside except for the mandatory morning counts, and even then she drifted in and out of a sense of bemused consciousness. She still played each day, but her efforts were lifeless as a leaf floating on a gust of wind. Her chair was occupied and her violin still cried with the rest of the orchestra, but Adele felt herself slipping away, further and further from reality.

Her will was no longer shaken; it was dead.

"Get up, Adele."

She turned slightly, her body too taxed to roll over on her side so she could look at her friend.

"Did you hear me?" Omara came over to the bunks and began tugging her shoulders up off the cot.

"What's the matter?"

"Get up. You must come with me now." Omara took a scratchy wool blanket from the overhead bunk and wrapped it around her shoulders. "Here. This will keep you from getting chilled."

Adele shook her head. "I'm hot."

Omara didn't mean to argue, apparently. She tucked the blanket around her anyway. "You can wear it under your coat and they won't even see it. Can you walk?"

"I think so." She tottered like a baby learning to stand for the first time, but was steadied by Omara's strong arms until her feet were firmly planted on the ground. "Where are we going?"

"To Canada."

"The warehouses?" Adele glanced out their small block window in the direction of the warehouse section of the camp. "But why there? Why now?"

"I have something to show you, Adele. Will you come with me?" Adele noted something strange in Omara's voice and though her gaze lingered beyond the last words, Adele felt compelled to obey.

She nodded and allowed her friend to lead her out into the broken, early morning light of dawn. Adele walked in a daze. They moved past the execution wall without a second glance. When had that sight become normal?

Omara ushered her to the back of the warehouse where she'd first stayed all those months ago. She remembered it now, that feeling of shock she'd had at seeing the overabundance of wares stacked ceiling high. Her ghostly pale hand ran over those piles now, the worn leather of the shoes in the pile feeling cold and withered against her skin.

They came to a door, small and insignificant as it was, tucked in the back corner behind a tall bin of clothing, its wood aged and shrouded in shadows.

"What is this?" Adele turned to look at Omara.

"Go inside." The elder woman tilted her head, giving the direction with a stoic expression on her face. Adele trusted her. And because of this, she placed her palm around the aged metal knob and turned. The door creaked, groaning as it opened.

She squinted. There was natural light from a frosted glass window set high up on the brick wall. As her eyes adjusted, Adele saw a small brick-walled room, tucked away beneath the wooden stairwell overhead. It was sparsely equipped, with only a small desk and chair in the corner, a single desk lamp in the back.

"What is this place?"

She stood, arms pulled in tight around her middle to ward off the damp chill in the air.

"It is there," Omara instructed, standing back in the doorway. She pointed toward the stairway. "Round the corner."

Adele looked at her friend and found her expression oddly void of emotion. She stood as a fixture in the shadowed alcove beyond the door. Omara nodded her forward. She obeyed, turning and walking, the wooden floor creaking with each cautious step.

When she got around the corner, Adele's mouth fell open, jaw dropping. Her heart rate quickened. Her hand flew up to cover her mouth.

There before her on the wall, seared with bright paint and hanging against the concrete background of the inner wall, was an image of her own face.

Adele approached it with caution, as if it were a mirage that would quickly vanish were she to even breathe. How could this vision of beauty exist in such an evil place? The painting was too stunning to have been rendered by an amateur. It was the face she'd seen in the mirror years before she came to Auschwitz—the ghostly image of a young woman who'd not been battered by the horrific truths of the real world. It was a woman who was young and strong and wide-eyed, confidently holding a violin.

Adele touched shaking fingertips over the image of herself, heart thumping, legs nearly unable to hold her upright. The only thing that didn't fit was that the girl in the image had been shorn of her hair. Adele ran her hand over the tuft of dirty hair at her nape, then touched cautious fingers to her cheeks. What did she look like now? Did she have pale skin and woefully sunken eyes like the rest of the girls? It had been so long since she'd looked in a mirror. So long since she'd seen that girl. Would Vladimir recognize his butterfly now? She was so . . . wounded.

Adele crumpled to kneel on the floor. Omara came up behind her and wrapped supportive arms around her shoulders. Adele looked past the painting of herself, noticing for the first time that there were other paintings—small drawings of the trauma-stricken faces of prisoners working under the dark shadow of armed guards, of stone-faced children in striped uniforms, all with a cold, lifeless sky behind them. Some appeared to be painted on makeshift wooden canvases, others painted on the walls of the closet-sized room. There were words, beautiful, poetic words too, etched in the wooden stairway and scratched even in the ground at her feet.

"What . . ." She sobbed on the words, looking back to the masterfully rendered painting of herself. "What is this place?"

"My dear child. This painting is how I see you. It's how we all see you. Do you understand? There is still beauty left in the world. It is here."

They looked around the room in unison. She was still in shock. Humbled. Taken by the beauty born from ashes that fell from the sky.

"Who?"

Omara seemed to understand that she was asking about the many images. Who created them? Whose words were those?

"The artist can't be killed, Adele. The men and women whose hearts have cried in this place—they couldn't stay away. The artists came here in droves. At risk of death . . ." Omara sniffed. Was she crying too? "Some are gone now. But their legacy lives on. There is art like this hidden all over the camp."

"And the painting?"

Omara tilted her head toward the door. "I found everything there, in that hellish warehouse out there. It wasn't enough to paint on the brick. The emotion wouldn't show like I'd hoped it would. I took wood slats from the bins for the canvas. Paints I found tossed in suitcases. A brush made from the piles of hair."

"Please," she mumbled. "Don't tell me any more."

Adele looked at the image of the beautiful violinist with the shaved head, wondering if she could ever be that beautiful again. She ran her fingers over the bottom of the painting, the paint somehow feeling alive as it grazed the scars on her palms.

"All this time, I thought you were a music professor. I just assumed . . ."

"That I could only play the cello." Adele saw Omara's face break into a smile next to her, the laugh lines creating deep creases at her mouth and eyes. Their cheeks rested together for the briefest of seconds. "Ah, and that is why God gives a variance of gifts. The cello may have kept air in my lungs here, but"—she pointed to the painting—"my heart has always belonged to the brush."

Omara released her for a moment and turned her shoulders so that they faced each other. "Adele, I brought you here for a reason."

She brushed a tear away from her cheek. "And what is that?"

"I must tell you that there is hope. Hope for tomorrow," she whispered, leaning to cradle Adele's face in her hand. "There is hope in God."

Adele's heart gave way then. In a rush, the vault she'd hidden deep within finally released the hold on the anguish she'd buried there. She crumpled against Omara, resting her cheek on her chest as the wounds she'd endured prompted fresh tears.

"I have prayed . . ." She sobbed, "I prayed the moment I stepped from the train. But this? This is a desert! You've shown me beauty. I see that it can exist in such a place. But why, after all of the agonizing prayers of His people—why is God silent?"

"Adele?"

Omara's voice was soft. A caress. A place of respite in the midst of their seemingly never-ending nightmare.

"Look at me, child." The woman's voice held such a tender note that Adele felt they could be miles away from Auschwitz in that moment. "There is to be a concert in early October. High-ranking Third Reich officials will be present."

Adele's voice hitched in her throat. She looked up. "My parents—"

"Calm down," she said, raising a hand to quiet her. "I know nothing of your parents' presence at the concert. That is not why we are here."

"Why then?"

"Now that Birkenau is joined by the first Auschwitz camp, they've asked that you play a solo in the orchestra concert. So you see, God is not silent. He has secured you another day. Now, you must get well so that you can practice. Alma is gone, God rest her soul, but it does not spell your end too."

"But how can I play?" Adele pulled at the dirtied uniform she now wore. "Like this? Look at me . . . I'm a ghost."

"I have asked the other girls for help. Marta has a friend in the kitchens and she will bring extra soup for you. They will smuggle potatoes into the block."

"No. Even if they could find any potatoes, I can't let them risk their lives for me. It's a death sentence if they're caught stealing food."

"Then they won't get caught."

Adele shook her head. "But they're starving. We all are. How can I ask them to bring me food?"

"They would do it for you, Adele, just as you would for them. The food will make you strong. Fränze and the others will watch over you as you walk to the gates each day, making sure you do not stumble or appear sick before the SS. Then we will all shield you from practice and allow you to rest in the block during the day. What I need you to do is to play the music in your mind. I need you to pray. Seek God. And above all, allow Him to heal you."

Adele's chin rose, pulling her eyes back to the images on the walls. She thought of the lost as her gaze traveled around the room. She heard the violin cry as scores of people walked the long road from the platform to the crematorium. Saw images of Dieter, and the Haurbechs, and her noble Vladimir, all flashing before her. She felt the coolness of the air in their secret garden, saw the butterfly tossing its kaleidoscope wings on a breeze as spring was renewed.

"You will agree to this?"

Adele decided then, with images of beauty cascading before her, that she must accept Omara's kindness, knowing she was going to die in Auschwitz. This would be her last performance . . . Finally, her soul spent, Adele was ready to let go.

"Yes," she said. "I will."

"And you understand why I have brought you here?"

Adele glanced up at the painting again, feeling the good-bye bleed over her insides.

This is it, God. Isn't it? You want me to play once more.

Just once—for You.

"I understand, Omara. And yes." She rose up from the floor with renewed strength, palms wiping the wetness from her face. "I will play."

CHAPTER TWENTY-SEVEN

— ✦ —

October 7, 1944

The explosions rang out in the afternoon.

Dust rained down from the ceiling with the force of the blasts and shook the walls around them. Adele's attention was ripped from the rehearsal in the music block, as was everyone else's, and was diverted to the sounds of screaming and popping gunfire that had erupted outside.

The orchestra froze into an eerie silence with instruments half raised, eyes and ears piqued with the awareness that something was very wrong.

Fränze breathed out into the silence, "What was that?" The tiny flute player's whisper was barely audible above the roar of activity outside.

When the walls shook with another loud boom, everyone dropped their instruments and flew to the only window in the block. Adele instead ran to the door, thinking they could get a better understanding of what was happening if she looked outside.

She poked her head out the door only to be yanked back a second later.

"Get back, Adele!" Omara stood with hands on hips and nostrils flared as she bellowed the order. "I have not fought to keep you all alive just to lose you now." She pointed to the back of the block and began ushering the group backward with forceful hands. "Everyone to the back wall. Don't you think bullets can pierce wood? Can they not destroy flesh and bone?"

More pops of gunfire in rapid succession and agonized screams made the group jump in unison. Terrified squeals permeated the air as several of the younger girls cried out. Marta stood over them, burying the younger Fränze under the protection of her torso as she looked up to Adele. The terrified flash of fear Adele saw there sent a sickening chill up her spine.

They stared, knowing what the sound was.

"*Machine-gun fire?*" Marta mouthed the words. Adele nodded, to which the older girl squeezed her eyes shut and whispered, "God help us."

The heart in Adele's chest quaked at the very thought of defenseless prisoners running from a hail of machine-gun fire aimed to mow them down. But why? Why now? She couldn't make sense of it. The Nazis had the gas chambers and their random executions. They had the harsh labor assignments, day in and day out. Even starvation and the rapidly spreading effects of disease worked in their favor. So why would they use up their artillery resources when they had so many other means of disposing of prisoners?

The orchestra was huddled together like sardines as each girl tried to burrow down against the girl squeezed up next to her. They were a terrified mass of muffled cries and trembling flesh, all lumped together as if the girl closest to the dirt on the floor would be safe.

Marta shouted over the noise, "Adele, what is happening?"

"I don't know," she said, patting a hand to little Fränze's head. The poor girl had taken to covering balled fists over her ears with such force that her knuckles were white. "Stay here," she instructed to the now silently crying Marta, and pecked a kiss to Fränze's temple. "All of you stay here. I'll find out what's happening."

Omara had moved to the door. Cautiously, she'd cracked it open and stared out at what Adele could only imagine as a new definition of Nazi horror. The woman must have heard her approach, as she turned with a dexterity that decried her advanced years and began shouting.

"Adele." Omara shoved her back again toward the corner with the other girls, a bit more roughly this time. "Get back! Do you not hear the gunfire? It's not safe!"

Adele righted her balance and took several cautious steps toward the door again. Something terrible had happened, that was clear to all. But unless she could find out whether it was safe to stay put, they could all be sitting ducks. Gunfire was frightening enough, but if their building was bombed and the walls burst into flames, their only hope might be to take their chances and make a run for it.

No one would survive if the wooden roof on the block turned into an inferno.

Omara had taken the scene quite badly. Adele could see the strain in a muscle that flexed in her jaw, as if she was grinding down her teeth with bottled emotion.

"Omara . . ." She reached a hand out to touch it to their block leader's shoulder.

The woman didn't respond to Adele's fingertips as she'd expected. Instead, she opened the door a few inches wider so that they might both look out and said, "There. If you must see it. Have another look at death."

The terror outside the block walls could only be described as a war zone. In seeing the carnage before her, Adele imagined somehow that the front lines of battle had been redrawn and the Red Army, as had been rumored by the prisoner population for weeks, had broken through to challenge the Germans on their own turf.

Is this it, God? Are we saved?

Another explosion sent a tremor to the back walls. More dust floated down from the aged wood ceiling as the younger girls cried out.

Adele's breath shuddered in her lungs. "Is it the Red Army?" She could scarcely speak with the hope of it all.

Omara shook her head.

"Then the British? Or the Americans? Please tell me they're here to save us."

The older woman scoffed. "Do you see? It is not someone who would save us! We are on our own here." Omara threw the words back in Adele's face, her usually controlled countenance now terse, her violently darting pupils looking almost manic as they searched her face.

"But this could be it—we could all be saved! Did you not hear it? Bombs exploding and machine-gun fire? What else could it be but that we are to be rescued!"

One of the girls shouted out in response to Adele's declaration, "Oh, merciful God! We are saved!"

Adele felt a rush of energy, a blast of adrenaline that instantly coursed through her veins, sending a shock to jump-start her limbs. She felt like she could fight, if need be. Whether born of courage or pure stupidity, she couldn't have deciphered. All she knew was that her legs wanted to run outside and her palms twitched, longing to be armed with a weapon that would allow her to fight back. "Surely God has sent—"

"Foolish girl! No one is coming."

Adele could see nothing beyond what she wanted to. "Omara, what would you have me see? Our hell here is over! Oh God . . . it's over!"

"It is a revolt, Adele!"

The words hit her like a fierce smack to the face.

"What . . . ?"

Her body froze, in panic or disbelief, and she stood numbed by the fact that the war zone in front of her could only have one winning side. She knew which side that would be.

The rest of the girls looked on from their perch in the corner, like a gaggle of frightened birds that couldn't hope to ever find themselves uncaged. They kept their eyes fixed on her, despite Omara's repeated order for them to lower their heads, and stared back as the truth suffocated all shreds of hope.

"What are you saying, Omara?"

The older woman closed the door to a miniscule crack when some of the activity again came closer to their door. "I am saying, Adele, that a prisoner revolt has begun. The members of the *Sonderkommando* at Crematorium IV made plans to fight back. They learned that they were to be executed and a new group brought in to take their place."

She shook her head. "But why? Why would the SS do that?"

"It is simple logic to them. I don't pretend to understand evil. But the *Sonderkommando* have seen too much. These prisoners can be elected to die the moment they step from the train or five months in the future. What choice do they have? They are charged with cleaning out the gas chambers and feeding the ovens with the evidence. They are witnesses to death, and a witness is a dangerous thing to the Nazis. The prisoners decided the time was right. The time to fight back is now."

It was shock all over again for Adele, but this time it connected to a memory—the memory of a night at the SS guards' Solahütte resort and the strange behavior of her usually wise and controlled friend. She thought of a morning the summer before when she'd snapped a string on her violin and come rushing back to the block, only to find that the odd behavior had returned with a visitor in the music block.

And it all became clear. Omara was involved in the revolt.

"You have been planning this, haven't you?"

Omara looked her square in the face and without hesitation nodded just once.

"Women have been smuggling supplies, weapons, and gunpowder from the ammunitions factory since before you arrived.

Little bits here and there—whatever could be hidden with the bodies of prisoners who died and were being carried back to the camp at night. They were smuggled to the men in the adjoining camp, on the bodies being carried to the crematorium. It was the only way."

Adele's heart sank.

They weren't saved. No one was coming to free them. No one was there to fight for them, except sorely weakened prisoners with makeshift weapons. And Omara, the only person she could rely on anymore, was involved. If they lost, which they would, the Nazis would surely take her to the gas chamber for it.

Oh God! I lost my family, my Vladimir . . . Am I to now lose the only person I have left in the world?

The physical pain caused by the heartache in her chest shocked her. As they stood by the cracked door, with hell erupting outside, she could see no way out. Except to fight.

Adele wiped at the tears that had been free-flowing from her eyes. "Fine. We fight," she said, and stepped up to Omara. "Give me a weapon."

"No."

"I'm ready, Omara. Let me fight with you."

Omara's face softened. As a mother might feel proud of her child, she raised her hand and brushed it over the lifeless hair hanging down at Adele's shoulder. Her fingertips brushed the strands as if they were made of the finest spun gold. The action inspired hope that she'd relent, but still Omara shook her head.

"No, Adele. Not this time. You must stay here."

"But I can do this! Let me help you," she begged as her hands curled around to pinch the skin of Omara's arms until her nails dug into the woolen fabric of her dress. "We've made it this far together. Don't you understand? There's not the least bit of hope left in this place. It has been snuffed out by evil. Surely your soul feels the absence of God in this place. Must I cry out to Him that . . . *I cannot go on?*"

She screamed the words with vehemence and, instead of showing courage, revealed anguish. She felt her hands ball to fists as the truth finally came out.

It had been building up for so impossibly long, through every march at the gates and the viewing of each family torn apart before her very eyes, that her soul had withered beyond repair. No amount of water could save it. And no revolt could make her fear death. She'd overcome losing everyone and everything that had mattered to her. She'd played. Practiced for the final performance that was now just days away. She'd even recovered from her illness with a renewed fervor to play in her final concert. But with the hail of gunfire popping outside the block, all melted away. Now she was ready to go down fighting instead of playing music.

Adele's chest rose and fell with such a ferocity that she wasn't sure she'd be able to keep breath in her lungs at all.

"Take me with you," Adele demanded. "I know you're going out there to fight. I beg of you to let me fight at your side."

Omara surprised her then, for her lips curved into the faintest hint of a smile. Even in moments of triumph—when they'd played at the SS guards' party or had reveled in the particularly beautiful moment of the music having carried them into communion with God—she'd not allowed it. The only time Adele had caught a ghost of a smile was in the shadow of the painted room.

"You have your whole life ahead of you." Omara's eyes seared as she spoke. "And I'll not allow that to be snuffed out, not when I can prevent it."

"I have no life ahead of me . . . I am already dead." Adele's sobs racked her body and she collapsed, face buried against Omara's shoulder.

"You are not, child. Hush. Hush now," she whispered, and ran a hand down the length of the hair at her nape. She continued soothing with honeyed words as the world exploded in fire around them. Adele clung to the older woman, her dear friend, their camp mother, and finally allowed the last two years to escape from the suppression of her walled heart. She cried for what seemed like hours, though the world had not stopped warring around them as mere seconds ticked by.

Omara whispered in her ear, speaking soft words of hope and restoration.

"You have been chosen for a special purpose." Her hand, trembling though it was, brushed over Adele's forehead until she was forced to look up into her friend's eyes. "Hear me, child. I never had a daughter. And I never had lofty dreams like most. I hoped to marry for love and perhaps, one day, to be gifted a child of my own . . . to find beauty in God's creation and worship Him all the days of my life." She stared off at some distant point on the wall, as if the memory of a dream had somehow come alive on the back wall. "But it wasn't to be, was it? I came here. Life never asked me what I wanted, so I gave up on those dreams. And because of the loss of them, because of the loss of so many others in this place, I now entreat you to listen to me as you've never listened before." She put her hands on Adele's shoulders. "Adele, you must go and make me proud by *living* . . . because God makes no mistakes. He gifted me with my heart's desire, here, in this place. He gifted me a daughter like you."

The words pierced Adele's heart.

Marina Von Bron was but a distant memory in Auschwitz. Adele had not thought of her in so long, but she pictured her now. Hearing the words solidified the fact that Omara was more a mother to her than she'd ever known, or would ever know again.

"You must promise me—you will live. That is all I ask. That is all that will make me happy and put my soul to rest," she said, and then turned to the group of trembling musicians in the corner. "This is your family now. Keep them safe, hmm? I charge this orchestra to you. You will play for both of us. You are their mother now."

"I can't . . ." Adele's heart wept right along with her eyes.

"You must. Lead them. Protect them. Stay together," Omara charged, her voice unwavering. "Do you hear me, Butterfly?"

Adele's head shot up at the mention of the nickname Vladimir had given her so long ago. Omara knew she'd taken her butterfly clip out each night, had turned it over in her hands, had clung to it in sleep. She knew it spoke of Adele's past. But the wisdom in mentioning it now had a far greater impact than if Omara had told her to live and, God willing, find that Vladimir had lived too.

"Tell me you'll keep our family together, Adele. No matter what. I love all of my girls."

Were Marta and Fränze crying too? Were the other girls' hearts breaking as hers was?

With a chin that trembled and eyes that clamped shut on emotion, Adele could speak not a word. But she nodded. With the barest measure of hope that could be scraped up from the bottom recesses of her soul, Adele committed to survival on behalf of her friend.

God only knew if she could honor the promise.

"Good." Omara said the single word as if it was a contract, then burst forth into action. She rushed over to her cello case and flung open the top. She pulled a small, rusted garden shovel from the recesses of the case.

"What are you going to do with that?" Had she possessed it all along? Indeed, it made a paltry weapon when Omara faced the barrage of machine-gun fire beyond the block.

"The time is now for me to do my job," she said, clutching the tool in her hand as if it were the sword of the archangel Gabriel himself. "I must go."

Adele felt the seconds ticking away, knowing they may never see her again. There were so many things she wanted to say, so many reasons to thank her.

"Omara, wait!" Adele reached out and grabbed her friend's elbow.

She turned then and, thinking of the only possession she had left in the world, darted to the pile of discarded instruments and chairs that had been overturned in the center of the room. Adele found her violin case and ripped open the velvet lining.

She ran her fingertips over the delicate wings of the clip.

Butterfly . . . Vladimir's voice whispered in her heart.

Adele crossed back over to her friend and, after kissing the clip to her lips, pressed it into Omara's free hand. "Take it—my promise to you."

Omara looked at her, then to the group of girls in the corner, and gave a last nod to them. And with that, she was gone, faded into the smoke and carnage outside the block.

Adele closed the door against the cries of chaos outside and rushed over to the family that remained in the block.

"Heads down, girls. Until it's over," she ordered, Omara's brand of courage feeling foreign to her heart. She wrapped her arms around the trembling group. "Heads down."

CHAPTER TWENTY-EIGHT

*S*era rushed from the subway back to the gallery, repeatedly checking her watch. It was nearly seven o'clock.

If she hurried, she'd have just enough time to grab her mislaid cell phone and get back to Manhattan's Upper East Side before her client's show ended.

A cool breeze brushed her face. The air smelled like rain.

Sera walked faster, though her heels were unforgiving for the pace. She tried not to think of the evenings she and William had walked past Roosevelt Park together. She blocked out the remembrance of hand-holding and soul-connecting under the overhang of the trees, and prayed that the memory of William Hanover would fade. She needed to get back to the Metropolitan Museum and she didn't need this distraction.

As if he'd read the words etched on her heart, there he was, sitting alone on the stoop, waiting under the glow of the streetlight. She squinted through the fallen shadows of dusk, trying to figure out if her eyes were playing tricks.

William hopped up off the stoop when he saw her.

She halted for a moment, her keys fused in a tight grip, feet frozen on the sidewalk. How was it that a West Coaster could drop into Manhattan whenever he pleased?

"William?"

"Hi, Sera."

"What are you doing here?" Her feet were somehow unable to breeze past him. She stopped an honest minute, long enough to wait for an answer. But feeling the prick of tiny raindrops from the laden clouds overhead, she took careful steps toward the stoop.

"Penny closed up. She said you were on your way back and I could wait, so . . ." He shifted his feet and came a step closer.

He looked nervous.

"I meant, what are you doing in New York?" she clarified as a soft rumble of thunder sounded in the distance. Their eyes sailed to that corner of the sky for a brief second before they came back to the awkwardness of conversation.

"I had meetings, lawyers and such. Business."

His hands were buried in his jeans pockets and his hair was mussed, as if he'd been running his hands through it for who knows how long he'd been sitting there, waiting for her to come back. She tried not to notice the cool spice of his cologne, or how close he stood.

Sera fumbled the keys and nearly dropped them before she found the right one. The gold key flashed in the dim light overhead and she took the stairs, two at a time, until the glass door was in front of her. She pushed the key into the lock.

The warmth of William's hand encased hers before she could turn it. Raindrops cooled the burning heat of her wrist and she froze, the nearness of him unexpected. The touch was swift in breaking down the careful defenses she'd been fighting so hard to maintain for the weeks they'd been apart.

"You are going to look at me eventually, aren't you?"

She exhaled and took a chance by tilting her chin in his direction. Her eyes met with the hopeful blue of his, though they were stormy now—seeking, even? She'd never be able to ignore them, it seemed. Something in them captured her even now.

"What are you doing here, William?"

"You haven't answered my calls."

She shrugged. "I've been busy."

"Busy for the last month?"

Sera could hear the roughness in his voice. His whispers held a tint of anger at having been put off.

Feeling the same hurt, she fired back, "How can you lecture me? You didn't call me for weeks after you left New York! Then I get a call from your lawyers?"

She looked him square in the face. She wasn't tough. He knew it too, or would the instant her chin quivered. But if there was any strength about her as Penny had said, Sera would stand up to him for how he'd lied. For Adele and Vladimir. For everything he made her feel again and then snatched away again just as quickly.

"I've called you at least a dozen times."

"I had a show to arrange." She wiggled her hand out of his grip to turn the key in the lock and then brushed past him, flicking on the lights as she marched into the gallery's front display room. Her heels clicked, creating a crisp echo against the tall ceilings.

"I know. I heard," he said, closing the door gently as he followed her inside. His shoes made light thuds on the creaking hardwood. "An installation at the Met? Congratulations."

"Yes. Well, finding lost paintings isn't all I do with my time." She dropped her evening bag and raspberry silk wrap on the oblong worktable, then moved into the office without turning round to face him.

Calm down, Sera.

It has to be this way. He lied to you.

She began sifting through stacks of papers and books that crowded her desktop.

This is your chance to make a clean break . . . and let him go.

She took a deep breath as she looked for her cell phone. After spying it under a vintage copy of *Gardner's Art through the Ages*, she snatched it up and turned to make a quick exit. What she didn't expect was to crash head-first into the man, his feet planted on the ground, standing sturdy as a redwood blocking her path.

"Please. Let me go."

William folded his arms across his chest—he wasn't going anywhere. "You can't put off talking to me if I'm right in front of you."

"Let me pass," she said, frustrated, her balance wavering on high heels.

"First, let me explain."

She exhaled and entreated softly, "Please. There's nothing to explain. Just leave it alone."

"Uh-uh." He shook his head and with a softened voice continued. "I won't let you shut me out, Sera James. Not this time."

"You used me, William," she reminded him, which seemed to create a twinge in him, but he said nothing. "You used me to pocket an inheritance. To find the owner of a painting so you could collect. You promised me you wouldn't do that."

"Sera—I never meant for any of this to happen."

"Well, it did, didn't it?" When he looked like he'd attempt to explain, she cut in. "And don't trouble yourself to make an excuse. The attorneys at Stahlworth and Martin have already told me everything I need to know. No doubt that's why you're here."

"I had no choice."

She turned to face him. "And by no choice you mean . . . ?"

He looked sick by it all. If she could judge the disheveled hair and painted circles under his eyes, she'd have guessed he hadn't slept in days. Or weeks.

Just like her.

"The company has less than three months of operating costs on the books, Sera. Our investors have been pressing me. The board is threatening legal action against the family."

"Why?"

He shook his head. "Why isn't important now."

"Did you—"

"No matter what you may think of me right now, I do have some integrity. I assure you that I've had no part in any wrong-doing where the company is concerned. But that doesn't change the fact that if I didn't do something fast, we'd go under. All of us. The family and my grandfather's legacy with it."

Sera stood there, the cell phone fused to her grip. Her hands trembled slightly. "So it's as simple as that?"

"No, Sera. It's not simple at all." He took a step toward her, cautiously so, as if he wanted to be closer but couldn't chance more than a few inches at a time. "I didn't want to do it. But after looking at the numbers, my lawyers couldn't see any other way. Everyone depending on me would have been wiped out. I couldn't let that happen. Can't you understand? My family would be left with nothing."

"I depended on you. You said we were partners in this, remember? Your grandfather depended on you to honor his wishes. And what about Adele and Vladimir? Don't we owe it to them to tell their story? If you go through with this, how will anyone ever know what happened to them?"

"They're gone, Sera. More than seventy years gone."

"You don't know that."

"I do," he whispered. "And I think you know it too. We've looked in every corner there is. You may want this to end differently, but their secret might have to stay in Auschwitz—"

"I'm going to Paris."

"What?"

"To Paris. To see the defendant in your case."

"Alone?" William asked, without the usual strength in his voice.

"Yes."

He glanced over at the worktable and the wooden stools upon which they'd once sat. Was he remembering the same night, the same conversation about the life they both longed to lead? Was he imagining what could have been had they lived it together?

Sera nodded. She was broken too. "How did you find her?"

"It was because of you."

It was the last thing she wanted to hear. "I don't understand."

"I called my father, just like you said."

Sera stood before him with arms crossed over her chest. "And what happened?"

"Nothing. He had nothing for me. So when I returned home to the estate, I began digging in boxes of photos in the attic—it was the only thing I could think to do. My mother had stored his old stuff up there when he left. And of course, it was a dead end. Just like I thought it would be. That is, until I found something none of the family had considered before. I found my grandfather's Bible discarded in a box. I blew the dust off the cover and flipped through the pages. And in it, I found a snapshot of my grandfather with a woman I'd never seen before. It was dated 1967." He tilted his head toward the ghostly image of Adele hanging on the wall behind them. "Believe it or not, our painting was in the background. The back of the photo had her name. He knew the one thing that would lead me back to it had to be turning to God."

Sera's pulse quickened. She felt a rush in her veins and almost grabbed the front of his shirt on instinct. "Do you have the photo? Is it Adele in the photo with him?"

He stood back for a moment, a rather curious look having taken over his features. "Is that all you care about, Sera? Finding the painting?"

"But don't you want to know?"

William shook his head. "Of course I do. And I did what I had to for my family. I didn't have a choice, Sera. But you do. You don't have to give up everything in the present to live in the past. You can choose to have a new future."

He was talking about the loss of her father. And her almost-wedding. It was *her* hurt. *Her* past. *Her* memory of pain that kept her from taking any second chance that could be handed to her.

"You don't know what you're talking about, William."

"I came back." His words were spoken quietly, almost as if it pained him to say them aloud.

"What?"

"That night—the last night before I left to go home to California. I was stupid and impulsive. I made the taxi bring me back and I stood out there, trying to think of the words." William paused, then tore a hand through his hair. "I was coming back to tell you that I . . ."

Sera wrapped her arms around her middle. Suddenly the room felt cold.

"To tell me what?"

He shook his head. "It doesn't matter."

"So why come back now? You dropped me completely. You dropped whatever was between us."

"Because I saw you." His words were heavy with feeling. It was unmistakable. "I *saw you* with him."

She swallowed hard, knowing what he'd witnessed through the gallery windows. An embrace from her ex-fiancé and a lingering kiss on the cheek, with emotion on both sides.

"Yes. Michael was here."

He seemed to scoff at the meager admission. "Now you tell me."

"It wasn't important. It didn't change anything."

"It looked important from where I stood, Sera."

"And this was your revenge? To break your promise, file a lawsuit, and cash in your inheritance—because you thought you saw something that night?"

"Tell me. What did I see?"

Sera swallowed hard. "You saw a good-bye, William. That's all it was."

He shook his head. "What if I wouldn't have come back? Would you have ever told me?"

"It was innocent, William," she cried, tears stinging her eyes as she shook her head. "He's getting married."

"Married?"

She nodded, unable to say anything for a moment. A pin could have dropped and it would have crashed through the silence loud as a thunderclap.

"Well, I'm happy for him. And his bride. But it doesn't change anything between us, does it?"

"He came to tell me he was sorry. For everything."

"Sorry for what? Leaving you at the altar? For casting you off like you meant nothing? Well, you meant something to *me*." William pounded his palm to his chest on the words. "He's a fool who will never know how much you're worth."

"You don't know what you're saying."

"Don't I?"

Sera closed her eyes tight, the image of his hurt too much to look at. "How could you make me care—only to betray me? After what I told you? I put myself out there! I exposed two years of pain and shared it with you because I thought you really cared."

"I did—" He paused. "Do. I *do* care."

"But you lied to me, and that trust—now it's broken. And you can't go back."

Soft thunder rattled the windows behind them and a flash of white light glinted off the glass. It was a punctuation mark on Sera's last words, though neither appeared to need such a thing.

Is this it, God? Sera's heart felt like it was bleeding. *Is this over?*

"When do you leave for Paris?"

"Tomorrow." She wiped at her eyes with the back of her palm

and sniffed before continuing. "I had to get through the show first."

He stared at her, a curious look taking over his face. She saw it. His eyes were guarded in much the same way they'd been that first day in his estate office. He'd been distant then, and clearly, he was distancing himself now.

"Did it ever occur to you that you don't have to find the end of Adele's story to have the beginning of a new one yourself?" He shook his head on the last words. "When you walked across the gallery that last night, I thought we were taking a step forward—together. That was more than enough for me. I'd have given up the chase if I thought you could too."

"But it wasn't enough, was it? It's easy to judge when you got what you wanted."

He surprised her then by taking a step closer until his mouth brushed up against her ear. She shivered when his breath warmed the side of her neck. "You have no idea what I want, Sera. Like everyone else—you never asked."

"William, I . . ." Sera couldn't think what to say.

It had never occurred to her that he might have understood a little more of heartache than she gave him credit for. She'd always been so wrapped up in her own pain that she hadn't thought much about his.

"We'll never find our own peace, Sera," he said, and brushed his hand over her arm from elbow to wrist, until it finally stopped at her fingertips. "I sat in that attic with my grandfather's Bible in my hands and realized that I don't have peace about any of this—not in my relationship with a grandfather who's now gone or with a father who's walked out on his family. I know I'll find the painting and save my grandfather's legacy, but at what cost? When all is said and done, will I have anything left that really matters?"

She closed her eyes on the image of him sitting in a dark attic with his grandfather's Bible in his hands, wondering about what might have been.

Could they move past regret? Or was it too late?

"I'm sorry, Sera." His words held sadness. "I came back that night to tell you something. But I need to tell you something else now."

"Which is . . . ?"

He squeezed her hand, then pecked a kiss to the tear on her cheek and turned to walk away. "I hope Paris turns out to be everything you hoped it would be."

CHAPTER TWENTY-NINE

---

*T*he aftermath of the revolt at Crematorium IV was staggering in its ability to silence the brave.

All the men who helped in the attack were rounded up and
killed before the burnt-out shell of the building had stopped
smoldering. The pile of brick and mortar, now charred and black,
continued to leak smoke that bled up into the sky like a menacing shadow, almost alive as it curled up to mingle with the tips
of the clouds. Adele watched it. Hated it. Felt that it mocked any
attempt the prisoners had made at escaping their cruel fate.

It was as if the scorched building laughed at them all for dar-
ing to hope.

And the men were gone. Just like that. In a hail of gunfire and
shouting guards, the prisoners' long-awaited attempt to fight
back had proven futile. They'd been gunned down. Attacked by
the dogs as they tried to clip holes in the barbed wire. Chased and
given not even a breath of freedom before they were silenced . . .
And now the women involved were holed up somewhere else in
the camp, placed in isolation, awaiting their own execution at the
hands of the SS guards.

Adele heard water drip somewhere behind her.

It was a cold day, wet and unforgiving for autumn, but she

hardly noticed. Her nerves were no longer raw. The threat of death no longer loomed. The daily terror had been replaced by despondence so that the chill was not bothersome, and the light tapping of the drops from the leaky roof became a reliable companion.

Adele felt the disconnection in her soul, if that was possible. Numbness had crept in and made a home. She felt cold. And empty. And hollow now that the painting in the stairwell was all she had left to connect her to Omara.

Adele was giving up.

She would still be required to play in tonight's concert to honor visiting members of the Third Reich. It was rumored that several high-ranking officials were making an appearance to show solidarity within the ranks, though that bit of news was speculation on the tongues of the prisoner population. Regardless of whether it was true, Adele was sickened by it. She was sickened by the senseless death the revolt had caused. And she was sickened still further that she must now play for the men and women who would celebrate the execution of the only person she had left in the world.

So she sat on the floor, the lovely dress they'd given her for the concert that night cradled in her lap, staring up at the ghostly painting on the wall. They'd once stood there together, she and Omara, and had talked of hope. Of God. Of the human spirit and the great beauty of creation. Adele stared at it now, transfixed as her hand ran the length of the beautiful ice blue fabric in her lap, wondering what would happen to Omara's masterpiece.

She told herself that to have something of worth in a world full of chaos was the very definition of beauty. It felt like a spiritual liberation that couldn't be silenced. These prisoners, the ones who painted or wrote poetry or played in the orchestra— they refused to let that spirit die. And this, she decided, is why the heart creates.

God plants the talent and it grows, sustained by a spirit-given strength to endure, even in the midst of darkness. It thrives in the valleys of life and ignores the peaks. It blooms like a flower when cradled by the warmth of the sun. It remains in a hidden stairwell in a concentration camp. It grows, fed in secret, in the heart of every artist.

The God-worship of every life—this was the art of Auschwitz.

The image of the painting was burned on her heart. This was Omara's legacy. This was the tribute to those who had lived and endured and died all around her . . . Adele could imagine Omara's hands, aged and knotted fingers moving with care over the makeshift canvas in the hidden stairwell, painting the image with as much pride as any artist in a modern studio. It was her art and here it would be lost.

Adele wiped at the tears that had pooled in the sunken skin around her eyes.

Would she play or should she refuse? Would she take a bullet in the head?

The young violinist in the painting looked back at her.

She looked pure, perhaps as Austria's Sweetheart had looked all those months ago when she'd first stepped off the train platform and into her new shadow of a life. But in looking at the shaved head, the sad eyes, and the hollow expression in the painting, it became clear; there was but one thing to do.

Adele rose up from the floor. And before she could talk herself out of it, she picked up the dress and shoes and walked out to the warehouse to retrieve a pair of scissors.

—

A general gasp permeated the crowd when Adele appeared on the concert hall stage.

She saw the sea of faces, some confused, others exclaiming at how the Germans could have allowed Austria's Sweetheart to have been shorn of her crowning glory. She heard their whispers, likely appalled by the loss of her dignity before such an auditorium of distinguished guests.

It was surreal, walking out before an audience of the Nazis' elite for the second time. And knowing what she must have looked like to them, with her trademark blond locks gone and her crown shaved smooth in replacement, face without powder or rouge, her skin translucent and pale as death. It was no wonder that the quiet murmurs sent a wave of shock to blanket the concert hall. She knew how she must look. Still, Adele kept her chin up as she stood tall before them, resolute and without shame now that her decision had been made.

No one had thought to check on her prior to the performance. Why would they? None of the guards ever had. The musicians had always been too terrified to do anything the least bit out of place. But not this time. Adele knew it was reckless but she didn't care. The feeling of taking scissors to her hair and shaving her head smooth had been freeing—she'd never imagined shedding that old part of her would minister to her soul. She fully expected to receive a death sentence because of it.

It didn't matter now. She'd already decided that regardless of her fate, this would be her last performance.

All she could do was think about God and how she would honor Him with her gift. For the first time in her life Adele felt beautiful in her weakness, a perfect creation with the shorn locks, feeling God's strength uplifting her from all sides. She was one of them now, the Jews and the other lost ones. Now that her former life had all but faded away, the prisoner population had become fused to her core. Her heart was with those who had died in Auschwitz and she would never, ever be the same person again.

Live or die—the outcome no longer mattered. Adele knew she would never leave Auschwitz.

In the echoing silence of the concert hall, she raised her bow and tucked the violin up under her chin. With her heart free and the scars on her palms burning to give the performance of her life, she waited for the crowd to quiet and the conductor to proceed, though he too appeared shaken. He looked to someone offstage, lifted his eyebrows in question, then turned to the orchestra with a look of subdued fear on his face.

He called them to attention.

And just as she'd always done, Adele breathed out deeply. She set her back poker straight. Her arms were fluid and ready to be used with proficiency. She looked at the crowd, the same sea of faces greeting her as a stranger, and tried to instead imagine Omara in the front row. She pictured the mothers who had walked the lonely path with their children, remembered the elderly who followed with bent backs and tired steps toward the gas chambers. She pictured everyone who'd been lost, urging her on, telling her it was okay to finally let go . . . that the Butterfly could dance with just one more song of praise lifted upward from her violin.

The rest of the orchestra sat at attention with her.

Adele was ready to play with every fiber of her being. Instinctively, like so many mornings at the camp gates or during the horrendous selections at the train platform, she looked up. Her eyes went to the second chair in the back row, just as they always had.

And in that perfect moment, all time stopped along with her heart.

Vladimir.

A breath of disbelief escaped her lips. Her fingers trembled and her feet twitched with their need to run to his side.

Is it really you?

She blinked once. Twice. No, her eyes weren't playing tricks.

His head was shaved. And he'd been beaten at some point, for a scar marred his forehead along his hairline and the telltale shade of purple darkened his left cheekbone. Appearing frail with a washed-out face, her love sat, quite alive but dreadful in appearance, on the same stage as she. Beaming at her with the same heart-stopping smile she'd dared not hope to ever see again.

Yes, it's me. She could almost hear his heart whispering to her. *I'm still here, Adele.*

Her Vladimir looked back with joyful tears freely dampening the eyes that blinked three times just for her. They couldn't talk. Couldn't touch. Couldn't do anything but know that they were onstage together. And whether they'd have a future together in this life or not, this one moment of worship they'd give back to God. They'd do so gratefully—together.

They had the past—it was all she'd been able to think on in the years she'd been in Auschwitz. And while they may not be gifted with a future, Adele was overcome by the present, the moment she'd always prayed would come. In that instant, she thanked God for second chances. He'd heard her prayers and had gifted her a last good-bye.

She blinked back. Quickly. Three times. And Vladimir nodded, ever so slightly, keeping his eyes fixed on her.

It was fitting somehow that she played Mendelssohn's Violin Concerto in E Minor, for it was one of the unique concertos to begin with the violin solo. The song called her to attention and she gave herself up to it. Longing for peace. Searching for God in such a soulless place. She played the crying melody with eyes closed and arms that moved swift as the wind through Birkenau's birch forest, her heart soaring in worship as the notes were carried from her heart to the strings on her violin, and echoed behind her by the orchestra.

And she felt the beauty in the music now, drank it in with tears streaming down her face. Never had she been so naked in worship before her Creator, allowing the adoration to bleed out her very fingertips onto the strings, playing her heart's cry for every single lost soul, for the loss of innocence every generation to come would possess as a result of what happened at the killing fields of Auschwitz.

Her final performance would be to honor God with every last breath in her body. And they played, she and Vladimir together, as if their symphony of thanks had been heard, for God allowed them to meet one more time.

Her body and mind floated through the fast-slow-fast pace of the concerto, the movements pacing first with the gentle notes of an ordered tranquility until they cascaded to a powerful, triumphant ending with all instruments awakened and orchestra strings blazing in unison.

The applause startled her, for Adele hardly knew when the notes had ended.

She'd been playing, crying, soul lost and heart soaring, and time had stopped, though she played for nearly thirty minutes. The moment the piece had ended, she dropped her arms and cradled the violin, head bowed. And they cheered. Whatever shock had been registered by her appearance was gone once she'd played so masterfully before the masses in the concert hall.

Abba . . .

Adele mouthed the words as the auditorium full of Nazis came to their feet and cheered.

Do You see, Abba? Do You see? It's not all evil, is it? There is beauty here too . . .

Beauty.

Awe-inspiring, sacrificial, and breathtaking beauty. Adele had been gifted this in what she believed was to be her last goodbye to life on earth.

CHAPTER THIRTY

———

*S*era arrived in Paris just as the sun was ducking down behind the great steel arches of the Eiffel Tower. The structure created a bronzed pillar on the skyline, stretching up to yawn through the low-hanging rain clouds as the curtain of evening fell around the taxicab windows. City lights dotted the sky beyond the streets, like fireflies dancing in between the raindrops that misted the glass.

The taxi driver turned corners too tightly, tossing Sera about the backseat as they traversed rain-slicked streets through the heart of the city.

"Nombre 58, Rue de la Concorde."

Sera felt the car slide to a stop, its brakes squeaking slightly. But it was the words William had spoken that echoed in her ears. She'd never find peace in her life without fully surrendering to God. Not if she found the painting. Not even if she learned what had happened to Adele and Vladimir. The answer she longed to find would mean little if she refused to yield to God's love in her own life.

Is William right? Have I learned nothing?

The thoughts tossed about the inside of her head almost as haphazardly as she'd been pitched about in the back of the taxi. She looked to the city lights beyond the window, feeling guilty that she'd ventured to Paris without having patched things up with William.

"*Mademoiselle?*"

"Yes?" She snapped her head up to look at the driver.

"*Voici. Nombre* 58," he said, and pointed to the awning-covered door of a white-brick, multilevel apartment building. Hanging flower baskets moved with the ebb and flow of the wind, casting ghostly shadows across the front steps. "Would you like me to wait, mademoiselle?"

"No." She shook her head and handed him enough euros to cover the trip. "*Merci.*"

The truth of what had happened to Adele and Vladimir was before her. There was nothing to do but climb the stairs to the woman's apartment.

William was right. She was poised to find the missing piece in the puzzle, but it didn't feel like she'd thought it would. The chase of the painting had captured her so that she couldn't see past it.

What came next? No matter the outcome, it wouldn't change the fate of a couple who had lived and loved more than seventy years before.

Sera ducked her head under the roof of the car and stepped out in the rain.

Without William, it wouldn't change her future either.

—

The door creaked open, and in the glow of lamplight that spilled out into the fifth-floor hallway, an elegantly dressed woman stood with a crocheted afghan draped over her shoulders. Her smile was soft and her features bordered by hair of a color so silver it reflected almost violet in the dim light. She stood with a frame of barely five feet in height, hands clasped in front of her in a demure manner, as if she'd expected a visitor in the midst of the rainstorm.

Sera looked at her, noting that she too had light eyes, though they weren't the same striking color as in the painting.

"Are you Adele?"

"No. I am not." The woman shook her head, though the hint of a knowing smile refused to fade from her lips. "But I knew her. We were acquaintances."

"Tell me? Please." Sera took a step forward, as if the anticipation of hearing the truth was too much to keep her away. "I have to know what happened to her."

The woman nodded. "You're the gallery owner."

"Yes," she said, relieved that the woman seemed welcoming. "Sera James."

"And you're looking for the painting?"

Was she? Was it only about the painting, or was it something more? She wasn't sure anymore. "Yes. I've come all this way because I wanted to speak with you about them. Adele and Vladimir, I mean."

"So you have," she agreed, and gave a gentle nod.

The woman opened her door wide, which revealed a classically decorated flat cloaked in shades of soft primrose and violet and lace trimmings that dripped from the drapery hooks and the tufted arms of a wood-framed settee. "I've a teakettle on the stove," she said as she walked into the living room to a door that led into a cozy French kitchen with slate blue walls and the smell of buttery cinnamon pastry wafting out into the hall.

"But what is your name?" Sera called out, leaning into the apartment because she was as yet unsure whether she'd been invited to step inside or not. "Ma'am?"

"And mind you wipe your feet," she called from an adjoining room. "The rain has been pelting the windows for hours. Paris in the springtime, you know."

No. She didn't.

She closed the door and stood in the entry, dripping rainwater on the woman's hardwood flooring as she stood. She tried to dry the tips of her hair with the edge of her sweater, but it was no use; she was drenched from head to toe.

"Caught in a Paris shower, were you?"

Sera looked down at the rain-speckled floor at her feet. In embarrassment, she brushed a lock of wet hair back from clinging to her cheek. "I suppose I was."

"Here you are," the woman said, and handed her a bath towel that smelled of fresh lilacs. "Dry yourself off and have a seat. I'll be back with the tea tray. Do you like shortbread?"

She didn't have a chance to answer. The woman puttered back to the kitchen.

Sera took the towel and began patting the drops from her hair and clothes as she walked into the apartment. The large living space was pleasant. It was a far cry from lavish, but certainly not shabby. The woman had floor-to-ceiling bookshelves on the back wall, full of carefully arranged books. There was a small writing table in the corner, complete with an antique chair and what looked like a 1920s-era Remington typewriter in remarkable condition on the desktop. There was a vase of bright peonies the color of April sunshine prettying up a low, circular coffee table in the center of the room.

The living room was bright and cheery, just as she'd imagined it would be. Her eye was drawn to the oversized whitewashed mantel on the back wall, its top lined with dozens of framed photos. She crossed the room, lost in thought. She ran her fingertips along the edge of the wood as her eyes scanned the photos for images of Adele and Vladimir.

There were dozens of photos. Some were small and unassuming in tiny, gilded frames. Others were more pronounced, such as an eight-by-ten vintage wedding photo of a beaming bride hidden beneath the curtain of an elegant, Spanish lace veil. The photos were beautiful, and Sera could see a lifetime of memories in them. And then she stopped. Her breath caught in her chest, for hidden behind several other photos was a small, wallet-sized photo of a young smiling couple.

Before she could even lift the frame, she heard the woman's voice behind her.

"Yes. I knew them."

Sera plucked the frame from the mantel and turned round, cradling the photo in her hands. "You're their daughter."

The woman gave a slight chuckle, which jostled the teacups on the tray in her hands. "No. They didn't give me life. But I suppose you could say that they did give me my life back." She placed the tray on the nearby coffee table.

Sera looked at the woman, hardly believing that the connection was real. "What is your name?"

"Sit. Let me tell you about them."

Sera found a spot on the nearby brocade settee and sat on the edge of it, the photo still clutched in her hands. She then looked up at the woman with the silver hair and the wise smile.

"I'm ready." And she was. Two years and a lifetime of living in between had ensured it.

"Good. Because I want to tell you a story about the night my family was killed. My name is Sophie, and Adele and Vladimir saved my life."

CHAPTER THIRTY-ONE

November 4, 1944

$\mathcal{I}$n a bitter cold the orchestra was pulled into line with the rest of the prisoners. They had no clue where they were going. Were they marching to their deaths? Adele couldn't have guessed.

Marta was lined up in front of her, Fränze behind. The other girls were around them, some looking woefully pale, others fighting to stand up like a reed against a violent wind. None of them said a word as they stood unmoving while the frigid November morning sent an icy wave of snow with each gust of wind. Adele shivered with each punishing wave.

"Where are we going?" Fränze asked, coughing into the wind.

Marta seemed to know and looked around for the SS before speaking up.

"They're loading us on trucks today," she said, and pointed out to the far end of the fencing. "They're abandoning Birkenau."

A long line of vehicles coughed exhaust in the cold morning air.

"But why?" Adele asked.

"Why ask questions, Adele? At least they're not feeding us to the gas chambers," she whispered. Fränze nodded meekly, her long lashes peeking out from bangs that fell down over her eyes. "If they're even still standing. They have been dismantling the buildings as quickly as possible."

"We can't leave Omara behind." She was still in isolation.

"They're not giving us a choice," Marta noted. "And we don't even know if Omara is alive."

"If the women had been executed, we would know."

"How, Adele?"

"They haven't had a public execution in a while, have they? They'd want to make an example of the prisoners who fought in the revolt," she argued. "They always do."

"So what happens now?" Fränze asked, her voice meager against the roar of the trucks in the distance. She glanced up at the top of the tower where uniformed guards still stood watch.

"Edith works in the kitchens and she told me they've been taking everything away—packing up what they don't burn." Marta paused long enough to give a cautious look around, then continued. "I've heard rumor that the Jews are being taken away somewhere. Anyone else"—she looked at Adele—"is being sent over to Auschwitz I. Christians. Political prisoners. Some of the Russian prisoners of war . . . We are leaving and they're to stay behind at Auschwitz."

Fränze hugged Adele's arm. "They'll separate us?"

Adele's thoughts went to the only options she had left.

Should she try to sneak onto one of the trucks? It didn't seem like a clear choice. Even now, as they watched prisoners being loaded on trucks and into the cattle cars at the train platform, she saw no food or water being loaded with them. It was likely they'd all be sent away and die in transit.

But to stay behind at Auschwitz? What would happen to the non-Jewish prisoners?

"I could pass for a Jew." She ran her hand over her head, the month's growth of stubble scratchy to her palm. "I could hide with you in the trucks." The line moved haltingly forward and she took care to stay directly behind Marta.

"You can't mean you'd come with us?" Marta asked over her shoulder. "How could you do that?"

Adele felt the fresh tattoo, a discipline for her stunt at the concert, burning into her left forearm. She was marked like the rest of the population now. Couldn't she somehow fade into the ranks of prisoners being shipped out? The SS were moving quickly, as if time was running short. Surely they wouldn't notice one out-of-place prisoner in a population of thousands?

"Look at how they're moving around. They are anxious about something. They've been dismantling and burning buildings for days, haven't they? They might not have time to gather all the administrative files on everyone. It's possible they wouldn't know who I am, especially with my hair gone."

Fränze looked up at Adele with doe eyes. "But what if they ask who you are?"

"Sweet Fränze." Adele pressed a kiss to the top of the kerchief covering her head. "I'll lie. We'll all lie if we have to."

"No. You're tattooed now, remember? They'll catch you and kill you for it. And they'll kill us for knowing about the deception and not coming forward." Marta made no attempt at softening the truth. Fränze lowered her chin on a muffled cry.

"We must stay together," Adele whispered, and they moved ahead a few steps, the lines being drawn nearer to the cavalcade of trucks before them. "We promised Omara, didn't we? Most everyone in the orchestra here is a Jew, so I have to stay where the majority of the girls are. That's on those trucks."

Marta glanced back at her for only a split second. "And what about your cellist?"

Vladimir.

Yes. Adele had thought about him. If she stayed behind, could they be reunited somehow? If the Germans were pulling out, which it looked like they might be, then maybe the prisoners could make a stand and fight. Wasn't that what she wanted to do—fight alongside the man she loved? What if she could feel his arms around her just one more time?

"I don't even know if Vladimir is alive. I haven't seen him since the concert."

She kicked at a stone on the snow-covered path.

How could she be asked to make a decision between a life-or-death promise she'd made to Omara and the chance that Vladimir was somehow still alive in Auschwitz I?

God, what do I do?

Except for a frozen, threadbare uniform and a now-tattered picture of Vladimir that she kept hidden in the seam of her shirt, Adele's worldly possessions were walking right next to her. Fränze, Marta, and the rest of the girls were something tangible that she could see and care for, as she'd promised Omara.

But seeing her Vladimir again?

That was a dream.

"Marta, what else have you heard about Auschwitz I?"

"They are setting fire to some buildings, blowing up others. And shipping prisoners out to other camps." When she lowered her eyes, Adele knew there was more.

"Go on," she urged. "What are you not telling us?"

Fränze seemed to hang on the questions as much as Adele did. They shuffled through the snow together, yet kept their eyes trained on Marta instead of the line of vehicles that grew closer with each step.

"The sickest prisoners are staying behind—we don't know why. Only those who can walk are being forced to go. And there are rumors that those going to Auschwitz I are being shot, that the SS are eliminating witnesses, especially those who may have privileged knowledge—"

"Such as the members of the orchestra who played at SS parties and concerts."

Marta nodded. "Yes."

The temptation to go to Auschwitz I and look for Vladimir was so great, Adele could scarcely stand it.

What do I do, God?

She looked out over the barren fields and ramshackle barracks that were now blanketed in snow, feeling as desolate as her surroundings.

How can I follow my heart if it goes in two different directions?

CHAPTER THIRTY-TWO

—

*T*he story behind Adele's painting was so much deeper than
Sera had ever imagined.

She pressed her fingers to her lips, covering the emotion. "I
had no idea what she went through."

The story that Sophie had relayed over the last hour was so
poignant that Sera struggled to make sense of it all. The atrocities. The fear they must have endured. The lives of Omara and so
many others, lost within the barbed wire walls. The world was
irreversibly altered . . . and for all that Adele lived through, this
humble little woman before her was now the only witness to it.

"What happened to Omara?"

"She was executed for her part in the revolt." Sophie lifted her
knotted hands, using them to emphasize the events of Omara's
death. "But not before making a great sacrifice. There were written accounts found buried near the site of Crematorium IV. Adele
always believed that was why Omara ran from the block with
nothing but a small shovel in her hands. It was her job to bury
the prisoners' accounts so that someday we would remember."

Sera's heart broke at the words. "How did she die?"

"There was a public hanging in January 1945. All of the women
who aided in the revolt were killed."

"Did Adele see it? Did the orchestra have to play for Omara's
execution too?"

"No. Thankfully, she did not." Sophie's voice was slow and steady, almost melodic. "The Jewish girls were taken on a death march to the Bergen-Belsen camp in Germany. Keeping her promise to Omara, Adele went with them. There they survived in horrific conditions until the camp was liberated months later."

So Adele had survived the war.

"She lived . . . I didn't know. We found no record of Adele after Auschwitz."

"No. How would you have? Adele never again played in public, not after the last concert she gave in October of 1944. And there was nothing to tie back to any of us after Auschwitz was liberated."

"That's the last record we found of her."

"Yes. And she wanted it that way. After the loss of Omara, Adele vowed that she would survive, but it would never be to go back to her old life. It just so happens that on the same day of the prisoner revolt at Auschwitz, Adele's home was destroyed when Vienna was bombed by Allied planes."

"So she never had to go back."

"No. She did not."

"But her parents? Did she ever see them again?"

"Her mother, yes. After some time," Sophie relayed, her eyes fighting back what looked like the evidence of tears. "Adele was able to forgive her parents, and I believe, having been freed of that bitterness, she was able to go to Marina and make peace before her mother died."

"And her father?"

Sophie shook her head. "Adele forgave him too, but he would never receive her again. Too much had happened during the war, with the loss of everything he'd built, and he could not forget what he believed was the treachery of saving my life."

"And that's why she never played in public again?"

"Adele kept her survival hidden. She was a new person after Auschwitz. This I can understand. I, too, have valued my privacy.

I expect you had great difficulty finding the painting, especially without any record of Sophie Haurbech ever having been tied to Adele Von Bron."

"I've wanted to find it again since I was a child."

Sophie's interest appeared piqued. "You've seen Adele before?"

Sera smiled at how a painting could be referred to as the person depicted. It reminded her that the art lived on as long as the story behind it did.

"Once. As a child. My father was an art historian and he brought me to a friend's gallery here. In Paris. I've tried to find him, but the gallery is long since gone. I could find no record of Adele's painting ever having been there. All I had was the memory of seeing her hanging in the back of his gallery and negatives of the borders of the original. The film strip of the borders was how we confirmed Mr. Hanover's painting was a copy."

"A very good copy," Sophie added, smiling.

"After my dad died, nothing made sense. I wanted to go back to that time in my life when everything was safe, when I wasn't hurting. I remembered the painting and became obsessed with searching for it. I kept thinking the painting was like my Holy Grail—that finding it would make me complete."

"But she was not ready to be found then, was she?" It was a rhetorical question to which Sophie required no answer. Instead, she stood and took Sera's hand in hers. "Come with me."

Sophie led them into a small sitting room adjacent to the larger living space. It had large windows draped with airy white lace, through which Sera could see the backdrop of the Paris city lights. It wasn't until Sophie washed the small office in lamplight that the meaning for the foray into the tiny room became clear.

It hung on the wall, in a place that lacked prominence, overlooking the busy street below.

"I've brought you here because of this, child. You had to be ready to see it."

Sera's eyes misted. She couldn't help it. After everything she'd researched, after every breath she held in waiting to learn the fate of this one remarkable woman—it was all there, right in front of her. The painting was real. It was real and Sera had all but unearthed her buried heart in the journey to find it.

Thank You, Lord, for this.

Sera took a step forward on impulse and asked, "I'm sorry, but can I please touch it? I just have to know it's real."

Sophie laughed softly. "I'd be offended if you didn't."

Sera shook her head, even closed her eyes for a moment as her trembling fingertips reached out and touched the uneven texture of the painted wood-planked canvas. She was inexplicably moved, knowing the story was real and that her hand was *this close* to living history.

"I'm sorry you had to come all this way, especially after your long search for the painting. But it was a last promise I made to a dear friend."

Sera did a double take and stared from the painting back to the woman's face. "Do you mean Edward Hanover?"

Sophie nodded as she slipped into a cushy chair opposite the painting. It looked as though it was positioned so that a viewer could sit opposite Adele. The old woman looked weathered and wise as she nodded, sitting in the chair with her hands gently folded in her lap.

"It's estimated that one and a half million people died within Auschwitz-Birkenau."

"Yes." Sera's chin quivered as she turned her attention back to the painting. She ran her hand over the coolness of the canvas.

"But Austria's Sweetheart did not," Sophie said, triumph evident in the elevation of her voice. "Adele led a full life. She passed years ago. Peacefully, in her sleep. With her beloved violin at her side and—she told me—with her Savior waiting to claim her with open arms." The old woman chuckled softly. "I thought she'd outlive me for sure, courageous woman. But she left me her most prized possession, a painting from within the same camp that almost took her life."

"How was it saved from Auschwitz?" Sera walked over to a settee at the woman's side and took a seat.

"Omara's painting of Adele was found hanging in a stairwell within Auschwitz-Birkenau. It was saved along with many other works of art from the warehouse section of the camp."

"Did Adele ever see it again?"

"She did. Edward Hanover used his contacts in Europe to look for the painting. He never forgot Adele, or her story, and wouldn't give up the search for it. And he did find it a few years later, and sent it to Adele. She cherished it and the memory of Omara so much that she'd not part with that painting all the days of her life. Upon her death, she left it to me. I lived in Prague at the time, so it hung in a small gallery in Paris until I could come home and look after it. The same gallery you visited as a girl." She reached out to pat Sera's hand. "I suppose it was God's plan all along that our paths would cross. Without the painting having been left in the gallery, you would not be here."

"And I thought it was lost all this time. It seemed to vanish into thin air after I saw it all those years ago."

Sophie chuckled. "It vanished to a Paris apartment, that's all."

"And what about the painted room? Did it survive?"

"Adele went back to what remained of the death camp many years later, but the warehouse that held the painted room had long since been demolished. It exists only in memory now."

Sera went to the painting again and thought for a moment, then turned to Sophie.

"There are still so many pieces missing . . . What happened to Vladimir? And I don't understand how Edward Hanover fits into all of this."

Sophie patted the settee next to her.

"Sit down, child."

CHAPTER THIRTY-THREE

April 25, 1945

By the time the British 11th Armoured Division arrived at Bergen-Belsen, there was almost nothing left, except for worn barracks made of cracked wood and tent cities that were tattered and falling to the ground around the tens of thousands of prisoners packed into the camp. The transported prisoners who had survived were a blink from death. Many were sick. Others were so malnourished that it would be a miracle to grasp them back from death's clutches. With no provisions, little water, and the stunning sight of soldiers vomiting as they looked around at the carnage of Belsen, many survivors didn't understand what was happening.

Adele had found some water that day. She'd stolen it, of course, half a bucket full, when one of the SS guards had turned to give attention to a convoy of trucks passing by. She was rushing back to the tent city where the orchestra had huddled together, trying to stay warm through the last freezing weeks of winter, and had been stopped in her tracks by the deafening sound of vehicles thundering into the camp.

Adele was terrified at first and nearly tripped over some stones on the path back to the orchestra girls' tent. She righted herself quickly, then ran the rest of the way. They'd been skeptical, even when loudspeakers announced that the British were there.

"This is the British army. You are liberated . . ."

Over and over, the speakers sang out with voices loud in triumph over the Nazis. They were liberated. Free. Death had been conquered.

That was ten days ago.

Adele ran her hand over her head, the prickle of pixie-short hair coarse against her palm. She sat on the ground now, staring at the sunrise, with a thin blanket pulled around her shoulders. It barely shielded the dew that had collected upon and frozen her striped uniform in the night, turning it into fabric that crackled like paper when she made the slightest move.

"Miss? Did you hear me?"

Adele was shocked back to reality by the Brit's words.

"Yes?" she answered, though she doubted she'd ever be able to hear a man's voice behind her and not feel a split second of fear that it might be an SS officer with a cocked pistol.

The gravel-covered ground crunched beneath the weight of the man's combat boots. He cleared his throat before continuing. "Pardon, miss. But it's time to go. The doctors have cleared you for transport. The rest of your group has been loaded in the trucks and the last group before them left an hour ago—"

She turned and looked at him. "Tell me, sir—where do I go?"

"We have shelter for you at an Allied camp just over the ridge. You'll be quite cared for. There we have food, provisions, medical care. We can help you locate your family."

He didn't understand what she meant. She studied his face.

No, she didn't suppose he could understand. He was young, maybe only twenty or twenty-two years old at the most. His hair curved around the ears and was black as night. The morning sun was just high enough to shine upon a sprinkling of freckles on the bridge of a strong nose and a noble brow, illuminating youthful eyes that didn't speak of experience with death. He looked innocent. And kind.

Adele wanted to know where she *could* go, not where she *would* go after the truck took them to the displaced persons camp. Where could she live now and not see Auschwitz around every corner? Her world had been forever altered, and locating her family wouldn't change it.

"What will happen to them?"

He clearly didn't understand, because he bent down and took her by the elbow to help her stand, trying to make her leave the barren fields of Bergen-Belsen. He looked out over the near-vacant tent city, his eyes scanning the nothingness that was left. "To whom, miss?"

"The camps," she said, forcing her weakened legs to support her as he steadied her. "What will happen to the warehouses in Auschwitz, to the walls of painted brick? Will they be torn down?"

"I've heard tell of other camps through the wire," he declared with a slight nod. "Is that where you're from? Auschwitz?"

"Yes. Birkenau."

"Well, you needn't worry about that now. We're getting you some help."

Teeth chattering, she continued, "Tell me. Is Auschwitz still standing? There were explosions when we left. Have they burnt it to the ground?"

"No, miss." He braced her elbow and, surprisingly, pulled a thick wool blanket up over her shoulders. She hadn't even known he'd held it. "The Red Army liberated Auschwitz months ago. The Nazis pulled out—tucked tail and ran. But I believe many of the buildings still stand."

"Liberated . . . *Auschwitz*?" She could scarcely imagine it. Auschwitz without guard dogs and watchtowers? The crematorium out of operation? No more trains . . . no more orchestra playing for the ghosts marching out to work each morning.

No more death.

"Yes. The Nazis destroyed many of the buildings before the Red Army moved in."

She saw the camera hanging round his neck and stared at it, then lifted her chin to look at his face. She leaned into him and gripped the lapels of his army jacket. His face registered surprise at the forceful action.

"Tell me—were there survivors at Auschwitz? Did anyone make it? You must have received news in regard to this, being with the press." Her voice hitched on the last words, her heart thumping for word on a young cellist she'd seen onstage months before.

She must have guessed correctly. He looked down at his camera for a split second, then reconnected his eyes with hers. "Have you lost your family?"

Her soul cried with the question.

Yes! She wanted to scream it out. *I've lost my family. My innocence. Even my heart is gone. I've lost everything. Except for God! He's all I have left . . .*

"Who survived at Auschwitz? Do they have prisoner lists?"

"They haven't told me, miss. I am merely following orders given to me here."

"But if we could find out?"

The young man shook his head. "The SS destroyed their administrative files before we arrived here. I can only assume they did the same at Auschwitz. But I promise we're here to help. No one will harm you again. We can begin the search for your family after you've first been properly taken care of." He pulled her hands from his lapels and cradled her arm at the elbow. He raised his eyebrows slightly and tried to offer her a nudging smile. "Come now, might you be able to walk with me? I'll hold you steady so you can get your footing."

She swallowed hard and nodded, her effort at walking quite feeble and her legs feeling as if they were attached to nothing but a weakened shell. He walked with her, as slowly as she needed, one arm around her waist and the other hand clutching her elbow. Step by step to the convoy of transport trucks, the young man held her in his care.

"What is your name?" she asked, their feet trudging along at a painfully slow pace.

"My name is Edward, miss." He looked as though he was trying not to connect with her gaze, for he kept his eyes fixed on a point out over the horizon of ramshackle barracks and leftover SS officers digging graves in the fields.

Edward, she thought. *You have kindness in your eyes.*

Adele allowed him to continue walking. She kept her head down, eventually leaning it against his shoulder when the strength to hold it up proved fleeting. "Edward, I have been praying for kindness for two years," Adele whispered against the thick canvas of his jacket. "And here it is. Surely God has heard our prayers."

A soothing hand cradled the back of her head, gently patting her nape, drawing her closer to the compassion of a stranger. She felt the nod of his chin against her brow. "You're safe now, miss."

"Thank you, Edward."

He loaded her on the back of a truck, even as her taxed legs trembled from the short walk to the line of roaring engines. Marta was there, coughing and miserably dirty, but took her by the elbow and pulled her down next to her in the truck bed. Fränze was there too, and curled up close to her side.

As Adele looked around, she realized that it had happened.

The promise had been kept.

The orchestra had survived. The girls were war torn and weary, dirty and likely unrecognizable now, but they were alive. Adele looked at their faces. Marta's strength was there, in the toughness of her set jaw. And little Fränze, still a child at fourteen, retained something of her doe-like innocence in the soft hazel eyes that were always searching. And the rest of the girls—Adele looked them over, one by one, the ones who were still by her side through it all.

Thank You, Lord. Her heart could have wept for the blessing of life.

And in an instant, a pang of fear dropped over her.

"Wait!" In the bustle to load the last of the survivors in the truck, she'd lost sight of the British officer.

Several trucks began moving away. In a moment of panic, she called out to the drivers through the kicked-up dust, "Wait, please wait!" Her eyes scanned the soldiers. They all wore the same clothes, all had the same forlorn expression and down-turned eyes. But Edward—he had a camera round his neck. Her eyes wildly searched for the distinction.

"They're taking us to safety, Adele!" Marta shouted, and tried to pull her back. "You'll fall from the truck—please sit down."

"Edward!" Her eyes scanned the crowd of officers, searching for the man with the kind eyes and the camera. She called out to him, over and over, praying she hadn't lost the one chance she and Vladimir may have had left.

Suddenly, he was there. His hands clasped hers and he moved her backward toward Marta's waiting arms. "You'll fall, miss. Please, do sit back. Sit here with your group. I promise they'll take care of you at the Allied camp. You have only to rest now."

"You are a photojournalist with British intelligence?" Her eyes searched his face.

He seemed surprised by her question but answered anyway. "Yes, miss."

Adele looked him straight in the face, hoping beyond hope that his kindness would stretch far enough for what she was about to ask.

"Then you may have contacts who can help," she said, tears welling in her eyes.

"Contacts to help with what?" He blew the words out, the sun not having burned off enough of the cool morning to keep his breath from turning to fog.

Adele hastily tore at the inside hem of her uniform until it gave way. She retrieved the worn photograph of Vladimir, her smiling cellist, and slid it into the young man's palm. "His name is Vladimir Nicolai. I'm asking you to find this man," she begged, eyes searching. "Find him and bring him to me."

CHAPTER THIRTY-FOUR

My Dear William,

I pray this letter finds you when you're most ready to receive it.

Take it from an old man; life is fragile. It's meant to be lived in service, with an abundance of love, in the gracious guidance of a Savior who leads each step we tread in this journey of life.

I'm sorry that you're reading these words and I'm not able to tell you this until after I'm gone. But you're clever. And a hard worker. You've grown into a fine man and I'm quite proud. But I also remember another William, a young man who talked often in his youth about the call upon his heart to become a minister. I remember the day that sixteen-year-old chap walked into my study with his Bible in hand, ready to tell the patriarchs of the Hanover clan that he had every intention of walking away from the family business in favor of walking toward a pulpit. I regret that your father and I rejected this path. I further regret that I remained silent and refrained from supporting this call upon your life. I aim to right that wrong now.

I've asked Ms. Sophie Haurbech-Mason to be a witness to my wishes. If you've found her, then your smarts are exactly as I'd thought them to be. You've learned the story of Adele.

I was indeed at Bergen-Belsen when the camp was liberated on April 15, 1945, and she was one of the prisoners who survived.

The events of that day have changed me to my core. I suspect they've changed you too.

You must know by now that the entirety of the Hanover estate is to be left to the owner of Adele's painting. That owner is Sophie Haurbech-Mason.

"So it's true." Sera stopped reading and looked up. "You're to inherit everything."

Her face must have registered the shock, because Sophie leaned forward and nudged her hand with an aged fingertip.

"Continue, my dear."

Sera obeyed, though the opinion she'd held of the sweet woman was in danger of fading if she was poised to take away everything William had fought so hard to keep.

Whether out of obligation to the company or to honor your responsibilities to the family, I admire your resolve. As the painting still exists, and you've found it, you have but to ask for it. If it's still what you want, you can take it home, run the company, and live your life.

I give you the choice.

But if, after learning of Adele's story, you've changed your mind at all, then I ask you to consider what brought you to Ms. Haurbech-Mason's door in the first place. If you choose it, this letter can free you, my boy. You can walk away from any sense of propriety with a heart that is full.

Our lawyers have a copy of a new will outlining alternative wishes. I've taken careful steps to ensure that my last will and testament is executed in the manner you choose when the painting is found. As for the family assets, Ms. Haurbech-Mason will have sole discretion to disperse the Hanover funds. She's smart and honest; she will ensure the family is looked after. The leadership of the company will be turned over to the board of directors, who will in their own best judgment appoint a successor as chief executive officer. And you, William, can finally walk away. Live the life you've always wanted with my blessing in it.

Money, position, and power—we both know they are a ruse. There's no lasting fulfillment in them, is there? I find shame that you learned this long before your foolish grandfather. I implore you to live your life for second chances, Will, because you shall always have one with Christ.

Your loving grandfather,

Edward William Hanover

Sera held the letter in her hands, moved by the fact that the man had cared enough to leave such a legacy behind.

"So Edward Hanover was there in Bergen-Belsen?"

"Yes, he was there on the day of liberation." Sophie nodded. "And he was there for the days afterward, when prisoners died from eating the food rations that had been given them. When disease still claimed victims. He was there, and I can tell you, the things he witnessed transformed him."

"I can't imagine what all of them went through."

"It was impactful enough that he remained close with Adele. They were friends for the remainder of their lives."

"All because of that chance encounter . . ."

Sophie shook her head. "There are no chance encounters with God. Adele brought Vladimir to my family. We'd hoped to all escape," she said, her voice taking on a softness that comes with the remembrance of memories from long ago.

"How did you survive the war?"

Sophie looked to the mantel and smiled at the sea of faces

staring out from the picture frames. "That is a story for another day, I think. But I had my own journey to take, just as Adele did, and we found each other after the war."

"How?"

A smile warmed her face, spreading pleasant wrinkles from the corners of her eyes. "Edward. He intervened. He found me too, just like Adele's painting."

Sera took a sip of her tea. *So it was William's grandfather who had been the connection all along.*

"I must tell you, Sophie, how sorry I am about what happened with the will being contested. Had I been able to prevent it, I would have."

"Life is a funny thing, my dear. We try not to take it for granted. The moment we do, it's gone. Wiped away on a memory." She shrugged delicate old shoulders. "Who knew I'd been named in a will to the tune of a hundred million dollars? I only agreed to help Edward because of our mutual affection for Adele. I did not expect him to have changed his will. That point we never discussed. I would have discouraged it. Perhaps that's why he told me after the fact."

"But you discussed the other things in the letter?"

She smiled over the rim of her delicate rosebud-sprayed teacup. "Yes. We discussed your William."

Sera found it difficult not to blush under the weight of the woman's words.

"He is a fine man, Sera."

"Yes," she admitted, and swallowed hard over the lump of regret that had formed in her throat. "He is."

Oh Lord . . . I think I've made a terrible mistake . . .

"We think we know what we want, don't we? We always believe we know better than God. We have our entire journey plotted out. We may have even packed our bags and purchased a ticket, but God always has His own plans. And His plans are infinite in wisdom." Sophie smiled on the last words and took a sip of tea. "He was here, you know."

Sera's head snapped up. "Who? Not William."

"Yes. Earlier today. He showed up on my doorstep asking for you, interestingly enough." She smiled over the rim of her teacup. "Seemed to think he'd find you here."

"And he read the letter."

Sophie nodded with a gentle air and replaced the cup in its saucer. "He did. Said he had to know for himself what happened to our Adele. Edward and I had a bet, you see." She looked to the lofty ceiling above their heads and chuckled. "I guess you won."

Sera raised her eyebrows in question. "I don't understand."

"Edward approached me with the idea of helping his grandson because he'd never forgotten what was truly important in life. God had anchored and steered him through everything. And he knew that his eldest grandson desired to devote his life to following God, but hadn't been able to because of the demands of the family business. And when he'd gone to the family about his wishes, Edward hadn't supported him. But time can heal a heart, can't it? He realized that William would never leave the business without his grandfather's blessing. Edward wanted to leave this world having done something about that."

Sera leaned forward to return the letter, hands trembling. "But he left the estate to you."

"He did." Sophie appeared pleased. "William may have contested the will, but it turns out he didn't have to. He had the choice all along. So he asked for enough to take care of his family. As for the rest—the stock, the assets for the family business, even the painting—he asked for nothing. He mentioned something about going back to an old career path he'd always been drawn to, exactly as Edward hoped he would. He told me to do with the money what I will. To perhaps give it away because it's what his grandfather would have wanted. It's what Adele and Vladimir would have wanted. Perhaps this money can give someone else a second chance?"

Sera's heart warmed just as tears misted her eyes. "Then it meant more than the money to him."

"Yes. And now, I believe your William hasn't a job or a family fortune to claim. I'm not sure whether that matters to you, but he sounds remarkably similar to a penniless cellist Adele and I once knew."

Sera jumped up from the settee. In a flurry, she grabbed up her purse and damp trench coat and apologized, "I'm sorry, Miss Sophie. But I have to go."

"But you haven't heard the rest of the story."

"I know . . . I want to! I need to know what happened to Vladimir. But . . ." Sera looked at the door and back to Sophie. "I need to find William."

"Yes, dear. That's quite all right." Sophie followed her to the door.

"Did he give any indication as to where he was going?"

"He said there was something he wanted to see before he flew back to America. A favorite piece of art?" Sophie winked.

Sera's heart leapt, and her body with it. She planted an impulsive kiss on the woman's cheek and sailed out the door as Sophie's charming laughter carried down the hall after her.

CHAPTER THIRTY-FIVE

$\sim$

Sera was near to breathless when she walked up the stairs, having run from her taxi into the Musée de Louvre through the rain. It was late on a Friday—nearly closing time—and she worried he'd have already gone. But in the instant she rounded the corner, William was there. She could see him from behind in his usual jeans, his messenger bag slung so casually over his shoulder, his broad back to her.

She stood there with tears in her eyes, looking at the scene. The *Winged Nike of Samothrace* was more beautiful in person. It was the way she'd always pictured it: magnificent and mysterious, free and beautiful as its every angle captured the light bouncing off the lofty cream walls. And it stunned her that while the ethereal sculpture reigned so majestically in the center of its grand portico, she hardly cared. The moment she'd always dreamed about was perfect because she couldn't take her eyes off the man who stood in its shadow.

She trotted up the stairs until she was standing close enough to reach out and touch his arm. "Beautiful, isn't it?"

He slowly turned from the sculpture and connected his blue eyes with hers.

"Sera."

She didn't know what to say. She'd thought of possibly a hundred things she wanted to tell him on the way from Sophie's apartment. How she was stupid and sorry and could he forgive her for being so hopelessly stubborn?

She wanted him to be who he was, who he'd told her God had called him to be once, before money and expectations got in the way. But oddly, none of that seemed important. Not when he'd said her name so sweetly and was standing before her with a contented smile.

"You're here." She smiled back and wiped some of the raindrops from her cheek. "You came all this way?"

"Well, I couldn't let you be in Paris all alone." His voice was soft, forgiving. "Could I?"

Though the crowds had thinned, there were other tourists still in the portico, some walking through and stopping to look at the statue while others breezed past the towering sculpture unaffected. A rather hurried older man walked in the space left between them and said, *"Excusez-moi,"* when he passed by and bumped her shoulder on his way down the stairs.

They looked at each other and grinned.

"It's what I thought I always wanted, to come back to Paris. To be standing right in this very spot one day. To have this exact view. And I always thought if I found Adele's painting, it would fill the void in my heart. But I wanted everything on my own terms. I didn't want to wait on God, for His perfect timing. For His guidance . . ." She stood just inches from him. "And strength . . ." A pause, and she inched forward. "And a reason to trust my heart to someone again."

He nodded, a genuinely tender look on his face. "Me too."

"I know you didn't take the money."

"No. I didn't."

"I think I understand why," she said. "Do you want to tell me?"

"I've known all this time I'm not who I'm supposed to be. I haven't been living the life God has called me to. I couldn't take the money," he admitted, and took a careful step forward, until the tips of his shoes just brushed hers. "Not if it forced me back into that life. And never if I lost my chance to have a new one."

She smiled, freeing her heart from the burden of the last two years, and allowed a tear to trail down and mix with the rain on her cheek.

"Sera, my beautiful, gifted friend. You saw Omara's painting as a child, didn't you? On your last trip to Paris with your father?"

"How did you know?"

"Sophie mentioned that it had been lost after the war, until my grandfather found it a few years later. He sent it to Adele and she kept it all the years of her life. When Sophie said it was left in a gallery in Paris after Adele died, I put the two together. Now it makes more sense. I understand why it was so important to you. I know you've been living in the past, just as I have." He reached up and brushed a tear off her cheek with the edge of his palm. "But I want a redefined future, a real one with the freedom to pursue God fully—and with you in it. Can you forgive me for breaking your trust?"

"Yes—"

"I know I've hurt you." He kept on as if he hadn't heard her. "That I've acted like a fool, and I know what's between us has just started, so I don't expect an answer right away . . . I don't even know if I could move or where I'll find a job, but . . ." William kept talking, rationalizing his thoughts aloud. "I'm not even sure what I'm trying to ask you . . . except that if it wasn't for what happened, would you consider—"

"Will?"

He stopped and took a deep breath.

"Yeah?"

"I don't care what the question is." She bit her bottom lip. "My answer is yes."

William's hands cupped the sides of her cheeks and he brushed her lips with his, connecting in a way she'd never thought possible. She melted into him, loving the familiarity when his arms wrapped around her. She felt somehow . . . home.

He pulled back from the kiss and for a moment dropped his arms open at his sides. "You realize I have nothing now, right? I have an old Bible and my grandfather's painting of an Austrian violinist. Beyond that, you're going to get me. That's it. Just William."

She stared up at the sculpture for a moment and smiled.

Paris is the city of love. But this, Lord? This is all I want.

Sera reached out to one of his waiting palms and laced her fingers with his. "Second chances, remember?"

He nodded at the reminder and dropped a kiss to her temple.

"Then she told you, about them. Adele and Vladimir?"

"Yes . . . wait, no! I still haven't heard what happened to Vladimir!" Sera looked up at *her* William. "I ran out the door to find you."

"You actually left without hearing the whole story? I'm flattered, Manhattan."

"You'll tell me, won't you?" She brushed a hand over his cheek, feeling the incredible weight of his arms around her as the winged marble statue stood watch over them.

"Do you remember when I told you their love story must have ended more than seventy years ago?"

She nodded.

"Well, I can admit when I'm wrong." He smiled and turned, taking her hand and walking slowly down the steps of the portico. "Are you ready for the best part?"

CHAPTER THIRTY-SIX

April 28, 1950

Paris, France

"Adele?" The young woman spoke directly into her ear, the hint of a smile in her voice.

Adele's eyes popped open.

She sat in her little music shop, the wonderfully worn old building with the tall, street-facing windows and the sun streaming in to warm the aged walnut floors. She lowered the violin and bow to her lap and turned, spying her assistant just behind her with a mock scold on her face and eyes that were bright even from behind dark-rimmed glasses.

Young Mariette leaned against the baby grand and tapped the toe of her spectator heel against the hardwood.

Adele summoned the courage to ask, "What time is it?"

The bow had touched strings, and Adele had found herself lost in the magic lull of her beloved music. She'd only meant to play for a moment, but what had begun as a few chords between appointments had morphed into a trip of memories . . . Her eyes had simply closed on their own, and her hands? They'd played without knowing.

"It's nearly noon."

"Noon?" Adele's attention was ripped from the music. She

rested the violin across her lap. "It can't be . . . ," she uttered as she checked her wristwatch. Sure enough. Ten minutes till. She was going to be late. Again.

Flustered, Adele replaced her violin in its case and began the task of shoving haphazard sheets of music down into her canvas satchel.

"Here. Let me." Mariette took a stack out of her hands and began evening out the pages. Adele smiled, knowing her assistant's methodical nature couldn't stand for paper to be stuffed in a bag when there were at least thirty good seconds that could be used to right them. "I shouldn't have let you play so long."

"No," Adele said, shaking her head. "Mariette, it's not your fault. A teacher should be on time without her younger but much wiser employee having to constantly check up on her. I don't know what came over me."

Mariette looked at her with a softness as warm as the sun outside. "You were there again, weren't you?"

Adele gave a slight nod. She'd told her assistant just enough for her to know she'd been in Auschwitz, but the rest she'd buried in the recesses of her heart. It was far too soon to talk of such things. She wasn't sure if she'd ever be able to.

"Yes."

When Adele played, she always went back to the same place—to Auschwitz. To her chair in the front row of the orchestra, with Omara at her side and Alma Rosé standing in front, leading their group through another one of the Germans' marches.

"Well. You're talking to a fellow musician." Mariette's shoulders lifted in a shrug as she continued flattening the sheet music. "No explanation necessary. Just go." She nodded toward the door. "Get your things while I do this."

"What do I need?" Adele sailed around the small studio, looking for her handbag. She found it discarded by a vase of flowers and stack of books on the sideboard in the entry. She snatched up the yellow leather purse and after rooting around for a moment plucked out a compact mirror and tube of poppy red lipstick. She set about quickly perking up her appearance.

She pinched her cheeks for color.

After she decided her face was as good as it was going to get in the one-minute window she'd left herself to get ready, she replaced the lipstick and compact back inside her purse.

"Food?"

Mariette brought the satchel that now had a stack of impeccably ordered sheet music inside, right next to the brown paper bag with her lunch, and swung it over her shoulder.

Adele's hands flew up to her brow. "Hat?"

Mariette shook her head. "Not today." She untied the pin-dot blue kerchief from round her neck and tossed it in Adele's direction. "Here." The light fabric caught the air and danced down to her waiting palms. "Wear this. It brings out your eyes."

Adele raised the dainty cloth up and, after balancing it over her blond, shoulder-length barrel curls, tied it in a knot atop her head. She turned round to glance in the floor-length mirror against the wall. Black-and-white striped blouse, a springy A-line skirt, and patent red flats. The outfit was Paris-perfect.

"Mariette, I know you don't have any lessons until tomorrow morning, and I hate to even ask, but do you think you could—"

"Sure." Mariette winked and turned the kerchief round until the knot was hidden at Adele's nape. "I'll take your afternoon lessons."

Adele grabbed her friend by the shoulders. "Really? Oh! You sweet thing!" She wrapped the girl in a quick embrace.

The smile melted on Mariette's face and made her freckles dance. "You honestly think I'm going to tell my boss to hurry back from her noon appointment?" She turned and looked out the sun-drenched front windows. "On a Paris day like this? Now scoot," she ordered, swatting the small of her back to usher her toward the door. "Get out of here. You don't want all the good sunlight to go to waste."

"Of course not," Adele agreed, and smoothed her hands over her skirt. "Losing the sunlight would only drag this out longer, wouldn't it?"

With one last wink, she hurried to the door.

"Adele?"

She turned back, her hand fused to the door's old brass knob. "Yes?"

"Is he ever going to be finished?"

Adele blushed, feeling the warmth spread from her cheeks to her mouth, the smile finding its way onto her lips with an unconscious effort. "Who knows?"

Her blue bicycle was waiting against the front stoop. It was the French kind, with the wide wheels and a woven basket for trips to the flower shop and buying baguettes on Sunday mornings. Adele dropped her satchel and purse in the wicker basket and hopped onto the seat.

She took off in the direction of the River Seine.

Mariette had been right. Adele had been lost in her music, thinking of that train ride she'd taken so long ago. The memories were always the same. She thought of what had changed her. Of Omara and the rest of the girls. Of the long days of playing and the even longer, sound-empty nights in which sleep never seemed to come. She thought of how fragile life is and how different things were now than she'd ever imagined in her charmed, Viennese youth.

Every time her eyes closed on the music, her mind flashed with images of them. All of them. The lost. The brave. The souls whose second chance never came . . . Her heart bled those familiar notes of Auschwitz.

Adele rode along, passing flower shops and her favorite boulangerie as she wheeled the bike past the Champs-Elysees, thinking about the life that Omara had made her promise she'd live. She remembered that day in the painted room, where Omara had told her that God was everywhere. The sky breathed Him. The sun gave His warmth. The music, haunting now and tied only to her memory of a place called Auschwitz—these things all remained as songs of praise to Him. Why, the very air she inhaled was created and willed by His hand. And as God is everywhere, she couldn't live but to carry Him in her heart, with the worship of daily life, using the gift of every second bestowed upon her to bring honor and glory to her Savior.

She came to the banks of the river and smiled. A perfect day.

There were people enjoying the sunshine. Children laughed as they chased a red balloon caught up on the lightness of a spring breeze. Lovers walked hand in hand. And artists were everywhere along the banks of the river, lost in their craft, each alive because there was a paint-dipped brush in his or her grip.

She raised her hand up to shield the sun from her eyes.

Her heart thumped when she saw the painter she was looking for. His tall form was there, carving out a steadfast image through the sunlight, stealing away her heart just as he always had.

There he was—her artist.

Adele dropped her bike and trotted down to the river. He was standing with his easel, canvas, and paints, as always when the light was good. He looked up before she said anything, able to tell she was there. A lock of hair fell down to shield the small scar on his forehead.

"There you are," he said, his heart-stopping smile gleaming with her approach. "I was beginning to worry that I'd be stood up today. Let me guess, Butterfly." Vladimir brought his hand up to his chin and rested it there, in a mock pensive manner. "Playing again? Lost with your violin instead of coming to see your husband? Or are you trying to pay me back for all of those nights I left you to wait in our garden?"

"I'll never tell," she joked, feet adding a little independent spring to her step when they were walking in his direction. He set the brush down on the easel just in time to catch her leap into his arms. Caring not that her poppy red lipstick would be mussed, Adele pressed her lips to his, thankful all over again that they'd not have to hide their affection from anyone.

Adele was the wife of a penniless merchant's son, and happy for it. Having him by her side was worth far more. She was saddened that her parents never realized that when they could. She looked over at the painting and saw the numbers he'd added to the left forearm of the image. It made her tattoo almost burn with the memory.

"What's this?" He tipped her chin up so that her eyes could meet his. "I just saw clouds move across your pretty face."

She rolled her eyes heavenward, lightening the moment. "Old ghosts, I suppose."

"Then let them pass by," he instructed, and placed a kiss to her brow. "They've no power over us anymore."

"Mariette was asking me again"—she smiled at the thought of teasing him and continued—"whether you'd ever be finished."

"With Edward's painting?" He turned his attention to the canvas and studied it, his eyes moving over the brushstrokes as she watched. "I'm not quite sure. The light is better outside. That's certain. And it looks right, for the most part—the lovely mouth, gentle hands, curve of the neck. I'd say they all look nearly the same as in Omara's painting." He turned back to her. "But I think . . ." He gave a sure nod. "It's the eyes."

"My eyes?" Adele raised her eyebrows to show them off. "What's wrong with them?"

"Nothing. We've promised something for our British friend, that's all, to thank him for what he's done for us. Edward did help us find each other after the war. And he helped us hide you so we could get married and leave Vienna behind. So we could have a new life together. Even if I am copying the painting for him, I want it to be perfect. I want it to show the beautiful eyes that blinked back at me onstage that last time."

"He's sent us Omara's painting," Adele said, and tilted her head while looking at the beautiful brushstrokes. "And you've done a fine job of copying it for him."

"I get the distinct impression that you believe I am stalling." He walked back over to face the canvas, studying it for a moment before turning back to her. "I think I need another appointment with my muse. Tomorrow at noon."

"But it's supposed to rain tomorrow," she gibed, and cracked an eyelid up at the blazing sun overhead. "Poor light."

"Then the next day? I'll buy lunch. Or bribe you with flowers for your pretty wicker basket over there."

"I have students. Appointments." Adele began shaking her head and took a few cautious steps backward as he drew nearer. "Oh no, you don't, Vladimir. We have work to do."

"This is pretty," he said as he caught up to her, a hand running over the light chiffon kerchief tied round her head. "It brings out your eyes."

"You have to finish the painting," she said, trying to fend him off but failing miserably the moment his shoes bumped hers.

He wasn't dissuaded. Instead, he reached out a hand for her. "I should have asked you to dance the night of your birthday. Remember?"

How could she forget?

Adele almost laughed about it now, how silly that broken birthday wish seemed now that she could feel the touch of his hand to her face, could feel the brush of his lips against hers without fear that someone might see them.

"Dance with me."

She looked around, thinking they'd cause a scene. "Here?"

"Yes."

As if she had to tell Mr. Picasso the obvious. "But there's no music."

Vladimir shook his head and pressed a soft smile to his lips, enough that only a whisper could escape them. "You and me? We've always had our own music. Haven't we, Butterfly?" He opened his arms wide.

She accepted the embrace and allowed him to lead her in a dance, their dance, the one they missed all those years ago. She melted when he held her close and brushed his lips against hers, as she'd always hoped to. "I'll ask you to dance every day for the rest of our lives together. I won't waste this second chance God has given us, not even if it rains tomorrow and the day after that."

She felt the graze of his chin against her forehead as he spoke.

And as if playing her violin, Adele was lost in the moment enough that her eyes closed on their own. With each step, each sway, each move of their feet with the silent song of her heart, Adele cherished the moment.

She worshipped God for it. Because of His grace in offering it.

Because they'd survived.

Because she'd kept her promise to Omara.

A soft breeze caressed her cheek. She turned her face up to greet it.

He broke into her thoughts with a barely there whisper. "Every morning, just as I saw dawn break over the skyline, I said a prayer for you. I regretted those times I'd stayed away. Wished like mad that I could take them all back—maybe add the moments up, just so I could exchange them for one chance to see you again."

She shook her head as if she didn't know. As if he hadn't told her dozens of times before.

"You were always with me. I prayed that if you were forced to play music as I was, you'd let it keep you alive. I prayed that you'd use it to come back to me, Butterfly. That God would keep you strong so you could."

Adele and Vladimir danced along the banks of the River Seine, the loveliness of spring a backdrop all around them. A breeze rustled the blond curls she'd tucked under her kerchief. The strands danced about her face, a grateful, delicate waltz about her cheek. Vladimir caught them, wove them back behind her ear with a delicate touch.

"And I was never without you. Or Him."

She knew the answer, but asked anyway. She'd never tire of hearing his voice with her ear pressed up against his chest. "Why?"

"Because even in winter, the Auschwitz dawns were warm when I thought of you."

Adele knew what he meant, that God was there, in the hearts of the lost, in the lives of the men and women and children who had lived for a new beginning. He was there in the painted room. She prayed that the generations to follow would never forget the lost. She prayed that it would be the Auschwitz dawns they would always remember.

AUTHOR'S NOTE

*B*etween June 1940 and the autumn of 1944, nearly a million Jews and tens of thousands of Roma (Gypsies), Soviet prisoners of war, religious dissidents, non-Jewish Poles, and other German, Austrian, Czech, French, Lithuanian, and Italian civilians perished at the Auschwitz-Birkenau killing center in Upper Silesia, Poland. On October 7, 1944, as the Red Army continued to bomb German targets mere miles from the electrified fences of Birkenau, a prisoner revolt began. Using handmade weapons and gunpowder smuggled from the ammunitions factory in which they worked, prisoners mounted a heroic resistance against the heavily armed SS military police guarding the camp. The group of prisoners included underground resistance fighters and *Sonderkommando* (Jewish crematoria workers) who learned they were to be killed and replaced by new workers in Crematorium IV. Brave men and women gave their lives to stand up to injustice, as Omara and Adele sought to do.

In advance of the liberation of Auschwitz by the Soviets in January 1945, members of the Women's Orchestra of Auschwitz were marched to the Bergen-Belsen camp in Lower Saxony, Northern Germany. There, the remaining fifty-three members of the orchestra survived to be liberated by British troops on April 15, 1945. Though many of those left behind at Auschwitz died from disease or starvation, the voices of the lost were not completely silenced. Found in the rubble of partially destroyed warehouses and old barracks of Auschwitz were more than 1,600 pieces of art that survive to this day, each telling a poignant story for the generations to come.

Many of the artists remain unknown.

It's been more than a decade since I learned of the art of the Holocaust. I remember the feeling of sitting in that college class, moved to reverence as our group of students looked at each slide image. We studied the sketched faces of prisoners, and the landscapes with depictions of hard labor while armed guards looked on from the background. We found ourselves hushed by delicate floating butterflies and cheery watercolor flowers that had no place within the camp's barbed wire walls. We were moved by the coexistence of evil and sheer beauty, seemingly both allowed to flourish in the same place.

As a student, I was captured by the innate need of humans to create. As a young Christian, I was inexplicably moved by the glimpses of light in the darkness. Even in the most evil of circumstances, the art of human expression was so powerful that it couldn't be overshadowed, not even by death. In *The Butterfly and the Violin*, I did my best to explore this theme. It's about worship through God's creation—our lives.

I am thankful to each of you for reading this book. It is in the generations following ours that the stories of the lost must be kept alive. And it is in the legacy we each leave behind that the love of Jesus Christ will continue to blossom in a fallen world.

ADDITIONAL READING

http://www.ushmm.org/—United States Holocaust Memorial Museum

http://en.auschwitz.org/m/—Auschwitz-Birkenau Memorial and Museum

http://lastexpression.northwestern.edu/—The Last Expression: Art and Auschwitz

http://sfi.usc.edu/about—USC Shoah Foundation: The Institute for Visual History and Education

Corrie ten Boom, *The Hiding Place*, 35th anniversary ed. (Grand Rapids, Michigan: Chosen Books, 2006).

Elie Wiesel, *Night*, rev. ed. (New York: Hill and Wang, 2006).

READING GROUP GUIDE

1. Adele's world was a sheltered existence of luxury and prominence before the war. It wasn't until she visited the Haurbech family's hiding place that her eyes were finally opened to the threats around her. How did Adele's view of the world change between the night at the dance hall in 1939 and her arrival at Auschwitz in the spring of 1943? How would her life have been different had she not offered to help the Haurbechs escape from Vienna?

2. As a member of the Women's Orchestra of Auschwitz, Adele's musical gift was valued by the Nazis and likely contributed to her survival. How much of an impact did Omara also have on her will to survive? Instead of marching to Bergen-Belsen, would Adele have stayed at Auschwitz if she hadn't promised Omara to keep the orchestra together?

3. Prisoners in Auschwitz felt compelled to write, paint beautiful pictures, and play musical instruments, even in the face of death. Why was the art of creation in these prisoners' hearts so important that they would take such a risk just to create? What images of beauty come to mind from Adele's story?

4. Sera and William were both seeking God in their lives and had to lay down several burdens of past hurts before they could love again. How did God use Adele and Vladimir's story to

awaken their hearts to a second chance at love? Is there a past hurt that He's helped you overcome in your life?

5. Sera's longtime dream was to see Paris again. That dream is realized at the end of the story, but in a different way than she'd envisioned. What are some of the factors that worked together to bring this dream to life? When you look back on your own life, how was the path laid out to get to your own dreams?

6. This book was written with a heart for the lost—those who perished in WWII, as well as anyone who has suffered from a lack of peace in their lives. Adele and Sera are women separated by decades, but united in the peace Jesus Christ brought, despite their circumstances. How was their faith affected by what they went through in the story? How has your own faith been affected by difficult times?

ACKNOWLEDGMENTS

A special debt of gratitude must first go to my husband, Jeremy, for his unending support in making this book a reality. You're the best half of anything I will ever be. And to Brady, Carson, and Colt, my little men with such big, big dreams and God-given smiles.

To my faithful friend and agent, Joyce Hart, for believing in me. Together with my publishing family, you helped this book come alive. A sincere thanks and extra hugs must go to the fiction team at HarperCollins Christian Publishing: Daisy, Katie, Ami, Jodi, Elizabeth, Becky, Amanda, and especially to Kristen, for an artistic eye in cover design that could rival van Gogh himself. To my intelligent and committed editors, Becky Monds, Amanda Bostic, and Rachelle Gardner: I thank you for reading this book and changing my life because of your belief in it. I will always be grateful for your counsel and heartfelt encouragement.

Writers are often students of history. I'm honored to be one who has had the investment of a gifted teacher in my life. To Anne Allen, PhD, my longtime mentor at Indiana University Southeast: thank you for investing your time and knowledge in the awakening of art history in my heart. A special thank-you also goes to Mrs. Eva Mozes Kor of the CANDLES Holocaust Museum, for breathing life into this author's understanding of Auschwitz-Birkenau and for teaching the world's children how to walk in forgiveness.

Thank you to my Christian Academy of Indiana and Humana Inc. families for the years we've spent together, and especially Marlene Blair and Libby Powers, for being my partners in a daily dose of laughter for so many years. A special thanks goes to Maggie:

friendship with you has been a pillar in my life. And to the authors of Regency Reflections, the BritCrits critique group, and my Novel Sisters, Joanna, Carol, and Jessica: you light my days with your love of the writing craft and with your wicked-fast British wit. I've learned so much about life from each of you.

Unending gratitude must go to my first readers, Lindy and Paula, for the hours you spent encouraging and brainstorming with me, and to my sister, Jenny, for dreaming with me through the bookstore aisles.

To my mom and dad, for battling leukemia and encouraging others in Christ along the way: you're the stuff from which heroes are made. I love you both so very much.

I thank you, my wonderfully inspiring readers, for reading this book. It's been the pleasure of my life to share this story with you. And to my beautiful Savior and best friend, Jesus Christ: this heart will always be imperfect, but it's still Yours.

In His Love,

Kristy

ABOUT THE AUTHOR

Danielle Mitchell Photography

KRISTY L. CAMBRON has been fascinated with the WWII era since hearing her grandfather's stories of the war. She holds an art history degree from Indiana University and received the Outstanding Art History Student Award. Kristy writes WWII and Regency Era fiction and has placed first in the 2013 NTRWA Great Expectations and 2012 FCRW Beacon contests, and is a 2013 Laurie finalist. Kristy makes her home in Indiana with her husband and three football-loving sons.